CW00497920

MOMENT OF
MADNESS

Una-Mary Parker

HEADLINE

Copyright © 2001 Cheval Associates Ltd

The right of Una-Mary Parker to be identified as the Author of
the Work has been asserted by her in accordance with
the Copyright, Designs and Patents Act 1988.

First published in 2001
by HEADLINE BOOK PUBLISHING

10 9 8 7 6 5 4 3 2 1

All rights reserved. No part of this publication may be
reproduced, stored in a retrieval system, or transmitted,
in any form or by any means without the prior written
permission of the publisher, nor be otherwise circulated
in any form of binding or cover other than that in which
it is published and without a similar condition being
imposed on the subsequent purchaser.

All characters in this publication are fictitious and any
resemblance to real persons, living or dead, is purely coincidental.

British Library Cataloguing in Publication Data

Parker, Una-Mary
  Moment of madness
  1. Suspense fiction
  I. Title
  823.9'14[F]

ISBN 0 7472 7078 3

Typeset by Avon Dataset Ltd, Bidford-on-Avon, Warks

Printed and bound in Great Britain by
Mackays of Chatham plc, Chatham, Kent

HEADLINE BOOK PUBLISHING
A division of Hodder Headline
338 Euston Road
London NW1 3BH

www.headline.co.uk
www.hodderheadline.com

This is for
Stéphanie Glénat

With grateful thanks for her
help whilst researching for
this book

One

They always made love on Sunday mornings. Hurriedly, almost furtively, Lucinda arching her back, Julian's breathing becoming laboured as they moved together, faster and faster . . .

'That looks fun! Can I join in?' piped a small voice from the doorway. Lucinda sneaked a peep over Julian's shoulder and saw Daisy, who had just turned six, watching them with undisguised interest. Julian lay absolutely still on top of her until his diminishing manhood allowed him to extricate himself and slide onto his side of the bed, where he lay, eyes tightly shut.

'You're up very early, darling,' Lucinda remarked weakly, pushing the pillow under her head.

'Jamie said you and Daddy are taking us swimming,' Daisy announced, clambering onto the bed, her feet emerging pink and chubby from the legs of her Peter Rabbit pyjamas.

'Yes . . . but later,' Lucinda pointed out.

'Why can't we go after breakfast?'

'Well, yes we will, but not just yet.'

'Come *on*, Daisy! I *told* you they'd be having S.E.X.,' admonished Jamie from the doorway. He was glaring at his younger sister who was bouncing blithely on her mother's legs. She turned to look at Lucinda, blue eyes round and trusting, golden curls framing her small face.

'Mummy, what's S.E.X.?' she asked, confused.

Julian opened his eyes and hauled himself into a sitting position. He looked exhausted. 'It's time we all got up,' he announced, trying to sound brisk. 'Who's going to have scrambled eggs for breakfast?'

'Yuck!' Daisy wrinkled her face in disgust. 'Daddy, what's S.E.X.?'

Jamie strode into their room. He was an amazingly good-looking eight-year-old, with clean-cut features, unwavering blue eyes like his sister, and a thatch of golden hair.

'It's what you do to have babies, stupid,' he announced with authority. 'Mothers and fathers have to have S.E.X. whether they want to or not. If you want children, Daisy, you'll have to have S.E.X. one day, too.'

'I don't think so,' she said politely, getting down from the bed. 'Daddy, can I have a boiled egg?'

'Kids asleep?' Julian enquired that evening without looking up from his position along the length of the living-room sofa, where he lay immersed in the *Sunday Times* holiday section.

Lucinda dropped into the deep armchair by the fireplace. Her long dark hair was scooped back into a pony tail, her jeans were stained with Ribena

1

down one leg, her T-shirt was crumpled and her lightly tanned face was devoid of make-up.

'Yes. Bathed, fed, read to and now out for the count.'

It was eight o'clock and a feeling of languor had spread itself through their little terraced house in Fulham. They'd had a lovely day, and it had been wonderful having the place to themselves, as Delia, their au pair, had gone home to her family for the weekend. After swimming they'd taken a picnic to Richmond Park, lazing on rugs on the soft springy grass, and watching the brightly coloured parakeets, now breeding in the wild, fluttering from tree to tree. Then Julian had produced some rackets and balls from the boot of the car and they'd played until it was time to go home.

Julian was almost looking forward to work the next morning. For the past twelve years he'd been with Heanage Antiques, an emporium just off the King's Road which sold everything from Empire beds to George II fire irons, and it seemed like a rest cure compared to entertaining two active children. But Lucinda had a cold sick feeling in the pit of her stomach, reminiscent of the days when she'd been small and the holidays were coming to an end and she'd had to go back to school. She wanted every day to be like today. She wanted to watch her children grow, spend all her time with them, be a real mother. They were fine; it was *she* who felt deprived. The need to earn money was robbing her of days like today and at times she felt resentful.

So what had changed her from being a seriously career-minded young woman? Eleven years ago, just before she'd met Julian, she'd joined D'Aussoire, the giant French cosmetic company. Determined to get to the top, she'd worked a twelve- or thirteen-hour day at the beginning. Marriage and then the birth of Jamie had slowed her down, but she still continued to work an average of ten hours a day. Her reward was to be made head of market research for D'Aussoire and the seven other cosmetic companies in the group.

And now it was Sunday evening, and tomorrow morning she'd have to be up at six thirty to wash her hair and apply her make-up to look like a perfectly groomed walking advertisement for D'Aussoire, and then don a neat dark suit and fashionable shoes in order to go to work.

She sighed deeply, fed up with always being tired and stressed. She was beginning to feel like a juggler, trying to keep all the balls in the air, and ending up with the dreadful thought that she was spreading herself too thinly, and wasn't doing *anything* well.

'All right, Bun?' Julian had lowered the newspaper and was looking intently at her.

She smiled quickly. It wasn't his fault she had to work. They were too financially stretched for her not to.

But Julian knew how she felt and it made him feel guilty. He, too, was working round the clock, driving to auction sales all round the country in his search for suitable furniture and objets d'art for Heanage Antiques. But if they were going to pay for Jamie and Daisy's education, plus all the other hundred and one hidden costs of family life, they needed Lucinda's salary as well as his.

'I'm fine,' she replied lightly, reaching for the *Mail on Sunday* but knowing she ought to be doing something about supper.

Julian rose to his feet. 'Shall I open a bottle?'

Her smile broadened, became genuine. That's what she loved about him. He could sense her feelings and he always knew what to say or do that would lift her spirits again.

As they drank the delicious red Bordeaux he'd bought through the wine club he belonged to, Lucinda felt herself mellowing. God, she was lucky to be married to Julian, she reflected, putting her feet up. While many of her friends were still going through the agonies of wondering if they'd ever find the right man at all, or, alternatively, going through nasty divorces, here she was, happily married with two adorable . . . well, most of the time . . . children, and a nice house.

And she had her grandmother to thank for it all.

Sarah Wells, now eighty-two but still as active as someone twenty years younger, had always played a large part in Lucinda's life. She'd been on hand throughout their childhood to help with Lucinda and her elder brothers, Tom and Harry. Trips to museums and art galleries had been turned into fun occasions when Lucinda had been as young as six, and as she grew older Sarah had taken her to places like Claridges for lunch and the Ritz for tea.

'Lucinda must know the ropes,' Sarah had said, thinking of her own youth in the thirties, 'so that when young men take her out, she's confident. There's nothing worse than a girl who dithers when faced with a menu, and who doesn't know where the loos are.'

It remained an unspoken fact in the family that Lucinda was Sarah's favourite.

When Lucinda was twenty-two, Sarah, who still entertained several times a week with the help of a housekeeper, invited her to a dinner party in her first-floor flat in Rutland Gate, Knightsbridge. Sarah's guest lists were omnifarious and might include a bishop, an actor, a foreign ambassador, a dowager duchess or a Rastafarian poet. It was as if she collected people at random; if they were interesting she invited them. If they proved to be amusing as well, then she invited them again. On this occasion she decided to invite some of 'the young', as she described anyone under thirty-five.

When Lucinda arrived, late from work and somewhat breathless, she received a warm welcome and a chilled glass of champagne.

'Come and meet a charming young man, darling. His aunt is a friend of mine and I needed an extra man to make up the numbers tonight,' Sarah whispered ingenuously, leading Lucinda by the hand until she was face to face with a tall, rangy man not much older than she was herself, with broad shoulders, untidy brown hair and a fan of laughter lines on his lean tanned face.

His hazel eyes seemed to brim with amusement as he looked down at Lucinda. 'So you're the granddaughter Sarah's always going on about?' he asked, smiling. 'I've heard so much about you I feel as if I already know you.'

'There you have the advantage over me,' she replied, trying desperately hard to look as if she wasn't particularly interested, and then hoping she hadn't sounded too crisp. 'I don't think I've met your aunt; who is she?'

'Maria Manners.'

'The actress?'

He nodded.

'Granny knows some amazing people, but I didn't realise she knew Maria Manners,' Lucinda said with genuine interest. 'She was wonderful in *The Lion in Winter*. Are you in the theatre too?'

As soon as she'd said it she hoped he wasn't a famous actor she should have heard of. There were moments, she reflected in panic, when she only seemed to open her mouth to move her feet.

'Lord, no!' He was laughing now and she let out a little sigh of relief. 'I'm with Heanage Antiques. I'm just a dogsbody at the moment, really, but I love the business,' he added with disarming honesty.

This she could cope with. He seemed easy-going and quite laid back. It would require no great intellectual effort on her part to keep the conversation going. And for once she wouldn't have to make an effort. All the young men she'd met recently had been pompous, arrogant, and out to impress. As a result she'd instantly backed off, feeling disturbed and unnerved, only realising afterwards it was because they reminded her of her father.

But in those first moments she realised Julian Cotterell was different. He was intelligent, amusing and very attractive, and there was a warmth about him which made her feel utterly comfortable in his company. In fact she had the strangest feeling that she already knew him. It was almost like looking in a mirror and recognising a part of her own reflection.

Afterwards he gave her a lift back to the flat she shared with two other girls in Gloucester Road. 'I'll give you a call,' he said, smiling down at her as he walked with her to her front door. Lucinda thanked him for the lift and then turned away swiftly so that he'd not see the look of hope in her eyes.

That night she hardly slept at all. She longed to ask Sarah all about him. Was he as nice as he seemed? What did his famous aunt have to say about him? What sort of track record did he have with women?

The next day, Lucinda was on the point of phoning Sarah when Julian himself rang.

'How did you get this number?' Lucinda blurted out in shocked delight.

'You did mention you worked at D'Aussoire,' he said mildly.

'Oh, yes. Of course.' She felt confused and excited.

'I wondered if you were doing anything tomorrow?' he continued. 'I thought we might take in a film and then have something to eat afterwards.'

'Yeah. That would be great.' Lucinda was desperately trying to get her head round the fact that Julian was actually asking her for a date.

'What would you like to see?' he asked. 'There's a new Bond movie?'

'I'd love to see that,' she said quickly. It would be safer than going to a romantic film which might make her weep with emotion; that would be too embarrassing.

'Excellent. I'll get the tickets. Shall we meet in the foyer of the Kensington Odeon at about seven twenty?'

She was so absorbed in listening to the rich timbre of his voice that she was barely paying attention to what he was actually saying. 'Yeah. Fine,' she said, quickly recovering herself.

And so began a whirlwind romance. They fell instantly and desperately in love. Soon they were spending every spare moment together and then Julian suggested she move into his tiny flat in Victoria. Without hesitation she agreed. After all she was twenty-two, she argued when her mother demurred. A year later Julian proposed with touching formality, although they both knew where they were heading. For ever after Julian joked about theirs being 'an arranged marriage' because Sarah had set them up to meet each other.

The only person to object was Miles Scott-Forbes, Lucinda's father. He'd scoffed at the fuss and expense of the wedding, and said that anyway Lucinda was far too young to get married and Julian would never make anything of himself and he just hoped they wouldn't come running to *him* for money when they got into financial difficulties, which they undoubtedly would.

Now, looking back at that time, Lucinda had the satisfaction of knowing they'd never had to go to her father for anything. And soon they'd be celebrating their tenth wedding anniversary.

The maddening shrill tones of the alarm clock woke her up at six thirty the next morning. The week had begun and Lucinda knew she'd be on a helter-skelter for the next five days. As she showered she could hear Delia getting the children up, pacifying them as they wailed for lost shoes or satchels, a missing hairbrush or a clean shirt.

'They're on the *chair*, Daisy,' Delia kept saying in a low patient voice, or: 'They're under your *nose*, Jamie!'

By the time Lucinda had slipped into a white lace bra and pants, sheer tights and a navy blue sleeveless dress with a matching jacket, she could smell the toast being made in the kitchen downstairs, and then the tantalisingly delicious aroma of freshly brewed coffee.

'Have you seen my keys anywhere?' Julian asked. He was casually dressed today in moleskin trousers, open neck shirt and a pale blue sweater because he was off to a house sale in Wiltshire.

Lucinda paused in making up her face long enough to glance around the bedroom. 'You had them last night so they must be somewhere,' she said, a touch irritably. What was it with men and keys, she thought, turning back to the mirror again.

'Could they be on the hall table?' Julian asked rather helplessly.

5

'If you looked you'd find out,' she replied tartly.

He slouched out of the bedroom moodily. Really, he was no better in the mornings than she was, she reflected.

By the time she got downstairs, Daisy and Jamie were fighting over whose turn it was to sit on the red stool at the breakfast bar in the kitchen.

'You had it yesterday,' Jamie shouted angrily, trying to tug it away from under Daisy's bottom.

She hung on to the bar with the tenacity of someone clinging to a rail of the *Titanic*. 'I *didn't*!' she screamed, scarlet in the face. 'It's *my* turn today!'

'No, it's not, you tart! It's *my* turn!' Jamie yelled back.

This battle happened every single morning and Lucinda had had enough.

'That's it!' she snapped, lifting Daisy off the stool with one arm, whilst removing the stool altogether with the other. 'I'm putting this seat in the broom cupboard and *neither* of you is going to have it.'

'That's not fair,' cried Daisy, bursting into tears.

'It's all your fault,' Jamie shouted at his sister. 'It was *my* turn, anyway.'

'And you are not to call Daisy a tart,' Lucinda shouted above the din. Then she grabbed herself a cup of coffee, which she stood drinking, leaning against the Welsh dresser.

Julian came shambling into the kitchen, a bigger but no less agitated version of his son. 'Delia, have *you* seen my keys? I've looked everywhere and I can't find them and I've got to be in Salisbury by ten.'

Delia looked at him with an amused expression. 'They're by the draining board.'

'So there!' Lucinda chuckled, catching Delia's eye. Two sensible women having to cope with two fractious males, their expressions seemed to say.

Daisy, now seated on the green stool, was sobbing quietly into her bowl of cereal. Lucinda put her arms round her and hugged her close. 'Cheer up, sweetheart,' she whispered.

Daisy clung to her, smearing her milky mouth against her mother's pristine jacket. 'I don't want you to go to work, Mummy,' she wept. 'Jamie's so nasty to me.'

Lucinda reached out and included Jamie in her embrace. 'He wasn't being nasty if it *was* his turn for the red stool,' she said reasonably. Then she kissed them both and for a terrible moment felt like weeping herself. What was she doing with her life? Working for some stupid cosmetic company when she should be bringing up her children?

Forty-five minutes later she arrived at the UK headquarters of the D'Aussoire Group. They occupied a block of purpose-built offices in the Gray's Inn Road, near the ITN building. Seemingly made of acres of glass, and mostly open plan, with glass lifts swooping up and down to the various floors at one end of the building, it was the last word in modern minimalism. Sometimes Lucinda felt she was floating in mid-air as she sat at her curved desk, in a padded swivel chair, surrounded by a stunning view of London under a sky of scudding clouds.

In the lift, already packed with a dozen or so other employees, she was whizzed up smoothly and silently to Market Research on the ninth floor, gliding through Artémis, Bagatelle, Galactée, Tazée, Mazeray, Idole and Archée, each a cosmetic company owned by D'Aussoire, each with its own division within the group. Between them all they produced 48 per cent of the world's cosmetics. And at the head of the far-reaching billion-dollar empire was its president, Jean-Paul Pruedom, who was due to fly in from Paris today.

There were moments when Lucinda felt enormously proud to be working in such a vast and successful company, but this morning wasn't one of them.

They hadn't planned to give a party. Just a few friends for drinks, Julian had insisted. She'd agreed. They were both working too hard to organise a big bash, he continued, adding: 'Anyway the house isn't big enough. A dozen or so people. That's enough.'

At that point Lucinda decided it wouldn't be tactful to tell him that what with his family and hers, plus close friends and work colleagues, that was already twenty guests. A glance at her address book made her realise that number would have to be doubled. At least. There were people they simply had to ask; friends who'd given them huge hospitality over the years, like Rachel and Ian Compton, who had even invited them all for weekends to their house in Sunningdale.

This was going to require discreet management, but she knew Julian would enjoy the party when it came to the point. He always did. It was also going to take careful planning. Most of the drawing-room furniture was going to have to be moved, and the double door that led to the small dining room left open, with the table pushed to one side for drinks.

In a casual voice she said: 'I'll get the champagne delivered, sale or return from Oddbins, if you like.' She'd pay for it herself and that way Julian wouldn't know they were going to need four or five cases.

'Excellent,' Julian replied. 'Better get some designer water, too. What about offering Pimms, if it's a warm night?'

Lucinda could tell he was already enjoying the prospect of the party. She studied the list again. She supposed her father would have to be invited because her mother would be terribly upset if he wasn't. The thought filled her with dread. Tom and Harry would almost certainly refuse to come if he was there and Julian wasn't going to be exactly thrilled either, but what was she supposed to do? Miles Scott-Forbes, professor of mathmatics and a recognised genius, was her father, and Anne, her mother, worshipped the ground he walked on. But she was, Lucinda reflected sadly, about the only person who did.

Miles threw the old-fashioned cream Bakelite phone forcefully onto the floor. There was a sickening crash.

'Stupid buggers!' he stormed through clenched teeth. 'Damned inefficient!

7

Why can't they tell me when they're coming? How are we expected to do anything without hot water?' His dark eyes blazed with fury.

Anne sat at the kitchen table, drinking coffee and pretending to read the *Financial Times*, the only newspaper he would allow in the house. She was used to her husband's tantrums, tried hard to appear indifferent to his yells of rage, usually over something trivial, but still, after nearly forty years, found them unnerving.

'What the hell are we supposed to do now?' he demanded, pacing around as if the expected time of arrival of the plumbers was a matter of life or death. He swung on her venomously. 'For God's sake, why didn't you get the boiler serviced? You never do anything right. I'm sick to death of living with your stupidity.'

Tall, very thin and stooping, he gave off an edgy nervous energy that threatened to explode at any time. Now was one of those moments.

Professor Miles Scott-Forbes's entry in *Who's Who* was impressive. Born in 1927, the only son of Colin and Mary Scott-Forbes, of Ripon, Yorkshire, it covered several inches as it listed his achievements in his illustrious career as a professor of mathematical statistics. Educated at Harrow and Queen's College, Oxford, he'd become a Fellow of Magdalen College, Oxford, before becoming a lecturer on a worldwide scale. Honours were heaped on him from Princeton to Jiaotong University, Xi'an. He had also published several books on higher mathematics and statistical science, which were now required reading for university students.

None could doubt his genius. In the scholastic world his was a revered name, spoken with awe. His grasp of mathematical statistics was phenomenal, but in the eyes of Lucinda his priorities were summed up in just one line in *Who's Who*, one small line among the dozens that spelled out his brilliant achievements.

M. 1958, Anne Judith Wells, two s one d.

Not even a capital D for daughter, she reflected indignantly when she first read the entry. Aware that personal details were kept to the minimum in *Who's Who*, she was nevertheless miffed, because it so aptly summed up her father and what he cared for most.

'What are you doing, sitting there, in that half-witted way?' Miles stormed at Anne now. 'God knows, I don't ask for much but I cannot abide inefficiency. You *know* I need a hot bath in the morning before I can function. It ruins my day if I can't start off with a hot bath.'

Anne smiled nervously. Her hands shook. 'I know, dearest. But these things happen. I expect the plumbers will be here soon. Why not have another cup of coffee?'

'I don't want another cup of bloody coffee. Christ, do I have to do everything myself round here? How am I supposed to cope, living in this bloody house?'

8

With that he turned and charged out of the kitchen, walloping the door shut behind him. Then Anne heard him go upstairs. Five minutes later the front door slammed and she could hear his feet stumping down the steps. Miles would be gone for several hours. She knew not where, but that didn't matter. He always came back eventually. And he'd been right about one thing. It was her fault. She'd meant to have the boiler serviced and she'd forgotten.

Never mind, she'd make up for it by cooking his favourite supper. It was better not to answer him back. She'd done that a couple of times when they'd first been married, but it had made things much worse. On one occasion he hadn't spoken to her for two months, only acknowledging her existence if there was someone else in the room, and she swore never to stand up to him again. She couldn't bear being punished by someone she loved as deeply and obsessively as she loved Miles. She was proud of his dazzling brilliance and the fact that a man like him should have married her in the first place; that still thrilled and amazed her.

When she first met Miles, he was the handsomest young man she'd ever seen. His hair was black as a raven's wing and so were his strong eyebrows. His jaw and sharp cheekbones were like carved ivory, and his eyes, to her romantic mind, seemed to burn darkly with fierce passion. Fierce, certainly, but over the years she realised the passion was mostly anger, directed at the stupidity of others.

Admitting she was stupid herself, she sympathised with his intolerance. For a brilliant man like Miles, anything less than acute intelligence could only be met with derision. How lonely and frustrated he must be, she thought, so intellectually isolated, on a high plane all by himself.

Nevertheless, her love for Miles had not diminished and she supposed it was because she'd never really *had* him. He'd never been hers, never belonged to her. That was why she'd always felt a desperate sense of unrequited love. And had he been happy with her? Had she satisfied him?

It was something she didn't want to dwell on. The answers might be painful. It would be terrible to know she'd never really made him happy.

Sarah was deeply worried about her daughter. Anne seemed to be getting more swamped and crushed as the years went by, and recently, probably because he was getting old, Miles's behaviour was becoming increasingly irascible. Anne, never a strong woman, seemed to be no more than a frail husk now, like someone in a faded sepia print: everything beige, the hair that had once been chestnut, the freckles on her pale face, her eyes, once blue, now a washed-out shade of ash. And for some reason she always chose to wear beige or cream, too.

Sarah hated Miles Scott-Forbes with a deep loathing for what he'd done to Anne, and the way he'd treated Tom and Harry. In fact she couldn't bear to set eyes on him, could hardly mention his name without bitterness, and never ceased to regret the day her only child had become bewitched and besotted by a man Sarah believed to have a great brain but who hovered dangerously on the brink of insanity.

Anne had been a pretty young woman full of high spirits and confidence until she had fallen under the deeply destructive spell of Miles when she'd been eighteen. He'd broken their eldest son's spirit, too, but their second son, Harry, had been more resilient. But he was badly damaged, and very immature, always chasing pie in the sky. Extraordinarily, only Lucinda seemed to have escaped her father's volcanic anger and sarcasm, although Miles's negative treatment of her was a form of abuse in itself.

Sarah thanked God for Lucinda's relative immunity, but was troubled by the fact that Anne had never done anything to protect her children from their father's cruelty. She'd stood silently by while he'd bullied them, taunted them and made their lives a misery.

There seemed only one explanation. Anne must still be in love with Miles. If her greatest fear was of losing him, no wonder she continued to turn a blind eye to what he was doing to their children.

Two

Julian's face gleamed with sweat. 'We've overdone it a bit, haven't we?' he gasped, struggling through the crush of people blocking the doorway into the kitchen, where Lucinda was frantically opening more bottles of champagne. She was surrounded by what resembled a tip of empty bottles, dirty glasses, and a stack of dishes that had once been piled high with canapés.

'You can't move in the drawing room or dining room,' he continued, plonking more empty bottles on the floor. 'How many people did we ask, for God's sake? Sarah and Aunt Maria are squashed up against the fireplace and can't move, and Delia is having to fight her way round, trying to top up people's glasses.'

'I didn't think they'd all come,' Lucinda replied, flustered, 'at least not all at the same time.' She was stuffing more bottles of champagne into the deep freeze, in an effort to chill them quickly. 'God, I wish we had a bigger fridge.'

'I wish we had fewer friends,' Julian retorted good-humouredly. 'Can you come and control Miles? He's insulting everyone, which I suppose is one way of ending up with fewer guests but not necessarily the way I'd choose.'

'I can't be everywhere at once,' she retorted in agitation. 'The chipolatas are burning. I've got to take them out of the oven before they get like cinders. Give those bottles on the table to Delia, will you?'

'That won't help those who haven't already got a glass,' Julian pointed out reasonably.

At that moment the front door bell rang again.

Lucinda pushed her hair back from her face and wished she had time to repair her make-up. 'Oh my God . . . who can that be?'

'Let's hope the person nearest to the front door will open it,' Julian shouted cheerfully over his shoulder, as he pushed his way back into the drawing room, clutching the bottles and some glasses, in search of Delia.

The sound of prattling voices in the low-ceilinged rooms had become a roar. Conversation was impossible. Lucinda, squeezing along the narrow hall past people holding their glasses aloft to prevent spilling, found herself shouting: 'Sorry about the crush. More drink is coming round. It's so lovely to see you.'

What she really longed for now was for the party to be over. The house quiet. Her stilettos kicked off. A hot bath. And bed. Then she spotted Jamie and Daisy looking well scrubbed and adorable in their pyjamas, peering down over the banisters from the floor above.

'You're supposed to be in bed,' she called up, knowing she might as well tell the wind to stop blowing for all the attention they'd pay.

11

'We just want to watch, Mummy,' Daisy pleaded, putting on her most angelic expression.

'Yes, we want to see everyone, especially Granny Sarah,' Jamie added with diplomatic craftiness.

Lucinda smiled, her heart melting at the sight of them. Maternal pride welled up inside her. Why shouldn't they stay for a while, providing they remained on the stairs? She actually rather wanted all their friends to see how beautiful her children were.

'All right,' she told them, 'as long as you stay there. Promise?' They nodded solemnly.

More guests were arriving.

'Darling, this is such fun! Here's a tiny anniversary prezzie . . .' Her best friend Carina Somerset squeezed in through the front door, kissing her on the cheek and thrusting a gift-wrapped package into her hand. 'My dear, *everyone*'s here!' she exclaimed, twisting her head this way and that.

Lucinda looked at Carina affectionately. She always looked chic and immaculate, as if she'd stepped out of the pages of *Vogue*. Tonight she wore a sapphire blue silk cocktail suit, with matching strappy shoes, and her short blonde hair was styled in a fashionably casual way. By comparison, Lucinda felt slightly plump and definitely not out of *Vogue*. More like *Nursery World*, she reflected ruefully, with the stains down the side of her dress where Daisy had spilt her yogurt just before the party began.

Lucinda had first met Carina twelve years ago when they'd both been staying at Ascot with some mutual friends. The Needhams had two daughters, Alison who was the same age as Carina, and Rachel who was six years younger and a contemporary of Lucinda. Rachel and Lucinda were still single at that time but Carina had already married Alex Somerset and had a baby called Charles. On that particular weekend, Alex had flown to Antwerp on business and the baby had been left with his nanny, and so Carina was on her own, and she and Lucinda had realised they got on extremely well. They had a similar sense of humour, loved the same films, adored clothes, and they both lived in London. It was the beginning of a lasting friendship and they'd remained in close touch, in spite of the differences in their lifestyles.

Alex had become fabulously rich; the Somersets lived in a mansion in Holland Park with nannies to look after their three children and a cook, housemaid and butler to look after them. Carina had never worked in her life and was on the A-list for all the best parties. Her rampant extravagance amused Lucinda, who found Carina immensely entertaining. At the same time Carina admired Lucinda's honest charm and kindness. She was also amazed that anyone could have a demanding career, as well as a husband and two children, and still remain cheerful.

'Darling, I *must* go and congratulate Maria Manners. She gave a riveting performance in *Relative Values* . . .' Carina plunged into the crowd and, stunned by her beauty, everyone made way for her, like the parting of the waters.

Minutes later, Julian's parents Jane and William Cotterell arrived. They'd flown over from their house in France, just for the party. Suddenly panic seized Lucinda. Practically all the food had been eaten, as if a plague of locusts had swept through the house, and they were getting low on drink. Should she send Julian to the off-licence for some sparkling white wine and a few packets of peanuts? Maybe not. Her in-laws lived unostentatiously but well. Dashing back into the kitchen, Lucinda grabbed one of the remaining bottles of good champagne, opened it quickly, took two of their best wedding-present glasses out of the cupboard and squeezed her way back up the hall.

'Ah! Champers!' exclaimed Edmund Wilcox, one of Julian's colleagues, seeing the bottle and glasses and reaching for them.

Lucinda hugged them to her chest, embarrassed. 'Sorry, these are for my in-laws,' she said apologetically. 'More supplies are on the way.'

'Where?' Edmund wailed. 'We've been here ages and we haven't had anything to drink at all yet.'

'I'll find Julian,' she replied hopefully, dodging and diving round Edmund's wife, a particularly large lady in a daisy-patterned dress.

'This is a complete farce. I'm going,' bellowed a voice at that moment. It was Miles, barging his way through the guests, shouting rudely as he elbowed past them. 'Why d'you ask such dreadful people, Lucinda? Cluttering up the place so that no one can move! It's absolutely ridiculous!' He glanced balefully at Carina who was laughing loudly amongst a group of people.

Anne followed, squeezing her way past other guests and smiling apologetically, as if to suggest Miles was really only joking.

'I'm sorry ... excuse me ... I'm so sorry,' she murmured, to which no one paid the slightest attention.

Miles swung furiously on Anne. 'What are you sorry for? Why are you apologising, you stupid woman? Come *on*! Come now or you can bloody well stay behind.'

'Anne was merely being polite,' Alex pointed out coldly.

Lucinda flushed with anger and embarrassment. 'Then go, Dad, and stop making such a scene,' she hissed in his ear.

'Why are you whispering?' Miles shouted. Then he looked over his shoulder at his wife again. 'What's the matter with you, for God's sake? Always lagging behind. Come *on*.'

Everyone had stopped talking, appalled by the way Miles had spoken to Anne, who looked very fragile.

'I'm sorry, sweetheart,' she whispered to Lucinda. 'You know how Daddy hates a crush. It's been a lovely party and thank you for inviting us.'

'Oh, Mum, I wish you could stay,' Lucinda murmured regretfully. 'Julian's parents have just arrived and they're hardly ever in England.'

Anne edged closer. 'You know Daddy can't stand them. He says they—'

'Anne! Are you coming or not?' Miles shouted, standing by the front door. 'Goddamn blasted cocktail parties! Who bloody needs them?'

'Such language!' Daisy exclaimed disapprovingly as she leaned over the banisters, her fat little arms folded across her chest.

Jamie nudged her. 'Be quiet.'

'I'll phone you tomorrow.' Anne gave her daughter a quick understanding smile as if they shared a secret, and turned to hurry after Miles.

Lucinda stood watching their receding figures for a moment, wishing with all her heart that her mother would stand up to her father. His rudeness, the way he'd spoken to Anne, was outrageous.

Behind her, in the packed room, she heard a buzz of scandalised whispers as the guests asked each other how Anne could stand being married to such an obnoxious bully.

'Everything OK?' Julian asked, on his way to the kitchen to fetch more drink.

'Apart from the fact that my father has insulted all our friends en masse, everything's fine,' she replied drily. On impulse she reached up and kissed him quickly on the corner of his mouth.

'What's that for, Bun?' he asked, pleased.

'For *not* being like my father.'

He pinched her bottom as he squeezed past. She gave a delighted little scream. Then the front door bell rang again.

'Oh, for heaven's sake . . .'

When the last stragglers finally left, Jane and William Cotterell insisted on taking Julian and Lucinda to dinner at the Mirabelle, while Delia finally got Jamie and Daisy into bed.

There were times when Lucinda envied Julian his parents, a happily married couple, who were easy-going and charming and not given to domestic dramas. It was not surprising Miles didn't get on with them, having once labelled them as 'boring . . . vapid . . . and appallingly bourgeois'.

William, who was in his sixties, was tall and pleasant-looking with blue eyes, thinning white hair and a rich tan from spending so much time in his garden in the Dordogne. Anywhere in the world he would have stood out as an archetypal Englishman, with his quiet manners and reserved way of dressing.

Jane was the absolute opposite of Anne Scott-Forbes, in every way. Strong and gregarious, her tanned, finely boned face was a network of lines, but her eyes were still a dazzling shade of blue and she had a wide enthusiastic smile and a warm confident personality. She also dressed with stylish chic in a very understated French way which accentuated her slender figure. Having no daughters of her own, she adored Lucinda and had welcomed her into the family from the beginning. And of course Jamie and Daisy came in for their share of spoiling as they were the only grandchildren she'd ever have.

'We've got to fix dates for you all to come and stay again,' she said eagerly, as soon as they were settled at their table.

'Let's order first,' William suggested. 'How about a champagne cocktail to start with?'

With expertise born of years of experience, he ordered the drinks and the food. 'I've been coming here for forty years and I must say it's kept up with the times,' he remarked, looking round admiringly. 'I'm glad we booked. We've never have got a table otherwise.'

'I'm longing to show you what we've done in the garden,' Jane said, sounding as excited as a girl. 'William and Jacques have been planting borders of lavender on either side of all the paths and it looks – and smells – heavenly. And we've built an arbour, by the side of the house, which will be perfect for eating out of doors when we need a bit of shade.'

'Jacques must be ninety by now,' Julian remarked. 'I'm surprised he can still lift a spade.'

Jacques had been the gardener at the Château St Laurent for the past fifty years. The Cotterells had inherited him from the previous owners when they'd moved to the area fifteen years ago, and his daughter and daughter-in-law helped Jane in the house.

'Seventy-eight to be precise,' William said, smiling. 'And he's fitter than me. He can out-garden me any day. God knows what we'll do when he drops off the perch.'

'He'll probably outlive both of us,' Jane joked, 'so I wouldn't worry. Now, dates. When can you both get away for a couple of weeks?'

Lucinda and Julian exchanged smiles. Knowing his parents were expecting them all during the summer, they'd already managed to arrange to take their holidays at the same time, although it meant taking the children out of school for two weeks.

Julian leaned forward, elbows on the table, his expression eager. 'Would May the sixth be all right? It's a Saturday, and if we leave at dawn we could be with you by the late afternoon.'

William thumped his fist on the table in delight. 'Perfect. Isn't that perfect, Jane? And you'll be staying a fortnight, won't you?' The hope in his voice was touching.

'Of course,' Lucinda rejoined warmly. 'That is if you can bear us all for as long as that.'

'My darlings . . .!' Jane's eyes filled with emotional tears. 'You've no idea how much we're looking forward to your staying. Daddy has a surprise for the children, too,' she added mysteriously.

William beamed. 'You bet I have. I can't wait to see their faces when they see what we've fixed up for them.'

'What is it?'

'Do tell them, darling,' Jane urged.

He took a deep breath, obviously enjoying the moment. Then he said, 'We've fixed up a playground for them, with a slide, a couple of swings, a see-saw and a climbing frame. Don't say a word, though. I want it to be a surprise for them.'

Lucinda's jaw dropped and all she could think was: my father never even gives Jamie or Daisy a Christmas present, or a birthday present either, and here are Julian's parents going to all this expense and trouble.

'That is so kind,' she burst out impulsively. 'We won't say a word, but my goodness, they're going to be thrilled.'

Julian looked at his parents, his eyes, so like his father's, filled with gratitude. 'Lucky children. Thanks, Mum and Dad,' he said softly. 'They're going to be over the moon.'

'We love to try and make it special when you come to stay,' Jane replied.

Living in France was something she and William had promised themselves years ago, and it was a perfect existence as far as she was concerned, except that they didn't see Julian and his family as much as they'd have liked.

'That's settled, then,' William said, raising his glass. 'Here's to May the sixth and a happy holiday to everyone!'

Three

It was 5 May and Lucinda was frantically trying to clear her desk before going on holiday. Their cases were packed, she'd stocked up on books to read, she'd bought masses of factor 15 sun lotion, and Julian was organising as a present for his parents a hamper filled with all the things they loved and couldn't buy in France, like Scottish oak-smoked kippers, Harrods sausages, English mustard and Keeler's thick cut marmalade.

She glanced at her watch. It was already three o'clock and she knew she'd never get through the stack of reports on her desk by six. One of the field research agencies they used had been doing a street survey in an effort to find out which age-group of women preferred loose face powder to pressed powder. Another report concerned the packaging of a new twenty-four-hour moisturiser they were bringing out. Should it be boxed in pastel pink with the Archée logo in silver and the name of the product printed in blue? Or was an all silver box more popular, with the printed matter in midnight blue, making the subtle point that it worked night and day?

'Oh, God . . .' Lucinda groaned, catching the bottom line which said the results were inconclusive because they varied widely from area to area. The sales department and the directors were going to want something more positive than that before they went into production. It was up to her to assess all these different finds and put them into her own report, so that at the next meeting with the production managers a decision could be reached.

Just when she thought she was making some headway her phone rang.

'Hi, Lucinda. Peter here.' Peter Harris, the director of marketing and her boss. 'I need some info,' he continued breezily. 'What was our share of the hair spray market in December 1998?'

Lucinda raised her eyebrows. Eighteen months ago. Why the hell did he need to know that now? She tapped her keyboard rapidly. 1996 – 97 – ah! 98 came up on the screen.

'I have it,' she replied. 'We had 58 per cent.'

'And the value of units produced? And the sales value?'

Experience had taught her they were not one and the same. 'Units' meant the value of the cans of lacquer that had been manufactured. 'Sales' value meant how many were actually sold, and how many came under the heading 'Buy one – get one free'.

She tapped away some more and swiftly gave him the figures.

'Thanks,' he said briefly, hanging up.

Lucinda had just immersed herself in the findings of another field research study on anticipated new trends linked to fashion/role models from the pop world/etc. when her phone rang again.

Cursing, she snatched it up. If she had to answer many more complicated queries she'd never get home tonight, and as tomorrow was going to be a long day, driving through France, she really wanted to get to bed early.

'Hello?' she said crisply.

'Lucinda? Lucinda, is that you?'

She froze. Her mother sounded distressed and agitated. 'Hi, Mum. What is it?'

'Terrible . . . terrible . . .' Anne wailed. 'Your father's had an accident. Can you come at once? I don't think . . .'

'Where are you? At home?'

'No, Chelsea and Westminister Hospital. In the casualty department. Can you come right away?' Anne's voice quavered dangerously. Lucinda could feel, with a dread sense of doom, that it was serious.

'Of course. I'll be with you in twenty minutes. What happened? Is he badly hurt?'

Her mother's words sent a chill down her spine. 'He fell. In the street. And he's hurt his head.'

'Try not to worry, Mum. I'm on my way.'

Hunched on a seat in the casualty department, Anne kept looking around fretfully, as if expecting someone to come and give her bad news at any minute. Where was Lucinda? Tom and Harry wouldn't be turning up, that was for sure. She'd phoned both of them but they 'couldn't get away at the moment', or were 'stuck in a meeting', but promised to 'keep in touch'.

Anne was hurt but not surprised. The boys had never been close to their father. They'd been a great disappointment to him. The trouble was, neither Tom nor Harry had done well at school, and once Miles realised they hadn't inherited his brains he wrote them off as hopeless and useless. From then on their relationship had deteriorated. Now they were grown men nothing had changed. She wished things were different, but her priority was Miles; it was up to the boys to get on with their own lives.

'Mum . . .! What's happening?' Anne looked up. It was Lucinda, her darling dependable Lucinda, her eyes anxious.

Anne immediately burst into tears. 'Oh, thank God you're here,' she wept. 'I'm so worried. Daddy's being X-rayed at the moment and they're talking of doing a brain scan as well. He was unconscious when they brought him in . . .'

Lucinda hugged her mother. 'I'll find out what's happening, but X-rays and scans are routine procedure for anyone who's had a bump on the head, so don't worry about that, Mum. I'm sure Dad'll be all right.' Right now she was more worried about her mother. Anne looked pale and haggard, as if she'd aged ten years, and her eyes were filled with fear. Miles was a tough old bird. No doubt he had concussion, and he'd probably be kept in hospital overnight as a precautionary measure because he was, after all, seventy-three. But Anne looked as if she were on the brink of collapse.

'Shall I get you a cup of tea first, Mum? Or a glass of water?' she asked worriedly.

Anne shook her head. 'I just want to know what they're doing to Miles,' she said brokenly.

Lucinda strode over to the reception desk, which was staffed by two nurses. 'Can you tell me how Miles Scott-Forbes is, please? He was brought in with head injuries after a fall.'

One of the nurses, small, quick and dark, gave a reassuring smile. 'I'll just check for you.' She turned to the computer, reached for the mouse and studied the screen intently. 'Nothing yet, I'm afraid. He's still in X-ray and they may do a scan as well. I'll let you know as soon as there's any news.'

Lucinda frowned. 'Can you tell me – I'm his daughter, by the way – did he have a serious fall? Or just a bit of a tumble?'

The nurse's reply was typical cautious hospital-speak. 'Until we see the results of the X-ray it's hard to say. But try not to worry. We're doing everything possible and I believe an ambulance was called right away so he received attention almost immediately, which is good.'

'Right. Thanks,' Lucinda replied doubtfully. Instinct told her the nurse was purposely making light of the situation. She moved away, out of her mother's line of vision, and took her mobile phone out of her bag. Then she tapped out Julian's number.

'Hi, Bun!' he greeted her, seeing her number come up on the screen of his mobile. 'How's it going?'

'Something awful's happened,' she said bluntly, and explained.

'Shit!' he said, shocked. He added immediately: 'How's your mother bearing up?'

'She's in a state, of course, but that's to be expected. Listen, about going to France tomorrow. You and the children must go ahead. I'll fly out to join you as soon as I can.'

'Oh, Bun!' he said, appalled. 'Sweetheart, we can't go without you.'

'You can't let the children down, or your parents. They're expecting us, and they'll have got everything organised, and anyway, Jamie and Daisy would be so disappointed. You've got to go. With any luck, I'll be able to get away in a couple of days.'

'I do hope so. God, what bad luck, when you need a break more than any of us,' he added wretchedly.

'That's the way it goes,' she replied. 'I've got to go now. I'm going to call Tom and Harry. They should be here.'

She phoned Tom first. He worked in the accounts department of Garson & Co, a large electrical company in Chiswick. When the switchboard put her through, his customary laid-back voice answered her wearily.

'Hello?'

'Tom, it's me.'

'Oh, hi! Any news about the old man?'

'You already *know*? Then why aren't you here? Poor Ma's demented with

19

worry. You must come, Tom. They're not saying much but I don't think it looks too good. Apparently he's still unconscious.'

There was a long silence, and she could sense Tom was thinking what a nightmare it all was. She knew exactly how his mind worked. He'd be inwardly groaning at having to drive in from Chiswick to Chelsea – the traffic would be heavy and it was a hot day – and then he'd have to find somewhere to park and there'd be the inevitable hanging around until they knew the details of Miles's condition.

'How bad is Dad?' he finally asked, with obvious reluctance.

'I told you, I don't know. But Ma's in a bad way, Tom. For her sake you should be here, if nothing else.'

There was another pause. 'OK,' he said finally, with a deep sigh. 'I'll come right away.'

Lucinda phoned Harry next. He was three years younger than Tom, and a year older than her. Ambitious, driven and always thinking up schemes that never took off, he was a complete contrast to his brother. His current plan was to set up an internet company which would trace people's family tree for them. He was sure it would appeal to Americans. Especially those who might have Irish ancestors. And especially those who were rich.

As soon as he heard Lucinda's voice, he launched into the quick-fire way of speaking he felt was impressive and showed how busy and stressed he was; a young tycoon on the brink of making his first few millions.

'What's the score with Dad, then, Lu? Mum phoned, bang in the middle of an important meeting. I've got this big deal coming up. I can't get away; I'm expecting a call from Dallas at any moment. All hell is breaking loose here. We're frantically busy.'

Lucinda was almost certain he was sitting alone in the bedsit in Baker Street he referred to as his 'office'. Here he worked out all sorts of fantasy 'projected sales graphs' with his mobile phone in one hand and a cigarette in the other.

'Dad's still unconscious and they won't know anything until they've seen the X-rays,' she snapped irritably. 'You really must come to the hospital, Harry. Mum needs you. It wouldn't take you long to get here and it's the least you can do in the circumstances . . .'

'Yeah, yeah. But can't you just keep me up to speed? I really am up to my eyes at the moment.'

'Don't give me that bullshit, Harry. He is our father, after all. You ought to be here.'

'It's all right for you,' he said angrily. 'He didn't make you suffer like Tom and me. We owe him nothing. Absolutely nothing. If we didn't turn up at his *funeral* it would be no more than he deserved.'

'Don't talk like that,' Lucinda said, distressed. 'Stop thinking about yourself, Harry, and think about other people for a change. Mum needs us, right now. You're just going to have to drop everything and get here, I don't care what you say.'

'Oh, Jesus! This couldn't have happened at a worse time.'

'Harry . . .!'

'Stop stressing, Lu. If I come I can't stay long. Casualty department, did you say? OK. See you shortly.' He sounded no more willing than Tom.

Anne was still sitting in the same hunched position, eyes flickering nervously. 'Have you found out how he is?' she asked, her voice breaking.

'They haven't told me the results of the X-rays yet, but the nurse sounded very reassuring,' Lucinda said, sitting down beside her. 'Try not to worry, Mum. Dad's very strong, you know.'

'But they're taking such a long time. What can they be doing? If only I knew what was happening . . .' She clasped her hands together to stop them from shaking.

'Does Granny know he's had an accident?' Lucinda asked suddenly. If anyone had a calming effect on Anne it was Sarah.

'I didn't want to distress her.'

Lucinda suppressed the ghost of a smile. A mishap befalling Miles would not have the power to distress Sarah Wells. Disturb her, maybe. Even worry her mildly, perhaps. But never distress. Lucinda was under no illusions about her grandmother's feelings towards her father, even though Sarah tried to hide them with diplomatic finesse.

'Don't you think she'll be hurt if we *don't* tell her?' she pointed out. Sarah, in fact, would hate to be left out of any family crisis.

Anne shook her head. 'I don't know. She must be told gently, then. Not the way I was. With a policeman coming to the house, blurting it out . . . just like that! I got the most dreadful shock.'

'Poor Mum.' Lucinda could just imagine how terrified her mother must have been. 'I'll call Granny. I know she'd want to know.'

When the phone rang that afternoon and it was Lucinda on the line, Sarah knew instantly that something was wrong.

'What is it, darling? Are the children all right?' she asked immediately.

'They're fine, Granny. It's Dad I'm ringing about. He's had a fall. A bad one, in the street. I thought you ought to know.'

'What about your mother?' Sarah's voice was sharp with anxiety. 'Does she know?'

'Yes. We're both at the hospital. Dad's got head injuries but we don't yet know how bad it is. Mum's distraught, so I've told Tom and Harry they've got to get here, but there's nothing we can do until we know the results of the tests.'

'Oh, my darling, what a worry for you. I'm so sorry. Would you like me to come? I can nip into a taxi and be with you in twenty minutes.'

'Would you, Granny? I mean, we may be getting worked up over nothing. Dad may only have a spot of concussion, but . . .'

'But you don't think so?' Sarah said intuitively.

'No, I don't,' Lucinda replied in a small voice.

* * *

Tom turned up first, crumpled-looking, as if the stuffing had been knocked out of him years ago. Although he was only thirty-seven he looked older, largely because his face was etched with lines of sadness. He was a grey man with kind eyes who hardly ever smiled. When he did, there was a gentleness about him that was disarming. He wasn't smiling now, though. Looking downcast, he walked over to where Anne was sitting and kissed her on the cheek, his lips hardly moving, as befits a man who is unused to kissing.

'Are you OK, Mum?'

'I want to know what they're doing to your father.'

Tom looked at Lucinda and raised his eyebrows.

'I'll see if there's any news,' she said. 'You stay with Mum.'

While she was waiting to speak to the nurse at the reception desk again, Harry came bowling along, with his jaunty walk and cheeky, boyish face.

'Any news, sis?' he asked, joining her at the desk. His blond hair flopped over his forehead, and he smelled of cigarettes.

'I'm just going to ask again.'

At that moment a white-coated doctor joined the nurse behind the desk and spoke to her in a low voice. Lucinda couldn't make out what they were saying, but then the nurse cocked her white-capped head in Lucinda's direction, and Lucinda caught the words '. . . the daughter'. The doctor looked at her hesitatingly.

She leaned across the desk towards him. 'I'm Miles Scott-Forbes's daughter, Lucinda Cotterell,' she said. 'Can you tell me how my father is?'

'I believe his wife is here, isn't she?' he asked, still hesitatingly, as if he didn't want to discuss her father.

'Yes, but she's very upset and rather . . . well, quite frail.'

He nodded. 'Yes, I understand. Maybe we could go somewhere quiet for a moment.'

Lucinda's heart suddenly started hammering against her ribs. 'Is he . . .?'

'No, but his condition is very serious. If you'd like to come this way.'

He led the way into an empty cubicle. Harry followed Lucinda, whose face was now very white.

'Your father apparently tripped on a pothole in the road and fell, hitting his head on a kerbstone.'

Lucinda winced, imagining the pain. 'And . . .?'

'Normally this might cause concussion, even a cracked skull, but I'm afraid there is a complication in your father's case.'

'What sort of complication?' Harry asked.

'We've done a scan.' The doctor paused, sizing up his words carefully, as if they were sharp dangerous flints that could fly out of his mouth and hurt them. 'Did you know he was suffering from a tumour?' he asked at last. 'A large brain tumour?'

Lucinda blinked, stunned. What had that to do with the accident, she thought stupidly.

'A brain tumour?' Harry echoed.

The doctor nodded. 'I'm afraid, as a result, your father has had a massive brain haemorrhage. He is in a coma at the moment.'

Lucinda sat down rather suddenly on the only seat in the cubicle. 'Will he come out of it?'

It took the doctor several moments to decide whether to be honestly blunt or not, but this young woman looked strong and capable, and she had her brother with her.

'No, I'm afraid not. He's sinking fast,' he replied.

'Fuck!' Harry drew out the expletive, making it a long word that fell from his open mouth.

'Oh, poor Mum,' Lucinda breathed, closing her eyes for a moment.

'If you like I'll arrange for you to be with him until . . . until the end. He's beyond the point of resuscitation, so it will be . . . quite peaceful,' the doctor said gently.

'Shit! Do we want that?' Harry asked, eyes wide, voice hoarse.

Lucinda nodded. 'Mum will,' she said positively.

The doctor became brisk, businesslike. 'Then I'll arrange it. If you'd like to wait with your mother in reception, I'll send someone to fetch you in a few minutes, to take you to him.'

Outside in the corridor, Lucinda turned anguished eyes on Harry. 'Who's going to tell her?' she asked, aghast.

'You, of course,' Harry replied. 'You're always good with her. I say, sis . . .' He grabbed her arm as she started to walk back along the corridor, to the reception area. 'Do I have to be in on this? I mean, Dad and I never got on. I don't see any point in—'

Lucinda cut him short. 'You're staying,' she said firmly. 'And you're staying for Mum's sake. We all must. She's going to need us as she's never needed us before.'

Julian had just arrived, hot and breathless. She saw him bending over Anne, Sarah and Tom as they sat huddled, asking them what was happening. Then he turned round and saw Lucinda, and knew from her face that the news was as bad as it could be.

Instinctively he went and put his arms round her and she leaned against him for a moment before whispering hurriedly, 'We've got to tell Mum he's dying.'

The nurse escorted them to a large cubicle in a quiet corner of the casualty department. Miles lay on the bed, covered by a green blanket. His face was like an old polished ivory carving, still, lifeless, a purple swelling on one side of his forehead the only sign of what had happened.

Anne went straight to her husband's side, as she had done all their married life, through cursing and criticism, bullying and bad temper, in success, failure and all manner of domestic strife, until death finally parted them ten minutes later when Miles slipped silently beyond her reach.

* * *

They all went back to the large rambling house in St John's Wood which Anne and Miles had moved into when they'd first got married. It hadn't been redecorated for years, and the faded curtains, worn carpets and heavy Victorian furniture Miles had inherited from his parents added to the atmosphere of gloomy darkness. Today it looked more neglected and unloved than usual, and Sarah's first thought was: Anne can't stay in a place like this now she's going to be alone.

The whole family, in their different ways, were suffering from a profound sense of shock.

Anne, as was to be expected by those who knew how much she'd loved Miles, was inconsolable, a shattered and broken woman who could only sob, 'Why did this have to happen?'

'Why don't you phone her doctor, darling?' Sarah whispered to Lucinda. 'Your mother needs a sedative. I'll get her into bed.'

Lucinda nodded, kissing her grandmother gratefully on the cheek. Julian, watching them, realised for the first time how alike they were. Both composed and calm in a crisis, with a strength of character that kept them going in moments of stress.

'I'd better phone my parents,' he told Lucinda when she'd spoken to Dr Keenan. 'Tell them we won't be coming tomorrow.'

'Yes. And can you phone Delia? She doesn't know what's happened. Tell her we may be back late this evening, and ask if she can put the children to bed.'

Julian nodded, squeezing her hand. 'Poor Bun,' he said sympathetically. 'I'm sorry.'

She gave him the ghost of a smile. 'I'm all right,' she said stoutly. 'It's Mum we have to worry about.'

In contrast, Tom had become hopeless and confused. 'What happens now?' he kept asking anyone who would listen. But Harry was recovering already from the shock. He wanted to get the whole business of death over and done with so he could see what Miles had left them all in his Will.

While Lucinda made tea for everyone in the kitchen, where the sink and units and gas oven dated back to the sixties, Julian went into Miles's study to phone his mother and father.

'I'm afraid we're going to have to postpone the holiday until after the funeral,' he told his father, knowing how disappointed they'd be, although they would absolutely understand.

'Of course, of course,' William said immediately. 'Let us know if you want us to fly over for it. Perhaps we could all come back to France together afterwards? Lucinda's going to need a break.'

'You're right, Dad. I'll keep in touch.'

'Please give her our best love, and our sympathies to the rest of her family, especially Anne.'

'I will, Dad.'

'Take care, old chap.'

The doctor arrived soon after, and administered a sedative that sent Anne into a deep sleep. Her grief-stricken face was swollen with crying, but at least her fevered emotions were stilled for a while.

'What happens about the funeral?' Harry asked, as soon as Lucinda carried the tea tray into the drawing room. Sarah and Tom were sitting in armchairs, and while Lucinda sank down onto a sofa beside Julian, Harry stood with his back to the fireplace, as if he already owned the house.

'As I see it, we've got two options,' Lucinda said. 'We either have a big funeral, attended by all his past colleagues and friends from the academic world, or we have a private family funeral, and then later on a big memorial service. Either way we've got to do it properly. When we announce his death in the newspapers that's not going to be the end of it. I'm fairly certain *The Times* and the *Telegraph* will do obituaries. There will be tributes from all over the place, and hundreds of letters to be answered . . .'

'Oh, God,' Tom groaned. 'Then let's have the big funeral and get the whole thing over with, in one go.'

'Hang on,' Harry cut in. His mind was working fast. A funeral would have to take place within a week. A memorial service could be postponed for a couple of months or so. Long enough to plan the whole thing properly. Long enough to make sure important people could find a window in their diaries on that day. Maybe even get the Secretary of State for Education to attend, and a few other bigwigs. Properly done, the whole thing could be turned, subtly of course, into a PR exercise for him and his new company. After all, his father had actually been quite famous in his own field; nothing like hanging on to someone else's coat tails – or in this case coffin and hearse – to get a lift, he reckoned. Aloud he said, 'We must arrange a beautiful memorial service. I think it should be at St Martin-in-the-Fields, and we should make out a guest list . . . because there are a lot of people who will be very hurt if they aren't informed,' he added swiftly, seeing Lucinda and Tom's expression. He turned to Sarah for support.

'Gran, you think Dad should be properly honoured, don't you?' His eyes were wide and round, giving him an appealing boyish expression that didn't fool her for one moment.

Sarah's expression gave nothing away, but ever since Harry had been a child she'd privately thought of him as a 'wide boy', slippery, crafty, flash and totally self-seeking. Now, only hours after his father's death, she knew she was right.

'That's up to your mother, really,' she said stiffly. 'When she's calmer you must ask her what arrangements she'd like.'

'I have a feeling, knowing Dad, that he's probably already left detailed instructions as to what's to happen,' Lucinda pointed out. 'I know he always said he wanted to be cremated, rather than buried.'

'Then we'd better get on to his solicitor right away,' Harry said eagerly, jumping to his feet, glancing at his watch and reaching in his pocket for his mobile. 'I'll do it now. Anyone got his number?' They all knew Bernard Clarke, who was a family friend and had been Miles's solicitor for over forty years.

Julian glanced at Lucinda, looking for her reaction. He personally found Harry's attitude distasteful. It was no secret that none of the siblings, Lucinda included, cared deeply for their father after the way he'd treated them all, but it was obvious that Harry was now after the main chance. He wasn't even pretending to be saddened by Miles's death.

Lucinda spoke. 'This has got to be thought through, and discussed with Mum. I mean, I haven't fully grasped what's happened yet. I keep expecting Dad to walk though the door at any minute, and ask what we're all doing here. It hasn't sunk in that . . . he's gone. That we're never going to see him again. I can hardly believe it.'

'Neither can I,' said Tom. There was an unmistakable note of heartfelt relief in his voice. 'D'you know,' he paused to look round at the others, 'he's been like a dark shadow hanging over me all my life. Ever since I can remember. I used to be sick with dread when I had to come home from school for the holidays. He tormented Harry and me, Lucy. You were younger. You probably didn't notice.'

'I noticed,' she said quietly.

'Well, there you go!' Harry intervened. 'You got off lightly, only because he didn't think you were worth noticing, while we got the full blast of his cruelty and rage. I'm damned if I'm going to pretend to be upset now.'

'As long as you hide your feelings from Anne,' Julian remarked. He was finding this whole scene difficult to accept. He so adored his parents that the very thought of their death was liable to bring tears to his eyes.

'I did notice,' Lucinda repeated, looking at Harry, 'but he was our father and presumably he did his best. I don't think he deliberately set out to be cruel. Mum wouldn't have married him in the first place if that had been the case.'

Tom and Harry snorted derisively.

'No, I mean it,' she continued. 'God knows, he drove me crazy, too, but I believe he thought he was doing the right thing. He thought he was toughening us up, preparing us for the real world. The fact that he got it all wrong is the real tragedy. But there's no point in holding it against him now. It's too late. We've got to go forward and try not to be bitter.'

'Easy for you to say that,' Harry scoffed. 'I reckon Tom and I have been scarred for life by the way he treated us.'

Sarah spoke softly. 'People are only scarred by life if they allow themselves to be.'

Harry ignored her. 'So what are we supposed to do, Luce?' he asked irritably. 'Mum's going to be out for the count for the rest of the day and even then she'll be in no fit state to make decisions.'

'Harry has a point,' Julian said. 'There's a hell of a lot to do when someone dies. One of us will have to pick up the death certificate from the hospital tomorrow, register the death, get on to an undertaker to make the arrangements, put announcements in *The Times* and the *Telegraph*, book a church for the service; then there's the cremation to be arranged . . . the order of service and hymns to choose . . . cars to be booked, people to inform . . . flowers to be ordered . . .'

Harry looked at him in amazement. 'You seem very up in all this; how many funerals have *you* arranged?'

Julian shrugged. 'When my uncle died I helped Dad organise the whole thing. He was a general in the last war and a bit of a hero, so it was a big affair, as this one will be.'

Lucinda shivered. The hideous reality of it all was sinking in. Her father was dead and nothing would ever be the same again, and meanwhile they were all going to have to endure the pain of the funeral. No funeral was easy. She wondered how her mother was going to survive.

As if she knew what Lucinda was thinking, Sarah leaned over and placed her arm round her granddaughter's shoulders. 'I think I'll stay here with your mother for a few days, darling,' she said. 'She can't be left alone, but you've got to be at home with the children . . .' Her voice trailed off, the unspoken remainder of her sentence more suggestive than if she'd actually said 'and Tom and Harry aren't going to be any comfort to her.'

Lucinda nodded in understanding. 'Can you really, Granny? Are you sure it won't be too much for you?'

'Of course not,' Sarah replied stoutly. 'We'll be fine.' She knew that Anne's daily, who came to clean the house and do the ironing, could also be persuaded to do a little shopping and cooking. One thing was certain. Anne couldn't be left alone.

Harry was still on his feet, jingling the loose change in his pocket with one hand, clutching his mobile with the other, shifting from foot to foot like a boxer warming up for a fight. The sooner the funeral, the sooner the Will would be read.

'I still think I should get on to Bernard Clarke. He might do all the boring ground work for us,' he said in frustration.

'OK, go ahead,' Lucinda said wearily, reaching for her shoulder bag which she'd dumped on the floor at her feet. 'I've got his number.'

As Delia was leaving the next day for her own holiday, which was supposed to have coincided with their departure to France, Lucinda returned home that evening to look after the children while Julian, Tom and Harry got started on making all the announcements and arrangements. Bernard Clarke had assured them that their father had left no particular instructions as to his funeral arrangements, so it was decided they'd try to arrange a private family cremation service for the next Thursday, and then organise a memorial service at a later date.

With Anne still sedated and the doctor expected to return in the morning, Sarah collected a few things from her flat and settled herself in the spare room, keeping in touch with Lucinda by phone.

'As soon as possible I'm going to suggest your mother comes and stays with me,' Sarah said. 'Who wouldn't be depressed in this gloomy old house? It's like a mausoleum. I think she ought to leave it in due course, and get herself a cheerful little flat, don't you? After all, she's only sixty-one! Time to start over again.'

'Like you did when Grandpa died?'

'That's right. I've been a widow for over twenty years, and very good years they've been too, although I still miss him.'

'Mum can stay with us,' Lucinda suggested, 'at least for a while. We could get a bed for the playroom, and she could sleep there.'

'Sweet of you, but I don't think so, darling. The children would exhaust her.'

Harry sat facing the undertaker across the desk. He was a thin, dark-haired, oily young man in his thirties, with an unctuous manner which Harry thought was unnecessary as he was getting the business anyway.

'Now, Mr Scott-Forbes, would you like to see our range of coffins? We have—'

'It doesn't matter what sort of coffin it is,' Harry cut in. 'They're all second or third hand, aren't they? I mean, you use them again and again, don't you? As long as the lining isn't stained, any in your range will be fine.'

There was a stunned silence.

Harry thought to explain himself. 'I told you we wanted a bake and shake, didn't I? That's what you call it, don't you? Everything gets recycled; you must make a tidy profit.'

From the undertaker's expression it was obvious he thought Harry was drunk. His tone became gently solicitous. 'We have a very nice mahogany model . . .'

Harry laughed. 'Not getting mixed up with Naomi Campbell, are you?'

'. . . with brass handles.' He paused, looked pained and then continued swifty: 'We will also provide four pall-bearers, a chauffeur-driven hearse, and how many other cars would you like, sir?'

'We'll use our own,' Harry replied nonchalantly.

'Now, about the ashes. Would you like to select an urn? Alternatively, you might prefer us to scatter them for you in the Garden of Remembrance?' He pushed a pamphlet across his desk with quiet deference. 'We can plant shrubs or spring bulbs to mark the spot. This gives you all the details.'

Harry's blue eyes widened. 'This is a really profitable scam for you, isn't it? I'd no idea.'

In an increasingly strained atmosphere, the undertaker continued to ask whether they required an organist, flowers for the chapel, and a priest, or were they bringing their own? Finally, as he ushered Harry to the door, he leaned forward to shake Harry's hand and make a final attempt at being courteous. 'I hope we shall meet under happier circumstances, Mr Scott-Forbes.'

'Oh?' said Harry, looking him straight in the eye. 'Is that likely?'

The undertaker forced a faint smile to his thin lips. 'I do have quite a social life.'

'Really? You surprise me,' Harry said bluntly, before setting off jauntily down the road. He knew he'd behaved atrociously but he simply couldn't help himself. He felt so *free* now his father was dead. It was like being released from prison after a life sentence. Never again would he be hauled over the coals for being stupid, a failure, badly behaved or a waster. He could do anything he liked in future because his father wasn't there, and would never be there again, to reprimand him as if he were still a child. The joy of being recalcitrant was now his, and he felt like dancing along the pavment.

The announcement in the deaths column of *The Times* and the *Telegraph* was simple and to the point.

> SCOTT-FORBES. Professor Miles Robert, DSc; FRS 1952. Suddenly, aged 73, on Friday 5th May, 2000, dearly beloved husband of Anne (née Wells) and father of Lucinda, Tom and Harry. Funeral private. No flowers please. Memorial service on a date to be announced later.

'Not even flowers?' Carina asked, stricken, when she phoned Lucinda as soon as she saw the announcement. She sounded shocked and distressed.

'I don't believe it!' she kept saying. Then her voice caught on a sob.

'Are you all right?' Lucinda asked in surprise.

'It's just that since Mummy died last year, I'm . . . I'm awfully wobbly about death,' Carina wept.

'I can understand that.'

'But is there anything I can do to help?' she continued, rallying. 'Would you like me to have the children for a few days? Charles is away at school, but Tara's home because she's hurt her ankle, and so is Michael.'

Tara was eleven and Michael was nine, and they'd known Jamie and Daisy since the latter had been born.

'Thanks, Carina, but they're fine here. I'm off work anyway and it's rather nice being at home with them,' Lucinda replied.

'Just a thought. Tara's as bored as hell being at home and missing all her friends at school. Maybe I can drop her off at your house for a few hours, so she can keep your two amused.'

Lucinda hesitated. While she adored Charles and Michael, she'd never taken to Tara and it made her feel guilty, because she'd no idea why. Tara was a pretty little girl, with dark hair and eyes and a quiet manner, but there was something about her that was unnerving. A certain slyness, a watchfulness, as if she were summing up all the grown-ups, wondering what made them tick. Compared to Daisy, who was as open as a sunny day, Tara had an altogether darker side.

Lucinda heard herself say: 'Can I take a rain check, Carina?'

'Fine. Just let me know. How's your mother bearing up? Your father was an incredible man, wasn't he? An absolute genius.'

'Mum is in a bad way,' Lucinda said. 'She's staying with Granny at the moment, because she says she can't bear to be at home. There are too many reminders of Dad.'

'I can understand that. So . . . the funeral is for family only? No friends at all? Not even close ones?'

'Just family. Dad didn't believe in God, you know. Really believed that religion was the opium of the masses and all that stuff. But Mum believes desperately; she's relying on being reunited with him in heaven one day.'

'I'm sure she's right, I mean, about being reunited in the next life and all that.' Carina sounded almost tearful, and Lucinda guessed she was thinking about her mother again.

'Yes, I'm sure there's something, some sort of afterlife,' Lucinda said carefully. She recalled with a smile Sarah's description of what she believed happened when you died.

'There's this long dark tunnel,' Sarah had said, 'with a light at the end of it. And when you get to the light, there are all your family waiting for you.' Then she'd cast her eyes up in mock horror. 'And then you're damn well stuck with them!'

At this moment Lucinda shared Sarah's feelings. So many people had said to her over the past two days: 'You're going to miss your father so much, aren't you?' and to spare their feelings she'd nodded, given what she hoped was a brave little smile, realising it would sound awful to say: 'Actually, no. It's a great relief he's gone.'

It *was* an awful thing to say and a worse thing to feel, but she simply couldn't help it. Just as she could never stop loving Julian, so it was impossible for her to suddenly start loving her father. She knew with all her heart that however much she might wish it, feelings of affection could not be forced. Far less love. Just now the only feelings she could summon up were ones of profound thankfulness that she would never have to see him again. And of course sympathy for her mother's grief which was genuine and heartfelt. She only had to imagine how she would feel if anything happened to Julian to realise how much Anne was suffering.

Tom, steeped in gloom, arrived at Lucinda's in time for supper that evening. In an effort to try to hold the family together she'd also invited Harry, but he'd said he was meeting friends and couldn't come. Well, she'd tried, she told herself. Anne had also refused, saying she couldn't face anyone, not even her own children, so Sarah stayed at home with her, getting her into bed in the spare room after giving her a large whisky and warm milk to try to get her to sleep.

Tom lived on his own, in one miserable room that had been advertised as 'a studio flat', which Julian said was how large cupboards or even cellars were described by estate agents these days. It was years since Tom had had a girlfriend, and Lucinda worried about him, feeling he was stuck in a lonely rut out of which he'd become unable to dig himself.

'Good to see you, Tom,' Julian said warmly when he arrived shortly after half past seven.

'I bought this, thought we could have it with dinner,' said Tom, handing him a bottle wrapped in cheap paper. Though not exactly penniless, and not intentionally mean either, Tom did not know how to lash out and enjoy himself. His idea of a good time consisted of treating himself to a double *café au lait* at the cafe near where he worked.

'Thanks, old chap.' Julian winced inwardly when he saw the label. He wasn't a snob but he was something of a wine buff and he knew the plonk Tom had presented him with was guaranteed to give them all a hangover before they'd finished the first glass. He belonged to a wine club which did wonderful monthly 'special offers' and Julian's cellar – in truth the cupboard under the stairs which he'd rigged up with racks from Homebase – included some fine Chablis and Pouilly Fumé, his favourite Côtes du Rhone and a nice line in red Bordeaux from the Château les Moines. Without hurting Tom's feelings he wondered if he could surreptitiously substitute one of his own botttles for dinner without Tom noticing.

'Thanks,' he said, nevertheless, 'that's really kind of you. Come through to the kitchen. Lucinda's putting the finishing touches to dinner.'

Tom could smell it; the delectable aroma of roasting lamb with rosemary. He sniffed appreciatively. God, was there anything better than home cooking? He lived on packets that called themselves 'Shepherd's Pie', or 'Beef Lasagne' which when removed from the microwave resembled, both in taste and texture, nothing so much as hot, wet cardboard.

'Can I get you a gin and tonic?' he heard Julian say.

'Thanks,' he replied gratefully. Fresh fragrances were assaulting his senses: roast potatoes and french beans, rich gravy and mint sauce . . .

'Hello, Lucinda?' he said, entering the kitchen, already cheered.

Lucinda looked flushed and contented, a big apron over her sweater and trousers, and comfortable loafers on her feet. She glanced at his grey face, which seemed to match his rather scruffy grey suit and tie, and knew that his father's death was affecting him more than he'd ever admit.

'Hiya, Tom.' She kissed him affectionately on the cheek, making a mental note that when the present ordeal was over she really must try to find him a nice girlfriend.

'Is Harry coming?' he asked, sipping his drink, the heat and the wonderfully appetising smells in the kitchen making him feel suddenly quite light-headed. Making him realise that this was what life should be like.

Lucinda shook her head. 'No. I just hope he comes to the funeral. He's in a funny mood at the moment.'

'He's always in a funny mood if you ask me,' Tom replied morosely. 'I think he's chucked Helen.'

'Really?' Lucinda stirred the gravy with a wooden spoon before deftly

31

pouring it into a gravy boat. 'What happened?' She'd liked Helen. She was an air hostess and had a calming influence on Harry.

Tom shrugged. 'She probably ran out of air miles,' he retorted drily. 'Before that, what happened with Michelle, Hildegarde, Carol, Aileen and Patricia?'

Lucinda stared at him in amazement. 'How do you remember all their names?'

'What I want to know is how does Harry get all these women? What do they see in him, for God's sake?'

'He's . . . well, pushy,' she said carefully. He's also got sex appeal, charm when he wants to impress, a wicked sense of humour and a forceful energy that women find attractive, she thought, looking sadly at Tom, because he didn't have any of these qualities. Tom was basically timid, shy and very low in self-esteem. That was why he'd been crushed by Miles, and Harry hadn't. Harry was a survivor. Poor Tom was a classic victim.

'I'm dreading Thursday,' he said suddenly. 'I hate funerals.'

'I don't think any of us are looking forward to it.' As she spoke, Lucinda was putting the steaming vegetables onto dishes, getting the leg of lamb out of the oven for Julian to carve, placing the warmed plates on the kitchen table. 'Can you help me carry these through, Tom?' The small square dining room was next to the kitchen and the children had helped her lay the table before they'd gone to bed, Daisy insisting she pick some flowers from the patio which she'd stuck in a jam jar in the middle.

Obediently Tom did as he was asked. 'But it's going to be hell, isn't it?' he continued. 'Mum's going to be a wreck, Harry will be making flippant remarks . . . Christ, I wish it was over.'

'What's this? The funeral?' Julian asked, coming into the dining room with a decanter, into which he'd secretly poured a bottle of Château des Annereaux in lieu of Tom's offering. 'At least it's family only.'

'I suppose so,' Tom replied doubtfully.

'Have a little salmon pâté, darling,' Sarah coaxed, as if Anne were still a child, 'and some warm toast.'

Anne had only slept for a short while and Sarah had heard her keening as she sat watching television. She had appeared in the drawing room a few minutes later, unable to bear being alone.

Sarah had settled her on the sofa and then gone to the kitchen to get out some tempting delicacies from the fridge, and a bottle of wine. She placed them on a tray with a bunch of grapes, and a little dish of handmade chocolates.

'I'm not hungry,' Anne protested weakly.

'You'll make yourself ill if you don't eat anything. At least have some wine.' Sarah filled her daughter's glass before pouring some out for herself.

'What am I going to do without Miles, Ma?' Anne asked for the umpteenth time.

'At first you're going to hurt like hell, but I promise you it will get better as time passes. It would be stupid to say time heals, but it does at least give you a chance to get used to the pain so that it hurts less and less. You'll be all right, darling. God never sends us a situation we can't cope with. Remember that, Anne. I felt just as bad as you when your darling father died, but I've managed to have a very nice and happy life, haven't I? A different sort of happiness, perhaps, but nevertheless a very rewarding one, which I probably would never have experienced had he lived.'

'But you're stronger than me. I depended on Miles for everything,' Anne sniffed. 'He was my life.'

'So what you have to do, my darling, is to get yourself a new life. You're only sixty-one, Anne. Some people start a new career in their sixties. You used to write such wonderful children's stories; d'you remember? Tom and Harry loved them.'

'Miles said they were rubbish and that we'd never get the boys to read anything decent if we brought them up on that sort of pap . . .' Anne paused, her face puckering, unable to continue.

Sarah's lips tightened as she inwardly wished her late son-in-law in hell. He'd stripped Anne of everything: a charming talent, self-confidence, self-esteem . . . and what in God's name had he given her in return? The role of a browbeaten victim who actually believed she'd been blessed.

Sarah opened her mouth to say something and then, looking into the tortured eyes of her daughter, she realised with a pang that she might as well save her breath. Just now, poor Anne was as incapable of carving a new niche for herself as a child was of becoming Prime Minister. It was going to take time, and a lot of patience and support before Anne would be even vaguely fit to emerge from under the shadow cast by Miles.

'You'll find a way, darling,' Sarah said at last. 'It will take time, but you *will* make a new life for yourself. You could start, once the funeral and everything is over, by offering to help Lucinda with the children. She works so terribly hard, and she's only got that au pair to help her. She'd find it a godsend if you took Jamie and Daisy off her hands occasionally. Or you could offer to do the shopping for her?'

Anne nodded, too weak to argue. Since Miles had died, she'd felt only half the person she'd been before, and the weaker half at that. She wasn't at all sure she'd be able to exist without him.

When she awoke in the early hours, remembering what had happened, she was seized by a mixture of grief and panic. The demons of the dawn, as she described them, attacked her and tortured her with doubts about her whole future. What was going to happen? How would she know what to do? Who was going to look after her? She'd lost the most marvellous man in the world and she grieved that their three children did not share her adoration of him. Miles had been rather hard on them; that she realised. But he'd wanted the boys to succeed, and it had been his way of teaching them to stand on their own feet and apply themselves to the matter in hand. Instead, they'd rebelled

33

and neither of them had made anything of their lives. Anne saw it as a betrayal of Miles's good intentions. Only Lucinda, although she didn't know it, had lived up to his expectations.

But if Miles had been a less than perfect father, he had been an ideal husband. Through tear-drenched eyes Anne recalled how, in all the years they'd been together, he'd never so much as looked at another woman. How many wives could say that? He'd loved, protected and provided for her in his own inimitable style, and once she'd got used to his funny little ways, knowing they were for her own good, she'd trusted him with all her being. She'd been so lucky, she thought humbly, to have been married to someone as loving and loyal as Miles.

Harry spotted Paula Maxwell sitting on her own at the bar in Harvey Nichols's fifth-floor restaurant. She was drinking a spritzer and looking awkward, as if she wasn't used to being on her own. Harry studied her, his interest quickened. He reckoned she was in her early forties and very sophisticated in a cream suit with matching high-heeled shoes and a scattering of diamonds. Her auburn hair was taken smoothly back and held in a pony tail with a cream silk scarf, and her lightly tanned face was delicately made up.

A classy number, he reflected. A bit old for him, in fact *very* old for him – he was more inclined to chase birds in their early twenties – but this one had something different. Money. She looked rich. And so far, she appeared to be on her own.

He picked up his drink and sauntered in her direction, pretending he was looking for someone. When he got to her side, he pointedly looked at his watch, shrugged and gave an impatient sigh. He could feel her looking at him. After a moment he turned, gave her a wry but impersonal smile and remarked: 'Annoying when people are late, isn't it?'

She smiled back, not replying.

Undaunted, Harry continued: 'A colleague from my company promised he'd be on time, but I suppose he's got held up.' He downed the last of his gin and tonic. 'Oh well . . . let's hope he's pulled off the big deal we're after.' He looked at his empty glass. 'I'm going to get myself a top up, while I wait. How about you? Can I get you the other half?'

This last phrase was one of the few things he remembered his grandmother instilling in him, when she'd coached him on etiquette during his youth. 'Never ask someone if they'd like another drink; that makes people feel greedy,' Sarah had intoned. 'Always offer them the other half. It's much more diplomatic.'

The woman hesitated and Harry employed his trick of looking boyishly innocent and appealing by opening his blue eyes wide and giving his head a little shake so his blond hair flopped over his forehead.

'All right,' she said, relenting. 'Thank you.'

Harry ordered their drinks, praying whoever she was waiting for wouldn't turn up yet.

'My name's Harry Scott-Forbes, by the way,' he said. 'Of Scott-Forbes & Masters.'

Her smile broadened. 'Hello. I'm Paula Maxwell.' Then she looked puzzled for a moment. 'Your name's familiar. I'm sure I've heard it recently . . .?'

'You've probably heard of us. We're quite big,' he added grandly. 'We've been really lucky in cornering the market for tracing people's family trees. I think it's because, in this changing, uncertain world, people at least like to know where they come from, because none of us can be sure where we're going, can we?' His smile was earnest but indulgent. 'Tracing one's ancestry can be so reassuring. It gives people such a wonderful feeling of security.'

'I suppose so,' she said uncertainly. Then her face lit up. 'No, it wasn't that! I read Professor Scott-Forbes had died; he was a friend of my father's and I met him several times. What a brilliant man he was. A great loss to the academic world. Are you related to him?'

Harry changed from being a City whizz-kid to looking suitably wistful. 'He was my father,' he murmured in a subdued voice.

'Oh!' Paula Maxwell's left hand flew up to her mouth and Harry noticed the large diamond solitaire next to her wedding ring. 'I'm so sorry. How stupid of me. I should have known. Oh, my deepest sympathy. I know what it's like to lose someone. You must miss him desperately.'

Harry hung his head and bit his bottom lip. 'I do. It's a terrible blow to us all. My mother's devastated, so the funeral is going to be private; we'll be having a memorial service later on. When we're all a little less upset.'

'Oh dear, I'm so sorry,' she said again, looking genuinely sympathetic.

Harry raised his head to look at her, his expression still wretchedly sad. 'You've lost someone, have you?'

'My husband, actually. He died nearly four years ago.'

A widow, no less! Harry looked horrified. 'That's dreadful,' he exclaimed, 'and you're so young, too. I'm most terribly sorry.' He dropped his voice to an intimate level but was careful not to lean towards her. 'Are you desperately lonely on your own?'

Paula spoke carefully. 'I am lonely at times, but I've got a lot of good friends and so I get by.'

'And you've got parents?'

'My mother died when I was twelve but my father's alive, and we're very close. I don't know what I'd have done without him when Neil died.'

Harry nodded seriously. 'Nothing like family in times of trouble.'

They sipped their drinks in silence for a few moments and Harry wondered if she was meeting a man 'friend'. And was he in with a chance if this 'friend' didn't turn up? If that should happen he'd have to 'cancel' the meeting with his 'colleague'. And if he got to know Pauline Maxwell better, he'd have to get round the Scott-Forbes '& Masters' bit, because there was no Masters. But he was racing ahead of himself. An idea was forming in his head and it had nothing to do with sex. Paula was a cool, classy widow and he had a strong feeling she was not looking for a quick fuck. He'd need to be sympathetic, supportive and go very, very slowly to get what he was really after.

'I think I'll have to be going,' he heard her say and his heart sank. 'My aunt's obviously been held up. Thank you so much for the drink, and my sympathies again over your loss.'

Harry gave his sweetest smile. 'That's very kind of you. I'm not the best company at the moment, I'm afraid, but I wondered . . . would you consider meeting me again?' He saw her look wary. 'For a drink, perhaps?' he added hurriedly. 'At the end of a long day it would be something to look forward to, you know?' The head shook and the lock of hair tumbled forward again. 'How about we meet opposite? At what used to be called the Hyde Park Hotel and now has some newfangled name, as my grandmother would say?'

He could see her hesitating. 'Well . . .'

'Oh, please. It would really help to cheer me up. You'd be doing me a real favour, you know. Take my mind off poor old Dad. How about Friday evening? Seven o'clock? Please?'

It did the trick. Paula smiled generously. 'All right. I'll see you then.'

'Cool.' Harry patted his pockets, frowning, as if feeling for something. 'I'm afraid I haven't any business cards on me but you can get me on my mobile. I'll give you the number.'

'Thanks.' She waited while he scribbled it on a blank page in his pocket diary, which he then tore out and handed to her.

'Have you . . .?' he began.

'No, I never have cards. I'll see you on Friday. Thanks for the drink.' And with that she smiled once more, turned and walked swiftly and with an attractive swagger out of the bar in the direction of the lifts.

Harry stared after her. He hoped she'd turn up on Friday. He wondered if she was listed in the telephone directory. He longed to know if she had a man in her life. And the first thing he must do in the morning was to get some business cards printed. One could get them done, he believed, instantly and inexpensively in a slot machine at the local post office.

The obituaries appeared the following morning, taking up a third of a page in both *The Times* and the *Telegraph*, with a photograph of Miles taken in his early forties, looking suave and striking in a dramatic way, with his dark penetrating eyes and pronounced nose and jawline.

Lucinda, scanning them quickly, saw they were fleshed-out versions of his entry in *Who's Who*, but once again the only mention of his family read: 'He married Anne (née Wells) in 1958. They had two sons and one daughter.'

Nothing more. Once again Lucinda felt as if she, Tom and Harry had been airbrushed out of the scene; they were of no importance, mere shadows in the background of a landscape dominated by Miles.

During the following days sacks of mail containing letters of condolence were delivered to Anne in St John's Wood, a lesser amount to Lucinda in

Fulham, and none whatsoever to Tom or Harry in their one room flatlets in Earls's Court and Baker Street respectively. That was because everyone Tom and Harry knew was aware they couldn't stand their father; to sympathise on his demise would be the height of hypocrisy.

The number of letters Anne and Lucinda received were exactly relative to their feelings, reflecting Anne's utter grief at the loss of her husband, and Lucinda's loyalty to a father she'd never liked but had been publicly loyal to.

'How am I going to reply to them all?' Anne wailed, when she went back to her house to collect some more clothes. She was overwhelmed by the endless stacks that arrived, from all over the world, and could not bear the thought of reading how admired Miles had been, and how greatly missed he was now.

I can't handle this, she thought in despair. Not now. Not yet. So without reading any of them she placed them in a series of plastic carrier bags, and put them in a corner of Miles's study.

'What you do want done with these?' her cleaning lady asked, as she hoovered around them.

'I'll have to reply to them . . . in time,' Anne stammered, scurrying up to her room to collect more black clothes and a black hat for the funeral. Alone, she sobbed uncontrollably. Every word of sympathy and understanding in those letters was like a knife through her heart. But as soon as the funeral was over she'd make a start answering them all. She'd have to. If she was ever going to be able to look at them again.

The cremation service at Golder's Green cemetery was minimalist in the extreme. Exactly six people were present, there was no music at Anne's request, because it would make the whole occasion even more painful, and no eulogy either for the same reason. The only flowers were a handful of white rose petals scattered on the coffin, which Lucinda had insisted on at the last moment, and the straightforward funeral service was taken by a clergyman who'd never heard of Miles anyway.

On the whole, Miles would have approved.

But as they watched the coffin shudder forward in silence on its final journey to the incinerator, Harry said in an aside to Tom: 'We might as well have put the old man out with the trash at this rate.'

But Tom was suddenly too convulsed with sudden grief to hear. Tears poured down his cheeks and he was racked with wrenching sobs as it dawned on him that the father he had always hated was actually gone and now he was without a father at all. The tears of hurt that he had held back as a boy had suddenly been released by the sight of the disappearing coffin, and he was inconsolable.

Lucinda, sitting between him and Julian, turned and put her arms round her brother. Tom clutched her hand in a fierce grip, like a drowning man on the brink of being washed away, and sobbed harder than ever.

Anne, sitting with Sarah on the other side of the aisle, turned to look at

Tom in shocked concern. His outburst of emotion was so unexpected, so utterly out of character, that she rallied, momentarily forgetting her own grief, and became almost composed as the clergyman spoke the closing prayers.

It hadn't occurred to her until that moment that anyone else might be suffering as much grief as she was, certainly not Tom and Harry. I should be thinking of them more, she thought guiltily, looking across the narrow aisle as Tom wiped his tears with the back of his hand. The trouble was she'd devoted her entire married life to looking after Miles, and it struck her now, with terrible clarity, that maybe she'd done it at the expense of her children's happiness.

I must try to show them I love them, too, she reflected, feeling for almost the first time the burden of parenthood, so wrapped up had she been in trying to be the perfect wife.

The little service had come to an end. Anne, Sarah and Harry led the way out of the chapel followed by Julian, with Tom clutching his arm. Outside the air was sweet and fresh and the sun was shining brightly.

At the door, Lucinda breathed deeply, thankful to be re-entering the world of the living. Then she turned and for the last time looked at the gap through which her father's coffin had disappeared. She felt a wave of immense sadness; not for what was, but for what might have been. Should have been. How terrible to say farewell to your own father and not grieve. At that moment she almost envied Tom. When it had come to the point and in spite of what he'd said, he had obviously felt a sense of grief and loss. All she'd felt was a sense of regret.

Her mother had said the previous evening that although Miles was dead he was 'still there' for her, and she found that immensely comforting. Well, Lucinda reflected, walking towards the car, he certainly wasn't here for *her* now.

But then he never had been.

The woman dressed in black lurked under the trees, watching Anne and Sarah and Harry, followed by Julia and Tom and, after a long moment, Lucinda, emerge from the chapel. As the family walked to the cars, she withdrew deeper into the shadows, her white face tearstained and half hidden by dark glasses, a handkerchief held to her mouth. She shouldn't have come today, and it was vital they didn't spot her, but she hadn't been able to stay away. Miles had meant more to her than anyone knew, or must ever know. She simply couldn't have let today pass without saying a final goodbye to him. They'd shared so much, she and Miles, dark secrets she was determined to take to the grave with her, but wonderful, beautiful secrets, too.

Meanwhile the cars were leaving, Harry driving Tom and Anne in his Ford Cortina, and Julian following in his BMW with Sarah sitting in the front beside him and Lucinda in the back.

The woman in black turned sharply away in case they spotted her, but as

38

soon as the cars had swept out of the courtyard and onto the main road she entered the chapel and knelt in the front pew, tears streaming down her cheeks as she looked at the place where Miles's coffin had lain only a short while ago. And she envied his family because they were allowed to grieve, and to show their grief, whilst hers had to remain hidden.

It had been decided that Jane and William Cotterell should attend the memorial service in due course, rather than fly over for the funeral, and they spent the next day making sure everything was ready for the arrival of Julian and the family.

Château St Laurent had originally been built in the seventeenth century, just outside the village of Berteillac, near Tremolat, and with loving care the previous owners had gradually enlarged and modernised it without destroying any of its character and charm. When Jane and William had first seen it, fifteen years ago, they'd fallen in love with it immediately.

The pale stone building with its steeply built slate roofs, all at different levels, and a small round turret at one side housing a staircase, nestled like a jewel in the hundred hectares of fields, woodlands and lake that surrounded it. Built on the foundations of a monastery, its neat square windows kept the twelve main rooms cool in the heat of the day, and in the winter wooden shutters kept out the cold night air while log fires flickered in the great fireplaces.

Now, in the second week of May, the sun shimmered on the garden William had worked so hard with old Jacques to maintain, and the lavender borders were alive with the activity of bees.

'I wonder what time they'll arrive?' Jane said, trying to keep the excitement out of her voice. They were sitting on the terrace, having had a swim. An English tea, with cucumber sandwiches and home-made scones, was already laid out in the kitchen.

'Shouldn't be long now,' William replied, stretching his long legs as he lay on one of the sun loungers. 'They were picking up a car at the airport, weren't they?'

She nodded. 'Thank God they were able to get away after the funeral. What poor Lucinda must have been through in the past week I can't bear to imagine.'

'Trust the old bugger to die just as they were going on holiday.'

Jane laughed. 'William, do be careful what you say in front of them. I know Lucinda never talked about her father, but she may have been extremely fond of him. She may be really upset.'

'I doubt it. D'you know what Julian once told me? That Miles completely ignored Lucinda when she was a child, and when she was in her teens he told her that if she couldn't think of anything intelligent to say, she was not to talk at all.'

Jane gave a sharp intake of breath. 'Surely not!'

'Apparently so. Lucinda told him that she became practically mute, because every time she opened her mouth she realised that what she had to say was utterly banal, so in the end she said nothing.'

'To see her now, you'd never think she'd suffered like that, would you? She's so assured and confident, and she holds down such a good job,' Jane remarked thoughtfully.

William nodded, gazing up at a peerless blue sky. 'She's had what they call, in the latest parlance, a big learning curve,' he said, grinning, 'and what we used to call growing up. There's no doubt Miles was a monster, Jane. Julian also told me he used to thrash the boys on the slightest pretext. One year, when Harry was eight, he'd been given a little radio for his birthday by his godfather, and Miles threw it out of the window, because he was playing it too loudly. Of course it was smashed to bits, which was his intention.'

Jane's eyes were filled with compassion, imagining the disappointment and hurt of a small boy. 'I always knew Miles was a rude bad-tempered man but I'd no idea he was so cruel.'

William shook his head. 'It's not surprising those young men are a mess.'

'Perhaps he was jealous of them?'

He gave her an incredulous look. 'Hardly, sweetheart. The man was a genius and they're as thick as two short planks. Julian has never understood why Lucinda got off scot-free in comparison but he thinks it's probably because she was a girl and not worth bothering about.'

'Lucky for her,' Jane remarked drily. Then she raised her hand, her head cocked to one side. 'Did you hear something? I think it's them! Yes! There's the car.' She jumped to her feet, wrapping a brilliant blue sarong over her bathing suit as she rushed towards them, arms outstretched.

'Hello, my darlings!'

Jamie and Daisy came scrabbling out of the car, screaming 'Granny!' in delight, before Lucinda had disentangled herself from the surplus bits of luggage on her lap that hadn't fitted into the boot. Then they were all hugging and kissing and William was whirling Daisy round and Jamie was asking if he could have a swim.

When the commotion had died down a bit, Jane had led them all indoors for tea.

'What was your journey like, darling?'

'Not bad,' Lucinda replied. 'We had thought of bringing the car over but the drive from Calais would have been a killer, so we arranged to hire a car at Bordeaux airport instead. The children slept most of the way, and as you can see they're hyper with excitement to be here at last.'

Julian fell into step with his father, while Jamie and Daisy dashed around like puppies.

'Been a helluva week, I suppose?' William asked.

Julian shot him a haunted look. 'Don't even go there, Dad.'

'Where?' William asked, puzzled.

Julian grinned. 'Let's just say it was a nightmare from beginning to end and thank Christ it's over. And d'you want to hear the good news?'

'Is there any?'

'Yeah. Both of us have wangled an extra week's holiday. If you and Mum can stand the pace, we're here for a fortnight after all.'

William looked delighted. 'Cold! I mean, cool! Isn't that what you say?'

'This is what heaven must be like,' Lucinda remarked as she lay in bed that night between pure linen lavender-scented sheets, resting her head on an enormous feather pillow.

After the excitement of their arrival, and the near hysteria of Jamie and Daisy when they were shown their newly installed playground, they'd all had a swim. Then the children had had supper in the large comfortable kitchen with its big ovens, collection of copper pans hanging from a beam, and dresser filled with pretty ceramic plates and dishes.

Tired after their long day, they fell instantly asleep in what Jane always referred to as 'their own rooms', where, over the years, she'd encouraged them to leave clothes, toys and books behind, ready for their next visit.

While Julian and his parents sat and talked, Lucinda had a hot scented bath, washed her hair, and put on a white T-shirt and a long wraparound skirt of Indian fabric. Her feet were bare and she relished the wonderfully warm flagstones and the cool grass beneath her soles. Chilled champagne was waiting for her on the terrace, and as she lowered herself onto one of the sun loungers London and all the drama and sadness she'd left behind seemed a million miles away.

'Have some foie gras, darling,' Jane urged, holding out a platter of delicious canapés, while William refilled her glass. Lucinda reached for Julian's hand, smiling at him.

'This is the life, isn't it?' she murmured. 'And to think that this time yesterday . . .'

'Don't even go there, Lucinda,' William remarked, pleased with himself for remembering the popular jargon of the moment.

'I won't,' she declared, seriously and fervently. 'I wish we could stay here for ever.'

'Oh, I wish you could, sweetheart,' Jane exclaimed. 'Wouldn't that be wonderful? Perhaps you can come for Christmas, though? You could bring your mother and your grandmother . . .' Then she caught William's warning eye and remembered Tom and Harry, too, and her voice faded away, before she added briskly: 'Anyway, you can see how you feel when the time comes, but we'd love to have you.'

Dinner, on the candlelit terrace under a brilliant moon, had been cooked by Jacques's daughter, Fleur, who delighted in showing off her culinary skills. The first course, a fragrant chicken consommé garnished with truffle and beetroot, was followed by roast partridge, served with grapes and segments of orange in a light orange curaçao sauce, with a variety of tiny home-grown vegetables, and finally an ice-cream soufflé flavoured with amaretto liqueur.

41

Afterwards, as they sat drinking coffee and cognac, a very gentle warm breeze wafted the scents of jasmine and nicotiana across the terrace. Lucinda closed her eyes, savouring all the sensations of taste and smell and the touch of the sun-warmed air on her skin.

Miles's death, her mother's heartbreak, Tom's hopelessness and Harry's rakishness belonged to another world now, as did D'Aussoire and the appalling work load she'd eventually have to return to. She only wished that her grandmother was here, knowing Sarah would relish every second of the elegant luxury as much as she did.

Now her eyelids were drooping as Julian kissed her tenderly on the mouth. There would be no lovemaking tonight because they were both exhausted, but there was a completeness between them that didn't need physical expression.

'Good night, Bun,' Julian whispered, curling himself into her back so that they slept like spoons.

' 'Night,' she murmured, taking his hand and holding it to her breast.

The moon slipped behind a cloud and the breeze stirred in the lavender, and the occupants of Château St Laurent slept on peacefully.

Four

'Was it ghastly?' Paula asked gently.

Harry had just described his father's funeral and she felt quite surprised that he'd wanted to meet her for a drink the day after such an ordeal.

He looked downcast, and bit his bottom lip. 'Pretty rotten. At least lunch at my grandmother's cheered us up afterwards. But we're all feeling stressed. My sister's legged it to France to chill out for a couple of weeks; wish I could do the same,' he added wistfully.

They were sitting in the newly refurbished Mandarin Oriental Hotel in Knightsbridge, its luxurious and extravagant interior glittering with gilt and chandeliers, its large windows overlooking the lush greenness of Hyde Park in the evening sunlight.

'Poor you,' she said softly. 'It's tough, isn't it? Coping with death.' She paused to sip the champagne Harry had rashly ordered before continuing: 'You should have put me off, Harry. The last thing you probably feel like doing is meeting someone for drinks this evening.'

Harry's whole face seemed to melt under her sympathy, and he looked up at her like a grateful little boy. 'Oh, you're so sweet, but I was really looking forward to seeing you again. I didn't want to postpone our drink, apart from which,' he gave a quirky little smile, 'you never gave me your number. I couldn't have got hold of you if I'd wanted to.'

'Oh! Neither I did.'

'And you aren't in the book.'

'So you *did* think of cancelling tonight?' Her smile was unfathomable. She crossed her legs and Harry heard the soft rasp of her nylons. She was wearing a slippy little dress, patterned with tiny roses, and over it a pink lace-edged cardigan. Her high-heeled strappy sandals were pink too, and Harry realised her whole appearance tonight was calculated to look much younger than on the evening he'd met her. Then she'd looked rich and soignée. Tonight she looked available and fuckable. It wasn't quite what he'd expected. It wasn't her body he was after, but if she was offering . . .? Well, what the hell.

'I was just curious to know where you lived,' he said, grinning. 'I might have guessed, as you're on your own, you'd take the precaution of being ex-directory.'

'Who said I was on my own?'

'You're a widow.'

Paula made a little moue. 'That doesn't necessarily mean I'm on my own.'

'No . . . I suppose not.' Talk about flirting, Harry thought, almost shocked.

Their eyes met and hers were dancing with amusement and something more.

'Would you like to have some dinner after we've had our drinks?' he asked, going for it.

'I'd love to.' she replied readily.

Again he felt a faint frisson of shock. Was she really that easy? Of course, he reminded himself, she was probably forty-one or two and maybe even lonely. Sex-starved, perhaps. And didn't women at that age go through a randy phase, a sort of premenopausal let's-have-a-final-fling-before-it's-too-late stage?

This could be trickier than he'd anticipated. At this rate she'd have him in bed before he'd finished his crème brûlée, and he'd never have a chance to interest her in his new company, never get round to murmuring that most magic of all words in the English language: *investment*.

'What are you thinking about, Harry?'

Harry didn't miss a beat. 'I was thinking how glad I am that I met you,' he said earnestly, his eyes wide and innocent-looking, a lock of hair tumbling onto his forehead.

Lucinda spent her first day at the château relaxing by the pool, while William and Julian played with the children, who couldn't be dragged away from the swings and slide and climbing frame in the meadow beyond the garden. Jane sat with her, sometimes talking quietly, sometimes sitting with her own eyes closed, drinking in the perfumed air and thinking how much she loved this place. The peace, the stillness, the wonderful countryside around them, the French food and the way of life were really all she'd ever wanted. To be here calmed her soul, and she very much hoped it would do the same for Lucinda, who seemed exhausted and stressed.

As if she knew what her mother-in-law was thinking, Lucinda turned to look at her, and smiled. 'It's bliss here, isn't it? I'm beginning to feel better already.'

'It's a very healing place,' Jane replied, smiling back. 'I could never go back to England now. William and I have made a life for ourselves here, and we love the place and the people, not to mention the climate.'

'What will happen when Jacques's too old to do the garden?' Lucinda asked, hating to cast a shadow over paradise.

'Fleur's husband, Younnik, will take over. He works in a factory now but he's a good gardener. And we're lucky to have Maria to help Fleur in the house. She's married to Jacques's son, Henri, who will inherit his cottage eventually.' Jane looked serenely around her at the old stone building and the beautiful garden surrounding it. 'The French are very family orientated. In this part of the world, jobs and homes are shared and handed down from generation to generation, which gives one a wonderful sense of continuity. All Jacques's relatives work locally, in Berteillac or Tremolat, so it makes it a friendly little community. They all get on with each other very well, too.'

Unlike my dysfunctional family, Lucinda reflected, wondering what Tom and Harry would be doing today. Anne was still with Sarah, of course, the one person who provided some sort of stability for them all, but even she hadn't been able to restore the much-needed family balance that Miles had systematically destroyed.

'I find myself thanking God every day for my blessed life,' Jane said humbly. 'I don't know what I've done to deserve such good fortune.'

Those words came back to Lucinda with fearful clarity a few days later, and it seemed to her that by speaking so, Jane had broken the spell of good luck that had cradled her for so long.

'Isn't it wonderful of Miles to have made sure I wouldn't have to worry about money?' Anne remarked to her mother as they sat drinking coffee after a simple but delicious lunch cooked for them by Mrs Morgan.

Bernard Clarke, not only Miles's lawyer but also one of the executors of his Will, had phoned her earlier in the week, to reassure her she'd been provided for, and to say that a copy of the Will would be sent to her in due course. 'You have nothing to worry about, although you can't sell the house, should you wish to, until probate had been agreed,' he had finished.

But Anne didn't care about that. She'd decided she would probably be happier staying on in the house which held such dear memories of Miles, but in the meantime, until she felt stronger, her mother had assured her she could stay in Rutland Gate for as long as she liked. She'd told Bernard that although Miles had appointed her as the other executor, she'd rather leave everything to him. He'd seemed relieved by this, and she supposed it was because he was a professional lawyer who knew what he was doing, whilst she hadn't a clue. Especially at the moment. She could hardly trust herself to write a shopping list without making a mess of it.

'Bernard said he's also left Tom and Harry fifty thousand pounds each,' Anne continued. 'Isn't that generous? It will be such a help to them.'

Sarah raised her eyebrows. 'And what did Miles leave Lucinda?'

Anne looked up, a figure from another dimension in a sepia print, all washed-out beige and cream, distant and flat and lifeless. 'Oh, I'm sure he'll have left her the same. He was such a fair man.'

Sarah found herself recoiling at the absurdity of the remark, and she turned sharply to look out of the window to cover up her reaction so that Anne wouldn't notice. The word fairness wasn't even in Miles's vocabulary. But there was no point in saying anything. At least Anne had begun to think more about Tom, Harry and Lucinda since the funeral, and that was something. But it would never stop her worshipping the memory of Miles and the false image she'd created of him in her mind.

As soon as Lucinda saw Julian's expression her heart did a little nervous flip. She swam across the pool, and pulled herself up to the surrounding stone edge.

45

'What is it?' she asked anxiously.

Julian dropped to his haunches and spoke in a low voice so that Jamie and Daisy, splashing around in their water wings, wouldn't hear.

'Dad's just had the most awful news,' he replied, frowning worriedly. 'He's breaking it to Mother at the moment.'

Lucinda clutched his arm and climbed out. Her hand, chilled from the water, felt icy to his warm skin. 'What's happened?'

'Dad sank a lot of money into ICC, and it's just gone pear-shaped. Dad may have lost the lot.'

'The Internet Central Company? Christ, I thought they were OK. What's gone wrong?'

Julian shrugged. 'Under-capitalised and lack of forward planning, I suspect. It's all very well setting up these new companies, but if all the other components from America are delayed and aren't in place in time, then the whole project's screwed up, for a start. The chairman's been kicked off the board and an emergency meeting of directors has been called.'

Lucinda frowned, her heart sinking. 'How much has he lost?' she asked in a low voice.

Julian raised his eyebrows and shot her a doom-laden look. 'Almost all he had,' he said heavily. 'He said it means this place will probably have to go.'

'Oh no!' Lucinda's hand flew to her mouth in anguish.

'What's happened?' Jamie called across the pool, picking up, with a child's instinct, the sense that something was wrong.

'Nothing,' Julian said firmly. 'Someone we know just got the sack, that's all.'

Satisfied, Jamie continued to splash about in the water with his sister. Watching them, Lucinda envied their capacity for being able to dismiss something instantly from their minds.

'So what happens now, Julian?' She remembered her conversation with Jane a few days previously. This was going to be the most tremendous blow to her.

'Dad's thinking of flying to London to find out how bad the situation is. He only heard about it because he happened to tune in to Sky News. He likes to keep abreast with what's happening back home, and suddenly he heard this announcement being made.' He shook his head. 'God, this is a bummer.'

Lucinda looked hopeful. 'Perhaps it's an exaggerated report? Maybe there is a problem with ICC but it's not as bad as it sounds?'

'I hope you're right.'

At that moment Jane and William emerged from the house. Jane's face was tearstained and William looked grim. Lucinda jumped to her feet and grasped Jane's hand.

'Are you all right?' she whispered.

Jane nodded silently, biting her lips.

'I'm going to London this afternoon,' William informed them quietly. 'I've already spoken to my stockbroker and it looks bad.' He turned to gaze at the view of distant wooded hills, richly green under a deep blue sky, and his eyes were filled with pain. 'I don't know what we can do to save the situation, but we're going to have a bloody good try.'

Jane slipped her arm supportively through his. It was a gesture of loyalty. It might be his fault that he'd invested unwisely, his fault that they might lose everything they held dear, but she would never utter a word of reproach. They were equal partners in a strong marriage, and Lucinda, watching them, could not help but compare their relationship to that of her own parents.

'Would you like to stay at our house, Dad?' Julian offered. 'I can give you the keys.'

William smiled wanly. 'Thanks, old boy. That would be great. The days of staying in five star hotels are almost definitely over.'

Tom pushed his trolley along the aisle of Waitrose in the King's Road, wondering what he should get for the weekend. Frozen dinners were the easiest but he was bored with them, longed for something freshly cooked, wondered if he might not phone Lucinda and invite himself for supper and then remembered she was in France.

He could open a tin, of course, and there was always salad. He tossed a lettuce, some marble-size tomatoes encapsulated in a plastic container, a cucumber and a bunch of spring onions into his trolley and then added a couple of large King Edward potatoes; he'd bake them for ten minutes in the microwave, and if he split them and shoved in a pat of salted butter they wouldn't be too bad. The skins wouldn't be nice and crisp, of course, but it was better than watching a potato bake in a conventional oven for two hours.

Then he added a bunch of bananas, four apples . . . his eyes were wandering across a selection of plums and peaches when suddenly his trolley seemed to jump out of his grip and slither away, banging into the dried fruit display.

'I'm so *sorry!*' a voice exclaimed. Looking round, he saw a woman he had seen several times before, also doing her shopping. She was in her mid-thirties, plump and motherly-looking, and they'd smiled and spoken on several occasions as they'd trundled their trolleys around. Today he noticed she was wearing a loose blue cotton shift which picked up the colour of her friendly eyes, no make-up and her brown hair tied back into a pony tail. Usually serene, she looked flustered at the moment, with a cluster of irritated lines on her forehead.

'These *damn* trolleys!' she swore, jerking hers towards her as if it was a wayward animal of which she'd lost control. It was piled high, as usual, and made the meagre contents of Tom's trolley look pathetic. 'Why do they *never* go straight? Did I give you a fright? I really am sorry.' Her apologetic smile showed nice white teeth and Tom noticed for the first time that she had a very pretty mouth.

'That's all right,' he replied easily.

Her smile broadened into a wide grin. 'Don't you just hate doing the weekend shopping?'

'It is a bore,' he conceded, 'but as you can see I don't have to get much.'

'Lucky you! I feel as if I'm stocking up for an army. I only have two sons to feed, but oh boy, do they eat!' She was laughing now, a rich fat chuckle.

Tom noticed her left hand was bare. 'You should get your husband to help,' he said slyly, testing the ground.

'I've never had one of those,' she replied cheerfully. 'What about you? You look as if you're catering for a mouse.'

Tom allowed himself a modest smile. 'I live on my own and I'm not very adept at cooking.'

'But you've got to eat!'

'Well yes, I do. Sort of.' Their brief exchanges in the past had alluded to the price of some of the goods, or how tiresome it was when the place was crowded. They'd never got to a personal level before. Tom moved on as if he had more things to get, and found she was pushing her trolley in tandem with his, falling into step beside him. He eyed the contents of her trolley with secret longing. Lamb chops. Minced beef. French beans. Pâté. A large wedge of Stilton. Streaky bacon, his favourite. Crusty bread. Fillets of smoked haddock. Fresh herbs.

'You obviously enjoy cooking,' he remarked, his mouth watering.

Again the rich chuckle. 'I enjoy *eating*. You ought to come to my place and have a square meal. You look as if you could do with it,' she joked.

Tom wished she meant it. 'How do you get that lot home?' he asked, as they strolled past a display of fruit.

She shrugged. 'The bus, usually.'

He looked horrified. 'How can you manage all that on a bus? Do you live far from here?'

'Why? Do you have a car?' she asked laughingly.

Something in his chest, just beneath his heart, blossomed and grew tender. 'Yes, I do actually. It's only an old banger but if I can give you a lift . . .?'

She stopped in the middle of the aisle to turn and look straight into his eyes. 'Tell you what. How about a deal? You give me a lift home and I'll cook dinner for you tonight. My name's Susan Murray, by the way. What's yours?'

As if mesmerised, Tom heard himself tell her his name, and accept her offer.

It transpired that Susan lived near the World's End, in a small council house. He also learned she'd never married the father of her two sons.

'He hit the bottle rather too often,' she said bluntly, as they drove along the King's Road. 'Then he became abusive, so I kicked him out three years ago. The boys are at school all day so I got myself a job in the local pub. What with that and Child Support, I was far better off without him, the lazy bugger,' she added, but without a trace of malice.

Later, leaning against the counter in her small kitchen, Tom looked at her with admiration. 'Which pub do you work in?'

Susan shot him a triumphant smile. 'I don't any more. I taught myself how to use a computer in the evenings when Dick and Steve had gone to bed and now I work as a secretary at Group Alliance. They have a branch at Hammersmith so I don't have to go far.'

'Good for you.' Tom watched as she prepared a steak and kidney pie, with mushrooms and a thick gravy that made him realise he was starving. By the time he'd told her about himself, Dick and Steve were home from playing football after school, also ready for one of Susan's 'square meals'.

Dick was nine and Steve seven. They were strapping lads but well mannered, fresh-skinned and blue-eyed like their mother, and Tom took to them immediately, especially as they seemed to regard his presence with nonchalant acceptance.

It was only when he was driving home, much later, after a dinner to dream about, that he wondered if their casual acceptance of him was because their mother often asked strange men home for supper.

William returned to the château three days later with little to cheer them.

'There's a rumour a rescue bid is going to be mounted to save ICC,' he explained, as they sat having drinks on the terrace before lunch. 'At Question Time in the House yesterday the Prime Minister said that too much was at stake to let the company collapse, but I honestly don't hold out much hope. The American division are denying the problem is their fault. They said they could have had all the hardware in place if ICC had liaised with them sooner.'

'When will you hear if the company can be rescued?' Julian asked.

William shrugged. 'These things can take months. Absolutely months.'

'So . . . what do we do in the meantime, darling?' Jane asked. There was a quaver in her voice, and dark shadows under her eyes. Lucinda knew she hadn't slept from worry since William had gone to London.

William took a gulp of his wine as if bracing himself for what was to come. 'I spoke to the bank yesterday. I'm waiting to hear if they'll grant us a loan so we can keep going for the time being, but I've had to offer this place as collateral. If ICC can't be rescued, then I'm very much afraid . . .' His voice drifted off and for a dreadful moment Lucinda thought he was going to break down, but he suddenly lifted his head and said angrily: 'It's my own bloody fault! I should never have been stupid enough to have put all our eggs in one basket. It's an elementary mistake and I've never done it before, but this time—'

'It's not your fault,' Jane said firmly. 'You were very badly advised, that's all. You were promised enormous dividends, an absolute fortune, when ICC was up and running. You mustn't blame yourself, William. If we have to leave here, then so be it. We'll just have to go back to England and start again.'

Only Lucinda, listening to those words, knew how much it was costing Jane to speak so bravely.

* * *

Lucinda found a message waiting for her when they returned to London a week later.

'I left it on the hall table by the phone,' said Delia, who'd come back two days before.

It was from Bernard Clarke, asking her to ring him.

'Oh, Lord, what now?' Julian asked, heaving their suitcases up the stairs, hindered by Jamie and Daisy who wanted to do their own unpacking in the hall. 'Don't tell me,' he shouted down from the half-landing, 'that Miles died intestate. That's all we need.'

A few minutes later Lucinda joined him in their bedroom. 'I've just spoken to Bernard, and Dad's made a Will all right. Mum's been left the house and Tom and Harry fifty thousand each, but I've got to go to his office to see him as soon as possible.'

Julian looked at her, puzzled. 'What the hell for?'

She shook her head. 'I've no idea. He said it was too complicated to explain in a letter or on the phone.'

Lucinda was early for her appointment with Bernard, so she walked past the offices of Blount, Middleton & Clarke, Solicitors, in Bedford Street, and turned left into Covent Garden. She'd have a cup of coffee at one of the cafés where in her childhood they'd sold boxes of Brussels sprouts and cauliflowers and the air was redolent with the fragrance of dawn-chilled apples.

In those days Sarah had made regular trips to Covent Garden when it had been a real market. She'd arrive by five o'clock in the morning, park her Citroën Safari in a side street, and set off with her list of fruit, vegetables, salads and flowers. She swore she saved herself a lot of money by going to the market, but in reality it was the romance of the place that entranced her. Sarah often invited her grandchildren to accompany her and that was when Lucinda, imagining herself to be Eliza Doolittle, became fascinated with the excitement of getting up when it was still dark, to enter the magical world of *My Fair Lady*.

'Tom and Harry can carry the boxes of fruit and vegetables and Lucinda can help me with the flowers,' Sarah would tell Anne when she picked them up from their home. 'It's educational for them. And the old market won't be there for ever,' she'd add as Miles protested vehemently at being awakened at such an unearthly hour by her arrival, and Tom and Harry sulked sleepily at having to do something so boring in the holidays.

But Lucinda never found those mornings boring. As she looked around now, at the chi-chi boutiques and cafés and bars, all geared to attract tourists, she felt saddened by the loss of something that had been full of vitality and atmosphere.

Covent Garden was not the same without the camaraderie of the cheery porters in the early hours of those mornings, as large lorries arrived up from the countryside bearing wooden crates of freshly picked plums and damsons, gooseberries and redcurrants, which were then transported on long narrow

50

barrows to the arched brick store rooms from which the vendors traded. The produce of the orchards and fields of Kent had been brought to the city. And the city, with all its cockney verve and good humour, turned the mundane transaction of selling that produce into a special event.

As Lucinda walked around now she tried to conjure up the remembered bitter scent of daffodils covered in dew, mingled with the tang of oranges and the earthy smell of potatoes. With nostalgia she recalled the hustle and bustle that had once taken place under a dawn that had gradually broken up the dark sky of night, and she wished it was still the same.

She glanced at her watch. It was ten twenty-five. She'd better hurry now, or she'd be late.

'Do sit down, Lucinda,' Bernard said. He was a tall grey-haired man with a long thin face and clever eyes half hidden behind thick glasses. With old-worldly charm he'd greeted her with a warm handshake and a slow but endearing smile. 'Would you like some coffee?'

Lucinda suddenly felt nervous. And very apprehensive. Why had he asked her here when he'd apparently told her mother and brothers outright about their inheritance?

'Yes, please. I'd love some,' she replied, her voice slightly shaky.

While he asked his secretary to bring two cups of coffee she tried to squint at the papers on his desk, see if they were anything to do with her father's Will, but the typescript was small, and she was trying to read upside down anyway.

'Now then,' Bernard said, sitting down and rubbing his hands together, almost, she thought, as if it was he who was nervous. 'How's everything going, Lucinda? You must all have been very shocked by your father's death. Very sudden and all that.'

'Very sudden.'

'But you've had a break in France, I gather? I'm sure you needed it. The children are well, are they? And Julian?'

Lucinda answered automatically and wondered with growing concern when he was going to get to the point.

'As you've been abroad, you won't, as yet, know the full contents of your father's Will.'

She shook her head.

Bernard then went on to repeat what he'd told her on the phone. 'But,' he continued, not looking her in the eye, 'it does become rather more complicated when it comes to yourself.'

With a wave of his hand he indicated a nineteenth-century writing case that was resting on a nearby table. It was eighteen inches by twelve and about six inches deep, made of cherry wood inlaid with mother-of-pearl, with a brass lock. 'Miles has left you this box,' he told her, 'and,' he paused for dramatic effect, 'here is the key.' He held out an antique brass key in the palm of his hand.

51

She couldn't help it; a wave of bitter disappointment swept through her. What was this casket? A pretty little antique case, of no practical use. That was all. So was this all she meant to her father? His only daughter? Nothing more?

When she thought what she could have done for Julian and the children with fifty thousand pounds, her eyes stung painfully. And it wasn't just the money; she now knew Miles had never cared for her. She'd been worthless in his eyes. Not worth bothering about, in life or in death. She clenched her hands and looked down, too shocked even to take the key from Bernard.

Then she looked up slowly, realising she was being rude and ungracious. He was looking at her with sympathy as if he knew what she was thinking.

'I'm afraid you must feel very disappointed, but I don't have to tell you how your father enjoyed manipulating people in his quirky way. I'm afraid what I have to tell you next will probably come as a great shock to you. I did everything I could to dissuade Miles from playing these games, but he wouldn't budge.'

'What games? I don't understand.' She had a fearful thought. 'What's in this box?'

There was a painful pause before Bernard spoke sombrely.

'Would you like me to give it to you straight? Or let you see his letter of instruction to you first? I have to say I believe he did all this in a moment of madness, and I greatly regret I couldn't stop him.'

'I want to know,' Lucinda said firmly. 'Tell me, please.'

Bernard cleared his throat. 'Very well. Macabre as this may sound, your father has actually left you several bundles of letters, which he placed in this writing case. They are from his former mistresses.'

Lucinda looked at him in stunned silence. 'Is this some sick joke of his?'

'Unfortunately not,' he said gravely.

'But I never knew he had any girlfriends in the first place. Are you sure you've got that right? And why in God's name should he leave their letters to me?' She felt confused and angry and deeply offended by her father's actions. 'There must be some mistake. I don't believe Dad ever had girlfriends. Not while he was married to my mother, anyway. I'd have known if he had.'

Bernard's sigh was deep and gusty. 'I'm afraid, Lucinda, all his affairs took place during the years of his marriage to Anne. Even up to a few years ago.'

'My *dad*?' Her mind was spinning, unable to grasp this extraordinary revelation. It was so unlike him; her cold, unfeeling father who never showed love or affection for anyone, not even his own family. He was the last person in the world she'd have expected to have had secret liaisons.

'I don't believe it,' she said flatly. 'No way. It's a wind-up. Was that his game? To tease in order to get me going? Which would be typical of him. I can just imagine him plotting this whole thing as a great joke. It's the sort of thing he'd find amusing,' she added in disgust.

'I almost wish that was true in a way,' Bernard said quietly, looking away from her again. 'But I'm very much afraid it's not. The letters are genuine. He showed them to me, filled in the details. And he has definitely bequeathed them to you.'

Lucinda sat staring at Bernard as if he'd suddenly grown two heads. Not in a million years had she expected anything like this.

'But why would I want them, for God's sake?' she protested. 'It's utterly sick. Even Dad can't imagine I'm perverted enough to appreciate such a thing.' She drew in a deep breath. Her chest hurt. 'Please take them and burn them, Bernard. I don't want them. And I don't want the case they came in, either. It will be nothing but an unpleasant reminder.'

Bernard looked deeply distressed. 'I'm very, very sorry, Lucinda, but I can't do that. If you will bear with me, I will explain that there is much more to this than being left some bundles of old love letters.'

'Such as . . .?'

'He has left detailed instructions. I can't tell you how it pains me to have to tell you this, and I wish to God I wasn't his lawyer, but . . .'

'Just tell me, Bernard.'

'He has stipulated that he wishes you to return these letters, *in person*, to the women in question.'

Lucinda drew a sharp intake of breath. 'You're kidding!'

He shook his head and picked up some of the papers before him. 'That is what he wants done.'

'*In person*? Well, he can forget it. If we have to, we can mail them, I suppose. Presumably he's provided their addresses?'

'Not exactly.' Bernard spoke carefully. 'Most of the letters have an address on the writing paper but not all, and many go back as far as twenty-nine years, so the writers may have moved, or died, anything. But his request is that you should trace them all, and, having done so, return their letters personally.'

Lucinda's face flushed scarlet with anger. 'But *why*? What's the point? I'm damned if I'm going to go along with his little game. This is the most outrageous and disgusting thing I've ever heard.'

'I think you're going to have to, Lucinda,' he said gently. 'There's a lot more I have to tell you, which will explain why it's important you carry out his wishes, mad though they may seem at the moment.'

Harry rolled over in the vast canopied bed, amazed by Paula's stamina. He felt absolutely knackered. They'd made love, if you could call it that – personally he'd called it rutting – three times in the past hour, which by his reckoning equalled a brisk ten-mile walk.

And still, after two weeks, she'd shown no indication that she'd be interested in investing in Relative Tracing, which was what he'd finally decided to call his company. He'd talked to her about it, outlined his plans, described his marketing campaign, stressed the importance of PR, but always, *always*, just as he was about to bring up the subject of her financial backing, she would deftly sidetrack him, almost as if she were doing it on purpose. But why should she thwart his attempts on the one hand, and make encouraging noises about what a good idea his scheme was on the other?

Harry had even bragged about his inheritance from his father, adding a nought to make it sound better and declaring he intended to invest the lot, he had so much faith in Relative Tracing, but she merely said, 'That's great,' and went on to talk about where they should dine that night.

As he lay beside her, Harry gazed up at the ceiling in frustration. He was itching to get his hands on some of her money and it didn't look as if she was going to part with a five p piece. And yet he knew for a fact she was worth millions of pounds.

He rolled onto his side again. The bedroom of her Eaton Place duplex was hot and stifling. He edged away from Paula's naked body, wishing he were somewhere cool, wishing he could take a deep breath of fresh air instead of scented air, wishing he didn't feel so fucking *smothered*.

A tiny part of him felt like getting up and leaving, going back to his one-room flat in Baker Street, where he could do as he liked: slob around in a T-shirt and jeans, remain unshaven, fart in bed, eat straight out of a tin or carton. But another part, a more powerfully obsessive part, knew that if he was careful he was really on to a good thing.

Paula was seriously rich. Not only had her husband left her the flat and a fortune, but she was rich in her own right, thanks to her father, Sir Humphrey Hodson, who had made money in property, and set up a large trust fund for her which she'd come into when she was twenty-one. She had it all, but it obviously wasn't enough. She seemed to need passion in her life as well, and that, thought Harry wearily, was exceedingly boring.

He turned to look at her and had to admit that even without make-up she was a looker. She lay beside him with a complacent smile on her lips, reminding him of a cat which hadn't just got the bowl of cream but a plate of salmon as well.

'Have you a busy day ahead?' she asked softly.

He sat up, nodding vigorously. 'Frantic. God knows when I'll be through. I've got meetings on the hour, every hour. I must dash now, because I've got to go back to my flat to get a change of clothes, but I'll ring you later.'

Her slender manicured hand reached out to stroke his thigh. Her nails were painted shell pink and Harry was shocked to see she wasn't wearing her wedding ring any more.

'You'll be back this evening though, won't you, darling?'

Harry hesitated and then was thankful that he hadn't said he was busy because she murmured: 'There's something I want to talk to you about.'

'As I was saying, these letters,' Bernard continued, 'are from five women. Four of them have written rather indiscreetly, I must say, giving their addresses on headed paper, but one of them gives no address at all. Your father has pencilled in their last names, so hopefully they won't be too difficult to trace, dead or alive.'

'How do you mean?' she asked, astonished.

'Some of them may well be in their sixties or seventies by now.'

This is becoming surreal, Lucinda thought, imagining herself trailing all over the country in pursuit of elderly ex-mistresses, maybe on Zimmer frames or in wheelchairs.

Bernard continued: 'You will have a problem tracing the fifth woman, I'm afraid. She wrote to Miles on blank writing paper, and signed herself "Pumpkin". Just that. Nothing more.'

'And Dad didn't pencil in her name, I suppose?' she asked with an edge of sarcasm.

Bernard shook his head. Lucinda was feeling sick now.

'This puts me in a terrible position with my mother,' she pointed out bleakly. 'What am I going to say if she asks what Dad's left me? I can never tell her in a million years. She's always been so proud that Dad never strayed, and always cared for her. I think she still believes that he loved no one but her. If she found out the truth now, it would kill her. And what do I say if Tom and Harry ask what I've been left? A writing case and a bunch of old love letters hardly equals their inheritance of fifty thousand pounds.' She tried to keep the bitterness out of her voice.

'Miles was very clever in the way his Will was worded as far as you are concerned. I haven't sent copies yet to the rest of your family, but when I do I don't think it will arouse their suspicion. All he actually puts is: "To my only daughter, Lucinda Clare, I bequeath an antique inlaid Edwardian writing case, containing some papers of mine, on my given subject. If she is able to dispose of them in an intelligent way, she will stand to benefit." Your family need never know what the papers are.'

'Oh, very clever,' she said drily. 'I'd like to know how I'm supposed to benefit from these letters, though. Except by suffering humiliation when I have to contact these women.'

'I'm very much afraid there's something else, my dear,' she heard Bernard say. Lucinda covered her face with her hands, wondering what else there could be.

He'd risen and gone over to a large grey metal safe in a corner of his office. The door was already ajar, and he opened it wider, and came back to her with several leather boxes, some small, a couple of them larger and flat. He laid them on the desk in front of her.

'Do you know anything about jewellery?' he asked, opening the boxes one by one.

'No, nothing.' With growing amazement she found herself looking at six exquisite pieces of jewellery, lying on their velvet beds like the contents of a treasure trove. There was a magnificent diamond brooch, a pair of beautiful gold earrings, a bracelet that twinkled like a fairy chain, a ring with a glowing dark stone, a pendant with sea-green jewels in a delicate gold setting, and a regal-looking pearl necklace. The pieces shimmered and sparkled in the dim lighting of Bernard's old-fashioned office, as she gazed down at them, speechless. Where had they come from? Whose were they? What had they got to do with Miles?

Bernard resumed his seat on the opposite side of the desk and watched her intently, saying nothing.

'W-what are these?' she croaked at last.

'Your father left them and he's given me instructions to keep them here, in the safe, until you have disposed of them all except for one piece; and that remaining piece of jewellery is for you.'

'I don't understand. Which piece?'

'That's up to you.'

'What do you mean . . . it's up to me?'

Bernard gave a quick sigh as if he wanted to get rid of the whole ghastly business as soon as possible. 'Your father has left instructions that when you return the letters to his mistresses, you are also to choose one of the pieces of jewellery to give to them, as a memento of his love for them. The last piece you keep for yourself.'

Lucinda raised her head slowly to look at him, her expression incredulous. 'He must have been completely out of his mind! No normal person would get his daughter to do all that,' she protested. 'Why couldn't he just have said return so-and-so's letters and give her *that* piece of jewellery, and return so-and-so's letters and give her *that* piece of jewellery?' She was suddenly very angry. 'Why the hell is he fucking me around like this?'

'This is where we come to Miles at his most . . . eccentric, shall we say?' Bernard replied smoothly, as if she hadn't sworn. 'I wish I'd been able to persuade him otherwise, but . . .'

Here comes the final killing sting in the tail, Lucinda said to herself, thinking she realised now how her father's mind had worked. Bernard's next words proved her wrong. She had had no conception of just how cruelly Machiavellian Miles could be.

Harry and Paula hadn't got back to her flat until after midnight. He'd started the evening by returning to Eaton Place with a bottle of Bollinger and the announcement that he'd managed to get a table at the River Café.

'How did you do that?' Paula asked, impressed. 'One usually has to book weeks in advance.'

Harry smiled wickedly. 'If you want something done, leave it to me.'

As it was a warm evening they were given a table on the floodlit terrace by the Thames. Harry, regardless of cost, urged Paula to order anything she wanted. As long as his plastic wasn't spat out by the restaurant's cash till, they'd have a wonderful evening. The only thing was, he hoped he had enough money in his bank account to cover the dinner. It would certainly be worth every penny of the odd couple of hundred pounds for two courses and a bottle of wine, because she'd said she had something to tell him, hadn't she? And it could only be one thing, couldn't it?

By the glow of the setting sun over the river he could almost see pound signs floating above her head with the fluffy clouds, dancing with the leaves on the trees as a breeze swept upriver, shimmering on the surface of the water. And so, relaxed after the champagne and excited by his prospects, he chattered on, mostly stressing how rich Americans would think it really really cool, not only to have their roots in England and Ireland traced, but, for an extra fee, to have coats-of-arms designed especially for them by the College of Arms.

'We could even find some titles – they're always coming up for sale – and flog them, too, at a nice profit,' he added.

Paula nodded and smiled, said very little but, he felt, appreciated having all the wheels and cogs of Relative Tracing explained to her in detail. She looked very nice tonight, too, in a simple little cream dress with no sleeves, and a choker of pearls and diamonds around her slender neck. Although he didn't actually fancy her, she was still very fuckable, he reflected.

'So-o-o,' he said finally, drawing out the word, as he stirred his coffee rather obsessively. 'I think I've told you everything I can about the company . . . so what are you in for?'

Paula looked puzzled. 'In for?'

'Well, you know.' He gave a nervous snigger. 'You're obviously interested. Want to get on board and all that. You said you wanted to talk to me tonight. So . . . what's it to be? One mill investment? Two?'

Her eyes were so blank Harry wondered if she'd had a stroke in the past thirty seconds.

'What are you talking about, Harry? Of course I'm interested in your ideas and plans. They're great. But I never said I'd invest a penny. I wouldn't even think of it without consulting my financial adviser first. What I wanted to talk about tonight has nothing whatever to do with your business.'

Harry felt as if he'd fallen off a ten-storey block and hit concrete. 'So-o-o . . . what did you want to talk about?' he said weakly.

Paula reached across the table and took his hand, which was now hot and clammy. 'I was going to ask if you'd like to move in with me. Permanently.' Her eyes glittered with feral lust in the gathering darkness and Harry felt as if he was being sucked down by quicksand. 'Don't you think it would be a good idea, darling?' she whispered.

'The trouble is,' Bernard explained to Lucinda, 'your father has left instructions that allow no leeway in which to manoeuvre. I have to keep the jewellery in the safe here, and when you've traced one of the women you have to come back to me and select which piece you want that particular person to have. It's then up to me to release that piece to you, and you must return to me a receipt signed by the recipient. That I may add was also your father's idea. I'd have trusted you, myself.' He sighed in frustration. 'Miles also stipulated that your original choice of the jewellery you're giving away has to be your final decision, too. In other words you can't go off with one piece and then come back the next day and say you've changed your mind and want to give another.'

'And this is because my father doesn't want me to know the value of any of it?' she asked.

'Exactly. Let me read you this paragraph in his instructions: "Lucinda must use her intuition to choose the five pieces of jewellery to give away, and keep the sixth piece for herself. One of the items is very valuable. It is entirely up to her what she does but she's not allowed to have them valued. She's not allowed to remove the jewellery from the office of my solicitor, Bernard Clarke, for valuation and no third party is to be present to try to influence her selection."'

'This is like a game we used to play as children,' Lucinda gasped. 'Winner takes all, but the clues were so loaded against us that it was usually Dad, who'd set up the treasure hunt in the first place, who won!'

Bernard gave her a strange look. 'That's exactly what he may have devised,' he said unhappily.

'So what happens? I could give away the valuable piece to a woman I've never seen before and will not want to see again, while I land myself with the booby prize?' She felt enraged. 'What a dirty trick to play on anyone. And why? He isn't even around to enjoy his own sick joke.'

'There *is* a point, abstruse though it may seem. If you do find your piece is worth the most, you will, according to Miles, have used your judgement, good taste, and recognition of value. You will also then acquire something else.'

Lucinda looked at Bernard glumly. She didn't know anything about jewellery. Rubies were red and sapphires were blue but apart from that they could be coloured bits of glass for all she knew. Miles had been aware of that, too.

'What else will I acquire?' she asked drily.

'Nearly three million pounds, which he's left on deposit to be given to you in the event of your being in possession of the right jewels yourself.'

Lucinda started laughing, a hysterical mirth that bubbled up uncontrollably inside her, until her face was scarlet and she was weeping openly. 'I don't believe this,' she gasped, pressing her hand to her mouth, struggling for composure. 'Dad didn't have that sort of money to leave.'

'He certainly did,' Bernard pointed out. 'He made a lot of money lecturing, you know, and from writing his books on higher maths, which are still compulsory reading in universities worldwide.'

'But I don't understand' – she gave a hiccuping sob – 'I don't understand any of this. I didn't know he had all these women. I didn't know he had all that money. We've lived with him all our lives and now I find we've been living with a complete stranger. I don't *know* him any more. I doubt if Mum would either! She'd never have been able to cope if she'd known he was like this. Never! And we've got to make sure she never finds out. The whole thing's crazy.'

'Miles was a man of many parts, and quite why he wanted you, in particular, to be made aware of his secret past is a mystery to me. As much of a mystery as why he didn't leave you this fortune outright.'

Lucinda wiped her eyes and blew her nose. 'That wouldn't have been any fun for him, though, would it?' she said. 'A straight legacy like he left Mum and my brothers must have bored him. But with me, it had to be convoluted and in the form of a game I'll almost certainly lose.'

Bernard nodded bleakly. 'I'm afraid it does seem that way, but with hindsight, I believe your father already knew he was a sick man. I remember thinking he looked ill when he brought in the jewellery, and it was as if he knew his days were numbered, but wanted just one more throw of the dice. Just one more game with life.'

'So what do I do now?'

'My dear Lucinda, I can only suggest you go home and think about it. Talk it over with Julian. I'm sure he'll give you good advice. Why don't you take the writing case and the letters with you now? Then you can decide if you want to go ahead or not. I mean, you don't *have* to abide by your father's eccentric wishes. You can put it down to a moment of madness on his part, burn the letters and forget it.'

Lucinda looked thoughtfully at the writing case. It was a beautiful object, with its intricate design of shimmering mother-of-pearl and the handsome brass lock, and she wondered where her father had got it from.

'Tell me, Bernard, if I refuse to play his game, or if I do as he asks, but I end up with the least valuable piece of jewellery, what happens to the money then? Who gets it?'

'The three million pounds?' He paused as if what he had to tell her was too painful to contemplate. He glanced down at Miles's Will again, trying to gain time. 'It goes to an animal sanctuary in the Midlands,' he said finally in a flat voice.

When Lucinda emerged into Bedford Street again, everything around her looked different. Her life had shifted and skewed in the hour she'd spent with Bernard Clarke, and now she felt she was facing an alien world. Nothing that had gone before bore any relation to what was happening now. Even her family, especially her father – oh God her father! – had become other people.

Surely her mother must have realised what was going on? How could anyone not know about *five* mistresses during the course of her marriage, she reflected as she walked to Covent Garden station. And yet Anne had continued to adore Miles, and even at this moment was probably at home in bed, crying her heart out because he'd died; the husband she'd always said was so loving, so loyal, so faithful.

The aspect that Lucinda found most scaring was that they'd all been oblivious of what had been going on. Miles had been living not just a double life, but a life that involved five other women, though not, she presumed, all at the same time.

How could Anne have believed him when he'd said he would stay overnight in some hotel after a conference or lecture, rather than endure the exhaustion of dashing home so late? Uncomfortably, she realised that she and her brothers had believed him, too. But then they weren't married to him; surely a wife would sense something wrong? She would know instantly if Julian ever played around, she reflected. She would sense it from him, smell it on him, feel it in her bones.

Boarding the train for Earl's Court and the change for Parson's Green, she was thankful she'd taken the day off and so could go straight home to gather her thoughts. The house would be empty. Jamie and Daisy were at school, and Delia had gone to Tesco to stock up on supplies.

Once home, Lucinda felt like a displaced person in someone else's house. Her furniture looked unfamiliar, her bed unslept in. Even the kitchen, cleaned and tidied by Delia that morning, looked like a set waiting to be photographed for a magazine advertisement, rather than the cosy chaotic heart of the house.

Unable to relax, she wandered from room to room not knowing what she was supposed to be doing. How could Miles have led such a life? There was a part of her that didn't believe what Bernard had told her. A bit of her brain that said she'd soon learn it was all a big mistake. Disjointed random thoughts flitted in and out of her mind, but pulsing repeatedly through her aching head was: Dad had all these women in his life. He deceived all of us, and now he is treating it like a game.

She pulled herself together with an effort. The first thing she must do was phone Julian. Disappointment left her weak when the gallery manager told her he was out at a furniture sale in St Albans, and, consequently, he'd have had to switch his mobile off.

It was absurd, but she felt like weeping. At that moment she needed Julian to comfort her and love her and be there for her . . . or was it her father she was crying for? Was there still lurking inside her the remnant of an ignored little girl who wanted Daddy to love her? Daddy who had now betrayed her and landed her in a living nightmare?

The phone suddenly rang, startling her. She grabbed it greedily. 'Julian?'

'No, it's me,' replied a bright female voice. 'I thought you must be back from France by now.'

'Carina!' Lucinda sank onto a kitchen chair, wiping her wet cheeks with the back of her hand. 'How are you?'

'Great. How are you? Did you have a good time? You sound funny.'

'No, I'm all right.'

'How were Jane and William? And their divine château?'

'They were fine. Awfully kind to us all as usual.' She didn't feel it would be right to gossip about their financial crash at this stage.

There was a pause before Carina spoke again. 'Luce, what is it? Is there something wrong?' They'd been friends for more than twelve years, intuitive to each other's moods.

Lucinda felt herself crumbling at the edges, unable to bear this new burden of knowledge on her own any longer.

'I've just come back from seeing Bernard. You know, Dad's solicitor, who's also a family friend.'

'Oh, yes?'

Lucinda could picture Carina settling down for a good natter, in the plush comfort of her large house. She'd be curled up on the white brocade sofa, wearing cashmere, surrounded by flowers, and no doubt the butler would be hovering, ready to take her orders.

'He's told me the contents of Dad's Will.'

'And . . .?'

Lucinda's tone was suddenly anxious. 'This is in the strictest *strictest* confidence, Carina. Mum must never know, and neither must Tom or Harry.'

'Cool. You know you can trust me,' Carina replied. 'I'm very good at keeping secrets.'

Lucinda did trust her. Fifteen minutes later she'd told Carina everything.

'Have you ever heard anything so diabolical?' she concluded.

There was a stunned silence. '*Five* mistresses?' Carina said, her voice shocked. 'What do you mean, five mistresses?' She sounded genuinely angry.

'I know, isn't it awful? I've got to prevent Mum finding out at all costs.'

'But you must have got that wrong,' Carina protested. 'How can Miles have had five mistresses?'

'He *did*, Carina. I've got all their letters! And they were all after he was married to Mum. It is shocking, isn't it? I could hardly believe it either, when Bernard told me.'

'The old bugger!' Carina exploded.

'And the worst thing is I've got to trace them all. I mean I think I must, though I don't want to. I can't afford to miss out on an inheritance like that. I want to give up work. Stay at home to be with the children. They're growing up so fast and I'm missing all these years.'

Carina sounded sympathetic. 'I know what you mean. I can hardly believe that Charles is thirteen. And Tara's eleven. She'll be off to Heathfield next year, and Michael will be soon going to Ludgrove. I don't know where the years have gone and I really miss them, but I could never have managed without a full-time nanny. I'm not that good at looking after children.' She laughed fondly. Then she became serious. 'So you're going to have to contact all these lady friends of your father's if you want the spondulicks? How the hell are you going to trace them?'

'Bernard has given me a list of their addresses.'

'What, all of them?'

'All except one. She's put no address, no date, anything.'

'Isn't that going to be a problem?'

'A hell of a problem.'

'My God, aren't the others going to be shocked when you turn up, out of the blue?' Carina asked.

'I'm going to have to be diplomatic, obviously.'

'So . . . none of the names meant anything to you?'

'Not a thing.' Lucinda reached for the list, which lay just inside the writing case. 'They are Miranda Warwick, Renée Hartman, Fenella Harrison, Isabelle Cronin, and the one who hasn't put her address signs the letters "Pumpkin". Obviously a nickname. I've no idea how I'm going to trace her and of course if I can't, then—'

'Then the game's up!' interjected Carina. 'Sorry; no pun intended, but Miles *has* set you a sort of puzzle to solve, hasn't he?'

'Tell me about it. What the hell am I going to say to them all?'

'It's pretty cruel on the women too, isn't it? Are the letters passionate?'

Shocked, Lucinda replied, 'I haven't read them.'

'But don't you want to? I wouldn't be able to resist the temptation.'

'No, I couldn't. Not possibly. I mean, I presume they're love letters. Very private. It would be awful to read them.'

'But if you have a problem tracing these old girlfriends, maybe they've mentioned something that would give you a clue as to their whereabouts. Maybe it would even help you to see your father in a different light; he can't have been all bad if he had all those lovers.'

Lucinda raised her eyebrows cynically. 'I'm not sure it doesn't make him appear even worse.'

Julian leaned forward, elbows on his knees, face buried in his hands. 'I wish to God you could tell your father's solicitor what he could do with all those bloody letters.' Then he raised his head and looked at Lucinda in anguish. 'If only I had more money, you'd be able to give up work without having to go through this fucking ridiculous rigmarole. At the end of which,' he continued angrily, 'you may *still* end up with nothing.'

Lucinda dropped onto her knees beside his chair and put her arms round him. 'Don't get upset. Of course I want to give up my job, but it won't be the end of the world if I can't. And it certainly won't be your fault. You're working flat out as it is. If I am lucky enough to end up with the right piece of jewellery then it will be truly wonderful, but if I don't we'll be no worse off than we are now.' She leaned forward and kissed him gently on the mouth.

Julian took her in his arms and held her close. 'It's you I'm worried about. You work so hard, you're always tired . . .'

'Not too tired,' she whispered, her eyes suddenly glowing. 'As long as I have you, everything's cool.'

He returned her kiss, stirring her deeply as he always did with the urgency of his lovemaking. She clung to him, her arms around his neck, breathing in the faint scent of lemon soap and warmed by the heat of his skin. A rush of desire swept through her.

'. . . Delia has got the night off, hasn't she?' she heard him murmur, as he slid out of his chair, and pulled her down on to the hearth rug with him.

'Yes,' she breathed, lying close to him. 'Oh, Julian . . .'

'I know. Me too.'

Their lovemaking was always good; sometimes it was wonderful. Sometimes Lucinda reached such peaks of rapture she felt as if this was the only thing in life that mattered, this searing, exquisite sensation that hovered between pain and ecstasy. Tonight it was going to be like that. She could feel it building, swelling, growing, she strained to reach it, but felt Julian holding back to prolong the moment so it would be even better, and then, just when she thought she couldn't stand the desperate longing any more, he brought her to a climax of such exquisite intensity that she clung to him, sobbing with emotion.

Five

Jane had spent another sleepless night, unable to find a comfortable position, fearful of awakening William, her head aching from tiredness but her mind in a fever of worry, going over and over the calamity that was likely to change their lives for ever.

William had told her the previous evening that it was no use fretting; if the bank were going to tide them over while they waited to see if the government could do something to rescue ICC, well and good.

'But if the bank refuses . . .?' she asked tremulously.

'We'll probably have to sell up sooner rather than later,' he replied, trying to sound matter-of-fact and unemotional.

'But what about Jacques? And Fleur and Maria? We can't just sack them. And Younnik has planned to spend his future working here.'

William patted her hand reassuringly. 'We took them on from the previous owners. I'm sure the next lot of people will do the same. In fact they're one of the main assets of the place.'

'Don't let's tell them anything yet, please,' Jane begged. 'There's nothing more unnerving and unsettling that having your whole future up in the air.'

'I know. No one feels more badly about this disaster than I do, because it's all my fault.'

Jane dabbed the tears trapped in the fine lines under her eyes and then she raised her chin. 'Stop talking like that, darling. It's the fault of ICC. They've screwed up and I hope this leads to an inquiry. It looks to me as if they knew this was going to happen, whilst still getting people to invest.'

William blew out his cheeks. 'Nevertheless, it's my fault that I threw practically everything we had at it. If I'd only bought a few shares, made a modest investment, we wouldn't be in this situation now.'

'Your stockbrokers are to blame, William. Why else does one use them, if it's not to advise on what's a bit of a gamble and what's more likely to succeed?'

William hadn't the energy to discuss the matter any more. He felt sickened to the heart. Through his own greed and the naive belief that he could make a quick fortune by making a few phone calls from the cosy haven of Château St Laurent, he'd blown their secure future, and the inheritance which would have gone to Julian in due course.

The mail arrived but there was nothing from the bank. Another day of waiting. Another day of uncertainty. Another day when the ring of the phone set their hearts racing.

Jane never complained but she wondered how much more she could take of this heart-stopping suspense.

* * *

'When are you going to find the time to chase up those women?' Julian asked, as he drove along the Fulham Road. They were on their way to one of Carina and Alex's dinner parties, a black tie affair, with fourteen guests, an extra butler hired for the evening, and caterers to help Cook with the five-course dinner. The women would be exquisitely dressed and bejewelled, and Carina would be the star of the evening, in a Versace dress and a blaze of diamonds. Lucinda usually loved these occasions. They were a glimpse into a world of shameless pleasure and were largely made up of the very clients who bought D'Aussoire products: the wealthy, the glamorous and definitely the A-list. But tonight she felt out of sorts and edgy.

'Don't ask,' she snapped irritably. She'd had a stressful day at work, studying survey reports from three field research agencies, the details of which she had to assess and present to the directors at a meeting in two days' time to discuss a new shampoo which D'Aussoire were planning to launch the following year. The reports covered public opinion from different areas of the country, and included the age of those who took part, as well as occupation and income bracket. This all had to be collated with further information which included people's preference for texture, smell, skin sensation and packaging.

She hadn't been able to get away from the office until nearly seven, which meant rushing home to have a shower, change into a long black beaded dress, kiss the children goodnight, and dash out again in order to get to Carina's dinner party not more than twenty minutes late.

'Oh, my hair's dreadful,' she exclaimed, as she put on her make-up in the small mirror on the back of the BMW's sun visor. 'I meant to wash it, but I had to work so fucking late . . .'

She gave a howl of frustration as Julian had to brake suddenly to avoid being sideswiped by another car, causing her to jab herself in the eye with her eyeshadow brush. '*Julian!*'

'Sorry, but I couldn't help it.'

She made a face, and reached for her lipstick. 'Now go steady, for God's sake,' she begged, through gritted teeth.

'I'll have to stop if the lights change to red.'

'Well, stop slowly. Oh, I feel such a mess. We really shouldn't go to parties in the middle of the week.'

Julian kept silent, only a slight tilt of his mouth showing his amusement. Lucinda always got in a flap when they were dining with Carina and he couldn't imagine why. Except of course Carina had the whole day to prink and preen herself, and Lucinda hadn't. But in spite of that, Julian always thought Lucinda looked by far the better of the two. She looked warmer and more vital, and there was something very sexy about her slightly thrown together appearance, whereas Carina's perfect grooming made her look untouchable. Puzzled, he wondered why she was a close friend of Lucinda's in the first place – Carina, in his opinion, was shallow and brittle, and very spoilt.

'What I was trying to say is, I can probably help you trace some of those women,' he continued blandly. 'If you give me a list of their names and addresses, I can find out from the electoral roll if they're still around.'

'But I'm not sure they will be. That's the problem. I glanced at some of the letter headings yesterday and some were written as long ago as the sixties.'

'Let me try, anyway. You have enough to do. Do any of the letters have a London address, by any chance?'

Lucinda was twisting her long brown hair up into a loose chignon, whilst holding two hairpins between her front teeth. She mumbled something unintelligible.

He grinned at her. 'Didn't quite catch that.'

She dug the last pin into her hair. 'Isabelle Cronin. She lives in London. Or did, anyway.'

'Right. Can you remember where?'

'North Street or something. I'm not sure. I do remember it was SW1.'

'Sounds like Lord North Street. Why don't you get the number from enquiries and ring her now?'

Lucinda threw Julian a horrified glance. '*Now*? But we're on our way to Carina's.'

'We won't be there for another five minutes. Go for it.'

'I can't.' Her hands were trembling and the colour had suddenly drained from her face.

Julian looked at her sympathetically. 'Why not get the phone number, anyway, and then you'll know whether she still lives at that address or not.' He took the mobile phone from its cradle and handed it to her.

'Julian, there isn't time. I'll do it tomorrow. Anyway, I haven't planned what to *say*, for God's sake,' she added in panic.

'But you don't have to talk to her now,' he pointed out mildly. He tapped in 192 himself. 'What's her last name?'

'Cronin.' Her voice was small and subdued.

A minute later he switched off the phone and glanced at her profile, as she clipped on her earrings. 'You're going to have fun with this one,' he said drily. 'It looks like Isabelle is the wife of Malcolm Cronin, Member of Parliament.'

As soon as Lucinda got home from work the next evening she went straight to the phone. She'd spent all day psyching herself up to make this call and she'd no idea why she felt so nervous. It was, she supposed, fear of the unknown, coupled with embarrassment and dread. After all, it wasn't as if Miles had been her husband and she was the betrayed wife. She was merely his daughter – but could that be why he'd put her in this tortuous position? So that she would understand the emotions of a wronged wife?

Self-analysis was getting her nowhere, she decided. This was only the first of the women she had to trace. There were four more to go after Isabelle. The bullet had to be bitten. Firmly and now.

She took a deep breath and tapped in the number Julian had scribbled on a piece of paper last night. A man answered.

'Could I speak to Mrs Cronin, please?'

'Who wants her?' His voice was blasé, indifferent, rather grand-sounding.

'Lucinda Cotterell.' There was no reason to suppose Malcolm Cronin would connect her with Miles Scott-Forbes ... always supposing he knew his wife had had an affair with Miles in the first place.

'Will you hold, please,' the voice boomed.

Lucinda heard him shouting to someone in the distance and her heart started hammering. The click-click of high heels on a bare floor was coming nearer. She heard the receiver being picked up.

'Hello?' The woman's voice had an Italian accent. 'Who is that?'

'My name is Lucinda Cotterell. I'm ... er ...' She found herself floundering, partly because she didn't want to give the other woman too big a shock. 'I believe you knew my father,' she continued cautiously. 'Miles Scott-Forbes.'

There was a stunned silence and then an angry hissing whisper. 'God in heaven! What do you want?'

'Perhaps we could meet? I have ... umm ... er ... your letters to my father.'

Isabelle Cronin gave a tiny scream. 'You try to get money out of me? Is that it? You dare to try to ruin me ...?'

'No. No, nothing like that. Please listen to me,' Lucinda begged. 'I have something for you. From my father. A piece of jewellery.'

But Isabelle wasn't listening. 'You try to blackmail me? Is that what you're playing at?' Her voice edged towards high-pitched hysteria as she threw caution to the winds. 'You can go to hell!' There was a sobbing sound and then a loud click in Lucinda's ear as she hung up.

'Well!' Lucinda sat, stunned, and then she carefully replaced her own receiver.

A moment later she heard Julian's key in the front door. 'Bun?'

'In here.'

He came bounding into the living room, looking very pleased with himself. Bending, he brushed her lips with his. 'Everything OK?'

'I managed to speak to Isabelle Cronin just now.'

'And?'

'She sounds Italian. Very excitable. She got quite hysterical. Thinks I'm out to blackmail her. In the end she hung up.'

Julian nodded in understanding. 'She probably fears a scandal. Why don't you drop her a line? Assure her you only want to give her back her letters?'

'I told her I had a piece of jewellery for her,' Lucinda complained ruefully, 'but she simply wouldn't listen. I have a feeling it was her husband who answered the phone. Let's hope he didn't hear her outburst.'

'He'll probably overlook it if he did, rather than figure as yet another MP with a sleazy marriage,' he remarked shrewdly. 'Why don't you phone her again tomorrow? She's likely to be on her own during the day. She might listen then.'

Lucinda nodded. 'Unfortunately we're frantic at work, so I'll have to try to slip out at some point and use my mobile.'

'Good idea. Now, I've got something to tell you,' he said, grinning. 'I picked up a pair of small inlaid side tables today, at an auction in Northampton. Very French, decorative pieces, with gold ormolu trimmings. They were in bad condition but I had a hunch so I took a chance, bought them for a good price. At best I thought they were good reproductions but when I got them back to the shop we discovered they're roughly 1630: Louis XIV, you know, the Sun King? Roy was ecstatic! I paid two thousand pounds for the pair, knowing we'd have to have them restored, but they're worth around forty thousand!'

Her face lit up with excitement. 'Well done! Clever you!' She reached up and put her arms round his neck. 'Congratulations, darling.'

'I've been promised a very nice bonus,' he said with boyish modesty. 'Meanwhile, I think you should forget all about your father for the moment. Let's go out to dinner to celebrate.'

She grinned. It was just what she needed. 'Have I time for a shower?' The thought of going to a restaurant on their own, choosing delicious food and wine from the menu, being waited on, and finally being able to get up and go and let someone else worry about the washing-up, was absolute bliss.

Julian smiled down at her. 'Yup. I'll have one too.'

As they went upstairs the theme tune from *Coronation Street* came wafting from Delia's room, and there was silence from Jamie and Daisy's room. Julian and Lucinda exchanged looks. Then they hurried to the bedroom and undressed quickly.

Julian lit a scented candle in the bathroom before turning off the lights. He placed it on the marble surround of the washbasin so that it was reflected in the mirrors around the walls, the flickering flame repeating itself over and over into infinity. Lucinda turned on the shower and the room became a glowing misty magical place. Then Julian tipped some baby oil into the palms of his hands, and stepping forward began to stroke her body gently and tenderly, so that her nipples hardened and a deep tug of desire shot through her. His tongue explored her mouth, loving the taste of her. She slid her hands over his broad shoulders and down his back, feeling the firmness of his rounded buttocks, pressing herself against him, feeling him swell and grow hard, wanting him to take her, possess her, fill her with his love. But he kept her in aching suspense while he ran his lips down her neck to her breasts, licking her, sucking her, and all the time his hands were working in her secret places.

I want this to go for ever and ever . . . it must go on for ever and ever, I will *die* if it doesn't go on and on, she thought. 'Can we do it again?' she breathed into his open mouth. 'I want to come now . . . now . . . oh God! . . . but I want to do it again . . . oh, Julian, Julian, don't stop. Don't ever stop.'

They were forty minutes late for their reservation at San Lorenzo, and Lucinda arrived looking flushed and dishevelled with red patches on her neck and chest, but her radiance and glowing eyes made all the men in the smartest restaurant in London turn and look, almost hungrily, at her as they made their way to their table.

'We'll start with champagne cocktails, please,' Julian told the waiter when they were seated. Then he looked into Lucinda's blue-grey eyes. 'We must do this more often, Bun.'

'Yes, please,' she said softly.

'Hi, sis!'

'Oh! Hi, Harry. Listen, I'm in the middle of preparing a presentation—'

'What's this about you being left a box of Dad's papers?'

'Harry, I'll have to call you back this evening. I really can't talk now.'

'But what sort of papers?' Harry persisted. 'I've seen Dad's Will and all it says is "papers on my given subject". But then he goes on to say that if you dispose of them in an intelligent way you'll stand to benefit. What does that mean? Are they mathematical papers? And if so, how much are they worth?'

That, Lucinda reflected grimly, was at the root of Harry's avid interest.

'I've no idea. Listen, I've got to go. I'm snowed under. Talk to you later.' When I've thought up a convincing story.

So the rest of the family had seen Miles's Will and for them Pandora's box had been opened a chink. Now she had to work at containing the contents for her mother's sake.

As she turned back to the latest findings on pressed face powder as opposed to loose powder the phone rang again.

'Yes?' she said abruptly, snatching up the receiver, thinking it might be Harry again.

'Peter here.'

'Oh, hello, Peter,' Lucinda replied, forcing her voice, because he was her boss, to sound friendly and professional. 'What can I do for you?'

'I want some figures, Lucinda. I need to know our overall market share for shampoo in 1998.'

'In the UK or worldwide?' She reached for her mouse, opened the Hair Care file, and got into the 'shampoo' section.

'Worldwide, please.'

Her fingers flew over the keyboard. The analysis for each month of 1998 came up on the screen. 'I have it. D'Aussoire took 46 per cent of the market, 6 per cent more than in the previous year.'

'Cool.'

70

'Anything else?'

'Not at the moment. Thanks.'

Lucinda went back to studying the face powder survey. Apparently 53 per cent of women preferred pressed powder. She wasn't surprised. The whole business of a compact full of loose powder, plus a powder puff, belonged to her mother's generation. Thirty-seven per cent of young women, however, didn't use powder at all, but preferred a matt foundation.

At five o'clock she phoned Julian. 'I'm planning to go and see Isabelle Cronin this evening. I'll probably go straight from here, so I'll be late home for supper.'

'Is that wise?' he asked, concerned.

'I saw in *The Times* today that her husband is speaking at a dinner given by the Confederation of Businessmen. It's an all-male gathering so there's a chance she'll be at home on her own.'

'And you're just going to go round? Unannounced?'

'If she knows I'm coming she'll definitely be out.'

Tom was engrossed in dealing with the usual boring mail – though when did an electrical company ever have amusing mail, he reflected – as the phone on his desk rang.

It was Susan, telling him in one long breathless sentence that she'd bought far too much beef mince and she was planning to make a shepherd's pie for dinner, and if he was proposing to hot up some disgusting fish fingers in his microwave he'd better abandon the idea and come over for supper.

'Are you sure?' Tom asked tentatively. Not because he wasn't delighted; in fact the idea of another of Susan's home-cooked dinners set his stomach rumbling. But he didn't want Susan to be asking him over because she pitied him.

'Am I sure of what?' she asked laughingly. 'That you won't steal the silver spoons? Turn out to be the Boston Strangler? Of course I'm sure. I'd like to see you again, anyway.'

Her candidness surprised him. Could she actually be inviting him to supper because she liked him? In his mind women weren't supposed to do the running. And he'd always been too shy, too scared of rejection, which was why, at thirty-seven, he was still on his own.

'Well,' he said slowly, 'that would be very nice. What time would you like me to come?'

'After work, whenever that is,' she said casually. 'We can always have a drink first if supper isn't ready.'

Tom spent the rest of the day wondering what he should take. A bottle of wine? Not very original. Chocolates? Too much of a cliché. Flowers? Too intimate. Susan might read too much into such a flirtatious gesture and be scared off. Not that that was likely, he reflected, on second thoughts. She didn't come over as a woman who scared easily. What about a plant? No, boring. A book? But what kind of book? A cookery book could be taken as

71

an insult to her culinary skills, whilst a trashy novel might imply the same about her intellectual ability.

By four o'clock he had a stress related headache. In desperation he turned to Ruby, who'd been a secretary at Garson & Co for nearly thirty years, and asked her what she thought he should take.

'Easy,' she replied, a wide smile lighting up her chubby red face. 'Take a huge box of mixed biscuits. That's something she couldn't have cooked herself, and you'll gain brownie points with her sons. Kids like nothing more than biscuits.'

Six

Isabelle Cronin couldn't stop crying. She seemed to have been crying for days now and her beautiful dark eyes were swollen and her golden skin was red and blotchy. The call from darling Miles's daughter had both frightened her and reopened the wound inflicted by his sudden death. It was killing her. She couldn't sleep. Couldn't eat. And all the time she had to pretend to Malcolm that she grieved for 'poor Aunt Ilaria' who had died in Rome a month ago.

Turning to the long mirror in her extravagantly decorated bedroom, which was hung with tapestries and furnished with red brocade hangings and an ornate four-poster bed, she realised she'd lost a lot of weight. Too much weight. She'd always prided herself on having the same measurements as when she'd been seventeen, but now she looked scrawny. At forty-five one had to be careful, she told herself. It could be a question of keeping your figure or your face, and looking at herself now she feared she might lose both. Petite, with small feet and hands and birdlike ankles and wrists, she would, however, always look chic and that was a great consolation. Especially when she compared herself to the wives of other MPs. They were so *big*. So badly dressed. And they lacked grooming. God knows where they bought their clothes. Hers, of course, were all couture – what else was there?

Malcolm was at least rich if nothing else; but God, he was boring. All he ever thought about was politics and all he talked about was his hope that a coup could be brought about which would make him Prime Minister if his party won the next election. But he was fifty-six, and looked it. Florid of face and sparse of hair, he was a great bully of a man driven by ruthless ambition. But time was running out for him. Younger and younger people were achieving power in the Party. Meanwhile he insisted Isabelle should appear at his side when they attended political and social events. He was determined to give the impression they were the Perfect Couple.

To console herself, Isabelle had taken to shopping with the dedication of an Olympic contender going for gold. Trips to Gucci, Fendi, Chanel, Louis Vuitton and Daniel Swarovski featured on her weekly shopping list because she was mad about handbags and luggage, while Jimmy Choo and Manolo Blahnik shod her dainty feet. And not a month passed without her ordering something from Givenchy, Donna Karan, Christian Dior, Dolce & Gabbana, or Ungaro.

Drying her eyes she looked at herself in the mirror again, fingering her new Bulgari gold and diamond necklace and matching earrings with the tenderness of a mother stroking her baby's face. Miles had told her that if she was going to spend most of her husband's money on herself, she should at least, from

73

time to time, buy things that were a good investment. In her head Isabelle could remember him adding: 'If you ever wanted to leave Malcolm, you could cash in your jewels. You never know, you might need the money, and you'd get nothing for your fripperies, lovely though you may think they are.'

How wise he'd been. And now he was gone. She'd lost her erstwhile lover, mentor and best friend and she didn't know how she was going to go on living without him. And then his daughter . . .! Wicked girl to try to blackmail her with her letters! Miles would have been so shocked and angry at such a betrayal. And suppose Malcolm ever found out?

Isabelle shuddered, the thought being too dreadful to contemplate. There would be a scandal. The story of the MP's wife's affair with a learned professor would get into all the newspapers. Malcolm might have to resign and then he'd blame her for ruining his career. She prayed she'd never hear from Miles's daughter again.

As she bathed her face in the black marble bathroom which led off the bedroom, she heard a tap on her door.

'Si?'

It was Ingleby, the butler. 'There's someone to see you, madam.'

'I see no one,' she snapped, coming out of the bathroom, and dabbing her face with a towel. She looked a terrible mess. Not even her most intimate friends could see her with her face all red and puffy.

Ingleby looked at her penetratingly, with the expression of a man who knows more than he should. 'It's a young lady, madam. She stressed it was urgent.'

Isabel flashed him a look of terror. 'Who is she?'

'A Mrs Cotterell, madam.'

Instantly Isabelle remembered the name. She thought quickly. Malcolm was out at a boring dinner. Maybe she should see Miles's daughter and get rid of her, once and for all. If she were to come back while Malcolm were at home . . .! Her heart fluttered in panic at the very thought. She covered her eyes with her hand as if she was going to faint.

'Show her into the drawing room, Ingleby. I'll be down in a minute.'

Lucinda looked around the drawing room with interest. It had obviously been decorated with entertaining in mind rather than comfort. Louis XVI chairs, and small inlaid tables from the same period, were grouped stragetic-ally about the beautifully porportioned room, which was softly lit, with cream silk walls. An Aubusson carpet in delicate shades of pink, blue and beige covered the floor, and cream silk curtains edged with pale blue braid and tassels festooned the two long windows.

There was a large vase of lilies and roses on the gilt console table between the windows, and more flowers, obviously arranged by a professional, stood at either end of the white marble mantelpiece, above which hung a magnificent landscape. Lucinda tried to imagine her father in this opulent setting, and failed utterly.

At that moment the double mahogany doors leading into the hall opened with a flurry, and a small woman in a tight-fitting black dress and huge dark glasses shot into the room.

'What d'you want?' She spoke aggressively, with a heavy Italian accent. 'How dare you come to my home like this? I can tell you, you are not going to get anything out of me.'

Lucinda stepped back, raising her hands in protest, but not totally surprised by this greeting after their telephone conversation.

'Please listen to me,' she said firmly. 'I don't want anything from you. Nothing at all. I've come to return your letters to my father; nothing more.'

Isabelle looked confused. 'But you say . . .?'

Lucinda reached into her shoulder bag and withdrew a neat bundle of letters held together by an elastic band. 'I only want to return these to you, as my father wished,' she said simply, handing them to Isabelle. 'I will also be sending you a piece of jewellery. He wanted you to have something to remember him by.'

Isabelle's face crumpled and she whipped off her dark glasses as the tears ran down her cheeks. 'Oh! Oh!' she sobbed, reaching up to fling her arms round Lucinda's shoulders and kiss her on both cheeks. 'How sweet of Miles. How adorable. I'm sorry I thought . . .' She stepped back, full of contrition.

Then she gripped Lucinda's wrist and dragged her over to the chairs grouped in the centre of the room.

'Sit. Do sit,' she said in a fierce whisper, pushing Lucinda down, and taking the chair opposite. She leaned forward conspiratorially, her slender legs crossed, her bejewelled hands clasped together. 'I was so afraid my husband would find out about Miles. It was a big secret for a long, long time. He was the love of my life, you know, and I was the love of his life. There was your mama, of course, but I was the only other woman he ever had; or ever even looked at.'

Lucinda glanced down at the soft shades of the carpet under her feet, unable to meet Isabelle's large, dark, penetrating eyes. So she thought she was Miles's only lover, did she?

'We had such good times together,' Isabelle went on. 'So many laughs! I shall miss him until the day I die,' she added dramatically.

Lucinda sat in silence, mystified and still unable to visualise her father being involved with this dynamic little woman, who was obviously very temperamental and excitable. Miles had hated displays of emotion, hated what he called the nonsense of pretty clothes and make-up, deplored feminine foibles and loathed gushing chatter.

'He was wonderful, you know, as a lover,' Isabelle said suddenly with a knowing look, and then, as Lucinda's face flushed with embarrassment, she stretched out and grasped her hand. 'You don't mind my talking like this, do you? My own papa, he was a wonderful lover, too. It is something to be proud of.'

Lucinda felt peculiar. Even though she was thirty-three, there was something vaguely obscene in listening to someone telling her how good her father had been in bed.

'Good,' she said shortly.

Isabelle gave a little gurgling laugh, smiling for the first time. Her teeth were tiny and even and very white. They reminded Lucinda of a vixen.

'You English; you are so shy! But I must tell you, Miles was a great deal more to me than just a lover. He was like a father to me, too. He advised me. He comforted me. He gave me books to read.'

That sounds a bit more like Dad, Lucinda thought drily.

'I was devastated when I saw his death in the papers. So unhappy I thought I would die. And I have to pretend my Aunt Ilaria has died, because I cry all the time and Malcolm wants to know why . . .' Isabelle's eyes brimmed again. 'It is so hard. Something inside me died a little, too, when I knew he was gone. You must be missing him so terribly, too.'

Lucinda smiled weakly, not knowing what to say. 'I must be going.' She rose, hitching her bag onto her shoulder.

'You said . . .' Isabelle hesitated, her hand on Lucinda's arm, 'you mention something about jewels? Miles, he leaves me something?'

'Yes.' Lucinda hadn't decided which piece to give her. It would need thought and consideration. She'd have to look again at the earrings and bracelet, pendant, brooch, ring and pearls before she could decide. And as she had no idea of the value of any of it, all she could do was choose a piece she thought would suit the recipient. Was that what her father had meant when he said she must use her intuition? Was he testing her skill of observation? Her knowledge of human nature? Her good, or maybe her bad, taste? Or was there some more complex angle to this game which had so far eluded her?

'I'll get the solicitor to send it to you,' she said.

'No, no. Not send.' Isabelle was agitated now, gripping Lucinda's arm once more, whispering urgently as she glanced round to make sure no one could hear them. 'Not send,' she repeated. 'My husband would wonder what it was. I meet you. Let's have lunch. I give you lunch at the Ritz? And we talk about your darling papa. Si? Isn't that a good idea? You give me jewellery then and we drink a little toast to his memory, si?'

When Lucinda finally escaped into the street she felt as if she'd been mauled by a heavily perfumed and over-affectionate little fox. And as for the idea of lunch . . .!

'What was it like . . . meeting her?' Carina asked later that evening as they talked on the phone. Lucinda had been describing the encounter with Isabelle in vivid detail.

'It was very strange. A bit creepy too, trying to imagine Dad . . .' Her voice drifted off before continuing: 'And, my God, you should have seen the house! It was simply horrible in a Buckingham Palace sort of way.'

'I think Alex and I have met them at some party or other,' Carina remarked. 'I remember Malcolm Cronin being perfectly foul. Very bumptious. Terribly ambitious. I can't say I remember her.'

'I simply cannot see what they could have had in common. She was everything Dad claimed to dislike in a woman.'

'She probably dug her claws in and wouldn't let go,' Carina pointed out acidly. 'That sort of woman usually makes all the running. Miles probably couldn't get away. Did she say how long she'd known him?'

'Not exactly. She just said a long time. I got the impression that once the passion had burned itself out, Dad became more of a proxy father and friend rather than anything else.'

'Which piece of jewellery are you going to give her?'

'I haven't a clue. I'm going to have to look at it again before I can come to a decision.' Lucinda groaned in frustration. 'If only I didn't have this damned job; it leaves me so little time for anything else. At the moment I'm sometimes not home until seven or eight at night. Luckily I can get to Covent Garden from Gray's Inn Road in ten minutes if I take a cab, so I'll have to see Bernard in my lunch hour.'

'Why don't you take some sick leave?' Carina suggested.

'I can't. I've just had three weeks off, what with Dad's death and then an extra week in France, and I daren't risk losing my job.'

There was a pause before Carina spoke, as if she was considering something. Then she said: 'Would you like me to help you? I haven't got anything on, and I might be able to do some of the leg work in tracing these women if they've moved to new addresses.'

'Would you really? My God, that's so good of you. Julian says he'll help, too. Once I know where they are, or even if they're dead or alive, then the worst's over. I'm going to have a serious problem tracing "Pumpkin" though.'

'Yeah. With nothing to go on you're a bit stuck, aren't you? And without the full deck of cards I suppose you can't meet the challenge Miles set?'

'That's the problem. Listen, once the president of D'Aussoire has gone back to Paris and the heat's off, I'll let you know, then we can get started for real.'

'That was nice of her,' Julian remarked when Lucinda told him about the conversation.

'I know.' She sighed deeply. 'I could get on with tracing the women right away, but you should see my desk!' Then she brightened optimistically. 'Maybe I'll find them all and I can forget all about D'Aussoire.'

Julian grinned. 'It would be nice to come home to a wife who isn't tired all the time.' As soon as he'd said it he could have bitten his tongue off. Of all the stupid, tactless . . .!

'I can't help being exhausted at the end of the day,' Lucinda protested, hurt. 'I wish to God I could be at home all the time. You know that. I don't work because I enjoy it.'

He pulled himself into an upright position and reached for her hand. 'I know, Bun. I wasn't criticising. I know you hate working and I wish you didn't have to. I wasn't getting at you; you know that, don't you?'

Lucinda nodded but didn't answer. Guilt; why did she always have such a sense of guilt? Why did she feel she was letting everyone down all the time? Including Delia. She had far too much to do and only stayed because she was so fond of the children.

Then there was Anne, newly widowed, grieving and no doubt very lonely. All these people with a claim on her time, her love, her attention. How was she supposed to keep everyone happy *and* hold down a stressful job? She was torn in so many different directions and everyone seemed to want a piece of her. And all the time life was slipping past, the childen were growing older, and she felt she didn't have a firm grasp on anything.

'Forget what I said,' she heard Julian say, as she huddled gloomily at her end of the sofa. 'You do a marvellous job, coping with everything. You do far more than I do,' he added generously. 'I don't know how you manage it all.'

'Stop flattering me,' she replied crossly, but a smile lurked at the corners of her mouth.

The biscuits had been a stroke of genius.

'Wicked!' Steve commented.

'Yeah. Cool,' Dick said.

Susan beamed. 'Thank you so much, Tom. The next time they ask me if there's anything in the house to eat I'll just point at this tin.' Tom was suitably gratified. Then Susan handed him a glass of wine, her expression serious. 'It's such a hot evening and this house is like an oven, so I thought we'd eat in the ten acre wood.'

Tom frowned, nonplussed. 'The ten acre wood?' His mind darted wildly around the idea of even a quarter acre wood anywhere near a two up two down at World's End.

There were smothered giggles from Steve and Dick, and Susan grinned sympathetically. 'Let me show you.' She grabbed Tom's hand and led him across the tiny kitchen and out through the back door.

Tom found himself in a back yard approximately twelve foot square. The kitchen table and four chairs had been placed in the middle, set for supper. There were a couple of tubs, overflowing with a mixture of flowers and herbs in glorious juxtaposition, and from a flower bed in one corner a tangled mass of old man's beard clambered along the wall that divided the yard from the one next door.

'How marvellous!' Tom exclaimed. Then he suddenly realised Susan was still holding his hand. He could feel his face turning red and the evening seemed hotter than ever.

'It *is* a warm night, isn't it?' he remarked, pointedly looking at the other houses which backed onto them. Some had lines of washing hanging like signal flags on a ship, fluttering from bow to stern, hitched over the mast

78

trucks. Others had window boxes and hanging baskets like the outside of a pub.

'Gorgeous,' Susan commented for no particular reason. Then she squeezed his hand before letting go.

After they'd had the delicious shepherd's pie, transparent pieces of onion mingled with gravy-laden beef and topped with soft and fluffy mashed potatoes, Susan produced a home-made apple flan and a big jug of creamy custard.

'Can we watch the telly now, Mum?' Steve asked, when the last little morsel had been eaten.

'All right, but only for an hour. There's school tomorrow.'

Tom was impressed by the manner in which they agreed, before bidding them goodnight. 'They're very polite,' he remarked approvingly.

'Manners cost nothing and it's the one thing I insist on. Coffee?' She'd risen and was clearing away the dirty dishes.

Tom rose also. 'Let me . . .'

'Absolutely not,' she replied, smiling. 'There isn't room in the kitchen, anyway. I'll only be a minute.'

As Tom sat in the fading light in the little back yard, he realised he felt happier than he could ever remember being. At least since he was a small child. And not even then, really. Miles had ruined every moment that might have been good. Spoilt every occasion. Loomed large like a great dark shadow just when he and Harry might have been about to enjoy themselves.

This new sensation, this sense of peace and pleasure, was so new to Tom that he tried to examine it carefully in his mind, like dipping a bare toe into unknown water to test the temperature.

A moment later Susan came out of the house carrying a tray laden with fragrant coffee and several lit nightlights in old jam jars. She put one in the middle of the table and then placed the others around the yard and along the top of the wall.

Suddenly the atmosphere changed and the yard became an enchanted place, mysterious and beautiful. The sky was a deep purple now and the white blossom of the old man's beard looked like the froth of distant incoming waves. The tubs of flowers glowed like jewels against a black velvet background and Tom sat wondering what he'd been doing for the past thirty-seven years. Had he been blind and deaf? Had he lacked an awareness of beauty?

Susan was watching him quietly.

'I like it here,' Tom said suddenly.

'I like having you here, Tom.'

The meeting had nearly come to an end. The heads of marketing strategy, design concept, distribution, merchandising and public relations had finalised the details for the launch of Mousseline-de-Soie, and another major product for D'Aussoire was under way. The copy for the blurb that would be enclosed in the packaging had already been written and translated into six languages.

The president of the company wound up the meeting with a curt word of thanks. In his view they'd merely done the job for which they were employed. Sometimes starting work at seven thirty in the morning and maybe not getting away until eight o'clock at night was not considered praiseworthy; it was merely getting the job done and done thoroughly.

On the way back to her office, Lucinda went to the restaurant. Avoiding the queue for hot dishes, she grabbed a sandwich and a cup of coffee and hurried back to her desk.

Mousseline-de-Soie might be about to be launched, but there was the new range of lipsticks they planned to bring out next year to consider. Their laboratories in Paris and Bristol were working on a lipstick and lipgloss combined but there were still problems about its 'bleeding' at the edges. Worryingly, the findings she was receiving showed that women preferred ordinary lipsticks, anyway, with a separate lipgloss they could add on top if they wanted to. That might mean aborting the concept altogether. All the signs had to be positive before millions of pounds could be spent on something new.

As soon as she sat down at her desk the phone rang.

'Hello?'

'Lucinda, is that you, dear? Is that Lucinda?'

'Mum!' Anne never normally phoned her at work. 'Are you all right?'

'I've just heard from Harry about your father's Will, dear. I was sent a copy but I haven't read it. It would be too upsetting. What's happening, dear?'

Lucinda's heart skipped a beat. Trust Harry to stir things up. 'Nothing really,' she replied, trying to sound casual. 'He's left me a beautiful writing case, quite old I think, and . . . erm . . . some of his papers. That's all.'

'But I don't understand.' Anne sounded agitated. '*What* papers, dear? Miles didn't have any papers that I know of, unless they're the manuscripts of his books?'

'I really haven't had time to look at them yet,' Lucinda replied evenly. 'Anyway, it was very nice of him to leave them to me.'

'Harry thinks they may be valuable.'

'As Harry doesn't know what sort of papers they are, I don't see how he can tell.'

Anne sounded fretful. 'Well, he thinks Daddy only left them to you because they *are* valuable. Apparently his Will says if you dispose of them you'll stand to benefit. Doesn't that mean they must be valuable? As Daddy left the boys fifty thousand each, it must mean the papers are worth that, too? Shouldn't you get expert advice before selling them? Daddy would have wanted you to get the full value for them. He was a scrupulously fair man. This is not going to cause any trouble, is it, dear?'

'Of course not, Mum. Everything's absolutely fine. Bernard is seeing to everything for me,' she added, think that was partly true, anyway. 'Look, I've got to go now, but I'll try to pop in and see you and Granny this evening, after I've settled the children and fed Julian. Would that be all right?'

'Could you, dear? Oh, that would be nice.' Anne sounded pleased. 'And bring those papers of Daddy's with you. I might recognise what they are when I see them,' she added.

Lucinda closed her eyes at the very thought. 'I'll see you later, Mum.'

When the phone rang on Tom's desk, he was certain it would be Susan. Having supper with her again had been so wonderful, he was certain she felt the same way about him as he did about her. He'd planned to call her and ask if she'd like to go to the cinema, but if she was ringing *him* . . .!

He grabbed the receiver eagerly.

'Have you spoken to Lucinda?' demanded Harry, not bothering with the niceties of any greeting.

Tom's heart sank with a disappointed flop. 'No.'

'Why not? She might tell you something. She's being very cagey with me. I presume you've received a copy of Dad's Will, too? What are these papers he's left her?'

'I've no idea. Why does it matter?'

Harry tut-tutted irritably. 'Haven't you read the Will properly? It says that if Lucinda disposes of them in an intelligent way she stands to benefit.'

'Yes, exactly. I don't know why Dad didn't leave her fifty thousand pounds outright, like he did us, but you know Dad. Got to make things tricky. As long as Lucy ends up with as much as us, what does it matter?' Tom asked calmly.

'But Lucinda's not a businesswoman. She wouldn't know how to maximise anything. Neither would Julian. If it's not made of mahogany and has four legs he's lost! What I'm saying is I could probably point her in the right direction, make sure she gets the highest price for selling them.'

'I'm sure you could,' Tom replied sarcastically, 'but Lucinda's not a fool. She wouldn't have that good job if she wasn't highly capable. Anyway, it's none of our business.'

But Harry wasn't listening. 'Why don't you give her a bell and ask her what it's all about? She talks to you more than she does to me. I spoke to Mum this morning and even she doesn't know what papers Dad's left. It's bloody mysterious if you ask me.'

'I hope you didn't get Mum worried? She's got enough on her plate.'

'Mum's fine. Dad's made sure she's all right financially,' Harry said dismissively, as if that's what Tom meant. 'What are your plans when your fifty thou comes through?

'I haven't made any plans. Listen, Harry, I was just about to—'

'You should invest it, Tom. I could probably put you on to one or two good deals. I've got plans for my company with the money I'm getting. Big plans. I bet you anything you like I'll have quadrupled that fifty thou within six months.'

'How very nice for you,' Tom said politely. 'I really must go now. 'Bye.' He hung up quickly so if Harry had been going to say anything more he wouldn't hear it. Harry made him uneasy. And very nervous.

'I'm going to have to say I forgot them, aren't I?' Lucinda said to Julian, as they got into his car. He'd offered to go with her to see her mother and grandmother, and if necessary to help her sidestep tricky questions.

'Better still, say *I* forgot them,' Julian suggested. 'We'll tell your mother you asked me to bring them with us tonight, and halfway here I realised I'd left them on the hall table.'

'That'll work for now, but what are we going to do next time she asks?'

'Have a word with Bernard and see if he can't produce *some* papers of your father's; contracts with publishers, business letters, legal documents, anything that will satisfy your family's curiosity.'

'Good idea. God! Why did Dad put me in this dreadful position? And trust Harry to make a big thing of it.'

Sarah welcomed them with her usual elegant warmth, but Anne was in a very highly strung state, and more faded-looking than ever. She'd gone back to wearing off-white; an ankle-length wrapover linen skirt, a chemise and a droopy beige cardigan. Her hands fluttered like moths as she greeted them, and she looked as if she might fade away like a displaced ghost.

'Oh, darlings. So sweet of you to come. I've been so worried.' She pressed a crumpled handkerchief to her trembling lips. 'Why did Daddy have to die? We were so happy and now I'm all alone.'

'Not entirely, dear,' Sarah said drily.

Lucinda put her arms round her mother and hugged her. 'Mum, you'll never be alone while all of us are around.'

'I know, dear, and Granny's been so kind having me to stay, but it's not the *same*, is it? I depended on Daddy for everything. How am I going to manage? Who's going to deal with the tax man? And the bank manager? And what shall I do about the house and everything? Oh, it's all too much.'

'We'll help, Mum, but it's you who's been running your house for years, you know. Not Dad. And surely you've already got an accountant? Let him look after the financial side for you, as he always has done. Dad never got involved doing his own tax, so why should you? And there's Bernard; he'll help.' Lucinda stopped and threw Julian an anxious glance. The sooner they worked out the same story with Bernard the better.

'Are you all right for money in the meantime, Anne?' Julian asked sensibly. 'Sometimes the deceased's assets are frozen until probate has been granted.'

Anne gazed at him with vacant eyes. 'I don't know. I suppose I'll have to get on to the bank and ask. Miles always gave me money for housekeeping, every week, but since I've been staying with Granny . . .'

Lucinda looked at her mother sadly, realising that most married women of her generation were sheltered by convention from the nitty-gritty of dealing with the money side of life. For a moment she could see the advantages of being a working woman with her own income; how awful to have to ask your husband for money, for everything from Tampax to his own Christmas present.

'Can we help?' Julian suggested gently. 'Do you want me to sort out these things for you?'

It was Sarah who gave him a grateful smile. She was finding it quite exhausting having her daughter staying with her, and she couldn't help feeling that Anne wasn't doing anything to help herself, either, at the moment.

'That's very sweet of you, Julian,' Anne was saying, 'but Harry has promised to give me a hand. He said I wasn't to do anything without consulting him first. The problem is he's so busy with his new company and I don't like to worry him. He's anxious to know what papers Daddy's left Lucinda. Have you brought them for me to see?'

'I don't suppose they're of any importance, Anne dear,' Sarah said gently.

Julian made an apologetic moue. 'I'm sorry, it's my fault. Lucinda asked me to bring them and when we were halfway here I realised I'd left them on the hall table. I had a quick glance at them and they only seem to be rough notes, contracts from his publishers, that sort of thing.'

Lucinda raised her eyebrows fractionally and at that moment realised Sarah was watching her closely. So she, too, suspected there was something special about the papers, but had obviously been trying to put Anne off the scent.

'Really?' Anne asked, puzzled. 'Not valuable? Harry was sure they must be. How strange. And they were in an old-fashioned writing case?'

How well Harry had sown the seeds of suspicion, Lucinda thought. She smiled at her mother. 'It's an extremely pretty antique writing case. I'm thrilled with it.'

'A charming little memento for you, darling, of his brilliant work,' Sarah remarked peaceably.

They exchanged looks, understanding each other completely: words that were not necessary now would be exchanged on another occasion. They stayed a little while longer, drinking coffee and trying to keep the conversation light, but it was obvious Anne was dispirited and Sarah was tired so they left after an hour.

'It's too much for Granny having Mum to stay,' Lucinda observed as they drove home. 'She's either got to have someone live with her to keep her company at home, or else get a flat.'

'Do you want to ask her to stay with us for a while?' Julian asked.

Lucinda contemplated the suggestion in thoughtful silence. The problem was that whilst her grandmother infused her with enthusiasm and inspiration and she loved having her around, her mother seemed to bleed her dry, drain away her motivation and drag her down to her own level of hopelessness.

'I think she'd find the children too much,' she said at last, ashamed at using them as an excuse, 'and she'd have to sleep in the playroom as we don't have a spare room; it wouldn't work.'

Julian nodded, remaining silent.

'But I should offer, shouldn't I?' Lucinda continued. 'It's dreadful to think of her, pining for Dad, while poor Granny tries to keep her cheerful.'

'It's up to you,' he said generously, privately wondering how long he could stand having Anne around the place himself.

As it turned out, however, Anne refused Lucinda's invitation to stay.

'That's kind of you, dear, but I've decided to return home. Granny's very sweet but she does rather exhaust me. She's always wanting to do things, ask people round for drinks, give luncheon parties. I know she thinks it will cheer me up, but I've never liked socialising. I've realised I'd rather be at home after all. I shall feel nearer to Daddy, there.'

'But you can't be on your own,' Lucinda protested, horrified.

'I'll be fine, dear. I know I will. Everyone has to cope with grief in their own way and mine is to stay quietly at home until I get adjusted to the idea of Daddy not being around any more.' Her voice was shaky but there was a strength in it that hadn't been there before.

Lucinda realised that she must accept her mother's wishes, although she doubted that Anne was ready to face the world alone yet, and secretly she felt ashamed at her own sense of relief.

'Mum darling, you will take care of yourself, won't you? Call us if you need anything, all right? We're here all the time, you only have to give us a ring, and perhaps you can come to lunch on Sunday? And see Jamie and Daisy? They're always asking after you,' she suggested, trying to compensate for her own selfishness.

She could hear Anne blowing her nose, obviously struggling for composure, but her voice was steady as she said: 'Thank you, dear. It's sweet of you but I really just want to be on my own right now. You do understand, don't you, dear?'

'Of course I understand, Mum,' Lucinda replied peaceably. 'You could ask Tom to stay with you for a bit, you know. He hasn't got much on, and I'm sure it would cheer him up to be at home with you for a while. His flat is so dreary and I think he's probably rather lonely.'

'I could ask him.' But she sounded doubtful. 'Poor Tom. I wish he'd get himself a nice girlfriend.'

Lucinda had been hearing those exact words about Tom from her mother's lips for the past fifteen years, but Tom was a loner by nature, she feared. His little romances in the past had petered out practically before they'd begun, and now he was getting set in his ways. It would be a miracle if he found the right woman.

'Give him a ring, anyway,' Lucinda urged her mother. If Tom moved back home for a bit it would be therapeutic for Anne to have someone to look after and cook for.

* * *

They lay before her on the desk again, the six pieces of jewellery. Which would suit Isabelle the most? Or should she be thinking, Lucinda corrected herself, which piece should I choose to keep for myself? Her whole future rested on such decisions. Five times over she had to make up her mind which piece she should give away and which would be the piece that would determine her future. With that one step into the dark, having no idea of the value of these jewels, either she would have to remain at work for another ten to fifteen years, or she could stay at home and join the growing band of women for whom care for their husbands and children had become more important than having a career.

Lucinda glanced up at Bernard, but his expression gave nothing away. His eyes were both anxious and sympathetic. He couldn't help her and she knew it. She breathed deeply and knew she must stay calm.

All she actually had to do was select the right piece in the first place and then it wouldn't matter how she dispersed the rest. But that was easier said than done. Instinct told her that would be too simple. Her father had probably worked it that the piece she liked the least was the very piece she ought to keep.

Seeing them all spread out again was a fresh shock. They glittered and glowed with more dazzle than she'd remembered. The diamond spray of trembling roses and leaves was a wonderful display of workmanship. The pendant, with its clear pale green stones, was delicately made, and the gold chain from which it hung the finest she'd ever seen.

As for the single string of large pearls, it looked so lush she felt like putting it in her mouth and sucking on those softly gleaming spherical orbs, licking the smooth glowing surface, like a sweet. The bracelet, that delicate strand, loose-linked, of alternate diamonds and pale sea-green stones which she presumed to be aquamarine, was very pretty. She'd thought it would suit Isabelle, but now she saw it again she wasn't so sure. Isabelle had worn a bold necklace and earrings which shone lustily; this bracelet was altogether too understated, too refined, not fiery enough. That left either the gold earrings, fine glistening strands worked into a basket weave, or the silver ring set with the blue stone that looked purple at certain angles and was surrounded by rather dirty-looking diamonds.

'God, I don't know . . .' she murmured, the madness of the situation suddenly hitting her with renewed force.

'I wish I could help you, Lucinda.'

'It's hopeless, isn't it? I've never been that interested in jewellery and my father never gave my mother any, so I've no idea what's valuable and what isn't.' She glanced down at the only piece of real jewellery she possessed, the ring Julian had given her when they got engaged. It was a small square emerald set with an equally small diamond on either side. It had belonged to his grandmother and was of great sentimental value. Julian had said it was insured for six thousand pounds, but then emeralds

85

were one of the more valuable stones, weren't they?

She glanced up at Bernard, frowning. 'Am I supposed to guess the value of the jewellery as if it was an heirloom? Or bought at auction? Or the replacement value for insurance purposes? There's probably a huge difference between the three.'

He leaned forward, resting his elbows on the desk. 'I can tell you one thing. You don't have to guess the exact value of any of it. As you say, the difference between buying it in Bond Street and getting it at even a top auction house like Christies would be enormous, because shops have to add on purchase tax. The point is that however you price them, one piece is considerably more valuable than the other five. What you're aiming for is to choose the best piece,' Bernard explained. 'The others are irrelevant.'

Lucinda smiled ruefully. 'Easier said than done.' She examined the earrings again. Good quality gold could be eighteen carat, couldn't it? Whereas she was sure cuff links or signet rings were more likely to be nine carat because that was harder wearing. On the other hand the earrings had no stones, just exquisitely worked gold.

'I'll give Isabelle the earrings,' she said, suddenly making up her mind. 'They'll suit her anyway.'

'Very well.' He closed the box containing the earrings and handed them gravely to her. She had no idea what he was thinking. Then, as he put the rest of the jewellery back in his safe, he spoke.

'May I wish you all the luck in the world, Lucinda. You deserve it, and I sincerely hope you will be able to inherit what should rightfully be yours.'

'Thank you, Bernard.' She stuffed the earrings at the bottom of her shoulder bag, together with a document which would have to be signed by Isabelle as proof of receipt. 'I'm not getting my hopes up too high, though. My chances of getting it right remind me of that game we played as children: pin the tail on the donkey.'

He nodded. 'That's exactly what it's like. By the way, I looked through your father's files, and I've put together some perfectly innocuous documents that you can say were the "papers" he left. It's not a complete lie, because he *did* leave them, in my care rather than yours, because he thought he might need to refer to them again at some point, but no matter. Here they are.'

'Thank you. I'm desperate to prevent the truth getting out.' She put the bulky A4 envelope in her shoulder bag.

Bernard, aware of Harry's money-grabbing attitude, knew it was her brother she feared. His greed was such that even the thought of hurting his mother would not prevent him exposing the true contents of the writing case if he thought they led to a fortune.

Leaving work a bit earlier than usual that evening, Lucinda decided to go to Peter Jones on her way home. The children needed some clothes and she could put everything on her account and pay later.

It was while she was going up the escalator to the first floor that she heard her name being called in urgent tones.

'Lucinda . . . *Lucinda* . . .!'

She turned round to see Isabelle, running between the displays of bed linen on the ground floor, waving her arms excitedly. Then she jumped on the escalator in hot pursuit.

Before Lucinda, waiting politely at the top, could say anything, Isabelle had flung her arms round her.

'I'm so glad to see you again,' she squealed, little vixen teeth flashing behind her scarlet lipstick. 'You know, I thought so much about our meeting the other evening. I'm sorry I was so horrid to you when you arrived but I was scared. It would be *catastrophic* if my husband were to find out about, you know . . .' she lowered her voice to a loud stage whisper, and glanced around nervously in case the upper class housewives from the Shires might be listening as they stalked the shop's aisles in Barbours and thick stockings '. . . about Miles.'

'Yes, I quite understand.'

'But how *are* you?' Isabelle peered into Lucinda's eyes as if looking for the Deeper Meaning of Life.

'I'm fine. Actually . . . I have something for you.' This was the perfect opportunity to give Isabelle the earrings and then be rid of her. She delved into her handbag and withdrew the small square red leather jewel box.

As soon as Isabelle saw it she gave a piercing scream, startling a passing elderly customer, who jumped as if she'd come into contact with a live wire.

'Oh, my God! Oh, my *God*, I can't bear this.' Isabelle broke into sobs. 'This means so much to me . . . I didn't expect anything, you know. Oh, God . . .!'

Lucinda held out the box to her.

'No! No!' she cried. 'I can't open it here! It's too special, too intimate, too emotional to open *here*. We must go somewhere quiet. Private. Where we can be alone.'

'Why don't you take it home with you,' Lucinda suggested, trying to hand her the box again.

But Isabelle shook her head as if that was the most awful idea in the world, as if the atmosphere of her home might contaminate the magical moment of receiving Miles's offering. She seized Lucinda's wrist in an iron grip and, dragging her in the direction of the down escalator, spoke urgently. 'I know where we go. We'll get a taxi . . .'

'I have to get home,' Lucinda protested. 'The children . . .'

'It won't take long. We will be very quick, si? We'll go to the Basil Street Hotel. You know it? It is very private,' Isabelle added gravely.

When she saw the earrings she looked as if she was going to faint with joy. Trembling, she took them out of their box and pressed them to her bosom.

'And he chose them for *me*,' she breathed ecstatically. 'I can't tell you,

Lucinda, how much this means to me. It makes his passing a little bit more bearable, you know? I feel not so sad now, because he remembered me at the end.' She fastened them to her ears. 'How do they look?'

Lucinda had to admit they looked very good. The earrings had been the right choice.

'Your mother doesn't mind?' Isabelle asked curiously.

'My mother knows nothing about this.'

'But Miles's Will? It must have said he wanted me to have these earrings?'

'He left them to me,' Lucinda lied smilingly. 'But he also left secret instructions for me to . . . erm . . . to give them to you.'

Well, that was partly true, she told herself, as long as Isabelle never found out about the four other mistresses. And Lucinda hadn't the heart to disillusion her. She'd obviously adored Miles and to find there had been others would hurt her deeply. A wife was acceptable. Another mistress wasn't.

'We meet again?' Isabelle pleaded, after she'd signed the receipt with a flourish. 'It would be *so* nice. You are your father's daughter, after all, so we have a great link, isn't that so? He was someone we both loved so we must keep in contact. Miles was an amazing man.'

Lucinda smiled weakly. She just hoped her father's other mistresses weren't going to want to be friends, too.

Seven

Carina studied the list of women with interest.

'You certainly had beginner's luck finding Isabelle Cronin so quickly, didn't you?' she observed.

'That's because I think Dad's affair with her was fairly recent, I mean within the past ten years, and she was still at the same address,' Lucinda replied, lounging comfortably in a padded garden seat with a leg rest.

It was Saturday afternoon, and as Julian had taken Jamie and Daisy swimming, with Carina's husband Alex and Tara and Michael, they were taking advantage of the warm weather by relaxing in the garden of the Somersets' Holland Park house, which had a lawn, mature plane and sweet chestnut trees, and manicured herbaceous borders around the perimeter.

'That was a bit of luck,' Carina agreed.

Lucinda noticed Carina had lost weight since she'd last seen her. Always thrillingly thin, even after three babies, she was now edging towards looking anorexic. Her designer white slacks hung quite loosely around her hips and her raised arms, as she clasped her hands behind her head, looked bone thin.

'Are you all right?' Lucinda asked with sudden concern. 'You've lost a lot of weight, haven't you?'

Carina raised perfectly plucked eyebrows. 'Have I? I never eat much in hot weather. At least I'll have a flat stomach for Ascot. I've bought the most gorgeous dress from Bruce Oldfield, but it doesn't allow for lumps and bumps.' She returned to studying the list again. 'So Isabelle Cronin was happy with the earrings and she really believes she's the only mistress Miles had?'

'Absolutely. And now I can't get rid of her. Poor Isabelle, she really did love Dad. Depended on him, I think, and turned him into a surrogate father.'

'Yes. From what you tell me she seems to be young enough to have been his daughter, too,' Carina remarked acidly. 'Who are you going to try to contact next? What about this one, Miranda Warwick? Or there's Renée Hartman; she gives her address as Wainsley, near York, but I wonder how long ago that was? Fenella Harrison sounds homespun, doesn't she? Living at Honeycomb Cottage, Little Tew, near Oxford. You've got a lot of travelling to do, haven't you?'

'So far I'm not going anywhere. They've all moved. At least, Directory Enquiries couldn't find current phone numbers for them at these addresses.'

'Shit, that's a bore.' Carina, frowning, topped up their glasses with white wine. 'How are you going to trace them, then?'

'I thought I might contact the people at the various addresses and ask if they know where the previous owners moved to.'

89

'There must be an easier way of finding them than that. Why don't you phone the local estate agents?'

'I think I may have to go to the actual areas where they lived so I can look up the local electoral roll to see if they're still in the same vicinity. It's going to be back-breaking, but I don't know what else to do.'

'Advertise?'

Lucinda paused, the wine glass halfway to her mouth. 'How do you mean, advertise?'

'Why not? Put a little ad in the personal column of *The Times* and the *Telegraph* and maybe in the various local papers where they used to live. Ask them to contact you.'

'Are you *mad*?' She removed her dark glasses as she stared at Carina. 'Everything's got to be conducted with the utmost secrecy in case Mum finds out. How can I possibly advertise? That would be like telling the whole world. Hey, you out there, the former mistresses of Miles Scott-Forbes, give us a call, will you? I've got the love letters you sent to him, and he wanted you to have them back!' She gave an incredulous laugh. 'I don't think so.'

But Carina was gazing at the tree tops and the blue sky beyond and not listening. 'It could work. Take Miranda Warwick, for example. Why not put: *Miranda Warwick, formerly of*, then the address, *please contact PO Box number* so-and-so, *to learn something to your advantage*. Who would know you had anything to do with it? Who would know she had anything to do with your father? It's a perfect way to trace them all, one by one.'

Lucinda looked doubtful. 'I don't know. Supposing these women are well known in their own circle? People might start putting two and two together and—'

'Get nowhere,' Carina cut in scathingly. 'It's the obvious thing to do and it'll work, providing of course none of them are dead.'

'I suppose it might work. What about "Pumpkin", though? There's still "Pumpkin",' Lucinda reminded her. 'Do I put in an ad for her, too? *Pumpkin, whoever you are, please contact*, etc.'

'Why not?'

Lucinda leaned back in her chair and thoughtfully surveyed the garden. It had not been designed with children in mind. There was no play area, no swing, no shed for bicycles or games. 'I really wonder who "Pumpkin" is,' Lucinda remarked thoughtfully. 'I can't imagine my father having an affair with anyone who called themselves Pumpkin, can you?'

'Hardly,' Carina replied, laughing. 'But you never know. Who'd have thought he'd had an affair with a passionate Italian?'

'I can't help wondering what all these women are like. I mean, Mum and Isabelle couldn't be more unalike. They're chalk and cheese.'

'Perhaps your father had more facets to his character than any of you realised. Maybe no one woman could have kept him happy.'

Lucinda closed her eyes. She couldn't get rid of the uneasy feeling that there was more to her father's philandering than met the eye. And more to this hideous game that he'd set up for her than she'd originally realised.

'Have you read the letters yet?'

'Of course not. Love letters are private. I'd be furious if, in years to come, someone read Julian and my love letters.'

'But as I said before, there might be something in the letters that would help you find the women. I really think you should, you know.'

Lucinda's heart sank. The idea of reading the letters, written by women in love with her own father whilst her mother sat at home in blissful ignorance, was sickening, and yet at the same time there was some morbid compulsion to see what they disclosed. It was like wanting to look at the aftermath of a terrible car accident. But what Carina said was true. It really might be a short cut to finding out something about the women which would help her trace them.

That night, as Lucinda lay awake, she couldn't help thinking about what Carina had said. Julian was slumbering beside her and she longed to wake him so she could talk to him about it, but she hadn't the heart. He'd left the house at five thirty that morning to drive to an important house sale in the West Country and he hadn't got home until nearly nine o'clock. He'd made some wonderful finds and bought, amongst other things, a George III table, a large nineteenth-century French mirror and gilt mantel clock, and an 1830s chess set made of 'vegetable ivory', apparently a South American nut substitute, making it currently politically correct. He'd been thrilled with his bargains, but also drained, and after he'd had supper he'd fallen asleep in front of the TV.

Maybe she ought to look more closely at the letters, she thought, as she tried to find a cool patch on the pillow. Maybe she should glance through them. Not to read them properly, of course – just to look for clues that might be helpful.

Lucinda slid out of the bed, and, because it was a warm night, crept barefoot down to the drawing room. The writing case stood on a side table, its inlaid pattern of mother-of-pearl gleaming softly as she switched on a table lamp.

The key was kept hidden in a small china vase on the mantelpiece. With hands that shook, and a feeling that she was breaking into the privacy of the past that should remain undisturbed, she unlocked the case. Apart from a hasty foray to remove Isabelle's letters, it was the first time she'd looked inside since she'd brought it home from Bernard's office.

There, neatly placed in the mahogany interior, were the four remaining bundles of papers.

Drawn by a fearful fascination, she knew she had to do more than glance through them. She had to read them, devour their contents, try to find out what sort of man her father had been in order to inspire love amongst these women.

As Miranda Warwick had been the first one on the list Bernard had drawn up, it was for her letters Lucinda reached first. Might as well start at the beginning, she thought.

The top letter was dated after Miles had married Anne. Miles would have been thirty-two at the time; nearly the same age as she was now. And he'd have been married to her mother for eighteen months. Only eighteen months and already unfaithful.

Her heart started to pound uncomfortably and she suddenly felt afraid, though she wasn't sure why.

Miranda's handwriting was small and twirly, and slanted with tiny looping flourishes to the right. Lucinda curled up on the sofa with the bundle on her lap, thankful everyone was asleep. If she was caught reading them she knew she'd feel as guilty as if she was stealing.

My dearest Miles, the first one dated 10 February began, *I was so sad to hear of your great disappointment. Life is so short and it seems dreadful that you should have to endure such unhappiness. Why did you wait until now to tell me? We've known each other for over a year and all that time you never explained . . .*

Lucinda's pulse quickened. What disappointment had her father suffered? Was his career going downhill at that time? Had he lost money? Or was it . . .?

The next paragraph provided her with the heart-stopping answer. *I so admire you for doing the honourable thing and marrying your wife when she discovered she was pregnant. That is the act of a really noble person, especially as you tell me you were never really in love with her . . .*

Lucinda felt the hairs on the back of her neck tingle and she shivered. Had her father never loved her mother? Had it been a shotgun wedding?

And what baby? Tom, the eldest, wasn't born until her parents had been married for over five years. She remembered Anne telling her how relieved she was to have a baby at last.

I felt like weeping when you told me what had happened. What terrible irony! All that effort for nothing and a lifetime of misery tied to someone you no longer love but are too noble to leave.

Lucinda let out a squawk of indignation and then quickly stifled it with her hand. The misunderstood husband routine! Surely not. Surely Miles with all his intellect could have thought up something more original if he wanted a fling on the side? Burning with anger, she skimmed through the rest of the letter, but it went on to describe a weekend Miranda had spent with her sister. Only at the end did she appeal to Miles to come and see her soon again.

I live for the times we can be together, my only love. Take heart and remember you are in my thoughts night and day, now and for ever. Let me know when you can get away again, for another 'lecture tour' perhaps?

Lucinda didn't know whether she wanted to go on reading any more. If they were all going to be in the same vein, she'd skip it. What was all this nonsense about a baby, for God's sake? Had Miles lied in order to seduce Miranda? Pretended to have married Anne out of a sense of duty in order to gain sympathy? She felt disgust for his machinations, and almost sorry for his victim. Miranda sounded like a nice, if naive, woman.

But then her eye caught a line in another letter and she picked it up to read it.

Thank you for your card of congratulation. At last I have my degree and I'm so thrilled. Now I'm determined to get my Master's. I feel this has brought me closer to you. Although I will never reach the dizzy heights of your achievements.

That was a shock. So Miranda was an intellectual? Yet aware she was not in Miles's league? Maybe this had been more a meeting of minds than a passionate physical relationship? But it was her last letter, written two years after the first, that brought a pang to Lucinda's heart and made her realise that maybe her father had been deeply disappointed in his marriage to her mother.

My heart is broken, wrote Miranda, *now that I know I cannot keep up with you, can no longer interest and amuse you, talk your language or have anything in common with you. You have moved on and I don't have the brilliance to follow. I was never going to be your equal, I always knew that, but now I feel I cannot even hold a candle to you when it comes to achievements. I could see I bored you the last time we met, and then I began to realise for the first time how your wife must feel and my heart breaks with sorrow for her, too . . .*

'Oh, my God,' Lucinda said aloud. And again, as Miranda's words sank in: 'Oh, my God.'

So Miles hadn't been portraying himself as the misunderstood husband. He'd genuinely been seeking someone with a brain to vie with his own, because for him Anne had proved to have no brain at all.

Lucinda could only guess at the appalling consequences of the marriage of a scholar to a sweet but dizzy woman like her mother. Suddenly it came back to her, the memory of her father's constant cry: *How can you be so stupid, Anne?*

And perhaps the more he'd said that over the years, the stupider Anne had become, until in the end she was an adoring but downtrodden ghost of the young woman he'd originally married.

Lucinda returned Miranda's letters to the writing case and locked it once more before replacing the key in the vase. She hadn't the heart to read any of the other letters tonight, although she was still wide awake. It was now half past two and she hurried silently upstairs again, longing to lie close to Julian once more. She needed to feel his warmth. She needed to press herself close to his side, to reassure herself that at least he was all hers and they had a happy marriage.

The next morning before she left for work, she phoned her grandmother. Anne, she knew, had returned to her own home the previous day.

'Granny, can I come and see you this evening, for a few minutes?' she asked, when Sarah had greeted her with her usual warmth and affection.

'Of course you can, darling. Come for a drink,' Sarah told her. 'It will be lovely to see you.'

Lucinda felt comforted. Miranda's letters had shaken her badly, and there were questions she had to know the answers to.

She went straight to Sarah's flat in Rutland Gate from work that evening. It was on the first floor of what had originally been a Victorian family home, set in a row of identical cream stuccoed houses with pillared porticoes, ornate black iron railings and large windows through which passers-by could catch a glimpse of large, opulently furnished chandelier-lit rooms. The houses had long since been divided up into flats, but Sarah's was the best, with a balcony overlooking the towering trees in the central garden.

Lucinda ran up the blue-carpeted stairs rather than take the lift and there was her grandmother, standing in the doorway of her flat, smiling warmly in welcome. As soon as Lucinda entered the exquisitely furnished rooms she was assailed by the aroma of jasmine and a buzz in the atmosphere that indicated Sarah was planning a party.

'Eight for lunch tomorrow,' Sarah said, in answer to Lucinda's question. 'I'd ask you, too, darling, but this is an old *old* group who are coming. You'd be fearfully bored.'

'And I'd never be able to get away from work,' Lucinda replied regretfully as she looked through the open door into the dining room. Her grandmother liked to do as much as possible the night before so that neither she nor Mrs Morgan was too rushed in the morning. The table was already laid, with a white cloth, green and white china, green glasses and table napkins, and the white starry flowers of a jasmine plant standing in an antique tureen in the middle. It looked as if she was expecting a photographer from *House & Garden* rather than an 'old group' for lunch.

'I don't know how you do it,' Lucinda said admiringly. 'Is there anything I can do to help?'

'No thank you, darling. Everything's under control. It's a very easy menu: consommé to start with, then a tian of crab and lobster with avocado and sour cream and a little salad, and after that elderflower jelly studded with blueberries for pudding.'

'*Granny*! You are amazing,' Lucinda exclaimed.

Sarah smiled as she led the way into the drawing room. She was wearing her favourite shade of silvery grey today, with a straight skirt, long belted cardigan and a bright silk scarf draped around her neck. 'It's not as grand as it sounds, sweetheart. It's light, which people who are old appreciate; no one of my age can digest meat any more. It's also easy for Mrs Morgan. She made the jelly yesterday, and the rest she just has to assemble. We don't go in for *cooking* in the house any more, we *assemble*. Now, how about a glass of wine?'

'Divine,' Lucinda replied, dropping into the softness of a cushiony sofa.

Drinks poured, Sarah turned to her with a questioning look. 'So what's happened, darling?'

'You'll never guess what Dad has asked me to do, in his Will,' she began.

'Probably not, but I imagined from your reaction when your mother asked about the papers he'd left you that it was something you'd rather she didn't know about.'

'That's the whole point.'

An hour later, Lucinda, with her shoes kicked off, was curled up on the sofa, feeling much better for having got the whole story off her chest. Sarah had listened gravely, nodding from time to time, but making no comment.

'Obviously,' Lucinda concluded, 'Harry must never know the truth because he'd drag Mum into the whole business. I trust Tom, but right now I think it's better he doesn't know either.'

'It would put him in an awkward position with his brother,' Sarah agreed.

'Granny, do you think Mum had any idea what was going on?'

'Some people don't see what they don't want to see. They can go for years and years in a total state of denial. Actually, as you obviously didn't suspect anything, and presumably neither did Tom or Harry, your father may have managed to be very discreet, which is to his credit. And you're right; Anne must never know. There's no point and it would shatter her completely at the moment.'

'There's something else,' Lucinda continued, flushing. 'I'm afraid I read some of the letters last night, from a woman called Miranda. They were dated eighteen months after Mum and Dad were married.'

'And you found out something that disturbed you?'

'Yes,' she said, relieved that Sarah wasn't shocked by her nosiness. 'Something she wrote really appalled me.'

'Go on.'

'It's not true that they got married because they had to, is it?'

The lines on Sarah's face grew deeper and for a moment she looked her age. She clasped her hands tightly together on her lap and there was a pause before she spoke.

'I'm afraid that's true,' she said at last, her voice shaky. 'I didn't want your mother to marry just because she was going to have a baby. After all, it's something that happens to princes and paupers, the rich and the poor, saints and sinners. It was an accident. I'd have brought the baby up myself if necessary rather than . . .' She paused and bit her lower lip before continuing: 'But she was madly in love with Miles and I sometimes wondered if she hadn't . . . anyway, she insisted Miles marry her.' Sarah paused again and a look of pain flickered across her face. 'Your mother even threatened to do away with herself if he didn't marry her. I'm not sure he really wanted to, but he was an ambitious man and his career was on the ascent, and I suppose he didn't want to be involved in a scandal. So they got married quietly in a register office. By then Anne had somehow persuaded herself he was as much in love as she was . . . and she went on persuading herself that was the case until he died.'

'But . . . what happened to the baby?' Lucinda asked fearfully.

'It was a little girl, and, sadly, she was stillborn. Anne had a very difficult labour and feared she'd never be able to have any more children. It was a further five years before . . .'

'. . . Tom was born,' Lucinda finished the sentence for her. 'Those letters suggested Dad was disappointed in his marriage, and that it had all been for nothing.'

Sarah's smile was sardonic. 'I very much doubt if anyone could have held Miles's interest for long. He was mercurial, like quicksilver. A volatile and unpredictable man who became easily bored. I imagine he moved on from one woman to another, as well as having a wife, for that very reason.'

'I think you're right. Miranda's letters were pathetic. She'd realised she wasn't clever enough to keep up with him. And she also said that she'd come to realise how Mum must have felt.'

'But, as I said, I don't think your mother *did* realise anything was wrong. Some people, you know, derive more happiness from loving a partner than they do from being loved. It's the *giving* they rejoice in. *Receiving* love can have its down side; it's a great responsibility, and I guess one that your father, at times, couldn't tolerate.'

Lucinda nodded in understanding. 'Mum's ability not to see what she didn't want to see has probably enabled her to keep her sanity.' But she felt confused, not sure where her sympathies lay. With her father? Frustrated because he couldn't find a woman who was his mental equal? Or her mother and all the other women who had been in love with him, who couldn't keep up with the comet that held their dreams, causing them to trail behind, to be eventually vaporised.

'I must go now,' she said, uncurling herself and putting on her shoes. 'Julian will be waiting for me. Thank you so much for letting me talk to you and for listening to everything. I'll let you know how I get on.'

'Do, my darling girl.'

When Lucinda had gone, Sarah slumped heavily into her chair, feeling exhausted. She felt shaken, too, though not entirely surprised. Miles had always been like a dark river with hidden depths and unexpected whirlpools, treacherous shallows and deceptive undercurrents. She had never liked him or trusted him, but for over forty years she had pretended to, for Anne's sake. Now he was gone, and yet he wasn't. He'd left Lucinda with a diabolical task and an unlikely inheritance. The man had been evil. A genius steeped in malice.

The first advertisement appeared in the personal column of the *Telegraph* three days later. As Lucinda read the text, which gave a PO Box number for a reply, she wondered how Miranda Warwick would react when she saw it. She'd probably link it to Miles's recent death, if she read the newspapers at all. But would she respond?

* * *

Miranda Warwick had sat in her chair by the window for over two hours now. In that time she hadn't moved a muscle. Her hands had remained folded on top of the newspaper that lay on her vast lap, while tears trickled down her wrinkled cheeks amd plopped into her maroon jumper. Miles had remembered her. That one, dazzling, thrilling thought kept flowing through her mind, causing her joy and sadness in equal parts, and moving her deeply. There was no doubt in her mind that the guarded notice in the personal column referred to a legacy of some sort. Miles hadn't forgotten her, even after all these years.

The reason Miranda was so sure that 'something to her advantage' came from Miles was simply because there was no one else, and never had been anyone in her life, who would leave her anything. Or even have reason to want to contact her. Her parents had died years ago and she'd never had any siblings. She was alone in the world, but she hoped people didn't feel sorry for her; she couldn't bear that. In a way it was her own choice anyway.

She'd have married Miles like a shot if he'd left his wife and asked her, but he hadn't. He'd grown bored and moved on. But for her the flame of love had continued to burn brightly, and she'd never even contemplated having another love in her life. Never been tempted by anyone else, either. The man who had taken possession of her roughly and thrillingly, and finally dropped her suddenly and harshly, had nevertheless left his mark indelibly on her emotions.

It had all happened a very long time ago now, but for her it could have been last month or last year. And now, near the end of her own life, and at the end of his, he had remembered her.

She sobbed with the bitter sweetness of it all, and resolved to write to the PO Box number given.

When the phone rang, just before lunch, Jane flashed a nervous glance at William. They were expecting to hear from the bank at any time now, and every call made her heart leap with both fear and expectation.

William picked the instrument up from the table, where they were sitting by the pool, and held it to his ear. 'Hello?'

Jane watched his expression, trying to gauge whether the news was good or bad, but William was very good at hiding his feelings. Very English stiff-upper-lip, at least when they were with other people. Only with her did his exterior ever crack, revealing just how vulnerable he was under his protective armour.

'Yes. Right. Yes, I understand,' he was saying, while his eyes searched the distant hills of the Dordogne which lay beyond their property, as if he were desperately trying to find some landmark to focus on. 'Yes. Quite. I know.'

Jane tried to catch his eye, desperate for some indication as to whether the bank was being helpful or not, but William wasn't looking her way, and she felt that was a bad sign.

'Well, thanks anyway. Goodbye.' William switched off the phone and finally turned to look at Jane. 'No go,' he said shortly.

She felt herself grow cold, as if the blood were draining out of her body, and somewhere, just under her ribs, a block of ice trembled before settling.

'They won't lend us anything to tide us over?' she asked faintly.

'There are problems about using a property in France as collateral for a bank loan in England,' William explained, walking slowly round the edge of the pool, his hands stuck deeply into the pockets of his chinos. 'Fuck. Fuck. Fuck,' he muttered under his breath. 'I could *kick* myself.'

'How are we going to pay Jacques and the others? What about food? And all the bills?' she exclaimed.

He looked at Jane with concern. It made him more wretched than anything to see her so upset. 'Things are not as bad as that, yet,' he told her, trying to sound reassuring. 'We do have some savings. We'll be all right for the next few months, but we don't have the money to stay here for any longer than that.'

'Then we're definitely going to have to sell up?' She looked around the pool area and the garden beyond, with its lavender-bordered paths, and thought how hard they'd all worked to make the place their paradise on earth, and how terribly hard it was going to be to leave it all behind. She loved every stick and stone of the château. It was the sort of home she'd wanted all her life. Even worse would be saying goodbye to Jacques and his family.

'I think we'd be wise to put the house on the market now,' William was saying sombrely.

'*Now*?' Tears sprang to her eyes, and she dug her nails into the palms of her hands, feeling sick with misery as she tried to control herself. The bottom seemed to have fallen out of her world; where would they go? What would they do with all their things?

For the first time in her life she felt deeply scared. She and William were in their sixties. Too old to start over, too old to make all the hideous adjustments that moving back to England would call for.

'Why so soon? Maybe the government will do something to save ICC?' she said, trying to keep her voice steady.

'And maybe they won't,' he said heavily. 'We can't rely on it, Jane. If we were to stay on here for too long, we could go bankrupt. Supposing we can't find a buyer for this place? Then we'll be in real trouble.'

She closed her eyes and rested her head back on the sun lounger, wondering how anyone could resist buying her beautiful home. She'd created each room as an oasis of peace and elegance, each with its own atmosphere; the formal drawing room was typically French, with its Louis XVI style furniture, long windows draped in caramel-coloured silk and rich tapestries and gilt-framed mirrors; the dining room resembled an indoor conservatory, with cool greens and soft yellows and limewashed furniture, whilst their bedroom was like sleeping in the clouds; pale blue and white with billowing white muslin draped over the four-poster bed and windows. How was she going to leave all this behind?

* * *

'Hadn't we better get on with arranging Dad's memorial service?' Harry asked irritably. Frustration was eating into him. No one seemed to be getting on with anything, nothing was moving. Paula hadn't committed herself to investing in his company, although she'd said she would discuss it with her financial adviser; Bernard hadn't been able to tell him how soon he might expect his fifty thousand pound legacy, and everyone seemed to be hedging about the so-called papers Lucinda had been left, which he felt was highly suspicious.

At least if they fixed a date for Miles's memorial service, he could start talking it up to all his contacts, and all his late father's contacts, too, mentioning at the same time that he was launching Relative Tracing in the immediate future. Who knows? One of Miles's friends might be interested in investing.

'Hang on a minute,' Lucinda protested. 'We don't even know when Mum wants to have it. She may feel it's too soon.'

'How can it be too soon?' Harry snapped. 'The sooner the better, I say. We want to make sure it's an impressive do, with a reception afterwards, and all the media there.'

Alarm bells rang in Lucinda's head. Harry made her nervous when he was pushing for something. 'What's the urgency? Memorial services don't usually happen until months after someone's died, and Dad only died six weeks ago. Mum isn't up to it yet, Harry. We should wait for a bit.'

'I'll have a word with her,' he said brusquely, as if that settled the matter. 'Listen, what about the papers Dad left you? Mum says they're notes for his books – is that right?'

'Partly right,' she lied coolly. 'And a few old publishing contracts, that sort of thing.'

'Not worth much, then?'

'I doubt if they're worth anything at all.'

'Bad luck. Anyway, I'll get Mum moving on this memorial thing. Got to go. Frantically busy.' There was a click and he'd hung up.

'Fuck you!' Lucinda muttered to herself, switching off her phone. Harry was really outrageous, the way he phoned her on her mobile at the office, tried to force her to agree to an early memorial service, then said 'Bad luck' when he'd inherited fifty thousand pounds, and he thought she'd only inherited a lot of worthless documents. He was so up himself it maddened her. And she knew exactly what was going to happen. Because Anne didn't have great organisational skills, Harry was going to hijack the whole event for his own purposes, yet expect her to do most of the work. And she'd end up having to, because there was no one else in the family who could.

She reached for the phone again, deciding she'd better ring her mother before Harry went blundering in, upsetting her.

At that moment the phone sprang to life, ringing shrilly. Too late, she thought. Harry's reached her first.

99

Lucinda was right in thinking the call was from Anne, but what her mother had to say caused Lucinda's mind to freeze with shock.

'*Who*, Mum?' she asked, her heart thumping with panic.

'Miranda Warwick,' Anne repeated. 'There's something about her in the *Telegraph* today.'

'M-Miranda Warwick?' Lucinda thought she was going to faint.

'Surely you remember Miranda, darling?'

Lucinda tried to get her brain into gear, fast. What the hell was going on? Was it possible Anne had always known about Miranda?

'No, I don't remember her,' she croaked.

'Don't you?' Anne sounded surprised. There was a pause and then she said: 'No, I suppose you don't. You were only about four at the time so I suppose that's why. It's strange though, isn't it, when you've known someone quite well, and then they go out of your life and you don't even think about them for years and years. And then they suddenly turn up again.'

'Yes,' Lucinda agreed weakly. Then her mother must have known about the affair. But how come she was so calm?

'I'd forgotten all about her, you know,' Anne was saying. 'Anyway, as I was about to tell you, there's this notice in the personal column of the *Telegraph* today; it looks as if she's come into some money, which is nice for her, because she was quite poor in the old days.'

'I see.'

'She was such a good teacher. She tutored Tom when he was eight. He was a bit backward, you know. Daddy feared he'd never be able to keep up when he went to boarding school, so he found this excellent teacher. She came to stay during the summer holidays . . .' Anne rattled on, energised by having something else to think about apart from her own grief.

When Lucinda was finally able to say goodbye and switch off, she sat at her desk, while the open plan office buzzed with activity around her, feeling completely stunned. It meant her father must have contacted his ex-mistress nine or ten years after their affair had ended, in order to ask her to tutor his son! What appalling gall, she thought. What an incredible lack of sensitivity. He'd brought this woman into the home, to meet his wife, and his small children . . . and had he resumed the affair? she wondered suddenly. If so, Miranda hadn't written to him again, or if she had he hadn't kept those letters.

Then, suddenly, seeing it from Miranda's point of view, Lucinda wondered how she'd coped, coming into his home, his family, knowing what she'd lost out on all those years ago?

It wasn't until Lucinda was on her way home that evening, having dropped into the little toy shop on the corner to buy some miniature animals for Jamie's farm which had now spread across most of the children's bedroom floor, and a new set of Barbie clothes for Daisy's beloved doll, that she was struck by another dreadful thought.

*   *   *

'What have you got for us?' Jamie demanded from where he sat at the kitchen table, eating beans on toast for his supper.

'Is that a present for me?' Daisy shrilled excitedly.

Lucinda had the unpleasant feeling that they were only pleased to see her when she got home because several times a week she brought back little things for them; a basket of raspberries for their supper, some sweets, maybe a toy, like this evening, or something to wear. She knew she was spoiling them but she did love giving them things and seeing their faces light up with pleasure and hearing their voices squeal with delight.

But tonight wasn't the first time she'd noticed they were expecting something, and she felt disturbed. Julian had ticked her off about this before.

'They're getting to the stage when they almost take it for granted that you'll bring them something,' he'd told her a few days previously, when she brought them each a kite to fly in the park and Jamie had asked: 'Did you bring us anything else?'

'I know you're doing it to compensate for not being at home all day,' Julian had continued when they were alone, 'but you're storing up trouble for yourself. Presents should be for Christmas, birthdays, and occasionally when something special happens. Not all the time, Lucinda. They're going to grow up into monsters.'

She'd wept then, knowing it was because she felt guilty at not getting home to bath them and give them supper, and sometimes not even seeing them into bed. 'But I can't help it, Julian,' she protested. 'I'm missing so much of their childhood, and the only way I can feel better about that is to try to make up for it in other ways. You don't really think they're growing into spoilt brats, do you?'

Tonight, seeing their grasping little hands reach out for the farm animals and the Barbie clothes, with barely a thank you, she realised Julian had been right.

'But that's it,' she said firmly, handing them their presents. 'It's costing me a fortune buying you both all this stuff, and from now on, no more presents except at Christmas and birthdays.' Then she looked down at their sad and disappointed little faces, and without another word she turned sharply and hurried out of the kitchen and up to her bathroom, where she wept behind the locked door as if her heart would break, for her children whom she hardly saw, and her overflowing love for them that she had no time to express except by lavishing presents on them in the hope, perhaps, that they'd forgive her for being absent and love her just the same.

'What's all this then?' Julian asked her gently, when she'd sniffed her way through settling Jamie and Daisy for the night, using a bright false voice, and was now doing her best to make a Spanish omelette for their supper.

'You were right,' she began sadly and then told him what had happened. 'I feel so mean now. Jamie looked at me with such reproach. And Daisy looked really hurt. I was too upset to tell them that it wasn't because I didn't love them any more, because I think that's what they felt. But I will tomorrow,' she added, her voice subdued.

'Oh, Bun.' He came and stood behind her, and wrapped his arms round her, pulling her close. 'They'll get over it. Probably quicker than you will,' he added perceptively, kissing the back of her neck. 'You know what children are like. Explain to them in the morning that you love them to bits, but that for their own sake you don't want them to become accustomed to getting presents all the time, because life's not like that.'

Lucinda leaned back against him, loving his warmth and strength, longing for the moment when she could curl up in bed beside him. 'I know you're right, darling. It's because I feel so dreadfully guilty at not being here all the time.'

'Next time you feel like that, remember all the fathers in the land,' he chuckled. 'We don't get home to bath our children and give them supper, but think what it would be like if we all started handing out presents on an almost daily basis too.'

She turned and put her arms round his waist and looked up into his eyes, giving him a watery smile. 'Maybe I'll get my inheritance and then I can stay at home, bake bread, help the children with their homework, and know we can still pay their school fees without my having to work.'

Julian made some joking remark but Lucinda wasn't listening. She remembered that she'd been struck by an awful thought after she'd talked to her mother, and it came back to her now. When she'd told Julian how Miles had brought Miranda Warwick back onto the scene as a tutor, so that Anne had got to know her, she added: 'Suppose Mum's met them all? Suppose they re-emerged in Dad's life as secretaries? Assistants? Acquaintances? Old friends, even?'

Julian frowned, perplexed. 'Would it matter, now?'

Lucinda looked at him askance. 'It would matter like hell if I advertise for them, one by one, to contact a box number in order to hear something to their advantage.'

It dawned on him what she was getting at. Anne might be cerebrally challenged but even she would surely start to link all the women to Miles's recent death.

Harry had been so embarrassed at his lack of clothes and possessions that when he'd moved his things into Paula's duplex he'd spun her a story about his flat's having been broken into and nearly everything stolen.

'That's dreadful!' she exclaimed sympathetically. 'Of course you were insured?'

'Oh, yeah. It's just a bore. I hate shopping. All that traipsing around choosing suits and shirts and all the rest. It's such a drag.' Harry put on his little boy lost look but was clever enough not to say any more.

The set-up with Paula was not what he wanted right now, but with his feet under her table and his head on her pillow he reckoned he had to be getting closer to her fortune. As long as he had the patience to play this slippery but very rich fish. As long as her financial adviser approved. It annoyed him, though, that she kept wrong-footing him. And in such a charming and sweet way that he couldn't say a fucking thing without revealing his real motive. He was fast running out of cash, too. He'd got a loan from the bank when he'd shown the manager a copy of Miles's Will, but a lot of that money had gone on wining and dining Paula, and he knew the bank weren't going to let him have any more. It would be some months, he feared, before his father's estate would pay out his inheritance.

Meanwhile his mother and Lucinda were stalling over the memorial service, as if it was going to be a quiet family affair instead of a fantastic occasion in which he could promote himself.

If he was going to get his scheme off the ground, he decided, swift action was required.

'I've got a meeting this afternoon,' he announced, gazing awkwardly at the empty closet space Paula had cleared for his things. 'I don't really want to go; it's a guy I don't much care for but he's desperate to invest a couple of million in my company . . .' Harry shrugged, letting his voice trail off.

'That's great,' Paula said enthusiastically.

'Great for *him* if I let him,' Harry replied. 'He's been pestering me for weeks now, but I'm quite reluctant to take him on board. You've got to be careful who you have as backers,' he continued in a knowing tone.

An hour later Harry turned up at Bernard Clarke's office, demanding to see him.

'Mr Clarke's with a client at the moment,' the secretary informed him coolly. 'He could be quite some time.'

Unabashed, Harry seated himself on the sofa in the reception area. 'I'll wait,' he replied loftily.

Paula, showered and immaculately dressed in cream trousers and silk shirt, put the finishing touches to her make-up. It was ten thirty, and she went to her desk, ready to phone her broker, Edward Havell. She'd already studied the latest share prices in the *FT* that morning but she liked to discuss the way the market was shifting, and she frequently made suggestions about buying and selling her stock holding in a variety of companies. Her flair for handling her portfolio was as much instinct as knowledge, inherited from her financier father, and she used Edward as a sounding board before asking him to make transactions on her behalf. Twenty-four hours was a long time in the market. What was booming yesterday could be going bust today. Edward was an excellent broker who had looked after her portfolio with acumen for several years, but she still liked to play the market herself.

Taking her gold Cartier ballpoint out of her handbag she picked up the phone and tapped in his number.

'Edward, good morning,' she greeted him when she got though.

' 'Morning, Paula. How are you today?'

'Fine, thanks. Listen, Edward, I want you to do some buying and selling for me, please, but I'd also like us to have lunch this week. There's something I want to discuss with you.'

They decided on the following Thursday, at Greens, in St James's.

'I'll see you then,' Paula said.

'Can you give me an inkling of what it's about?'

'It's too complicated to start explaining on the phone but I'll tell you all about it when I see you.'

'I'm sorry, Harry,' Bernard said kindly, though his blue eyes were frosty, 'but these things take time. It can be years before monies can be paid out of a deceased person's estate.'

'Surely you can hurry up the process?' Harry asked sullenly.

'Probate hasn't even been granted and I'm not expecting it to be for probably another few months.'

'Bloody hell!' Harry stamped his foot like a spoilt child. 'What am I supposed to do in the meantime?'

Bernard Clarke's eyebrows shot up and he looked across his desk at Harry with deep distaste, and thought how different he was from his sister. 'I imagine,' he said coldly, 'that you will continue to do whatever you would have done if your father hadn't died.'

Harry didn't even look embarrassed. 'But I'm on the brink of clinching a really good deal for my company. An extremely rich backer is very interested in investing several million pounds. In the meanwhile, I've got to appear solvent.' He gave a false laugh, harsh and cocky. 'You know the old saying? You've got to spend a buck to make a buck.'

Benard spoke smoothly. 'I'm sure if your potential backers are interested, they will understand that a legacy can't be rushed through to aid a business venture. I'm afraid you'll have to wait like the rest of your family.'

'Could you advance some of it to me, then? I'm prepared to pay the going rate of interest.' There was a note of desperation behind Harry's brash manner.

'We're not moneylenders,' Bernard replied stiffly. Then he rose, bringing the meeting to an end. 'In due course you'll be hearing from me in the normal way but in the meantime I'm afraid I'm unable to help you. If you're short of funds, why don't you go and see your bank manager?'

As Harry strode angrily out of his office Bernard could have sworn he heard him mutter under his breath: 'Fucking arsehole.'

'Are you doing anything this evening, Lucy?' Harry asked when he phoned her on his mobile from an open-air cafe in Covent Garden, a few minutes later. 'I want you to meet my new girlfriend and I wondered if we could drop in for a drink?'

'OK,' Lucinda replied reluctantly, thinking that all she really wanted to do when she got home tonight was see the children, change into comfortable jeans and a T-shirt, and relax. 'Who is she? Do I know her?'

104

'You don't know her but you're going to love her.' He sounded enthusiastic and boyishly proud. 'Her name's Paula Maxwell, and we've been living together for a few weeks now.'

'It's serious, then?'

'I think so.' He sounded wistfully hopeful and Lucinda smiled to herself. Maybe the right woman would be the making of Harry, and get him to settle down to a proper job instead of always dreaming up new schemes and scams.

'Cool. Why don't you come round at about seven and stay for supper?' I'll do a pasta dish with salad, she thought, and there's plenty of fruit and cheese, and Julian can open some wine. 'Where are you living, by the way? Have you given up your flat?'

'Yes. Paula's got a duplex in Eaton Place.'

Lucinda's mind clicked with a nasty jar when she heard those words and she realised exactly what Harry was really after. 'I've got to go now, one of the directors is heading for my desk,' she said hurriedly. 'I'll see you tonight.'

'This is Paula,' Harry said, wide-eyed and grinning. 'Paula, this is my sister, Lucinda, and my brother-in-law, Julian.'

They all shook hands in the narrow hallway, while Jamie and Daisy came rushing out of the kitchen at the far end; Daisy had a half-eaten apple in her hand and Jamie's mouth was rimmed with peanut butter.

'Hello!' they chorused, looking up wonderingly at Paula. She looked cool and elegant in a pale blue silk trouser suit, with strappy shoes that Lucinda knew must have cost several hundred pounds. Her hair looked as if she'd come straight from a hairdresser, her hands were pale, the nails manicured and painted dark red, and her make-up was exquisitely applied. Her whole appearance suggested she was a woman who did little else but look after herself.

So what the fuck's she doing with Harry? was Lucinda's first thought.

'Come in,' Julian said, sharing Lucinda's surprise but slipping into host mode. 'Can I get you a glass of wine?'

They all trooped into the drawing room and at that moment Lucinda realised her fatal mistake. The Edwardian writing case was still standing on the side table, and Harry would be sure to notice it and realise what it was. What a fool! she thought, furious with herself. She should have hidden it before they arrived.

'White wine?' Julian was saying. Lucinda tried to edge Harry to a chair which had its back to the writing case, but he was obviously wanting to show Paula that he was a frequent visitor to his sister's house and completely at ease, and so he strolled over to the fireplace, and stood with his back to the mantelpiece, hands dug deeply into his pockets.

'How are things at D'Aussoire, sis?' he asked, before turning to Paula and continuing: 'Lucinda practically runs D'Aussoire. She's been there for more than ten years, and she's in charge of all their market research. You know they also own Archée, Artémis, Bagatelle, Galactée, Tazée and Mazeray. Oh! and

Idole.' He gave Paula a chummy wink. 'Be nice to her and she might get you some free samples.'

Paula looked at Lucinda and their eyes locked, and Lucinda instantly realised they were sharing the same thought: isn't Harry an embarrassing jerk? Lucinda looked away quickly, and Paula put up her guard again, saying with sincerity: 'My God, you must work hard. How do you manage with having children, too?'

Feeling disloyal, Lucinda tried to make a joke of Harry's boasting. 'Trust a brother to exaggerate wildly,' she said with a thin smile. 'I'm merely one of the market research team for the UK. Nothing special.' She gave Harry a for-God's-sake-shut-up look.

'Can I have a crisp, please, Mummy?' Jamie piped up.

'Can I, too?' Daisy echoed, as Julian handed round glasses of wine.

'Just one, darling,' Lucinda replied, 'after you've offered them round to everyone else first.'

Suddenly she noticed Harry's eyes had widened even more than usual, and she realised with an icy feeling of impending disaster that he'd spotted the writing case. Paula, looking at Harry, had followed his gaze. Fuck! How stupid to have left it there. Lucinda cursed inwardly.

'So tell me, Harry,' she said swiftly, 'how's your new company doing?'

'Cool,' he replied absently, his eyes still glued to the case. 'Is that what Dad left you?'

'What?'

'That!' he said, pointing. 'Is it a genuine antique?' And with that he strode over to the table, and started examining it. Julian shot Lucinda a look of warning. For a moment she held her breath, praying she'd remembered to lock it after she'd put back Miranda's letters.

Harry tried to lift the lid. 'Where's the key?'

Lucinda flushed scarlet and tried to busy herself seeing if there was any wine left in the bottle Julian had placed on the coffee table.

'I've mislaid it,' she lied. 'I had it just the other day and then I put it somewhere safe, and now I can't remember where.'

'I know where it is!' Daisy crowed triumphantly.

'So do I,' Jamie added. 'You put it in that vase on the mantelpiece.'

Julian stepped forward. 'You're quite right, old boy, it *was* there, but then I remember Mummy taking it upstairs.'

Daisy was trying to climb onto the seat of the club fender that surrounded the fireplace, her small hand outstretched to grasp the vase. With a swift movement, Julian picked her up in his arms and lifted her away. 'You're not allowed to stand on that,' he scolded. 'Supposing you slipped? And there was a fire burning in the grate?'

'I only wanted to . . .' she wailed, but Julian was cuddling her now, and offering her another crisp.

Even Harry did not have the gall to get the key out of the vase with everyone watching. They all resumed their seats but the atmosphere, uneasy from the start, was now tense, the writing case on one side of the room and the key on the other like unexploded time bombs ticking away.

'I knew your father, you know,' Paula said conversationally to Lucinda, as she sipped her wine.

'Did you?' Lucinda looked at her brother in surprise. 'Did you know that, Harry?'

He nodded. 'Paula's father and Dad were friends.' He smiled at Paula. 'You'd all known each other for ages, hadn't you, honey?'

'Yes. My father and I were very saddened to read about his death. It was a awful shock,' Paula replied, adding softly: 'It must be a great loss to you all, Lucinda. I know Harry was absolutely devastated. We met just after the accident, didn't we, Harry? I'd seen it in *The Times*, so I recognised your name immediately.'

'Really?' Lucinda looked from one to the other, observing their secret exchange of smiles and glances.

'Miles was an amazing man,' Paula remarked reflectively.

Something in Lucinda's chest fluttered and gave a nervous flip. A cold tingle flew down her spine and she looked at Paula more closely. She was older than Harry, at least eight or ten years older, although only another woman would have spotted the telltale signs of the slightly slack line of her jaw and the skin on the back of her hands. Harry usually went in for blonde, busty chicks in their early twenties. Paula couldn't be more different, and again Lucinda wondered what she was doing with Harry? Unless . . . unless . . .

Lucinda felt quite weak as a thought grew stronger, more positive, until she was almost certain she was right. And *why* was she so certain? Where had she heard that comment about her father before? 'Miles was an amazing man'? Spoken in the same tones of awe?

She looked more closely at Paula Maxwell. What did she know about her? The name meant nothing. She was an elegant, beautifully dressed woman, cultured and intelligent-looking. In her middle forties, with a home in the most expensive part of town. Who did that remind her of? The answer sizzled in her mind like a hot iron on ice. Isabelle, of course! An English version of Isabelle.

Lucinda could feel her heart pounding in her ribcage, certain this was the missing mistress. The one who had given no address but had signed herself 'Pumpkin'. It all fitted: P for Paula, P for Pumpkin. They'd met through Paula's father. She even lived in the same area as Isabelle and shared many of the same attributes. Lucinda was now certain Harry had unwittingly brought the fifth mistress into their midst. With a feeling of mixed excitement and revulsion she realised all she had to do was think of a way of confronting her without arousing Harry's suspicions.

Eight

In reply to the notice placed in the personal column of the Telegraph . . .

The writing, Lucinda saw, had hardly changed in nearly forty years. A bit smaller, perhaps, less meticulous, with the address in Hove handwritten, but the tiny twirls were the same. The quality of the writing paper was poor, though. It was the type, with matching envelopes, that was available from newsagents.

'Look,' Lucinda said triumphantly, handing the letter across the breakfast table to Julian, who was munching his way through grilled bacon and tomatoes.

He took the letter and skimmed its contents before handing it back to her, remarking: 'Two down, three to go.'

'Pity I can't advertise again,' she observed.

'Advertise what?' Jamie asked, cereal spoon in mid-air.

'It's something to do with D'Aussoire,' Lucinda said briefly, shocked at how easily she could lie. It was becoming a dangerous habit; lying to her children, her mother, her brothers. And she hated it. Even as a child she'd been truthful and it was against her nature to deceive, even apart from making life so complicated. She was forever having to watch what she said in case one of them overheard her.

'What three to go, Daddy?' Daisy piped up. 'Where are they going?'

Julian stroked her wild halo of blonde curls and smiled into her upturned face. 'To school, I expect, darling.' He caught Lucinda's eye. 'Shall I take them this morning?'

'Could you?' She looked at him gratefully. 'I want to make a couple of calls before I leave for the office.'

'But *which* three?' Daisy persisted, getting down from the table.

'They'll never tell you,' Jamie remarked resignedly. 'Grown-ups never tell you *anything*.'

As soon as they'd left, and Delia had gone upstairs to make the beds, Lucinda poured herself another cup of coffee and dialled Directory Enquiries.

'Which name?'

'Maxwell. Paula Maxwell. The address is Eaton Place, Belgravia.'

Lucinda waited, hearing the tapping of a keyboard in the background.

'Sorry, the number's not listed,' the operator told her.

It damn well wouldn't be, would it? Lucinda thought with irritation. Paula Maxwell was just the type of woman to have an ex-directory number. She'd have to find an excuse for getting it out of Harry without his knowing why.

Then she read Miranda's letter again, studying those fussy twirls, trying to picture what she looked like, dreading making this call yet horribly

109

fascinated to know she'd be talking to another of her father's mistresses in just a few moments.

A softly spoken woman answered the phone.

'May I speak to Miranda Warwick, please?' Lucinda asked, trying to keep her voice steady.

'It's me speaking.' She sounded like a timid little mouse.

'Hello. This is Lucinda Cotterell. You answered my notice in the *Telegraph*.'

'Hello, Lucinda.' Miranda didn't sound at all surprised at hearing from her. 'The last time I saw you, you were just a little girl.'

'How did you know it was me?'

'It just had to be,' Miranda replied calmly. 'There is no one else it could be. It's about Miles, isn't it? I read that he had died.'

Lucinda felt embarrassed and filled with pity. How dreadful to go through life with only one person who was important to you, and that person not even your husband. And when the phone rang, to know there was only one person who would be ringing.

'Right. Yes. I see,' Lucinda stammered. 'Erm . . . er . . . I'm not sure how you're going to feel about this, but he's left all your letters. He wants—' She broke off as she heard Miranda give a piercing little shriek.

'My letters! He kept my letters . . . Oh, my God! I'd no idea he'd do that. I've kept all of his, of course, not that there were many, but I never thought he'd keep mine.' She sounded as if the breath had been knocked out of her body.

'He wants me to return them to you,' Lucinda explained, hoping she hadn't given the older woman too great a shock. 'I've also got—'

'But what about your mother? Does she know about Miles and me? Is she still alive?' Miranda cut in, agitated, almost frightened.

'My mother's still alive but she doesn't know about . . . the letters or anything,' Lucinda replied firmly, unable to bring herself to say words like 'affair' or even 'close friendship'. Having to even talk to these women was an agony she was finding increasingly difficult. Words like 'betrayal' and 'lies' sprang to mind when she thought of her father, and she now felt that even she was betraying her mother by talking to them, by accepting them, in the knowledge that they were Miles's mistresses. It was pandering to her father's outrageous demands, and she was beginning to despise herself for going along with it, even though, for her, the stakes were so high.

'My mother does however remember you staying one summer to coach my brother, Tom,' she added lightly.

'Ah, Tom!' Miranda sighed. 'He and Harry were such sweet boys and you were such a dear little girl, so pretty. Your mother was a very, very lucky woman.' There was a pause, then she said, her voice achingly raw with longing: 'I never had any children, you see.'

There was an awkward pause and Lucinda didn't know what to say. A part of her couldn't help sympathising with Miranda.

110

'Have they done well?' she was asking. 'Harry was quite bright, I remember.'

Lucinda replied briefly. 'They're fine. Now I also have to tell you that my father has left a piece of jewellery for you to remember him by.'

'Oh . . .!' There was the sound of soft weeping. 'Oh, I don't think I can bear it.'

Lucinda waited, and in spite of herself and her protective feelings towards her mother, she was filled with pity for this woman who was still grieving over a man she'd had an affair with nearly forty years ago.

'I would send everything to you by registered post, but my father insisted I give them personally,' she said tentatively.

'Oh, yes, Of course.' Miranda blew her nose. 'I'm just so touched. When can you come? I'm confined to the house so it'll have to be here, I'm afraid.'

Lucinda glanced at the address again. Hove, on the south coast. Damn, it would take the best part of a day to get there and back. She didn't want to go at the weekend and she couldn't ask for time off, so the only answer was to drive down in the early evening. The sooner the better, too. Get it finished and done with.

'I could come next Tuesday? It would have to be at about seven o'clock in the evening because I work.'

'Very well. I'm afraid I can't offer you supper or anything, but I could manage a cup of coffee.'

'Please don't go to any trouble,' Lucinda assured her. 'I'll just drop these things off, as I have to get back to Town.'

'She sounds quite frail,' Lucinda said to Julian that evening, leaning back on the sun lounger. The children were in bed, asleep, and Delia had gone to the cinema with her boyfriend. The heatwave was unabating and the evenings seemed even hotter and stickier than the days. Trying to catch a breath of fresh air, they'd taken their cups of mint tea out onto the patio, but the humidity seemed to be pressing down on them, making Lucinda's head ache.

'How old is she?' Julian asked.

'If Daddy was seventy-three, then I think she's probably about ten years younger, unless she was quite late in graduating. She was very emotional, too. I have a feeling Dad must have been the love of her life.'

'Unbelievable, isn't it? Who would think it, knowing your pa?'

'I began to feel quite sorry for her, after we'd spoken. Mum at least has all of us, but apparently she's got no one. Not a living soul. I don't know what I'd do if I were entirely alone in the world,' she added sadly. 'I wouldn't be able to hack it.'

Julian glanced at her affectionately. 'Oh, Bun.'

She smiled. She loved him calling her Bun. Now it made her feel safe just as she'd been fantasising what it must be like to be in Miranda's shoes.

'I wonder which piece of jewellery I should give her?' Her head told her she ought to be giving away the least valuable-looking pieces, but her heart

111

was telling her it wasn't that simple. The jewellery had to be *right* for each mistress. It should suit their lifestyle. Their personality. It had been easier with Isabelle because she'd had the chance to meet her first, but she'd no idea what Miranda even looked like. All she'd got from their phone conversation today was a picture of someone who seemed to be incapacitated and was extremely vulnerable.

There were five pieces of jewellery left. In her mind's eye she tried to visualise them. What about the diamond flower brooch? Too showy, too Queen Mother. The bracelet? Too young and delicate and something you'd only wear for a party. The ring? Too flashy. That left the necklace and the pendant, and the necklace definitely wasn't right. It was too smart for someone living by the seaside, too *Vogue*-ish.

'She'd probably like a sentimental keepsake rather than anything else,' Julian observed, when she asked for his advice.

Lucinda nodded slowly. 'Something she can keep close to her heart.' As she said it, she knew what she'd give. Something that was delicate and pretty and could literally be worn next to her heart. Miranda would get the gold pendant, set with clear pale green stones, hanging on a gold chain.

Tom had decided he must repay Susan in some way for her generosity and hospitality, which had recently extended to asking him round for supper at least twice a week. He always arrived with something, a flowering plant for the garden or a pot of growing rosemary or mint, a scented candle, a box of liqueur chocolates or some wine, but he needed to do more. Take her something that would move their relationship forward onto a more intimate footing.

Fear of rejection had held him back from giving her anything more than a peck on the cheek, and although she'd squeezed his hand once, at the beginning, she too had seemed reluctant to show any physical affection since.

Tom considered his options: the cinema? the theatre? a concert, maybe? Or a romantic restaurant, and blow the expense? But then, for once in his life, and because the weather was so blisteringly hot, he had a brainwave. He reached for the phone and keyed in Susan's number.

'Are you doing anything this evening?' he asked her, after they'd exchanged the usual banal greetings.

'No, I'm not. Why?'

'Then I'll pick you up at six thirty and we'll go out,' Tom replied, a shade importantly.

There was laughter in her voice. 'Where are we going?'

'It's a surprise.'

'What sort of surprise? What do I have to wear?'

What did it matter, Tom thought. Why were women, even someone sensible like Susan, so obsessed about their clothes and how they looked?

'Something . . . erm . . . comfortable, casual,' he said lamely.

'Half past six, then?'

'That's right.'

After he'd hung up, he had an awful thought. Supposing Susan hadn't understood he'd meant he wanted to take just *her* out? Supposing she'd presumed he'd meant her boys as well? He couldn't very well ring her back, that would look too gauche.

But supposing he turned up and Dick and Steve were standing there, in their best clothes, expecting to be taken out, too?

In his lunch hour Tom went to Sainsbury's and did his shopping, and just in case Susan's sons took it for granted they were expected as well, he took the precaution of buying more than was necessary. Loading up the boot of his car afterwards, he wondered why he wasn't like other men. They took their girlfriends out without any of this angst. They wined and dined them, took them to Paris for the weekend, always said and did the right thing, and never had any problems. Whereas his courting had always been fraught with difficulties, misunderstandings, botched arrangements and finally total rejection.

He would hate to lose Susan, he thought with sudden anguish. Not that he actually *had* her. But to be on the safe side, and to make sure he'd covered all eventualities, he hurried back into Sainsbury's to get a few more things. Just in case.

Jane was sitting reading in the shade of the lime trees at the end of the lawn from where there was a breathtaking view of the smoky blue hills of the Dordogne, when she became aware of voices coming from the terrace. She frowned, puzzled. They weren't expecting anyone, and William was holed up in his study, writing endless letters to London, in a bid to try to retrieve their financial disaster.

'. . . we'd have to make the pool bigger,' someone was saying grudgingly, 'but I suppose if we extended the terrace . . .'

It was the voice of an American woman. Jane turned her head sharply but from where she was sitting she couldn't see who it was. Then there was another voice, a man's, also with an American accent.

'D'you think they'll come down in price a bit? It's going to need a lot spent on it. I mean, it's kinda cute, but everything's so *old* around this place.'

Jane jumped to her feet. Who the hell were these rude people, criticising her beautiful home like this? She strode purposefully across the lawn, an elegant figure in cream linen trousers and a navy blue T-shirt. As she turned the corner she came face to face with a middle-aged couple, the woman smothered in emeralds and diamonds, the man large and sweating in Bermuda shorts and a floral shirt. Beside them stood the French estate agent, to whom William had entrusted the selling of Château St Laurent. He was holding a glossy brochure containing coloured photographs of the château, its interior and the grounds.

'Oh-h-h!' Jane gave a loud gasp of dismay. Dear God, had things gone as far as this? A brochure? Prospective buyers? Strangers tramping through the place, loudly proclaiming the alterations they wished to make? She didn't know whether she was going to burst into tears or be sick.

'I – I didn't know . . .' she said weakly. 'I didn't know you were showing people round so soon.'

'*Pardon*, Madame Cotterell.' The agent, a handsome young man with a moustache, bowed politely. 'I'm just showing Madame and Monsieur Kernahan around the property. We did not intend to disturb you.'

'No . . . well,' Jane floundered. 'Does my husband know you're here?'

'*Ah, mais oui, certainement.*' The agent waved his hand dismissively in the direction of the house. Then he turned his attention back to the Kernahans and gave them a gracious smile. 'If you will follow me?' he said suavely. 'I will show you the garden and the orchard. There are some very fine old olive trees, too, and I did mention there was a gardener who comes with the property, didn't I?'

Jane wasn't going to stand and listen to another word. She turned and hurried into the house to find William.

'Did you know the agent was showing people round the house already?' she asked him as he sat at his desk. 'They're complaining the pool's too small, the price is too high, and the place is too *old*! William, get them out of here. We don't want people like that, who don't appreciate the house. Tell that agent to get rid of them, now.'

William looked up at her wearily. He'd aged ten years in the past week or so, and there were watery pouches under his eyes and deep lines down either side of his mouth.

'Jane darling, we can't be choosy about who buys the place. Unless a miracle happens we've got to sell, whether we like the people or not. And if they're keen to buy, then thank God.'

'I heard them tell the agent we're asking too much, so maybe they won't,' Jane said hopefully.

William sighed. The house was Jane's Achilles heel and he knew the most painful thing that had ever happened to her in her whole life was the prospect of having to sell up and leave. In part he felt the same, but not with such a depth of passion. Jane had always adored the château and all her energy over the years had gone into perfecting each reception room, each bedroom and bathroom, the large, functional but beautiful kitchen, and all the colour schemes and furnishings throughout. Guests who came to stay at the Château St Laurent knew they were in for a few days of luxury and a unique experience. Even Jane's table settings, whether in the formal dining room or on the terrace by the pool, were executed with beautiful china and wine glasses, flowers in low bowls and candles in crystal holders. And now it looked as if they might have to leave it all behind and settle for a little cottage under the rain-filled clouds of the cold English countryside.

William spoke gently but unwisely, he feared, because he offered her a strand of hope, hating to see her so despondent.

'If they make a good offer we will have to accept, darling, but we can delay exchanging contracts for a while, just in case a miracle does happen.'

Jane's face lit up, as he knew it would, and he could see her secretly crossing her fingers. 'Let's pray,' she said fervently. 'Let's pray for a miracle.'

Susan was ready when Tom arrived. She was wearing a blue summer dress with shoulder straps, revealing smooth tanned shoulders that had hitherto always been covered by a shirt or a sweater. There was no sign of Dick or Steve.

'The boys out?' Tom enquired casually, realising the house was very quiet.

Susan looked surprised. 'Yes, it's their night for bowling with their school. Why? Did you expect them to be here? Oh! Is the surprise meant for them? I'm so sorry, I'd no idea . . .' Her voice drifted off and she looked flustered.

Tom beamed reassuringly. 'The surprise is for you, not them. Come on, let's go.'

Once in the car, Tom headed west, caught up in the homebound evening traffic, which he'd overlooked. It didn't matter too much though, because Susan was soon regaling him with something funny that had happened at work that day. He wasn't listening, actually, he was concentrating on negotiating the mass exodus of commuters, but it was all right because she didn't appear to expect him to answer. Which meant, he hoped, she was relaxed and at ease in his company.

At last they reached the gates of Richmond Park and Susan gave a little crow of delight.

'It's years since I've been here. Isn't it lovely? What a wonderful place to come for a walk.'

'We're doing a bit more than that,' Tom replied, pleased.

When they got to one of the car parks, he entered and pulled up neatly beside a row of other cars. He obviously wasn't the only person who'd had the same idea this evening. There were several dozen cars, and in the distance he could see people walking their dogs, lovers strolling hand in hand, and even a few children still playing.

Susan got out, sniffing the air appreciatively as if she'd found herself in the depths of the country, and it was only when he opened the boot and she saw boxes of delicious-looking food and wine that she realised they were going to have a picnic.

'Tom! How fantastic. What a brilliant idea, especially on a hot night like this.'

'I thought it would be fun,' he said modestly. On the way to her house, he'd stopped off at his flat and picked up a rug and a couple of cushions, two wine glasses and a corkscrew, and some cutlery and plates.

'You've thought of everything,' Susan exclaimed in delight. 'God, I can't even remember when I last had a proper picnic.'

They chose a secluded spot beyond a patch of waist-high bracken, Tom making two trips to the car to collect all they needed. Long golden shadows stretched across the grass. There wasn't a breath of wind, and the heat of the day still lingered in the air.

Susan settled herself on the rug while Tom opened the wine. 'I feel as if I'd died and gone to heaven,' she murmured wonderingly. 'I'm glad it's just us this evening, but do you think we could bring the boys one day?' she added wistfully. 'They would so love it here.'

'No probs,' Tom said with sincerity. 'We could bring lunch and spend the day. They could bring a football to kick around.'

She nodded. 'That would be nice. Did you come here when you were a boy? Did your dad play football with you?'

Tom suddenly went cold and he felt sick. The weather seemed to have changed from a balmy golden evening to a darkened horizon filled with pain. The brightness of the hours ahead, so full of hope a minute ago, had been obliterated by memories that had left him more damaged than he realised. It was only now, when he'd seen for the first time a glimpse of happiness and fulfilment, that he realised what he'd been missing all his life.

He averted his face so that Susan wouldn't see the tears pricking painfully at the corners of his eyes before sliding down his cheeks, tears that he hadn't shed then but were forcing their way out of his body now, just when he wanted to make a good impression, when he was desperate to appear cool, suave like Harry, competent like Lucinda, when he longed to be interesting and amusing.

And all that had happened was that a wretchedly unhappy little boy was surfacing, and the tears were coming so fast he couldn't begin to control them.

'*Tom* . . .!' Susan was aghast, appalled in case she'd said the wrong thing. 'What is it? What's happened?'

Tom covered his face with his hands, unable to speak, almost unable to breathe, his shoulders shaking as wrenching sobs were torn from his throat.

With the swiftness of a mother reaching for a child in distress, Susan got to her knees and put her arms round Tom, pulling him close, cradling him and patting his back, while she made comforting noises. They stayed like that for several minutes, and Susan stroked his hair, her expression concerned, her eyes filled with sympathy for this man who'd suddenly become as distressed as Dick or Steve when they'd been small and their favourite toy had broken or they'd fallen down and hurt themselves.

Gradually Tom's sobs ceased, and as he became calmer he also became aware of how badly he'd humiliated himself. Susan wouldn't want to have anything to do with him after this, he thought, straightening up, unable to look at her, reaching for his handkerchief and blowing his nose. He got to his feet, looking lost and disorientated. He wished a great hole in the ground would appear and swallow him up. He wished he was home, alone, where no one could see him making a fool of himself.

'Here, have some wine,' he heard Susan say in a matter-of-fact voice. 'In a few minutes you'll feel a lot better for having got *that* out of your system.'

Tom still couldn't look at her. He was red in the face, embarrassed beyond belief, and didn't know what the hell to say.

'I'm very sorry I said the wrong thing,' she continued. 'Stupid of me and insensitive, when your father only died a few weeks ago. Trust me to open my big mouth. I won't do it again, I promise; that is if you ever want to risk taking me out again?'

Then Tom did look at her, and saw her gentle motherly face looking smilingly up at him. He sat down on the rug beside her.

'Of course I want to take you out again and thank God this isn't the Ritz or I'd be *really* embarrassed,' he replied, with a spark of unaccustomed humour. Somehow, extraordinarily, he no longer minded that he'd broken down in front of Susan. He'd no idea why, because he'd behaved like a demented hysteric, but the wonderful thing was she seemed to understand. She'd shown complete empathy and the relief was enormous. No one, not even his mother, had ever comprehended the pain his father had inflicted. In fact, Anne had seemed to take Miles's side when he'd been brutal to his children. For years he'd buried the anguish and lack of compassion he'd felt when he was small, because there'd been no one around who understood.

'Do you know how I learned to swim?' he asked suddenly.

Susan shook her head.

'We were on holiday in Scotland. I was three. My father hired a rowing boat. When we got to the middle of this big loch, he picked me up and threw me overboard into the icy water. Then he rowed away,' he said succinctly. There was no bitterness in his voice. No rancour. Then he raised his eyes and looked at Susan. 'That was his way of teaching me to swim.'

'I see,' she said quietly. 'Then there's a lot of pain inside you, and I think I'm going to make it my business to help you get rid of it.'

Then she got on her knees again and, reaching over, took Tom's face in both her hands and kissed him very firmly on the lips.

Sitting in the train on her way to Brighton, Lucinda checked the contents of her shoulder bag, as she had already done several times that day. Yes, she had the bundle of letters which she'd slipped into a big brown envelope, with the document Bernard had given her for Miranda to sign as a receipt. And yes, she also had the little leather jewel case containing the pendant, which she'd also put in an envelope so it wouldn't get damaged against the detritus that made up the contents of her bag.

She was beginning to feel nervous and wished that she'd accepted Carina's offer to come with her, but she'd insisted she'd be all right, saying she'd rather go alone because she wanted to keep things simple and had decided to go by train instead of taking her car. This meant taking a taxi to Hove, and asking the driver to wait while she dropped off the stuff at Jasmine Cottage.

But to have gone with anyone else, even Julian, would have made an occasion of the visit, which for her own sake she was trying to play down.

117

This way she could relegate it, in her mind, to a rather boring errand, without, she hoped, emotional overtones.

But as the train clattered along, packed with commuters going home at the end of the day, she began to see that if this was going to be difficult for her, how much worse was it going to be for Miranda?

Maybe it had been the pain in the woman's voice when she'd said she'd never had children that had melted Lucinda's heart, because now she was beginning to feel quite sorry for her. Lucinda tried to put herself in Miranda's shoes, and it didn't take much imagination to make her realise that this was going to be a deeply emotional ordeal for the older woman. The man she'd loved had stayed with his wife, even though his marriage hadn't been happy, and she'd been forced to accept his decision and get on with her life as best as she could. It seemed she'd never met anyone else, or if she had they hadn't matched up to Miles, and so she'd stayed on her own, alone and childless, for the rest of her life.

She felt hot and grubby when she eventually arrived at Brighton. A stream of commuters got off the train and charged out of the station into a salty gale blowing in from the sea. On impulse Lucinda went into a tiny flower shop next to the station and bought a bunch of yellow roses. Their stems were so straight and stiff they looked artificial, but the assistant swaddled them up to their necks in white paper which made them look better. She caught the last taxi on the rank, and sank into its sheltered depths. 'I'd like you to wait for me, and bring me back to the station, please,' she told the driver after she'd given him Miranda's address.

Jasmine Cottage turned out to be a small brick bungalow, with mean-looking little windows and a door painted blue.

Lucinda pressed the bell and there was a long wait before she heard movement from inside. Then the door opened a few inches.

'Hello. I'm Lucinda,' she said to the dark crack.

'Can you wait a moment before you come in,' she heard a woman say in a quavering voice. 'I have to get my chair out of the way first.'

Lucinda waited, hearing chains being removed and locks turned, then there was silence and after a few more moments she gingerly pushed the door open.

'It's all right now,' said the voice.

Miranda was sitting in a wheelchair in the middle of a narrow passageway. Thin and bony, with sparse grey hair and deeply wrinkled skin, she faced Lucinda with frightened tear-filled eyes and a trembling mouth.

'Lucinda? It's very good of you to come all this way.' As she spoke she manoeuvred the chair backwards, and then with hands blue-veined and covered in liver spots she wheeled herself into a sitting room that was dominated by books and a single bed in the corner. There were several small tables, also cluttered with books, papers, reading glasses, mugs, a box of tissues and, on one, a snapshot in a frame. It was of a man in a white open-necked shirt with the sleeves rolled up sitting on a garden seat. Beside him was a plump and pretty girl, one arm round his neck, her face wreathed in smiles.

Shocked, Lucinda realised it was her father and Miranda. Taken when he'd been in his late twenties or early thirties, looking so jolly and cheerful it seemed he hadn't a care in the world.

Miranda turned and realised Lucinda was staring at the picture.

'He was so handsome, wasn't he?' she said wistfully. 'That was taken in Cornwall.'

So where did this nice, happy-looking man go? was Lucinda's first agonised thought. What had happened to him? Why had she never known him? She'd have given anything to have had a father like the man in the picture. He would have been someone she could have loved and learned from; a warm and affectionate father and not a crotchety critical man who had showed none of them any affection but had struck fear in all their hearts. Where had that laughing person in the photograph gone?

For a dreadful moment Lucinda felt consumed with jealousy. Miranda's only memory of Miles must be of a man who was charming, warm and carefree, while the rest of them, Anne, Tom, Harry and herself, had had to endure the irascible person he'd become and was to remain until he died. Miranda had known the best of him; his family had known the worst: the tyrant who had bullied and psychologically abused his children, or ignored them completely which was almost worse. None of them had ever seen this relaxed, normal side of Miles.

'You must miss him terribly,' she heard Miranda say sorrowfully.

Lucinda ignored the remark. 'I've brought you these,' she said stiffly, handing Miranda the roses. Then she fished in her bag and produced the letters, and with bitterness rising like bile in her throat she placed them on the table beside the wheelchair. This woman had taken all her father's love; that was obvious from the photograph. Even though the affair hadn't lasted, even though he'd heaped humiliation on her by employing her as a tutor for his son in years to come, it was Miranda who had been the first one to take his love away from his wife. And it had changed him, because he'd never been happy and carefree like the man in the photograph again.

At that moment Lucida hated her. Resented her. This was quite different from meeting Isabelle, with whom Miles had obviously had good sex but she doubted much else; an amusing diversion with a lively Italian, to whom he'd eventually become a father figure. But this was different. Quite different.

Miranda was weeping quietly as she took the letters out of the brown envelope, placing them tenderly on her lap. Then she looked up at Lucinda. 'It was a long time ago, you know,' she said, almost gently, as if sensing Lucinda's bitterness.

Lucinda didn't reply, couldn't reply. She kept looking at the photograph, consumed with envy because her father had never loved her as he'd so obviously loved this woman who sat before her now. A little girl inside her was crying: *Daddy, why didn't you love me like that?*

It was a picture of a man she'd never known, a father who had turned into someone else by the time she'd been born. Tight-lipped with misery, she handed Miranda the second brown envelope.

'This is the piece of jewellery he left you as a memento,' she said shortly.

'He left me . . . *this*?' Miranda asked, holding the small leather jewel box with shaking hands.

Even in her jealous rage Lucinda hadn't the heart to clarify the point with the explanation that in fact he'd left jewellery to all his mistresses and it was up to her to choose which pieces to pass on. So she merely nodded and turned away while Miranda opened it.

Then Lucinda heard a little cry, almost like a cat's miaow, followed by a sob.

'Oh! . . .' she wept. 'After all these years! This is unbelievable . . .'

Something in her tone made Lucinda look back. Miranda was holding the pendant and staring at it as if she couldn't believe her eyes. Then she looked up at Lucinda again.

'Do you know something?' she whispered brokenly. 'I saw this pendant in a little jewellery shop in Barnstaple . . . why, it must be nearly forty years ago now! And I admired it, said to your father that it was so pretty. I remember the unusual setting. These stones are peridots, you know. And there's a little catch at the side and the back opens like a locket, and there's a tiny coil of blonde hair in it.'

Lucinda looked at her, stunned. 'So he bought it for you?'

Miranda shook her head. 'We went into the shop and examined it, but he didn't buy it. Told the assistant he'd think about it and I suppose he must have gone back afterwards . . . I was a bit disappointed, actually. And now, after all this time . . . He'd obviously been keeping it for me.' Her tears had dried and her face was flushed with pleasure. 'Isn't that the most wonderful thing?'

Lucinda didn't know what to think. She could have chosen any of the other items of jewellery to bring with her today. What had made her choose the very piece her father had bought for Miranda all those years ago? It felt strange and spooky and she had no way of explaining it, except that it had seemed the most suitable thing for an obviously older woman.

'I'm glad you like it,' she said, unbending slightly.

'Would you like a cup of coffee, Lucinda? The district nurse made some when she was here this morning, and put it in a Thermos. It's on the table in the window. Do help yourself. I think she put some biscuits out, too.'

It would be ungracious to leave now, Lucinda thought, although she longed to. 'Can I get you a cup, too?' she asked instead.

'Thank you, my dear. Now I want to hear all about Tom, and dear little Harry.'

The taxi would be waiting, ticking up an enormous fare, but Lucinda reflected that to talk to this woman for another few minutes wouldn't even begin to compensate her for all the years she'd spent alone, pining for a lost love.

Nine

'What's wrong, Harry?'

Paula, coming into the drawing room after her bath, saw Harry sitting slouched on the sofa, watching the television with a blank expression.

They'd been out to dinner, at The Collection this time, and Harry had told her he'd left his wallet with all his credit cards back at her flat, when he'd changed to go out. She'd paid the bill, not minding at all, but Harry had looked sulky, especially when he saw the waiter give him a dirty look when she'd signed her Amex slip.

He glanced at her now, his brow furrowed. 'I'm just pissed off by the bloody family solicitor,' he complained. 'Somehow he's managed to block the money Dad left me, and I really need it to kickstart certain parts of Relative Tracing. I told him what I thought of him, but these old solicitors . . .' His voice trailed off irritably. 'I mean, who the hell does he think he is? Dad left everything cut and dried so there wouldn't be any problems. I think he's just trying to milk the situation. You know how solicitors love to do that. They're the ones who make the money.'

Paula sat down beside him and took his hand. She was wearing a slithery blue satin nightdress and robe from Rigby & Peller that her aunt had given her for Christmas, which she knew Harry found a turn-on. She eyed him judiciously now.

'But has probate been granted? When Neil died it took nearly two years for all the loose ends to be tied up. I didn't get anything in all that time. I'd have been a penniless widow if I hadn't had my own money. Or I'd have had to get a job.'

Harry still looked disgruntled, but nevertheless he gave a tight little smile.

'I don't think the solicitor's doing his job properly, though. God knows why Dad used him in the first place. He should have gone for a young chap who's up to speed on tax and capital gains and all that stuff. It's so frustrating.'

'You're just going to have to be patient, Harry. Put your plans on hold for a while.' Paula paused reflectively for a moment and then her face lit up. 'I know! Why don't we take a trip somewhere? A real getting away from it all break? You've been under such stress for the past few weeks, with your father dying and all that. How about a week in Barbados?' She moved closer, putting her arms round him and resting her cheek against his shoulder. 'Wouldn't that be wonderful? I think it's the most romantic place in the world.'

Harry was appalled. Even if they went Dutch, it would cost him a couple of thousand pounds he didn't have. Paula would expect to stay at the best hotel and wine and dine at the top restaurants. And she'd want him to buy her amusing accessories at those expensive little shops that were always attached to smart hotels. It was out of the question unless he was certain she was going to invest in Relative Tracing.

'What is it, sweetheart? Don't you like the idea?' she asked, her voice heavy with disappointment.

He rose, as if to bring the conversation to an end. 'I can't, Paula. I've got too much on. I've got important meetings practically every day for the next couple of weeks. I mean, this company is going to go worldwide, big time. It's not some piffling little outfit. I need to be here to prepare the ground. It would be madness to go away at the moment.'

Her forehead puckered. 'But you could keep in touch with what's happening, wherever you are.'

'I have things to do,' he said stubbornly, 'but you go. You're obviously dying to get away so don't let me stop you.'

'But we should do things together, Harry. We should share our lives, your work, your plans for the future.' She paused poignantly. 'Perhaps I'm rushing you, Harry. I don't mean to, but . . . well, it would be wonderful if we could be . . . sort of partners in everything, wouldn't it?' She reached up and laid her hand tenderly on the side of his face. 'But maybe I *am* rushing you?' she said sadly.

Harry was reeling with shock. For Christ's sake . . . was the woman proposing to him? Did she mean – God forbid! – marriage? But what if that's what she was doing? Forget about the company, as her husband he'd be set up for life, but . . . but . . . but at what God-awful price?

'What are you thinking about, Harry?' she asked softly.

He took a deep breath as he tried to pull himself together. Was this half-veiled suggestion on Paula's part the only solution to his financial future? It was, he had to admit, a fairly terrible thought, but maybe he should go for it. Rich women, crazy for his body, didn't come two a penny. He made a split second decision, on the basis he could probably get out of it in due course.

'You're right, of course, Paula. I'll see if I can find a window in my diary' – I'll see if I can borrow a couple of thou from Lucinda or Mum – 'and we'll take a trip, work out our future together, OK?' I'll try to find a way of screwing you for some money without having to marry you.

Paula flung her arms round Harry's neck with a little cry of joy. 'That would be wonderful, Oh, we'll have such a marvellous time, I can hardly wait.' She turned and closed her mouth over his, her demanding kisses leaving him breathless. Pulling at his clothes now, she reached for his manhood with hungry hands, then she slithered on top of him, enveloping him in a swath of blue satin.

'Paula . . .' he croaked, coming up for air.

'Hush,' she whispered, 'you've no idea how happy I'm going to make you.'

He very much doubted if he did.

* * *

It had become an almost regular thing; Lucinda or Carina phoning each other at least twice a week, to catch up on the latest gossip. On this particular evening, Lucinda couldn't wait to tell her about the latest developments in tracing her father's mistresses.

'I'm almost certain I've discovered who "Pumpkin" is,' she announced triumphantly.

There was a moment's stunned silence before Carina asked in astonishment, 'Who? What's happened?'

'You'll never believe me. She's actually living with Harry at the moment. Isn't that sick?'

'But who is she?' Carina sounded intrigued.

'Her name's Paula Maxwell. I spoke to Mum last night, because Paula had told me—'

'You've *met* her?'

'Yeah. Harry brought her to supper. She said her father had been a great friend of Dad's, and she used exactly the same phrase to describe him as Isabelle: "an amazing man".'

'That doesn't mean . . .' Carina began, and then continued: 'Does Harry know about this?'

'No way, and he must never know, or he might tell Mum. He says he picked Paula up at a bar . . . actually, I think she picked *him* up. She pretended to me she didn't know who he was until he told her his name, but I don't believe that.'

'How extraordinary.' There was doubt in Carina's voice. 'What's she like? And why would she want to latch onto Harry?'

'I don't know. It's also odd that Harry is interested, because although she's beautiful, she is in her mid-forties.'

'She's beautiful, is she?'

'Pretty fantastic-looking. Especially for her age. Of course she's very rich, apparently, so that could be the attraction as far as Harry is concerned. You know what he's like.' Lucinda's voice was bleak. There was a plate of biscuits in front of her on the kitchen table. To hell with her figure, she thought, munching one.

'So what makes you think she's "Pumpkin"?'

Lucinda hesitated, unsure herself why she was so convinced she'd found the mystery mistress. 'It just seems to add up,' she said lamely. 'If Isabelle is anything to go by, I believe she's the type of woman Dad was interested in in recent years.'

'But that's fantastic, isn't it? Have you spoken to her about Miles yet?'

'There was no opportunity, with Harry never leaving her side, and then I had a nightmare moment when he spotted the writing case and wanted to know what was in it. I don't know her address either, and she's ex-directory.' She picked up another biscuit and started nibbling that, too.

'Lucinda, she *must* be "Pumpkin".'

'I have a gut feeling she is,' Lucinda agreed. 'Maybe she's latched onto

Harry because she's missing Dad, or something, and Harry's mad about her because he's desperate to find an investor for his new company.'

'God, this is the breakthrough you need, isn't it? So what happens now?'

'I think I'm going to have to invite her to dinner with Harry, and then get her on her own during the evening, and ask her outright.'

'Wicked!' Carina shrieked with laughter. 'Oh, Lucinda, *do* ask us, too. I'd kill to be there to see what happens.'

'OK, but I want to keep it low key. If she *is* "Pumpkin" it could be a sticky evening,' Lucinda pointed out.

'Yes, but what a fascinating one.'

'You're coming to lunch on Saturday, aren't you?'

'Yes, please. Alex has got to work and the children are spending the weekend with his parents, so I'll be on my own; is that all right?'

'Of course it is. If this heatwave goes on we'll eat in the garden.'

'Can't wait, and keep me posted about "Pumpkin", won't you?'

Tom awoke and for a few seconds wondered where on earth he was. Then he felt a movement beside him and realised with shock that he'd spent the night with Susan. In her bed. Having sex. The memories came thudding back, one by one, fantastic, mind-blowing memories that made him catch his breath, and wonder at the passionate warmth of Susan. In his experience of awkward fumbling and cold mechanical fucking, followed by embarrassing attempts at conversation when he had nothing to say and his mind was planning the nearest escape route, to awake beside Susan was a revelation. Almost as strong as discovering God, Tom reflected, smiling to himself.

As he turned towards her she opened her eyes and smiled immediately, her face rosily flushed and her hair tumbled on the pillow.

'Sleep well?'

Tom grinned and felt most unlike himself. 'Yes,' he replied, his voice surprised. 'Very well.'

Susan snuggled closer. 'Good. I slept well, too.' Her naked body was soft and warm and Tom caught a drift of jasmine perfume. Then he felt her hands, those strong capable hands that cooked such delicious food, reach for him, stroking his hips and thighs, cradling his manhood tenderly in her palms.

With a mixture of emotions, part arousal, part a desire to weep because he felt so happy and so grateful, Tom took Susan in his arms and kissed her deeply. She was everything he'd never had but always longed for: lover, mother, companion, friend.

Unable to believe his good fortune he continued to make love to her with care, holding himself back although it was the most difficult thing he'd ever had to do. Then . . . 'I want you . . .' he heard her say, her voice laced with yearning and a note of pain, and as he entered her she shuddered and clung tightly to him.

'Take me . . . take all of me,' he whispered, and as he moved inside her he vowed to love her for as long as she'd let him. For as long as there was breath in his body and blood coursing hotly through his limbs.

'What you need is this,' Carina told Lucinda. 'And I don't know why we didn't think of it before.'

Lucinda slowly turned the pages of the book Carina had given her. 'Gems' it was called, and it listed every stone in existence, as well as composition, specific gravity, hardness, system and form.

Intrigued, Lucinda turned to peridot, wondering with a pang of anxiety if, in her ignorance, she'd given Miranda the most valuable stones in the collection.

' "The Peridot or Chrysolite",' she read aloud. ' "Chemical composition: Silica 39.73. Magnesia 50.13. Ferrous oxide 9.19. Nickel oxide, etc. .95." But does that mean they're rare or special stones?'

'If they're part of the Chrysolite family it means they're semi-precious,' Carina told her.

'Does it? How do you know?' She started reading aloud again. ' "Specific Gravity 3.35. Hardness 6.5. Crystalline system . . . Trimetric. Form . . . generally in water-worn pebbles." Shit! It's all very interesting, I'm sure, but it's beyond me. I never knew there were so many stones, for a start. Listen to this lot. Apart from Diamonds, Rubies, Sapphires, and Emeralds, they list Opal, Oriental cat-eye, Turquoise, Agate, Alexandrite, Amber, Amethyst, Aquamarine, Bloodstone, Carnelian, Garnet, Iolite . . . which is sometimes known as "water-sapphire" . . . Jade, Jasper, Moonstone, Lapis-lazuli, Labrador . . . I thought that was a dog but it says here it's a "dull grey or greenish brown stone with internal reflections of prismatic hues, especially bright blue and green". This is fascinating, Carina. My God, the list's never ending; there's Onyx, Topaz, Tourmaline, Zircon, Jacinth and Jargoon. I could get quite interested in gemology, you know. It certainly makes a change from foundation creams, eye-shadows and lipsticks.'

'Well, I thought you ought to know *something* about the stuff you're giving away. As you're not allowed to have it valued, or to ask anyone's advice on what it's worth, you're working in the dark, aren't you?'

Lucinda nodded. 'I was looking at the fake jewellery in Harrods the other day, and some of it looked absolutely real to me. I honestly couldn't tell the difference. I even chatted to one of the assistants, and she agreed that unless you were an expert you wouldn't be able to tell the difference between a real diamond and a fake one.'

Carina raised her finely plucked eyebrows. 'I think I would,' she said drily. She held out her hand, exposing the fine solitaire diamond ring Alexander had given her when they'd got engaged. 'The setting is the first thing to look at. The second is the depth and fire in the stone itself. Here.' She took it off and handed it to Lucinda. 'Take a look.'

Lucinda examined the ring closely. The large diamond did indeed seem to have millions of glittering facets. But was that just because it was ten times the size of the diamonds in her own engagement ring?

'It's beautiful,' she acknowledged.

Carina reached for her Filofax, a bulging black leather book filled with not only her diary of social engagements, but lists of contacts that might be useful, from florists and caterers to people who did alterations, dyed fabrics, made lampshades or hair pieces to match your own hair, and even a few make-up artists, for special occasions.

'Now,' Carina said, settling down, pen poised. 'Try to describe each of the remaining pieces of jewellery to me, and I'll do some research. Of course we don't know how many carats the stones will have and that makes an enormous difference, but tell me as much as you can. At least you've already given away what sounds like the least valuable pieces.'

'That's a bit of luck, isn't it?' Lucinda leaned back, eyes shut, forehead creased in concentration. 'There's a pearl necklace. The beads or whatever you call them are quite large. Like small marbles, perhaps, or very large peas.'

'Have you tried to nibble them with your front teeth?'

Lucinda's eyes flew open and her jaw dropped. 'What?'

'You need to test the surface of the pearls with the edges of your front teeth. Feel very gently if each pearl is smooth or rough,' Carina said authoritatively.

'Are you kidding? What'll that tell me?'

'If they're creamy smooth they're false, and if they're just faintly rough they're real. Unless they're genuine baroque, in which case they'll be massively bumpy and irregular, but you'd see that, you wouldn't have to feel it.'

'This necklace looks like the ones by Butler & Wilson that cost around twenty pounds,' Lucinda observed helpfully.

'What's the clasp like? That's always the giveaway with fake jewellery, whether it's necklaces or bracelets.'

'It's a little knob, covered in tiny diamonds.'

Carina nodded, impressed. 'Sounds good. Check on the surface. Now what's next?'

'There's the ring. It has a dark blue stone, a sapphire I imagine, except it has purple lights in it at certain angles, so maybe it's an amethyst. It's surrounded by what look like diamonds but they don't sparkle much. Not even as much as the ones in my engagement ring.'

Carina made rapid notes. 'Is it set in gold?'

'No, I think it's silver.'

'Silver?' She sounded shocked. 'It's not worth anything if it's silver. It must be either yellow gold, white gold or platinum. You've got to notice all these things carefully, Lucinda, if you're going to get it right.'

Lucinda sighed heavily. 'Oh God, give me some slack, Carina. I've got Bernard sitting there, watching me all the time, waiting for my decisions, and I don't know anything about jewellery, and so much depends on my getting it right.'

'Well, you'd better get interested now, darling,' Carina remarked drily. 'What about the bracelet you mentioned?'

Lucinda went back to look at the book of gems, flipping the pages until she found what she wanted. 'Here we are,' she exclaimed triumphantly. 'I thought the stones were aquamarine and I'm right. Granny has a pair of aquamarine earrings, so that's why I was pretty sure. It's a link bracelet, Carina, made up of these pale blue-green stones, interspersed with tiny clusters of diamonds in between.'

Carina scribbled hastily. 'That should be easy to price. What's next?'

'There is a very grown-up diamond brooch,' Lucinda admitted. 'It's not to my taste but it's pretty impressive.'

'Ah-h-h!' Carina drew out her exclamation knowingly.

'What do you mean, ah-h-h?' Lucinda asked, grinning at her friend. She could see Carina was actually enjoying herself. She loved anything that was expensive and glamorous.

'What's it like, this brooch?'

Lucinda used her hands to describe it. 'It's a spray of solid diamonds, with a large rose and two smaller roses and several leaves. It's probably three or four inches long and some of the diamonds are quite big. It's too Queen Mum for words.'

Even to her own ears she sounded impressed.

'Bingo,' Carina said in a hushed voice. 'That's bound to be it. What's the setting like?'

Lucinda shrugged. 'Silver again.'

'No, no, *platinum*. Look at it very carefully next time. See if there's a deep fire in the stones. See if they're claw set. Is there a safety catch or chain?'

'I didn't notice.' By now she was beginning to feel seriously ignorant on the subject.

'If it's what I think it is,' Carina told her with a look of satisfaction, 'it's probably worth around a hundred thousand pounds or more. Depending on the carats. But it does sound like an important piece.'

Lucinda eyes widened with amazement. 'Bloody hell! Where did Dad get all this stuff? Apart from the pendant, which he bought for Miranda and then never gave her.'

'Perhaps he inherited it from his mother?'

Lucinda looked surprised. 'His mother?' she repeated questioningly. 'I suppose that's possible, except that some of it doesn't look old enough. The earrings I gave Isabelle, for instance. I'm sure they're modern.'

'You don't remember your grandmother wearing any of the stuff?'

'I never knew her. She died before Dad was married. He was an only child, so I suppose if she did have any jewellery it would have come to him. I'll ask Bernard. He'll probably know its provenance.' Lucinda reached for the notes Carina had been making. 'Can I have a look? See if there's anything I can add?'

Carina picked up her Filofax and closed it briskly. 'You'd never make out my hieroglyphics. My writing's so terrible I have to phone everyone! Now, if you think of anything else, give me a ring. And next time you're at the solicitor's, *really* look at the stuff, Lucinda. Study the settings. Examine the stones.'

'I will. And thank you for this book,' Lucinda said gratefully. 'I've certainly got a better idea of what I should be looking for.'

'Not before time, my dear!' her friend quipped amusedly, as they strolled into the garden, where Lucinda had already laid a table for lunch.

'Oh, I meant to tell you,' she said suddenly, as she opened a bottle of chilled white wine, 'Dad's memorial service has been arranged for July the nineteenth, at St Martins-in-the-Fields. Mum's at last had the courage to fix a date, and now it's up to us to arrange the service and put an announcement in the newspapers.'

'I'll make a note of it.' Carina gave a sudden sigh. 'That's going to be quite an occasion, isn't it? There'll be hundreds of people there.' Then she brightened. 'Have you decided what to wear?'

'Harry, what a surprise, darling. How lovely to see you,' Anne exclaimed. 'I was just going to make some tea. Would you like some?'

'Thanks.' He followed his mother into the big dark kitchen and watched as she plugged in the kettle. He hated this house more than he could ever express. It was gloomy. It was oppressive. It was filled with so many hideous memories he felt cold and depressed the minute he entered.

'How's everything going?' Anne asked, making her voice sound bright and interested because she knew anyone who was despondent annoyed Harry.

'I have got a slight hitch and I was wondering if you could help me out,' he replied breezily.

An anxious cloud seemed to film over her eyes and she spoke diffidently. 'I don't know, dear. What do you want?'

Harry perched chattily on the edge of the big kitchen table, one leg swinging easily, eyes wide and blue, hair flopping over his brow. 'I've got a bit of a cash flow situation at the moment, Mum, which is a real bummer because I'm just about to sign up the biggest deal *ever*. Not only will it set up my company, it will provide me with a livelihood for the rest of my life!'

'That sounds very nice, dear.'

'It's bloody marvellous, actually. But in the meantime, I need about three thousand pounds to cover some vital expenses. Without it, I won't be able to proceed.' He dug his hands deeper into his trouser pockets and smiled widely at his mother.

'Oh, I don't know, Harry. Your father's money's been frozen, you know.'

Harry frowned. 'Frozen?'

She nodded nervously. 'Until probate has been agreed, none of us can inherit anything.'

'Shit!' he swore, in horror. 'I thought that only applied to Tom and me. I

128

thought *you'd* be able to get your hands on a few spondulicks. When Bernard said—'

Anne blinked, her sand-coloured eyelashes flickering like nervous moths. 'Why were you talking to Bernard?'

'Because I was stupid enough to think he'd help,' Harry snapped, annoyed. 'Everywhere I turn I'm being hemmed in by bloody stupid people with their bloody stupid rules and regulations. How am I supposed to get my company off the ground at this rate? You'd think people were out to deliberately sabotage my future, wouldn't you?'

'So what do you want me to do, dear?'

'Can you lend me three thousand, Mum?'

'Three thousand *pounds*?'

Harry gritted his teeth and mentally counted to ten. 'Well, not pence,' he said, attempting to be joky.

'But at the moment I've only got the money I put aside . . . out of the housekeeping your father gave me.'

'Well, that'll do,' Harry retorted breezily. 'It's only a loan, I promise you. You can have it back within . . .' he looked at the ceiling and moved his lips, as if he were making calculations '. . . within six weeks. Six weeks max. That'll be all right, won't it? And I tell you what. I'll cut you in on the deal with my company. Give you 5 per cent of the profits. What do you say?'

Anne said very little but looked as if she'd heard it all before. As she'd feared Miles's anger when he'd been alive, so now did she fear Harry's wrath. She hated unpleasantness, bad feeling, a nasty atmosphere or anything approaching friction.

'Very well,' she said with a reluctant tremor in her voice, 'but I would like it back as soon as possible. The money I've put aside is all I've got to live on until . . .' Tears trickled down her cheeks and she couldn't continue. Then she suddenly burst out: 'Oh, I miss your father so much! He looked after everything and I never had to worry about money when he was alive.'

Harry helped himself to a biscuit from a tin on the table in front of him. 'You can flog some of the stuff in this house, can't you? Some of the silver, which you never use, anyway. Who's going to know? And it would keep you going if you're stuck, surely?'

Anne shook her head in silent anguish, but her thin shoulders were hunched in abject misery and she didn't answer him. He watched as she made the tea and wondered if, when he returned from his trip with Paula, it would be a good idea to move in with his mother for a while. It might make Paula all the keener if he wasn't around all the time, and it would certainly give him some breathing space from her. He remembered there was a pawn shop only a few streets away. If his mother wasn't prepared to raise money on the silver . . . well, he reflected with a secret smirk, what the eye doesn't see, the heart doesn't grieve about, does it?

Ten

Lucinda glanced surreptitiously at her watch. It was five o'clock. The meeting with the production manager of Bagatelle, Quennel Strange, had been going on for what seemed like hours, and she wanted to get home. But Alain Loubet, who had recently been seconded from the Paris office of D'Aussoire to take over the running of Bagatelle, was nit-picking over every little detail of the new aftershave they were planning to launch.

'. . . But this is a product for *men*,' he said, glaring at them all. 'We're calling it Zing by Bagatelle and therefore the design of the packaging must *have* zing. It must be striking, eye-catching, sexy. Very sexy.' He threw some prototypes down on the boardroom table. 'This is rubbish! Faux black marble for packaging has been done. It's *so* twentieth century!'

Geneviève, a new recruit from the Paris office who now worked in market research under Lucinda, referred to her notes.

'Forty-eight per cent of men questioned in our phone survey favoured a metal look. And 39 per cent liked the idea of darkened glass jars, like darkened car windows.'

For research purposes they'd set up various focus groups, targeting different prospective customers, divided into various age groups and income brackets.

Alain Loubet nodded. 'Brushed steel . . . darkened glass . . . something simple but exotic . . .'

Lucinda looked at her watch again. This could go on for hours and Delia had especially asked for the evening off to go to an amateur production of *Private Lives* in which her boyfriend was performing, and Julian hadn't been certain what time he'd get back from an auction sale in Somerset.

'. . . as this is a product for men,' Quennel Strange was saying, 'we have to consider the strategy and the design very carefully, but we also have to remember budgets.'

'But we have to break new ground in terms of concept,' Alain argued.

Lucinda was having a problem concentrating today. Julian had said last night that he didn't know how they were going to afford private education for the children. Their school fees were already steep; the looming twelve thousand a year each, not including extras, was far beyond their means. No matter how hard he worked. And even if she stayed at D'Aussoire they'd be stretched. The vision of that damned three million pounds from her father kept dangling tantalisingly in front of her eyes. She'd never get it, of course. In her bones she knew her chances were about as good as winning the lottery.

'. . . what were the findings of the report on the different age groups, Lucinda?'

Startled, Lucinda looked at Alain, and realised she'd switched off completely during the last few minutes and hadn't heard a word of what they were saying.

'Umm . . .' She fumbled among her papers, desperately trying to catch up.

'They're here,' Geneviève said, handing her the report.

'Thanks.' Flushed and breaking into a sweat of relief, she passed it on to Alain. It was divided into men under twenty-five, from twenty-five to forty, and from forty to fifty-five.

The group round the table studied the figures and started arguing again. What men in their early twenties liked in the way of aftershave was very different from what men in their forties liked, especially when it came to the smell. Older men were prepared to pay more, too, and were fussier about the style of packaging, whilst younger men preferred a product that was inexpensive and came in a functional container.

For the rest of the meeting Lucinda did her best to stay with it, telling herself that as soon as she got home she'd try to address the problems in her personal life in a sensible way.

First and foremost, though, she had to confirm that Paula Maxwell was 'Pumpkin'. Then she must try to trace Renée Hartman and Fenella Harrison, before she could hope to find that pot of gold.

'At *last*!' Lucinda exclaimed, when Harry answered his mobile later that evening. 'I've been trying to get hold of you for the last ten days. Why has your mobile been permanently switched off?'

'We've been in Barbados,' he replied with a casualness that didn't fool his sister; she could sense the suppressed excitement in his voice.

'Nice for some!' she rejoined, trying to keep the envy out of her voice. 'You obviously had a good time.'

'Oh yes. Very.'

She longed to know what was going on between him and Paula but was determined not to ask. But could this unlikely liaison be getting serious?

'I was wondering if you'd both like to come to dinner one night next week?' she asked, as if it was the most natural thing in the world to ask Harry, whom she'd hardly had any contact with for the past few years, to bring his much older girlfriend round for a meal.

If he, too, felt her invitation was surprising, he didn't show it. 'Cool. Which night?'

'Wednesday any good?'

'Fine.'

'Hadn't you better check with Paula first? She might have arranged something else.'

Harry chuckled smugly. 'I make the arrangements round here.' Lucinda then heard him say in an aside, presumably to Paula: 'Don't I, babe?'

Babe? In no shape or form did Paula resemble a 'babe', Lucinda reflected. Aloud she said: 'Eight o'clock, then?'

'Cool. 'Bye.'

Lucinda turned to Julian, who was watching television. 'We're on for Wednesday night,' she told him. 'I'm also going to invite Carina and Alex, and what about Ian and Rachel?'

'Yeah, good idea. We owe them.'

'We certainly do,' Lucinda replied, reaching for the phone again. Ian and Rachel Compton were the most generous and marvellous hosts, and Lucinda and Julian had spent several weekends with them in the lap of luxury in their beautiful house, near Rachel's parents, in Sunningdale. Jamie and Daisy were also invited, and had the Comptons' two small boys to play with.

Ten minutes later Lucinda had her dinner party organised.

'They've all accepted,' she said delightedly. 'This could be the unveiling of "Pumpkin"!'

'Which you will handle discreetly, I presume?' Julian asked, suddenly worried. 'We don't want to embarrass Paula.'

'Of course I'll be discreet,' Lucinda retorted. 'What do you think I'm going to do? Jump to my feet in the middle of dinner and say to her: "You were one of my father's five mistresses, weren't you?"'

While Julian sat gripped by the TV, watching a repeat of *Morse*, which he'd already seen at least twice, Lucinda decided to unlock the writing case and have another look at the letters. There were only three bundles left, and she took them all out, deciding to hide them in her bedroom, so there would not be a repeat of Harry's wanting to know what was in the case on Wednesday evening. In fact she'd leave it unlocked now. That would fool him if he got nosy.

Sitting on the bed before hiding them in one of her drawers, she glanced at the top bundle, and was struck by the small handwriting, in perfectly straight lines, and neat even margins down both sides. There was a calm purposefulness about this writing, she decided. Whichever one of the mistresses had penned it, she was a decisive no-nonsense type.

Slumping onto the bed, she decided to see what these letters would reveal. Yet another angle of her father's multi-faceted character? She looked at the signature first. Renée. So this was Renée Hartman.

Lucinda started reading the top letter. It was dated 27 August, 1971. Twenty-nine years ago. Lucinda realised with irony that she'd been four at the time and Miranda Warwick had been staying with them to coach Tom through the summer holidays. Had Miranda guessed Miles had got another mistress? The agony she must have suffered made Lucinda feel sickened by her father's capacity for hurting other people.

How are you doing, you old rogue? Renée's letter began. *Rogering half of England while the other half waits, I suppose? But then you're the king of rutting, aren't you, you old scoundrel.*

Lucinda leaned back against the pillows on her bed, feeling quietly amazed. If Isabelle had been the passionate Italian, a possessive, driven diva, and Miranda had been a gentle dowdy wannabe intellectual, Renée, by

133

comparison, seemed more like another bloke. Lucinda imagined her as a hard drinking, heavy smoking, sporty type who probably wore trousers in an age when most women didn't. The next line caught her eye and nearly made her laugh out loud, so near the mark had her observations been.

I nearly shat myself on the fairway yesterday when I thought I saw you in the distance. Jesus! It spoilt my whole game. From that moment on all I wanted was to be fucked senseless by you. No messing. Right down to it, as you always do, like a raging stallion, thrashing and bucking, no matter where we are.

Lucinda put the letter down again, unable to read on. She had a feeling that all Renée's letters would be in the same vein and there wouldn't be a word about affection or caring, and certainly not love. She got off the bed and went to the bathroom next door for a glass of water, to remove the sudden bad taste in her mouth. When she came back she bundled Renée's letters together again, and hid them with the others under her sweaters in a drawer.

The whole situation was, in her opinion, becoming more distasteful and disturbing by the minute. It was one thing knowing about other people's love affairs, but when it was her own father it made her feel like a Peeping Tom. I don't want to know about his sex life, she thought unhappily. But it seemed, for some bizaare reason, that Miles was forcing her to recognise him as a sexual being, and the notion made her feel more nauseated than ever.

Paula wrote 'Dinner at Lucinda's' in her diary, and wondered vaguely why they'd been invited. She'd got the feeling last time that Lucinda hadn't liked her much; and she gave the impression she didn't care for her brother either. In spite of Harry's efforts to appear chummy with his sister, the atmosphere between them had been very strained.

She shrugged; Harry's family was his business and nothing to do with her. She had affairs of her own to think about. Today she was meeting her broker, Edward Havell, for lunch, this time at Le Caprice. She hoped that by now he'd made all the arrangements she'd asked him to, just before she'd flown off to Barbados. Edward was very good at his job and knew what he was doing, and if he didn't he quickly found people who did. In any case he'd been working for her in conjunction with her accountants for a long time now, so she expected to hear that her plans for the future were already up and running.

Harry was going to get a surprise, but she believed in keeping an element of surprise in all things and her relationship with Harry was no exception. What Harry didn't realise was how aptly suited they really were. He'd met his match but he didn't know it. In his shoes she'd have behaved exactly as he was doing; using other people, manipulating situations to get what he wanted, scheming, plotting, employing sex as a weapon.

There was just one difference. She had the money to do it in style. He didn't.

* * *

As Sarah came out of Peter Jones on Saturday afternoon, having bought some more champagne glasses for her planned little drinks party the following week, she saw Tom striding along the King's Road, laden with carrier bags and accompanied by a comfortable-looking woman in her thirties, and two little boys, their hair cropped as close as a newly mown lawn, wearing trainers that looked too big for their feet.

'Hello, Tom!' she called out.

'Granny!' Tom smiled, then looked embarrassed and pink around the ears, and finally stammered nervously, 'H-how are you? Erm . . . erm . . . do you know S-Susan? And . . . erm . . . Dick and Steve. Her sons,' he added as an afterthought.

'How do you do?' Sarah said warmly, shaking them all by the hand with the graciousness of an elderly member of the Royal Family. 'How good to meet you. So, Tom, how is everything going?'

Tom looked with diffidence into her penetrating blue eyes and realised with relief that his grandmother was neither shocked nor patronising. Unlike Lucinda he'd always been in awe of Sarah. She seemed so grand, so sociable, so different from the rest of them. He found it hard to believe that his timid mother, who was quite unable to inspire awe in anyone, was Sarah's daughter.

He grinned at her, relaxed. 'Everything's great,' he said, putting his arm round Susan's shoulders as he spoke. 'You're looking very well, Granny. Is everything all right? Have you seen Mum lately?'

'She's coming to lunch tomorrow. She wants to discuss the details for your father's memorial service, which is good because she's refused to even think about it up till now, except for fixing the date.'

Tom nodded in understanding and Susan smiled and nodded gently, knowing the tricky dynamics of the Scott-Forbes family.

'Harry rang me to tell me he's thinking of moving in with Mum, to keep her company,' Tom continued guilelessly, too naive to realise that Harry's ploy was to keep in with Anne and to lay claim to her, his sub-text being: Keep off. I'll look after her – and myself.

But Sarah knew what Harry was after and she stiffened, her face becoming drawn and pale. 'Really?' she said, looking at him sharply. 'And whose idea was that?'

Tom shrugged. 'Harry's, I suppose. Mum never asks for anything.' Susan, standing close to his side, was looking up and watching him as he spoke, and her face was filled with tenderness. Then she turned to Sarah.

'Tom and I thought we would invite his mother to lunch one Sunday. We could pick her up and take her home afterwards; the weekends can seem so long when you're alone,' she added, experience giving depth to her remark.

'That's very good of you, my dear,' Sarah replied, liking this younger woman with her direct manner and sincere expression. So Tom had got himself a real girlfriend at last, had he? And a ready-made family, too, it seemed.

135

'When you've got a minute you must come and see me,' Sarah continued. 'Perhaps brunch one Sunday?' She looked smilingly at Steve and Dick. 'I expect you like things like sausages and chips, don't you? And gallons of Coca-Cola? I usually give that to my great-grandchildren when they visit me. So much more fun than boring old meat and two veg.'

Steve and Dick looked uncertainly at their mother and then turned to Sarah, their little faces stretched into wide grins.

'And cheesy-toast,' Dick piped up.

'I'll remember,' Sarah assured him gravely.

'That would be really nice, thank you,' Susan said with genuine pleasure. 'I've heard so much about you from Tom.'

'Don't believe a word of it, my dear!' Sarah chortled, as she waved frantically at a passing taxi which had its For Hire light on. 'We'll be in touch. Take care of yourselves.' And with that, she stepped gracefully into the cab, telling the driver to take her to Rutland Gate.

'She's amazing,' Susan remarked, as the taxi pulled away from the kerb.

Tom grinned, a touch proudly. 'Not bad for eighty-two, eh? Still entertains in the old formal way, too.'

'We'd better not invite her to my place, then,' she chuckled. 'Alfresco in a Fulham back yard overlooking other people's washing hanging out to dry is not exactly her style, I imagine.'

Tom roared with laughter. 'It's exactly what she *would* like, providing the people are interesting and amusing. That's what it's all about as far as she's concerned.' They'd reached his car which he'd parked down a back street, off Sloane Square. Bundling their shopping into the boot, Dick and Steve clambered into the back.

'Can we go home now?' Dick asked. 'I want to watch the match on telly.'

'So do I,' Steve echoed, suddenly remembering Manchester United were playing.

'You can if you help unload the car first,' their mother warned. The Saturday traffic was sluggish, the roads and pavements crowded. Families like themselves were doing their weekend shopping, Tom reflected, and a warm feeling enveloped him at the realisation that by some miracle and with a bit of help from Waitrose he'd actually acquired a family for himself. No more microwave dinners for one. No more small loaves that would last a week and then have to be chucked out because they were mouldy. Now he had a real sense of belonging and he felt quietly exultant at the thought.

They were able to park right outside Susan's little council house, and while the boys and Tom got the shopping out of the boot Susan went ahead to open the front door. Once inside she frowned, raising her head and sniffing like a cat scenting something. Following right behind her Tom stopped, asking: 'What is it, love?'

She didn't answer, and a moment later she had no need to. A tall figure appeared at the top of the narrow stairs, and stood looking insolently down at them. He was a big man, tall and muscular, with a menacing air. He gripped

136

the banister, his large knuckles gleaming through the skin. His other hand was clenched into a fist.

Susan gave a stifled cry, her hand flying to cover her mouth. But the man wasn't looking at her. He wasn't looking at Dick and Steve either, as they stood dumbstruck in the doorway. He was glaring threateningly at Tom.

'What the fuck d'you think you're doing here?' he roared. 'Get the fuck out of my bloody house and don't you dare show your motherfucking face around here again.' Then he started to come down the stairs. One step at a time.

Tom looked up at him. 'T-this happens to be S-Susan's house,' he stammered, shocked but trying not to show it.

'Like fuck it is!' the man growled, and with two bounds he was down the stairs, his hands gripping Tom's shoulders, his breath fetid in his face.

'Jim!' Susan screamed. 'No!'

But Jim was manhandling Tom, pushing him back into the wall of the narrow hall, shaking him like a rag doll, so that Tom's head kept banging against the wall, and although he tried to fight back he was no match for Jim.

Steve was crying now, an expression of terror on his face, but Dick was lashing out with his small fists, yelling: 'Dad! Stop it, Dad! You'll kill Tom.'

As soon as Sarah got back to her flat she phoned Anne, and, as always, couched what she had to say in diplomatic terms. After explaining how delighted she'd been to bump into Tom, who seemed to have such a charming female companion, she continued seamlessly: 'I gather Harry may be moving in with you?'

There was a pause before Anne answered. 'He's thinking of it . . . but I'm not sure.'

'Would you like him to?'

'I don't really know how to stop him. I mean, he was born in this house, it's always been his home.'

'But he's not a boy any more, is he, darling? He's thirty-four. Only let him stay with you if you want him to,' Sarah added reasonably.

Anne spoke as if she were deeply tired. 'He's starting up a company. Something to do with tracing people's family trees on the Internet or something. I suppose he needs a base.'

A rent-free base, Sarah thought. Aloud she said: 'Well, do think of yourself first, darling. Have you made up your mind about selling the house or staying on?'

'I think I'll sell, Ma. You were right. The place is too big for me, anyway. Harry said that as soon as probate had been granted he'd help me find a buyer.'

Alarm bells clanged in Sarah's head. 'All you need is a good estate agent, Anne. You'll have no problem getting rid of it, and then you can come and stay with me again, if you like, while you find yourself a flat,' she said firmly. Harry would do his level best to wangle a hefty cut for himself by selling the house for one price, and telling Anne it had gone for much less. And then she was struck by an awful thought. How sad, to have to protect your daughter from her own son.

Sarah had been very careful never to interfere in Anne's family life, but now that Miles was dead someone was going to have to guard Anne's interests.

Through a haze of pain and the taste of blood, Tom could hear Jim ranting at Susan. 'The boys are *mine*, d'you hear? Get that fucking toe-rag out of here . . . this is *my* fucking home and these are *my* children. I won't have him playing happy-fucking-families with *my* sons. And you can say what you fucking well like but I'm moving back . . .'

'Over my dead body,' Susan yelled back at him. 'Call yourself a father? Who's looked after them and fed and clothed them for the past nine years? Who's protected them from your violence? Your abuse? Your drunkenness? Get back to where you belong, Jim, in the flaming gutter. With your women and your booze and your drugs. You're not coming back here.'

Tom began to struggle to his feet, giving an involuntary groan as an agonising pain shot across his chest, almost taking his breath away. His head was spinning and he felt weak and sick. Then he felt Susan's protective hand taking hold of his arm as she helped him up.

Jim stood towering over them, dark and dangerous-looking, fist raised and ready to strike again.

'Get out! Get out!' Susan was screaming now.

Tom tried to collect himself, look round to see where Steve and Dick were, hoping they weren't witnessing this brawl, but they'd vanished.

'You get this fucking pansy out of my house,' Jim was jeering nastily. 'If I find him still here when I get back I'll make sure he ends up in the fucking mortuary.'

Suddenly, the sharp wail of a siren coming nearer filled the air and Jim looked murderously at Susan.

'If you've called the busies I'll break your fucking neck!'

Tom leaned back against the wall of the narrow hall, relief sweeping over him like a warm comforting wave. The police must have been called by a neighbour. Jim would be arrested and that would be the end of that.

But the wailing faded away and the three of them were left standing, rigid, like stone statues dumped in an alleyway.

With a swift movement Jim seemed to peel himself away from the staircase, and with a muttered 'I'll be back' he charged out through the open front door and clattered away down the street.

'Oh, Tom . . .' Susan took him gently in her arms and led him into the kitchen. 'I'm so sorry, are you badly hurt?' She was weeping now, the first time he'd ever seen her cry.

'I'll just sit down for a moment,' he replied, sagging into a chair. He was sure his ribs were cracked, and his jaw hurt as if all his teeth had been knocked loose.

'I'll just check the boys are all right and then I'll take you to Casualty,' she said, tearing off a piece of kitchen roll and blowing her nose on it.

'No, don't worry. Stay with the boys.' He touched his temple tenderly, fairly sure he was heading for a black eye.

'Nonsense.' Susan was brisk and in control once more. 'I bet they're hiding somewhere outside,' she said, leaving the kitchen.

Tom stood up carefully and made his way to the kitchen sink, where he splashed his face with cold water. He was shocked to see it ran red.

Susan had hardly ever mentioned her ex, except to refer to him as 'lazy' and 'no good'. Had he always been violent? Had he beaten her up in the past? Was that why she'd originally kicked him out? And what sort of father was that for Dick and Steve?

Susan came back with the boys at that moment, an arm round each of them. 'They were hiding on the floor of your car,' she announced with forced cheerfulness, 'and they said they'd rather come to the hospital with us than stay here, so we'll unload the rest of the food from the boot and then get off.'

'There's no need, really,' Tom protested unconvincingly.

'Yes, there is,' the boys chorused.

'There most certainly is,' Susan echoed.

'Are you going to call the police, Mum?' Steve asked, his face pale. 'Dad's really hurt Tom.'

'No,' Tom interjected, before Susan could reply. 'I've no intention of bringing charges against your father. He was obviously upset and he'd been drinking, so let's hope that's the end of the matter.'

Susan looked upset. 'But Tom—'

'No, Susan. He is the boys' father and for their sake I think we should try to forget about all this. Who wants any more unpleasantness? I certainly don't.'

She gave Tom a long, lingering look. 'Thank you,' she mouthed quietly. 'I'll have the locks changed first thing tomorrow. I'd forgotten he still had a key.'

When Tom arrived at work on the Monday morning with his face grazed and bruised and a black eye, there was a chorus of alarm from everyone in his office. Ruby, who'd been watching his romance with Susan from afar with a proprietorial interest ever since she'd suggested he take a tin of biscuits on that first occasion, which she was sure was the Beginning of Everything, looked ready to cry herself.

'Oh, lovey! Whatever's happened to you?'

Tom smiled wanly because his face still hurt. 'I was mugged,' he replied briefly.

'You never!' she exclaimed. 'Where?'

'Not far from where I live,' he lied, wanting to keep Susan out of it.

'Did they take anything?'

'Nothing worth speaking off,' he said dismissively.

139

As the oh-oo-ing and ah-aa-ing and looks of sympathy continued around the office, he seated himself at his desk, embarrassed because everyone in Garson & Co was looking upon him as a bit of a hero. In the circumstances, it made him cringe. He'd been terrified when Jim had lashed out at him. He was no match for the brawny six-foot-three thug.

Beside Jim he was a weakling, a puny desk-bound nerd who hadn't even been able to protect the woman he loved. What must she have thought of him? Crumpling like a rag doll against her skirting board? Half conscious and groaning in pain, leaving her to stand up to Jim by herself.

Shame and depression were causing him more pain than his injuries now. And what about Steve and Dick? The only way he'd been able to retrieve something of his reputation with them had been to make light of the whole thing and say he wouldn't press charges against their father, the interpretation being, he felt, *I can look after myself*, and *I'm big on the forgiving stakes*.

But it was with a heavy heart that Tom settled himself down to a day's uneventful work. No one would argue that Saturday afternoon had certainly not been his finest hour.

'So everything's in place?' Paula enquired.

'Everything,' Edward Havell confirmed. 'All the arrangements have been made. There's nothing for you to do but sit back, and in due course reap the profits.'

Their lunch meeting at Le Caprice had gone brilliantly, and Paula was smiling with delight. 'And you believe, as I do, that we'll do well?'

Edward was gazing at her with admiration. She knew she looked good in a pale grey Armani trouser suit, but she hoped it was her business acumen that was winning his approval, and not just her appearance.

'The profits will be good,' he told her, 'because you had a fantastic idea in the first place. You've really thought it through, haven't you? I must congratulate you, Paula. I bet your father's impressed, isn't he?'

'Daddy's delighted, and, yes, quite impressed too, I think,' she admitted.

After lunch, she said goodbye to Edward and decided to walk home through Green Park as it was such a lovely afternoon. She also decided she'd keep the surprise from Harry until after Lucinda's dinner party.

Eleven

The report that had landed on Lucinda's desk was a shareholder's delight. No wonder the president of D'Aussoire was pleased. Every one of the companies in the group had achieved record sales, and for Lucinda the best part was that all the products were now environmentally correct. There was no more animal testing for cosmetics, and synthetic chemicals had been substituted for animal musk. And CFC gas, which had at one time caused so much damage to the ozone layer, was no longer a component in hair spray, either. All the ingredients used by the company were harmless and natural now, so natural and so freely available in their original forms, like fruit and vegetables and herbs and pure olive oils, that Lucinda still wondered at the stupidity of some women who paid hundreds of pounds for a cream that promised magical rejuvenating properties from no more than the contents of a basket of groceries.

'What are you thinking, Lucinda?' Geneviève asked her smilingly from her desk across the aisle. She'd become a sweet and perky member of the team, using her French accent to great advantage when she asked for favours and adored by everyone for her helpfulness.

'I was just thinking what a long way the cosmetic business has come in the past ten years,' Lucinda replied thoughtfully. 'We are now able to produce everything from hair spray to eye-liner, or nail varnish to astringent, without having to resort to either experimenting on poor animals or wrecking the environment.'

'*Mais oui*, but one must remember that before they found a substitute for CFC gas, hair spray was one of the most profitable products on the market. D'Aussoire could not suddenly stop production because . . . how you say . . . someone tell them it makes a hole in the ozone layer? It was inconceivable!'

'Even if they knew it was destroying the environment?' Lucinda said, appalled. 'Well, I can tell you one thing, Genevieve, if D'Aussoire hadn't immediately found an alternative when the danger was recognised, I for one would have left the company.'

'That is very high-minded, maybe, but you can't overlook profit margins; anyway, what would women do if there was no hair spray? They cannot do without it.'

Lucinda looked at her askance. 'When my mother was a young woman, there was no such thing as hair spray.'

'*Mon dieu*, that cannot be.' Geneviève looked genuinely perplexed.

'My grandmother used to make a paste of sugar and water,' Lucinda said laughingly. 'Then she dipped her comb in it and it held the hair in place just as spray does today, even if it was a bit sticky.'

141

Her phone rang at that moment. It was Carina.

'Sorry to bother you at work, sweetheart, but I wanted to check: is it black tie tonight?'

For a split second Lucinda didn't know what she was talking about. Then she remembered. Tonight was the night Harry was bringing Paula to dinner.

'No. Just ordinary. Julian hates changing.'

'Oh, really?' Carina sounded disappointed. 'But you'll be wearing something glam, won't you?'

'I hadn't really thought about it. Probably not, as I'm doing the cooking.'

'But Paula Maxwell will be dressed up to the nines, surely?' Carina insisted.

'I'm sure she will. Listen, Carina, I can't talk now . . .'

'OK, darling. See you tonight. Eight for eight fifteen?'

'Yeah. See you then.'

The dinner party tonight. Lucinda had been determined to try to put it to the back of her mind while she got on with her work, but now, remembering, she felt a frisson of nerves. She hadn't yet planned how she was going to approach Paula, or how she was going to broach the subject of 'Pumpkin'. It was probably the most embarrassing thing she'd ever had to do, and no doubt Paula was going to feel the same. For that reason she had to catch her alone, maybe after dinner, if she could persuade Paula to leave the others on the pretext of 'being shown round the house'. All of four up and two down, Lucinda reflected drily. Not exactly impressive to someone who lived in a duplex in Belgravia.

By the time she got home, Delia had not only bathed Jamie and Daisy, but prepared the vegetables and set the table.

'Delia! You're a marvel!' Lucinda crowed in delight. 'I've only got to assemble the smoked trout and rocket as a starter, and then pop the leg of lamb into the oven.'

Delia dried her hands and looked bashfully pleased. 'Would you like me to take the pudding out of the deep freeze?'

'Good thinking.' Lucinda had made several summer puddings a few weeks previously. Thawed and served with double cream they would win her a mass of brownie points, especially with Rachel Compton, for whom cooking had become an art form; every ingredient had to be organic, she'd only buy beef from Scottish cows who'd grazed on grass, she made her own bread, jams and marmalade, and the most annoying thing of all was that she seemed to do it effortlessly, in spite of running a large house, albeit with staff, having two young children and a husband who loved having people to stay.

Julian had already put some champagne and white wine in the fridge, so, having arranged the flowers she'd bought on the way home, Lucinda hurried upstairs for a shower.

Jamie and Daisy were waiting for her on the landing, their sweet faces clean and rosy and Daisy's unruly curls brushed like a halo round her head.

'Mummy! Mummy!' They flung themselves at her, little hands clinging, small soft mouths pursed to be kissed.

Lucinda dropped to her haunches and took them both into her arms, her heart melting with love. 'How are you, my darlings? Have you had a lovely day? Come and tell me all about it, and you can help me decide what I should wear tonight.' She led them into her bedroom and Daisy ran over to the closet and flung open the doors. She tugged at a long dark red chiffon evening dress.

'I like this one. Mummy. It's pretty.'

'That's a frock for *big* parties,' Jamie told her, with an air of authority.

'Delia said this *was* a big party,' Daisy said, crestfallen. 'I want you to wear this one, Mummy. *This* one.' She gave the dress another tug and it slipped off its hanger and dropped to the ground.

'Now look what you've done,' Jamie scolded.

Daisy's eyes filled with tears. 'Mummy said we could help her choose,' she wailed.

Lucinda picked up the dress, her best, and put it back on the hanger. 'It's all right, Daisy. Don't get upset. You've got good taste, because this *is* my prettiest dress, but it's just *too* good for tonight. I'd probably spill something down the front, and that would spoil it, wouldn't it?' She gave Daisy a reassuring hug and, instantly mollified, Daisy turned to Jamie in triumph.

'See? Mummy says it *is* her prettiest dress.'

A diversion was needed before world war three broke out.

Lucinda seized a short black skirt and a black top with a scooped out neckline. Her standard outfit when in doubt.

'How about this?' she asked. 'With the silver earrings Daddy gave me?'

Jamie looked doubtful, but Daisy hopped around clapping her hands in delight. 'And your silver shoes, too!'

Lucinda decided to ignore that suggestion, hoping Daisy would have forgotten about it by the time she went to bed. Then she told them to go and watch television for fifteen minutes whilst she had a shower.

'If you're good I'll read you a story when you're in bed.'

They went reluctantly, their faces etched with sadness and disappointment. Lucinda was filled with remorse. Everything in her life seemed to take priority over her children these days, and it wasn't right. They deserved better. And as a mother, so did she.

Harry and Paula arrived first.

'Sorry, sis,' he said jovially, breezing into the drawing room, hands in pockets, hair floppier than usual. 'Meant to come earlier but we had to have drinks with some friends of Paula's.'

'I *do* apologise,' Paula said, extending her hand.

Lucinda realised Carina had been right; Paula was dressed to the nines . . . tens . . . and elevens in a pale grey beaded cocktail dress, with a matching pashmina artfully draped over one shoulder, and a blaze of diamonds in her ears and at her throat. Lucinda decided that here was a woman who had never cooked dinner for eight and then dished it up after a frantic day at the office. Paula looked far more glamorous than on the previous occasion, and, beside her, Harry resembled a rakish second-hand car salesman.

Julian poured the champagne just as Rachel and Ian Compton arrived. Lucinda introduced Paula and Harry and they all said How-do-you-do and then there was an awkward silence, and a slight shuffling of feet. It was obvious everyone was thinking: what's *she* doing with *him*?

Then Rachel, mistress of small talk as well as cooking, broke the ice. 'What a beautiful dress you're wearing,' she said to Paula. 'It's *such* a lovely shade of grey.' Her enthusiasm was obviously sincere.

Paula gave a little self-deprecating smile, a clear signal that she was used to getting compliments. 'Oh, how sweet of you,' she said, slightly patronisingly.

A few minutes later, Carina and Alex arrived.

'Darling, isn't this fun!' Carina said, kissing Lucinda in the hall, and presenting her with a beautiful orchid in a white china *cachepot*. 'Has she come?' she said in a stage whisper.

Lucinda nodded. Then she greeted Alex, who was looking suave as usual. 'Come and have a drink.'

They already knew Rachel and Ian, of course, and Harry.

'This is Paula Maxwell, and these are my old friends, Carina and Alex Somerset,' Lucinda said, introducing them.

Carina looked intently at Paula. 'How do you do? I hear you knew Miles.'

'He was a great friend of ours,' Paula replied graciously.

'Ours?' Carina queried, feigning a frown.

'My father and I. It was so sad when he died.'

'How's it all going then, Carina?' Harry butted in brashly.

But Carina didn't answer because she was still staring at Paula, and she looked quite put out. She was used to being the centre of attention, the best-looking, the best-dressed, the best-bejewelled woman at social gatherings, and she certainly hadn't reckoned on being upstaged by a girlfriend of Harry's, of all people.

Julian charged into their midst. 'Champagne?'

It was going to be, Lucinda realised with a sinking heart, a very long evening. Alex Somerset and Ian Compton, she noticed, were standing as if mesmerised by the sight of Paula. Ian had a silly smile spread all over his face, but Alex looked like a man who'd spotted something and intended to have it. A flicker of worry crossed Lucinda's mind; did Alex sometimes stray from Carina? It was something she'd never thought about before, but her father's unexpected past had made her look at other married men in a new light. Perhaps lots of the husbands they knew had mistresses? Maybe she and Julian were the only ones faithful to each other?

* * *

144

'The lamb needs another twenty minutes,' Delia whispered urgently, as Lucinda slipped into the kitchen, ready to serve up dinner.

'Are you sure?'

Delia opened the oven door and prodded the large leg, which was swathed in sprigs of rosemary. A trickle of blood oozed into the pan.

'Hell! That's a bit too fashionably pink, even for this lot,' Lucinda said, turning up the oven. 'I'll get Julian to top up everyone's glasses again. We'll have to take the vegetables off or they'll be mushy. What a bore. I thought I'd timed everything perfectly.'

'The starter's ready,' Delia said helpfully. 'They're just going to have to eat it slowly, aren't they?'

Back in the drawing room she found Harry had opened the writing case, and was peering into its empty depths. 'Where are Dad's papers?' he demanded. 'What have you done with them?'

Everyone stopped talking and turned to see what was going on. Paula, Lucinda thought, looked particularly interested. Did she know about the letters? If she was indeed 'Pumpkin', Miles might well have told her his plans for his Will.

'Until I decide what to do with them I've put them in a deposit box at the bank,' she lied coolly.

'At the *bank*?' Harry echoed incredulously. 'Why? Are they *that* valuable?'

Lucinda didn't miss a beat. 'They are to me. For sentimental reasons. They're all Dad actually left me,' she continued, which so far wasn't a lie, 'and I'd be very upset if we got burgled and they were stolen.'

'Humph!' Harry grunted suspiciously. 'I want to know when Bernard Clarke's going to get off his arse so we can have our money. Why do solicitors make such a meal of everything?'

'Oh, it's typical,' Rachel trilled laughingly, launching into small-talk mode again. 'They're so expensive, too. When we bought our house . . .'

The rest of her words became lost as everyone started chattering in an effort to smooth over Harry's unpleasantness. Lucinda looked at Paula, but she was observing Harry smilingly, as if something amused her.

'Top up everyone's glasses, dinner's not ready,' Lucinda hissed in Julian's ear. She was already hating this evening, wishing she'd never asked all these people to dinner.

'. . . no, Harry doesn't resemble his father at all,' she heard Paula say to Rachel, and suddenly the evening veered away from being boring to becoming very interesting indeed. Lucinda moved nearer, pretending to fetch a bowl of nuts from a side table.

'So you knew the famous professor?' Ian asked. 'I'm afraid I never met him. What was he like?'

'He was a very complex man,' Paula replied slowly. 'A genius, of course, with many facets to his character. In a world of his own, sometimes . . .'

'You seem to know a lot about him?' Carina said in a challenging voice. Lucinda shot her a warning look but Carina didn't seem to notice.

145

'I did see quite a lot of him at one time,' Paula replied calmly.

'And when would that have been? Recently, or some time ago?' Carina persisted.

'A little while ago.' Paula sounded vague.

'Why don't we have dinner?' Lucinda announced, an edge of desperation in her voice. She was annoyed at Carina for trying to goad Paula into admitting she'd been more than friends with Miles. It wasn't up to her, for a start. And certainly not in front of a roomful of people. Lucinda had arranged this dinner as a stepping stone. Maybe she was only going to be able to extract Paula's phone number or address from her tonight, but that would be a start.

'I thought you wanted me to top up everyone's glass?' Julian pointed out rather crossly, a newly opened bottle of Bollinger held aloft.

'What?' she asked distractedly. 'Oh yes, I suppose so. I'll go and light the candles. But try to keep Carina and Paula apart,' she whispered, slipping out of the room.

The dining table, set for eight, with white candles and flowers, and classical white china, looked cool and elegant. Earlier Lucinda had worked out a seating plan, but now she began to think it would be a disaster. The trouble was, the dynamics between the guests had changed in the last ten minutes, and now she didn't dare put Carina and Paula near each other, whereas she'd planned to have them on either side of Julian. She wasn't sure she ought to put Alex next to Paula, either. But that meant changing everyone round. It also meant that Harry and Paula would have to sit together. Oh, well . . . Thank God it was a round table, she thought, checking on the leg of lamb, before announcing dinner was ready.

Carina, sitting between Julian and Ian, proceeded to get drunk, which was unlike her. She picked at the smoked trout, pushed the now perfectly cooked lamb around her plate and emptied her wine glass rather rapidly. Something had rattled her tonight and Lucinda could only suppose it was jealousy of Paula, who was certainly the centre of attention as far as the men were concerned.

The main course had been cleared away. Lucinda was just about to fetch the summer pudding when she heard Carina saying loudly: 'I presume you're giving us pumpkin pie for pudding? *Pumpkin* pie, get it?' She winked broadly.

Paula didn't appear to have heard, or if she did she gave no indication, but Julian seemed to think it was very funny. He leaned back in his chair, guffawing with mirth, while the others looked at him quizzically.

'We're having something much better,' Lucinda said lightly, but this sent both Carina and Julian into further gales of uncontrollable laughter.

'For goodness sake, Carina!' Alex snapped reprovingly.

Rachel and Ian were looking bemused, but Harry's little sharp eyes had picked up something and he followed Lucinda into the kitchen.

'Is Julian knocking her off?' he asked, helping himself to a chocolate from a bowl on the coffee tray.

'What . . . Carina? Don't be so bloody stupid,' Lucinda retorted. 'They've just had too much to drink.'

'Too much of something,' he muttered darkly.

'That was the worst evening of my life,' Lucinda exclaimed when Rachel and Ian, the last to leave, had finally said goodbye and gone.

'Oh, Bun. You just had a massive sense of humour failure,' he said sympathetically. He tried to put his arms round her, but she pushed him away irritably.

'Carina was a complete cow tonight,' she said angrily. 'She really embarrassed me and you encouraged her. She knows how important it is for me to trace all these wretched women. Her remarks must have put Paula on her guard. When I asked her for her number, she said something vague about letting me have it some time. How am I going to get hold of her now? Harry will smell a rat if I ask him. How am I ever going to confirm she was one of Dad's mistresses?'

'Oh, sweetheart.' He looked repentant, digging his hands into his pockets and hanging his head, reminding her of Jamie when he'd been scolded.

'Why did you encourage Carina? Harry even suggested you were having an affair with her.'

Julian's head shot up, his face flushed. 'And of course Harry's word is gospel, isn't it?'

'No. But I wish you hadn't sided with her tonight. No one else understood the reference to pumpkin pie. It was very rude of you to join in an in-joke in front of the others.' As she spoke, she switched off all the drawing-room lights and headed for the stairs, her head held high and her back straight with self-righteousness.

'But Lucinda . . .'

'I'm tired and I'm fed up and I'm going to bed.'

For a long time Lucinda lay in bed gazing into the darkness, unable to sleep. The evening had left her with a uneasy feeling on several levels, and an almost literally bad taste in her mouth. Carina's behaviour had been appalling, of course, but it was the crass attitude to sex, displayed by the men, that had disturbed her most. Even Julian had behaved like a teenager, giggling at the play on words which Paula couldn't have failed to notice even if she pretended not to.

Alex had ogled Paula all evening which had clearly irritated Carina, while Ian had simpered stupidly every time Paula had looked at him, which Rachel had ignored with seeming amusement, as if to say boys-will-be-boys. As for Harry, he'd been even more arrogant and cocky than usual, prattling on about his new scheme to make millions, like a schoolboy announcing his intention of becoming an astronaut.

And all the time Lucinda kept remembering her father and all his mistresses. Were all men basically penis-driven? Tossing and turning, tired but unable to sleep, her mind twisting this way and that, sickened by how her father had lived, she longed for the oblivion of slumber, but it evaded her.

She fervently wished that Miles had not forced her to confront the sordidness of his past. But knowledge acquired can never be forgotten and she was stuck for the rest of her life with a set of facts she wished she'd never been aware of. Most irritating of all was the fact that the whole evening had been a waste of time and money because she still wasn't certain whether 'Pumpkin' was Paula Maxwell or not.

'Sorry about last night,' Carina said contritely on the phone the next morning. 'I was feeling dreadful so I decided the only thing to do was get pissed. Did you find out if Paula Maxwell was "Pumpkin"?'

'I never got a chance. Why were you feeling bad? Are you ill?'

Carina's voice was flat and expressionless. 'I've found out Alex is having an affair, and when I saw Paula, and all the men ogling her, I suppose I had a massive attack of loss of confidence. She looked so bloody *good*, and I wished I'd worn my new black beaded dress, especially when I saw Alex gobbling her up with his eyes. I'm feeling really unattractive at the moment; Alex has obviously found someone who turns him on more than I do.'

'Oh, Carina!' Lucinda felt horrified. She'd always thought they had a strong marriage. 'I'm so sorry, but if it's true it's probably only a passing fling. Alex will never leave you. He adores you. You're his wife and the mother of his children.'

'Yup. You're right, but it still hurts. The bastard's having it off with some bimbo in his office who's about seventeen. It makes me feel like I've passed my sell-by date. How can he be so stupid? How can a man risk everything for a pair of big tits and a young arse?' She sounded tired and wretched. 'I didn't mean to embarrass you last night, though.'

'That's all right,' Lucinda said, immediately forgiving. 'I'm just so sorry you're having such a bad time. What are you going to do about it, Carina?'

'Do? Why, nothing. There are worse crimes than infidelity, though right now I can't think of one. Anyway, I'd lose more than I'd gain if I left him. I love my lifestyle. I like this big house and having staff to run it. I like being able to order a new designer wardrobe twice a year. I like my car, my social life, going to top restaurants and having money to spend. What's a little damp wriggle in the dark between Alex and some tart compared to all that?' she added pragmatically.

Lucinda felt stunned. If Julian slept with someone else she could never brush it aside like that . . . but was it remotely possible Anne had done just that? Said to herself, I have what really matters? But Lucinda didn't think that was likely. Anne, she was sure, had been naive and trusting, refusing to acknowledge what was before her eyes.

'So you're not going to say anything to him?' Lucinda asked.

'Certainly not. I don't want to dignify his sordid little adventure by appearing to *mind*. I just got a shock yesterday, finding out about it, you know. That's why I drank so much.'

They said goodbye and Lucinda got down to work again, but whilst studying the latest research on the public reaction to a new perfume Artémis were planning to launch called Aquamarine, Lucinda's mind kept going back to Paula Maxwell. Could she really have maintained such an unconscious air last night if she had been passionately in love with Miles? Maybe her story was true, and she had only known him through her father, a casual acquaintanceship that was on a cocktail party level rather than a cohabiting level. And surely Harry, always nosing into other people's affairs like an inquisitive terrier, would have found some link between Paula and Miles if there'd been one?

Deeply disappointed, Lucinda decided she'd put Paula on the back burner as a possible 'Pumpkin' and concentrate on tracing the other remaining two, and that as soon as she got home tonight she'd get out Renée Hartman's letters again and see if she could track her down.

Paula was already up, showered, immaculately made-up and dressed in white flared trousers and a pale blue cashmere sweater, when Harry finally awoke.

'What's up with you? It's still early,' he murmured, wandering sleepily into the living room, where she was sitting at her desk. 'Where are you going?'

'I'm not going anywhere,' she said, sipping her coffee. 'You look hungover.' There was an edge of criticism in her voice.

'What do you expect? Julian was filling our glasses every two minutes. Carina was well away, wasn't she? I thought she and Julian were rather cosy.' Harry flopped onto one of the oatmeal silk sofas, and lay supine along its cushioned seating.

'Her behaviour was certainly odd. What was all that about pumpkin pie? I didn't get it, but Julian seemed to think it was very funny.'

Harry stuffed another pillow under his head. 'Lucinda didn't, though. She was giving Carina filthy looks.'

'Oh, well.' Paula shrugged her slim shoulders. 'I've got something to tell you, Harry.'

'What?' His eyes were closed, his hands behind his head.

'I thought your idea, of starting an Internet company tracing people's family trees, was such a clever idea that I—'

Harry sat upright as if a spring had suddenly propelled him into a sitting position.

'Yeah? And . . .?'

This was it, he thought in triumph. Bing-fucking-o! After all these weeks his persistence had paid off. She was going to bloody well invest at last. He was on his feet now, looking down at her eagerly, all traces of sleep vanished. 'So . . .?'

'Well,' she began in a leisurely fashion, 'with advice from my father, my accountant and my financial adviser . . .'

'Yes?'

'I've developed your original idea and formed my own company. It's called Family Lines. We have our website set up, and I've opened an office in Brook Street from which the company will operate. I've also acquired, under contract, the services of a previous editor of *Debrett's Peerage*, and someone who has worked on *Who's Who* for several years, and a strong contact in the College of Arms.' Paula smiled at him sweetly. 'I must thank you for giving me such a good idea, Harry. I was wanting to start a business of my own, and this is perfect. I'm planning, with the help of an agent I've just taken on, to tour America quite soon, giving talks about the importance of family trees. My agent thinks she can get me on several chat shows including *Oprah*, which would be terrific.'

Harry stood with his mouth gaping wide and his chin almost touching his chest. Noises came from his throat but he couldn't speak.

Paula looked at him, still smiling. 'It had to be done professionally, you see, Harry,' she explained simply. 'And I have to know exactly where every penny is going.'

'You . . . you *bitch*!' He clutched his head, reeling as if he was ill, his bare feet suddenly striking her as very vulnerable as he staggered across her deep pile carpet. Then he wrapped his arms around his waist and bent over, hugging himself, his breath coming in sobbing gasps.

'How could you *do* this to me?' he choked, when he could say anything. 'You vile, sneaky, fucking *bitch*! You've pinched my idea! The best idea I've ever had! Christ, I'm going to sue you for this. I'm going to drag you through every court in the country. I'm going to expose you as the scheming, rotten, cheating . . .'

'Harry, you didn't even *have* a company,' she said gently. 'We did exhaustive checks. You hadn't registered it. In fact you hadn't done anything! Not even a website! What did you think was going to happen? That I'd hand over a couple of million pounds, so that you could live the life of Riley, whilst pretending you had a business that was making money? I'm not as cabbage as I'm green, you know.'

'You *used* me,' he shouted accusingly, not listening to a word she'd said.

'And you tried to use me. Doesn't that make us two of a kind, Harry? Can't you see that? I realised it the moment we met. You've done everything you could to get money out of me for a project that hadn't and never would have got off the ground if it had been left to you. In my shoes you'd have behaved exactly as I've done.'

'But you *seduced* me, wheedled all my business plans out of me, you took my whole concept, lock, stock and barrel, and then set up on your own. How *dare* you!' He was beside himself now. 'All you wanted was to get me into bed.'

'Doesn't that sound rather girlie, Harry?' she remarked quizzically. 'This is the twenty-first century, you know. Rich older men have kept young women since time began. Why shouldn't a rich older woman do the same?'

150

'My life's in tatters now,' Harry sobbed. 'I've given up my flat. I'm in debt . . . that trip you insisted on, and all those expensive restaurants you wanted to go to, they cost me a fortune.' He looked at Paula accusingly. 'You've *ruined* me,' he added, wiping his eyes with the sleeve of the silk pyjamas she'd given him.

There was a moment's silence, broken only by his weeping.

Then Paula spoke. 'You're still very good in bed, Harry.'

Twelve

'Do I look all right?' Susan asked Tom. She was wearing one of the black suits she'd bought for work, teamed with neat black shoes and a small black straw hat she'd found at Accessorize. She'd been worried about the hat. Most of them looked as if they were only suitable for weddings, but this was the plainest one she could find, and she hoped it made her look dignified.

'You look wonderful,' he said appreciatively. 'I'm so glad you're coming with me. I've been dreading today for weeks now.' It was true. Every time Tom remembered his father's memorial service was getting nearer, his stomach plummeted and his heart lurched painfully. Lucinda had warned them there might be several hundred people there. Not that they'd be looking at him, of course, but nevertheless it was still going to be an ordeal.

Thank God he wouldn't be on his own, though. Tom leaned forward and kissed Susan gently on the cheek. 'What would I do without you?' he whispered.

'I think the boot's on the other foot, actually,' she retorted cheerfully.

Ever since the scene with her ex, Tom had been living with her, and now she could hardly remember a time when he hadn't been a part of her life. He'd got rid of his miserable flat, brought his few belongings over to her little house, and as she said to a colleague at her office, 'sort of melted into the very fabric of the place, books and all, like he's always been with us'.

Dick and Steve were delighted with the arrangement, too. Now there was always someone around in the evenings and at weekends who would play Monopoly or rummy with them, take them swimming or to the zoo, or arrange picnics in Richmond Park, where they could kick a ball around.

'I wish we didn't have to go to the reception afterwards,' Tom said now, as he straightened his black tie and smoothed his hair nervously with the palm of his hand.

Susan fervently agreed though she didn't say so. For her, it was a baptism of fire; her first meeting with all Tom's family. What would they think of her? No doubt there'd be a feeling that Tom was with someone socially beneath him, an unmarried mother at that, living in a council house, and working as a mere secretary at Group Alliance. That was why she wanted to look at least dignified.

Tom slipped his arm around her waist. 'We'd better go, then,' he said, squeezing her. 'God knows where we're going to park, but let's hope we find a meter.'

The boys were spending the day with school friends, as they'd broken up for the summer holidays, so Susan locked the front door carefully. All the locks had been changed but she wasn't taking any risks. She didn't want that scumbag getting into her house again.

Jane and William Cotterell were breakfasting in their room. They'd arrived from France the previous evening, and were staying at Bailey's Hotel, in Gloucester Road, because it was much cheaper than the hotels they usually stayed at when in London. These were the days of belt-tightening. The Château St Laurent was now under offer, but William was delaying exchanging contracts because that's what he'd promised Jane. It was going to have to be sold, sooner rather than later, but Jane was praying for a miracle and he hadn't the heart to tell her just yet that there wasn't a chance that ICC might be saved.

Today they were going to Miles's memorial service and the reception afterwards, and in the evening Lucinda had asked them to supper, but tomorrow the search for a modest cottage, somewhere in the home counties, must begin.

They drank their coffee and crumbled their croissants in silence, each deep in thought about the future. For a terrible moment William almost wished it was his memorial service today. Miles was out of it now. No more worries. No more responsibilities. No sickening feelings of guilt and self-recrimination. Miles had never done anything stupid or rash in his life. In consequence, Anne was well taken care of now. Whilst if anything happened to him . . .! There had been moments in the past few weeks when William had felt like jumping the queue, taking some pills laced with whisky and getting the hell out of the torturous situation in which he'd landed them both. He hardly slept, and when he did he had terrible mixed-up dreams of losing things and not being able to find them. Then he'd awake in a sweat, his heart pounding, his brain panicking and his thoughts desperate. Jane didn't know, of course. He tried to protect her as much as he could from the hideous reality that faced them, but sooner or later she was going to have to accept that their lives had changed irrevocably.

Jane went to the dressing table of their modest room to put the final touches to her make-up, which as always was subtle and did more to enhance her good bone structure and fine eyes than anything else. She was trying desperately hard to put a brave face on things, but even this neat little room depressed her when she compared it to the suites at the Berkeley where they used to stay. Where the manager arranged for flowers, fruit and a complimentary bottle of champagne to await their arrival. And where Room Service was a fingertip away, to bring a snack, send someone to press their clothes, polish their shoes, or produce a hairdresser at short notice.

What was going to happen to them next? Jane knew she must be strong and sensible about what was going to happen next. Otherwise people would think she was a spoilt old woman, who was making a fuss because she was probably having to face the future in a four-roomed cottage set in half an acre of land instead of a fifteen-roomed château surrounded by a hundred hectares, which included avenues and lawns, arbours and orchards, a walled garden, a large terrace and a pool.

She *would* be brave, she told herself, as she swept her hair up into a chignon, before putting on her small black hat. She was just being selfish. William was the one who was suffering the most, no matter how hard he tried to hide it beneath a veneer of calm joviality. At least, she thought, as she finally applied pale coral lipstick to her trembling mouth, none of them had a terminal disease, none of them had lost their sight, or a leg or an arm, none of them had *died*. Except of course for Miles.

Anne sipped the brandy and soda Harry had given her, and hoped she was going to be able to manage. All eyes would be on her today, all those terrifically clever intellectuals who had been Miles's friends, and they'd be thinking: there goes his widow. Such a stupid woman. What did he ever see in her?

Anne had asked Lucinda to organise the whole thing, and now she couldn't remember who was doing the eulogy, who was doing the reading, what hymns had been chosen . . . who was going to be there . . . Never mind. It didn't really matter. Miles wouldn't be there and that was the worst part of all. She took another gulp of brandy and prayed for it all to be over.

'OK, Mum?' Harry asked, refilling his own glass. He was much more subdued these days, Anne reflected. She wondered what he was up to. Still, it was very kind of him to say he'd stay with her for a bit. Just until she got over Dad's death, he'd promised. It did mean she had to cook breakfast, lunch and dinner for him, when all she wanted to do was slip into bed and not bother about eating, but she must be grateful. After all, he was probably giving up a lot in order to be stuck with her in this big old house. He took her glass from her now.

'Time for another quick one before the car arrives,' he said. 'That'll keep you going until the reception afterwards.'

'The reception . . .' Anne echoed, closing her eyes in horror. She'd forgotten about the reception.

'Drink up,' Harry told her.

Sarah Wells was an old hand at funerals. In her eighty-two years she'd been to so many, they'd become a part of life, like Christmas and Easter. In recent years the number had increased as her friends and acquaintances had died, but each time she couldn't help feeling slightly triumphant. It was as if heaven could only take a certain quota at a time, and if you managed to dodge the grim reaper, you'd scored! You were still here, enjoying life, and not a handful of grey ashes that resembled a box of cat litter And now, greatest triumph of all, she'd even outlived her unpleasant son-in-law.

Sarah took a last look at herself in the long hall mirror before going down to get into the hired car. She was wearing a beautifully cut black dress with a matching jacket. Pearls gleamed around her neck and in her ears. Her broad-brimmed hat was made of fine black straw with a bow in the front.

Some memorial services were very sad, she reflected, getting into the lift. This was one that wouldn't be. Not as far as she was concerned, anyway.

She'd been to Miles's funeral, though no one knew that. She'd had to hide some distance away, under the trees, watching the hearse arrive, followed by the cars that brought Lucinda and Julian, Anne and Sarah, Tom and Harry, to that grim place, where the details of cremation were closely guarded secrets. She sometimes wondered if the ashes given to the families afterwards were really the ashes of their departed relative. She imagined them all being dumped in some enormous dustbin and given a final shake before being divided up to be put into dinky little plastic 'urns'.

Today, though, she could be an accepted part of the congregation at St Martin-in-the-Fields, without her presence causing speculation. No one would know what had passed between her and Miles all those years ago and they must never know. The secret would go with her to her grave, as it had with Miles. She had someone else to think of now, and their life must not be disrupted.

In a melancholy frame of mind, she buttoned her smart black coat-dress, checked that her black pillbox hat was securely held in place with a hatpin, and then picked up her gloves and handbag. It was time to leave; time to say her final farewells to Miles.

'But *why* can't we go, too?' Jamie whined. He and Daisy were going to be spending the day with Delia, who had promised to take them to Whipsnade zoo.

'Because for one thing, you wouldn't enjoy it,' Lucinda explained, as she distractedly tried to fix her hair in a coil to fit under her stetson-shaped black hat.

'Yes I would,' he insisted stoutly. 'Everyone else is going.'

'Everyone else is *not* going. It'll be all Grandpa's friends, and even I won't know who they are,' she mumbled between the two kirby grips she was holding between her front teeth. Jamie did a cartwheel on the bed, nearly knocking over the lamp on her bedside table.

'Be careful!' she warned irritably. 'Why don't you go and find Delia? She's making a picnic for you all. You could help her choose what you want to take.' Her hair wasn't going as well as usual, and any moment Julian was going to shout up to say they ought to be leaving.

Jamie hung about looking at her thoughtfully. 'Are you sad?' he asked suddenly.

'What?'

'Are you sad because your daddy's dead? Is that why you don't want me to come with you today?'

'Oh, Jamie.' She turned and held out her arms to him. He came to her slowly, not sure whether he wanted to be hugged or not. 'I love having you with me, and I'd have you with me all the time if I could, but today will be a sad day for lots of people. Granny, Granny-Sarah, Uncle Tom and Uncle Harry, and of course I'll be sad, too, and I don't think it would be much fun for you to be surrounded by a lot of sad people, do you? You and Daisy are going to have much more fun at the zoo, and I'll do a special early supper this evening, so we can all have it together before you go to bed.'

'You always say that, but you're always late and then Delia says we can't sit up any longer.' Jamie wriggled out of her arms and went and sat on the edge of her bed.

'I'm not always late, Jamie. I do my very best to get home in time to see you in the evenings.'

He scuffed the carpet with the heel of his small trainers and stared down at the carpet, bottom lip stuck out. 'You're *never* here,' he said, his voice choked. 'I bet . . . I bet . . .' His small chest rose and fell quickly, 'I bet if I were to die, you wouldn't be any more sad than you are 'cos your daddy's died.' Then he turned and fled from the room, and she could hear his feet stomping across the landing to his bedroom.

She heard Julian calling up from the hall below. 'We ought to be going, Bun. It may take us ages to park the car.'

'I'll be down in a minute,' she called back, trying to control her own sudden flood of tears. Is that what Jamie really thinks, she wondered, feeling deeply hurt. That she didn't love him? That she was away from home such a lot because she wanted to be? She heard Julian bounding up the stairs.

'Come on, or we're going to be late.' He stopped in the doorway, staring at her. 'What's the matter, Bun?'

Lucinda rose and rushed into his arms. Between sobs she repeated what Jamie had said. Julian gripped her wrists and pushed her very gently away. 'Leave this to me, Bun. Fix your face and get into the car. I'll be down in a moment.' Then he turned and hurried out of the room.

By the time he came back, her appearance had been transformed from tearful harassed mother to cool sophisticated-looking woman.

'All under control,' Julian whispered cheerfully. 'I told him it's time he started thinking about other people instead of himself, and he's fine. He winds you up, you know, Bun, to see how far he can push you. He probably hoped you'd bring him back a present if he could make you feel guilty. Little wretch,' he added, laughing, half indulgently.

'Well, he can,' she said quietly, clipping on her pearl earrings. 'I spend most of my time feeling guilty because I'm at work and I feel I should be at home.'

'I know, but you shouldn't. They have a great life, and we're taking them to the ice rink on Saturday; they're jolly lucky children,' he said sturdily. 'Now let's hit the road.'

They wanted to be early, because Julian, Tom and Harry, and three of Julian's friends were going to be handing out service sheets to the congregation as they arrived.

'You look smashing, by the way,' he added.

She smiled. 'Thanks. I'll be so glad when today's over. It's going to be quite an ordeal, isn't it? There are going to be so many people.'

'You'll be fine, Bun. And I'll be so proud of you.'

'Will you?' she asked, surprised.

He nuzzled her neck, bending to reach her under the brim of her hat. 'You know I will.' Then he gave her a playful pat on the bottom.

'Is there going to be S.E.X. at the memorial service?' Jamie piped up, hanging over the staircase banisters from where he'd been watching them.

'No,' his father replied gravely, 'although I'm sure God wouldn't mind if there was. He likes people to love each other.'

Daisy came plopping down the stairs in her bunny rabbit bedroom slippers. 'I like Jamie, but I don't have to have S.E.X. with him, do I?'

'It's strictly for mummies and daddies,' Lucinda said firmly, 'and we've got to go or we'll be late.' She reached up to kiss them. 'Have a lovely day and we'll see you this evening.'

The service was due to start at eleven o'clock, and by ten forty-five St Martin's was packed, as Lucinda had expected, with colleagues and friends of Miles, accompanied by their wives, who were dowdy and unassuming and looked as if all the sparkle had been squashed out of them forty years ago. Beside them, the younger generation looked positively starry by comparison, the men lively and dashing, the women glamorous and spirited.

Most crushed-looking of all was Anne, swaying slightly and glassy-eyed from too much brandy. Most stately was her mother, looking as if she was on loan from the Royal Family. Lucinda took her place in the right-hand front pew with Sarah; Julian would join them at the start of the service, when Harry and Tom joined their mother in the opposite front pew.

The organ struck up 'I vow to thee my country'. The service had started and for the next forty-five minutes Lucinda sat and followed the prayers and hymns, and listened to the eulogy in which her father was praised for his genius, his achievements, his contribution to the world of intellectualism, and the way he had been revered by his peers.

Only Lucinda, Tom and Harry noticed that there were no words of praise for Miles as a husband and father. They'd been written out of the script of his life, and he was only going to be remembered for his academic brilliance. Sudden tears pricked Lucinda's eyes. She wished she had a father who would be remembered as a warm and loving person. But no one was able to do that and no one did.

At last it was over, and Harry was guiding Anne down the aisle, followed by the rest of the family. Within moments everyone else followed, and the portico of St Martin's became crowded. Old men were greeting each other, surprised that they were all still alive. Wives followed meekly, smiling wanly, and wondering how soon they could get away.

Lucinda felt a hand on her elbow. It was Tom.

'I'd like you to meet Susan,' he said eagerly, pushing her gently forward, his arm round her waist. 'This is my sister,' he told her.

The two women looked at each other, and liked each other immediately. Impulsively Lucinda leaned forward and kissed Susan on the cheek.

'It's so good to meet you,' she said, and Tom could tell by the way she said it that she really meant it.

'And you too,' Susan responded in her calm cheerful way. 'Tom's told me such a lot about you.'

'He's told me a lot about you, too.' Lucinda grinned. At that moment she froze as she spied a petite, exquisitely dressed woman making her way towards her, wearing a black mink coat, a tiny chic black cocktail hat and a pair of familiar gold earrings.

'I just had to come, Lucinda,' Isabelle said in a hoarse, emotional whisper. 'Such a beautiful service. So moving. And what they said was so true . . . your papa . . . he was such a magnificent man.'

'Y-yes,' stammered Lucinda, her cheeks flushed.

'You are well? We must meet again, soon.' The fierce little hand that Lucinda remembered so well closed around her wrist like a clamp. 'I was re-reading my letters . . . you know,' she whispered urgently. Then she sighed, eyes brimming. 'Such passion. Such love. I will never, never know the like again, you know?'

'I'm sure.' Lucinda glanced round nervously, making sure her mother wasn't nearby. What she wanted was a quick escape route.

'You're very brave,' Isabelle continued. Lucinda could smell her perfume, feel her hot breath on her cheek. 'Which is your mother?'

Lucinda's eyes flashed her a look of panic. 'I think she may have gone,' she lied. 'If you'll excuse me . . . I must find my husband.' She could see Julian's back through the crowds. His head was bent forward and he had his arm round a woman's shoulders. He seemed to be talking earnestly to her and for a moment Lucinda vaguely wondered who she was. She pushed her way through what had become a dense crowd by now, rather like a strange cocktail party without the drink. To people passing on buses and in cars, or feeding the pigeons in nearby Trafalgar Square, it must look as if a flock of elderly black crows were having a get-together.

As she approached Julian from behind she heard him say to the woman: 'Why are you so upset? I didn't think you even knew him that well.' Then he turned, sensing her presence.

Beside him stood Carina, her face awash with tears, her immaculate make-up ruined.

'Carina!' Lucinda said, shocked. 'What's the matter?' She dropped her voice to a whisper. 'Has Alex . . .?'

Carina shook her head, unable to speak. Julian answered for her. 'The service upset her,' he murmured, raising his eyebrows as he caught Lucinda's eye. 'She'll be all right in a moment, won't you, Carina? Come and have a strong drink at the reception. That'll cheer you up.'

Lucinda looked at her friend, puzzled. Carina never cried. It just wasn't her style. In fact she had the reputation of being a tad too hard boiled.

'Are you all right, Carina?' she asked softly.

Carina dabbed her eyes. 'I shouldn't have come. It reminded me of Mummy's funeral last year. So silly of me,' she said, pulling herself together.

'Are you two getting cosy with each other again?' asked a brash voice just behind them. It was Harry, surveying Julian and Carina, his eyes alight with mischief.

'Grow up, Harry,' Carina said, suddenly ratty. She moved away, squeezing Lucinda's arm as she did so. 'See you later, sweetheart.'

'See you later,' Lucinda replied.

'When are we leaving for the reception?' Julian asked. Certain people had been invited to drinks at a house in Belgrave Square which let out large rooms for private functions.

'In a few minutes,' she replied. 'I'm just going to see if Mum's all right.'

At that moment they were joined by another member of the congregation and it was Harry's turn to look stunned.

'Paula!' he croaked.

Paula stood with a distinguished-looking older man, smiling confidently at Harry. She was wearing an exquisite shade of lilac, with a hat in a deeper tone.

'Hello, Harry. This is my father. You haven't met before, have you? Daddy, this is Harry Scott-Forbes, Miles's son.'

Harry found himself looking into the candid and clever eyes of a man in his late sixties, with grey hair and a humorous mouth.

Sir Humphrey Hodson shook Harry's hand. 'My condolences, Harry. Your father was a good friend of mine, and he'll be greatly missed. He was a very brilliant fellow.'

Harry put on his mournful expression. 'Yes,' he said, nodding. 'It's a great loss.'

'The service was very inspiring, though,' Paula observed.

The cheek of it, Harry thought, covertly glaring at her. She'd cheated him, betrayed him, used him, and yet here she was, cool as a cucumber, introducing him to her father as if nothing had happened.

Sir Humphrey spoke again. 'I've heard a lot about you, Harry. I'm told you're a very clever young man,' he said warmly. 'And I must thank you for giving Paula such a brilliant idea. She needs something to do, and this is a perfect opportunity for her to form her own business.'

Harry opened and closed his mouth several times, not knowing what to say.

Paula came gracefully to his rescue. 'This must be a very sad and stressful day for you, Harry, so we won't keep you. But my father and I very much wanted to pay our respects to your father's memory, and that was a beautiful service.'

'Right. Yes. Thanks,' Harry said, feeling completely out of his depth.

160

The level of noise was rising. What with the roar of passing traffic and the number of people milling around, everyone was starting to shout in order to be heard. Lucinda was easing her way past a group of women in a corner by one of the pillars as she went in search of Anne and Sarah, when she heard a voice say loudly and distinctly: 'Of course I was Miles's mistress for years, you know, so this is a heartbreaking day for me . . .'

Lucinda stopped in her tracks, transfixed, swivelling her head to see which of the women had spoken. A rake-thin woman with red hair, who looked to be in her fifties, raised her eyebrows at a blowsy-looking earth mother with a shock of grey hair and a grubby shawl over an ethnic caftan.

'Really, how fascinating,' the thin woman said acidly.

'It was fate,' retorted the earth mother. 'I healed him, you know. One day he—'

Suddenly, with the velocity of an Exocet missile, a small figure hurled herself into their midst.

'You *lie*!' she shouted, her face scarlet with rage, her smart gold earrings quivering. 'Miles had no other woman!'

In total horror, Lucinda watched helplessly as Isabelle laid into the earth mother, hammering her with angry words.

'He would never have looked at you!' Isabelle said shrilly, her accent heavy. 'I was the only lover he took. I was his great love. We shared everything. How dare you say he was *your* lover?'

'Now look here, lady, I don't know who you think you are, but Miles and I were together for four years . . . four years . . . get that?' Earth Mother shouted belligerently, her vast bosom heaving with indignation.

Isabelle burst into hysterical tears. 'How can you say that? Today of all days . . . when we b-bid him goodbye . . . for ever,' she sobbed.

People around them had stopped talking and were turning to see what the commotion was about.

Lucinda looked round wildly. Had her mother heard what was being said? Where had Julian gone to now? She caught sight of Sarah, standing in the entrance to the church, watching the scene with a grave expression on her face.

'Isabelle.' Lucinda grabbed her arm and spoke urgently. 'Come with me. We can talk about this later. This isn't the time or the place,' she said desperately.

'But this woman, she *lie*,' Isabelle wailed. 'How can she say Miles loved her? He was *my* lover . . . he was everything to me.'

'There are people listening, Isabelle,' she pleaded. 'Come with me.'

'And who the hell are *you*?' Earth Mother demanded, her gypsy earrings swinging as she rounded on Lucinda.

'I'm Miles's daughter,' she said firmly, 'and you are . . .?'

'I happen to be Fenella Harrison.'

For a moment Lucinda felt as if she'd been punched in the chest. 'Please wait a moment,' she said in an urgent stage whisper. 'I have to speak to you.'

161

Hanging on to Isabelle, Lucinda dragged her over to Julian, and begged him to look after her for a couple of minutes. 'This is Isabelle. Keep her away from Mum. I'll be right back.'

She could see Carina about to head off alone down the steep steps of the church.

'Carina,' she called, racing after her. 'I want you to do me the most enormous favour. There's a desperate situation going on. Two of Dad's mistresses have turned up, and one of them is Isabelle and she's just realised she wasn't the only one. I've got to get her out of here before chaos breaks out and Mum discovers everything. Can I introduce her to you . . . and can you take her off, somewhere? I know it's a lot to ask . . .' She was gabbling breathlessly, feeling as if she were on the verge of hysteria herself. There was Isabelle, gesticulating wildly as she talked tearfully to Julian, while Fenella Harrison, who looked as if she might cast an evil spell on anyone who crossed her, was marching around like the Incredible Hulk on speed.

Carina's mouth tightened and she hesitated, as if about to refuse.

'*Please*,' Lucinda begged. 'I'm desperate, Carina. Something awful is going to happen if I can't get Isabelle out of here. And I must talk to Fenella Harrison.'

'OK,' Carina said resignedly. 'I was going home because I don't feel like joining the reception, but I'll take her to the Savoy for a drink or something. I suppose I'll have to hear all about her affair with your father.'

Lucinda gave her a quick hug. 'Carina, I'm indebted to you for life. I can't tell you how grateful I am.' She hurried her friend back into the mêlée and dragged her over to Isabelle.

'Isabelle, this is my best friend, Carina. I want you to meet her, and get to know her,' she said firmly. 'Carina suggests that you and she go off and have drinks. She's a family friend, and' – she lowered her voice to a whisper – 'she's the only person who knows about . . . about you and Dad. You can tell her all about him, while I deal with . . . erm . . . this other lady.'

'She no lady!' Isabelle spat furiously. 'She lying bitch.'

'What's up, sis?' Harry was at Lucinda's elbow again like a tiresome terrier.

Lucinda turned on him fiercely. 'Go and find Mum and take her to the reception *now*, Harry. And take Granny, too.'

'But what's going on?' He looked from the tearfully distraught Isabelle to Carina, who was standing grim-faced.

'Nothing's going on, Harry. Just go. Get Mum and go.' Lucinda turned her back on him. 'Carina, if you could . . .?'

Carina took Isabelle's arm. 'Come along, Isabelle. Let's go and have lashings of champagne and you can tell me all about it.'

'I come. I come.' She allowed herself to be led away like a child worn out with grief. Lucinda watched them go down the church steps together. Two women of about the same height, one blonde, the other very dark, both in their late thirties, and married to rich men, as was obvious from their couture outfits. They had so much in common that it struck Lucinda it might be the beginning of a great friendship.

'So what *is* going on, sis?'

'For God's sake, Harry, will you get off my case? Where's Mum? Has the car arrived for her and Granny, or do you propose popping them on a number nine bus?'

'Take a chill pill,' Harry retorted sullenly. 'Why did that woman, and the fat old bag over there, say she had an affair with Dad?'

'You don't know what you're talking about. Now, please go and find poor Mum . . .'

'You're up to something, Lucinda. You can't fool me. But believe me, I'll find out.' Harry turned abruptly away and with a sigh of relief she saw him heading in the direction of Anne, who'd joined Sarah by the church entrance. Now she could have a word with Fenella Harrison. She had to get her address and phone number from her.

As she stepped up to talk to Fenella she felt a tap on her shoulder.

'Lucinda, how are you, darling?' It was Jane, with William. They both kissed her, and told her she looked well, and said they were looking forward to catching up on all the news at supper that evening, and what a beautiful service it had been, but how sad for Anne to have to go through the whole thing again, and how were Jamie and Daisy . . .

Lucinda could see Fenella Harrison saying goodbye to her friends, about to depart. She had to speak to her before she left or she might not be able to find her again.

'Excuse me,' she blurted out to her in-laws, 'there's someone I must catch before she goes.'

She hurried forward, and just as she was about to catch up with Fenella, Anne passed in front of her. Harry was by her side, and Sarah, looking worried, was following.

'We're just off, dear,' Anne told Lucinda. 'Are you coming with us? We ought to get there before everyone else.' Her speech was slurred, and her eyes had faded to the colour of damp sand.

'Are you all right, Mum?'

'I'm fine,' Anne answered carefully.

'Coming with us, then, sis?' Harry had the look of a trouble maker. He knew she was trying to get to the fat old bag, and he was holding on to Anne's arm, barring Lucinda's way.

She glared at him and tried to step round him. A tall man she didn't know got in her way. By squeezing past, saying 'Excuse me' in a loud voice, she finally managed to get through to the group of women. Fenella was no longer with them.

'Shit!' she muttered under her breath in despair and anger. It seemed as if everyone was trying to prevent her from getting to this former mistress, and for a second she felt like weeping with rage. She looked around wildly, her eyes searching the dwindling group of mourners, seeing only the thin woman with the red hair Fenella had been talking to.

In desperation, Lucinda dashed over to her. 'Where's Fenella gone?' she asked breathlessly.

'Home, I think,' the woman replied dully.

'Which way did she go?'

She pointed vaguely in the direction of Trafalgar Square. 'That way, I think.'

Lucinda strained to see, amongst the stream of passers-by, any sign of the departing figure of Fenella.

'What's the matter, Bun? You look demented, rushing around all over the place.' It was Julian, looking at her anxiously.

Briefly she explained what had happened. 'Now she's gone and I may never get a chance to get hold of her again. Harry kept me back on purpose by blocking my way as she was leaving. He knows something's up and I bet he'll make mischief and tell Mum what's happened.'

'Fuck.'

The thin woman was still standing at the top of the steps, gazing out across Trafalgar Square with sad eyes.

'I've got to ask her if she knows Fenella's address. It's my last hope.' Lucinda hurried up to her.

'Sorry, dear,' the woman told her, 'but I've no idea. I only met her coming out of the church today.'

'God, will I be glad when this is over!' Lucinda exclaimed, as Julian parked the car up against the railings of the central garden in Belgrave Square. They'd given a lift to Jane and William, and on the way there Lucinda had decided to take her in-laws into her confidence, up to a certain point. She'd told them that two of her father's mistresses had turned up unexpectedly at the church, neither having known about the other, and Anne knowing nothing about either of them.

'And now Harry's sussed the situation and I'm scared he'll tell Mum,' she concluded despairingly.

'But why should he? For what purpose?' Jane asked, horrified.

'He enjoys a sense of power, amongst other things,' Lucinda said drily. 'It'll make him feel important, knowing something like this, when Mum doesn't.'

Jane and William exchanged glances. They'd never liked Harry and found it hard to believe that a sweet person like Lucinda could have such an objectionable brother.

Inwardly Lucinda was cursing with frustration at having let Fenella Harrison slip through her fingers. Tracing five mistresses in the hope of eventually inheriting a fortune was something she hadn't told Jane and William. And so, as they walked from the car to the large Victorian house where the reception was being held, Lucinda was silent and only Julian understood why.

'I could kick myself,' she muttered, as they walked side by side. 'I was trying so hard to be discreet, and people kept coming up and talking to me and I had to be polite . . .' She didn't add that his parents had been among them.

Tight-lipped, and feeling ready to scream at anyone who got in her way now, Lucinda entered the white stuccoed mansion and climbed the elegant staircase to a large reception room on the first floor, overlooking the central gardens. Anne, Sarah and Harry had already arrived, and so had Tom and Susan. Champagne and canapés were being handed round by several waiters and a strange atmosphere of euphoria pervaded the room.

Lucinda kissed her mother. 'Are you all right?' she asked gently. Anne looked flushed, as if she had a fever.

'I'm spil . . . erm . . . spel . . . erm . . .'

'Splendid, Mum,' Harry prompted.

'Yesh,' Anne said with a beaming smile.

Tom leaned towards her, frowning worriedly. 'Mum, have you been drinking?'

She blinked, and looked at him as if she'd never seen him in her life before.

'She needed a little steadying before we left,' Harry explained.

Nearby, Lucinda and Sarah faced each other. Sarah looked shocked, her face pale.

'That was a near one, darling,' she said softly.

'Tell me about it. Imagine *two* of them being there . . . and then finding out about each other! For a moment I actually thought they were going to have a fight.'

'Don't.' Sarah closed her eyes at the thought.

'The damnable thing, though, is that one of them slipped away before I could get her address, or set up a meeting. Now I don't know how I'm going to trace her.'

Guests were starting to fill up the room. Lucinda had invited the people listed in Miles's address book, which numbered about a hundred, but it began to seem, as time passed, that a lot of people who'd been in church and had heard about the reception had decided to come along, too. The young waiters were looking alarmed at the speed of new arrivals, as they opened bottles with feverish haste and hoped they wouldn't run out of glasses, while others replenished platters of food as fast as they could.

'Bloody lot of locusts in there!' an elderly waitress remarked tartly.

Tom and Susan stood close together, knowing only Tom's family, but more interested in each other than anyone else.

'I like Lucinda,' she announced. 'Do you think she and Julian would ever come to supper with us? I bet she's never been in a council house in her life,' she added laughingly, without a trace of rancour.

'I know they would,' Tom affirmed reassuringly. 'She's very down to earth, just like you.'

William and Jane sat by the open French windows which led onto a balcony and talked to Sarah, who had felt like sitting down ever since she'd arrived. Her heart had nearly stopped when she'd heard those two women, the excitable Italian and the earth mother, squabble about their affairs with Miles. At his memorial service, too! Thank God Anne had been too drunk to take it in.

'Very tiring, these occasions, aren't they?' William remarked. 'I prefer parties given in honour of the living. Definitely more fun.'

Sarah smiled wanly. 'I couldn't agree more. Are you going to be in London for long?'

'We're here for a week.' Jane didn't add their mission was house-hunting. She believed that as long as she didn't mention leaving France, it might not actually happen.

'Then you must come to dinner,' Sarah said, rallying. 'Are you free on Monday? I'll ask Lucinda and Julian, and I've got an absolutely charming couple coming called Davenport. Do say you'll come?'

'We'd love to,' Jane replied. 'Your dinner parties are always memorable.'

Lucinda had been stuck for nearly fifteen minutes with an elderly professor who was rambling on about global warming, which had at first interested her, reminding her of the argument she'd had at the office with Geneviève, who had thought that profits were more important than preserving the environment, but the longer he rambled the more he seemed to lose the plot and she was desperate to get away.

Just as she was about to excuse herself she felt someone tapping her on the back. Glad of a reason to get away, she spun round and, seeing it was Anne, spoke with relieved delight.

'Hi, Mum. Everything all right . . .?'

She felt the blood drain away from her head in a dizzying icy rush, as she saw who was standing beside her mother, their arms linked. It was Fenella Harrison.

Anne was swaying dangerously, clinging to the arm that supported her.

'Thish is Fenella Harrison. A colleague of Daddy's in the old daish,' she slurred. 'She heard about . . . about this resheption so she came along. Ishn't that nice?'

'Yes,' Lucinda replied faintly. The shock of Fenella's proximity again had given her an instant headache, and she felt quite ill. 'How do you do?' she said automatically, looking into the dark gypsy eyes. The raddled face, framed with a wild tangle of grey hair, reminded her for a ghastly moment of Grizabella in the Lloyd-Webber musical *Cats*.

Lucinda struggled to breathe normally, while her mind tried to grapple with this new hideous twist. How much did her mother know? Then she realised Harry was hovering just behind Anne and Fenella, and she wondered if he'd orchestrated the whole thing.

'I had wanted to talk to you outside the church, but you left before I had a chance,' Lucinda heard herself say, hoping she didn't sound as fraught as she felt.

'Whash . . . whash did you want to talk about?' Anne muttered.

Oh, God, where was Julian? Where was Tom? Where was *anyone* who would take Anne off to some quiet corner and pour coffee down her throat. At that moment William appeared through the throng. Lucinda signalled urgently to him.

'William, Mum's really tired. Could you take her somewhere so she can sit down?'

William summed up the situation. 'I'd be delighted.' He took Anne's other arm. 'Tell me, my dear,' he said, leading her over to the window, 'how are you getting on? Do you have plans . . .'

As Lucinda saw them go, she turned in relief to Fenella.

'We can't talk here. Let's go into one of the side rooms.' She led the way out of the reception room, across the landing, and into a small, empty ante-room.

'Who was that hysterical Italian woman who said she'd had an affair with Miles?' Fenella asked belligerently.

'Let's not worry about her, she's of no importance,' Lucinda said hurriedly, realising this woman was no cupcake. She was tough. A fighter. If she were to realise Miles had had five mistresses in total, she looked as if she could go ballistic.

Briefly, Lucinda explained that her father had requested Fenella's letters be returned to her, and that he'd also left her a piece of jewellery which the solicitor was at present holding.

'What sort of jewellery?' Fenella asked crisply. 'I'm into crystal. I use it for healing people. I don't want anything else. It's what I do. I first practised on Miles, when no one else knew the power of crystals. If it's not crystal I'm not interested.'

Lucinda was taken aback. This woman was a mixture of Earth Mother and Hitler's mother. She took a deep breath and decided to go for it. 'It's an aquamarine and diamond bracelet.'

Fenella made a face. 'I suppose that would be all right,' she said ungraciously. 'Mail it to me.'

'It was my father's wish that I hand you the letters and the piece of . . . the bracelet, in person. Do you live in London?'

'Certainly not. Ruination for my chakra. Yours too, I'd say. You seem very rattled.'

Lucinda had to privately agree that the woman was right, and that she was the cause of it. 'I'm fine. So where do you live?'

'Bristol.'

'*Bristol*?' Lucinda echoed in dismay. 'Are you by any chance staying in London tonight?'

'By no chance,' she snapped. 'I'm catching the train back in an hour's time.'

'Can I have your address and phone number, then? I'll be in touch early next week, to arrange to come and see you.'

After groping in a large bag designed for holding knitting, Fenella produced her business card, on which she advertised herself as a Healer. 'You'll find me here. You should make an appointment for a session at the same time, because you've got a lot of negativity, haven't you? You need earthing, anchoring to the energy field of the earth. That would stop you being all over the place. It's quite simple. You need to get to a higher light vibration in order to maintain a spiritual frequency. I will surround you with crystals, placing an earthing crystal under your chair to heal your base chakra.'

Lucinda blinked. 'Right.'

Fenella reached into her ravine-deep cleavage, and brought up a pale yellow crystal on a chain. 'I wear this all the time,' she announced. 'It prevents me from absorbing other people's negativity; it's an energy protector.'

'I see.'

'I taught Miles how to perform self-healing.' Fenella shook her head sadly. 'There must have been blockages in the patterns of his energy field that caused him to fall on that last fatal day. Do you know if they found any crystals on him?'

Lucinda felt she was fast losing her grip on reality.

'I don't know,' she replied blankly. 'Should there have been?'

Fenella nodded vigorously. 'I told him to tape a crystal to his groin in order to restore his usual vigour. Much better than Viagra.' There was a pause before she added, mournfully, 'He must have left it off, that day.'

As they walked to the door, Lucinda asked, 'Were you really a colleague of my father's? That is, as well as . . .?'

Fenella looked at her as if she were a complete fool. 'What do you think? Of course I wasn't a colleague. I only said that to spare your poor old mother's feelings.'

'Thank you. That was good of you.'

'Well, she wouldn't want to know it was me he really loved, more than anyone else in the world, would she?'

At last people were starting to leave. Anne was sitting meekly by the window, looking dazed and sleepy. Beside her Sarah sat stiffly, watching everyone warily, missing nothing. As soon as Lucinda had made sure Fenella Harrison had left, she walked slowly back into the main room, feeling absolutely drained. Her head ached with the stress of the past couple of hours and she was still suffering from the shock of seeing her mother and Fenella standing arm in arm.

Julian came over and, looking down into her face, put his hand gently on her shoulder. 'Are you OK, Bun?'

Harry came up to them. 'What was that all about, sis? I gather that woman slept with Dad at some point, and now she's trying to blackmail you; am I right? Is she threatening to tell Mum?'

Lucinda looked at him coolly. 'I don't know what you *think* you saw,

Harry, but you couldn't be wider of the mark.'

'Oh, come on! And what about that foreign-looking woman who was creating a scene outside the church; she was one of Dad's bits on the sides, too, wasn't she? How come you knew her? Why did you send her off with Carina? Something's going on, Lucinda, and I want to know what it is.'

Julian suddenly turned on him angrily. 'For God's sake, Harry, don't be a little shit all your life. Take today off.'

Harry's eyes narrowed and he raised his chin and looked as if he were sniffing the air, like a dog scenting something very interesting.

'You can't stop me finding out and I will,' he retorted. 'I've always been suspicious about those so-called "papers" Dad left you. Why haven't you shown them to me? What are you hiding?'

Lucinda decided to try another tack. 'Harry, the only reason they're confidential papers is because I want to protect Mum from being hurt. *Please* don't let her know about those two women today. It would be mean, cruel, and utterly pointless, and if you tell Mum anything, I'll never speak to you again.'

'But what has any of it got to do with you?' Harry persisted.

'Some day, maybe, I'll tell you, but only if you get off my back right now and mind your own business.'

'That was definitely the worst day of my life,' Lucinda exclaimed, flopping onto the sofa and kicking off her high heels, when they got home. 'I thought I was going to die about a dozen times.'

'At least you've found Fenella Harrison, so that only leaves two to go, doesn't it?' Julian asked, sinking into the chair opposite.

She nodded. 'Renée Hartman, and of course "Pumpkin".'

'Did you see Paula at the church? I think it's all over between her and Harry.'

'Yes, I think she's probably sussed him by now. I wonder why it took her so long? God, I wish he wasn't such a con man. I'm amazed by the number of women who fall for him. I knew he was after Paula's money, but why did an intelligent woman like her fall for it in the first place? She's either appallingly needy, or she's completely la-la.'

'The world is full of sexually attractive men preying on lonely rich women.'

'I know. I just wish my brother wasn't one of them.'

The heading on the Court Circular page of the *Telegraph* was *In Memoriam*.

Sitting at the breakfast table, coffee cup in hand, Lucinda read on:

A service of thanksgiving for the life of Professor Miles Scott-Forbes was held at St Martin-in-the-Fields on Wednesday 19 July . . .

Lucinda skimmed the details listing those who had officiated or given eulogies or readings to the line that began:

169

Among others in the congregation were Mrs Scott-Forbes (widow), Mr Tom Scott-Forbes, Mr Harry Scott-Forbes (sons), Mr and Mrs Julian Cotterell (daughter and son-in-law) . . .

and then there was a column nine inches long, made up of all those who had attended, their names taken down as they entered the church by representatives of the newspaper. As she read on, she saw her grandmother was listed, and Willian and Jane, Carina, and Susan Murray, which she presumed was the full name of Tom's girlfriend; then there was Sir Humphrey Hodson and Mrs Paula Maxwell, and so the list continued, name after name, most of them professors, a few knights, several judges . . .

'Oh no! No! I can't believe it!' Lucinda yelped, looking aghast.

'What is it?' Daisy asked, looking up from spreading honey on her toast.

Jamie left his seat and ran round the table to look over his mother's shoulder.

'Jamie.' Julian's voice was stern. 'Kindly sit down.'

'But I want to see,' he protested.

'Can I see, too?' Daisy asked, wriggling down from her chair.

'Sit down, at once, both of you. You're becoming extremely spoilt.'

With great reluctance they returned to their chairs, amid murmurings of 'It's not fair' and long lingering looks at the newspaper Lucinda was holding. Her hands were shaking and her face was scarlet.

'You'll never believe this,' she exclaimed in frustration.

'Do we want to know right now?' Julian asked carefully.

She paid no heed. 'It doesn't only list Isabelle and Fenella at Dad's memorial service, but *Renée Hartman*, too! *She* was there as well and I missed her!'

'Who is Renée Hartman?' Jamie demanded to know and the clamouring started all over again.

Lucinda phoned Carina as soon as she got to work. 'Can you believe it?' she demanded in aggravation. '*Three* of them were there. And if Paula really *is* "Pumpkin" that makes four out of five! I could have found out where they all lived and got this nightmare over in one fell swoop, but at least I've made contact with Fenella Harrison.'

'I suppose it's not surprising,' Carina reasoned. 'After all, you announced the memorial service in *The Times* and the *Telegraph* several weeks ago and it was open to the public; anyone was free to turn up. Isabelle certainly made her presence known, didn't she?'

'Oh, Carina! I haven't thanked you for taking her off my hands. I'm really grateful. Granny realised what was going on, but Mum didn't, thank God, and that's the main thing. How did it go?'

'I plied her with champagne and she was fine,' Carina replied drily. 'What a nightmare woman she is. What Miles ever saw in her I can't imagine.'

'What did she say about him?'

Carina sounded bored. 'Oh, you know, he was the love of her life . . . and he felt the same way about her . . .'

'That's what they all say.'

'. . . and that Fenella Harrison was a lying whore. Isabelle absolutely refused to believe she'd been Miles's mistress.'

'Let's be thankful she doesn't know about all the others! What else did she say?'

'Nothing much. She wants us to meet for lunch. As if!'

'Carina, I owe you one. You saved my life.'

'That's OK. So what are you going to do next?'

'I'm going to Bristol to deliver the things to Fenella, and then I can tick her off my nightmare list.'

Carina sounded sympathetic. 'Would you like me to come with you?'

'You've already done more than enough by looking after Isabelle,' Lucinda assured her. 'I'll be fine.'

Touched by Carina's concern, she thanked her and said goodbye. Lucinda sometimes wondered what chemistry bound them together. It certainly wasn't a shared lifestyle. They actually had little in common, yet Carina was loyal and took the closest interest in what she was doing, especially at present. How many friends, she wondered, would offer to accompany her to Bristol to visit her late father's ex-mistress?

Thirteen

As soon as Lucinda arrived at the office the next day she knew something was up. Everyone in the market research department looked anxious and there was an air of uncertainty in the atmosphere.

'What is it?' she asked, nervously. There'd been a rumour going round that they were going to be taken over by a giant American cosmetic company, a move none of them welcomed. Many feared there would be redundancies.

'I haven't a clue,' Geneviève said dolefully. They'd been absorbed in work and were about to bring out Mousseline-de-Soie, and all their energies in the past few weeks had gone into making sure the launch went without a hitch. Millions of pounds rested on the success of any new product, and as the day drew near it was normal for everyone to get uptight. For months the various divisions, which included laboratory tests, marketing strategy, design concept, distribution, merchandising, advertising, promotions and public relations, had been flat out preparing for the big day when the face cream hit the major stores worldwide. From London to New Delhi, from Paris to Tokyo, from New York to Sydney, Mousseline-de-Soie must be the big cosmetic story, the one moisturiser every woman, no matter what her skin colour or her age, would want to rush out and buy.

Everyone involved felt a huge sense of responsibility, too. D'Aussoire's reputation would suffer if target sales figures weren't reached. Beauty writers had to be wined and dined and given samples in order to encourage them to write in glowing terms about this sensational cream which promised to 'lift away wrinkles, restore a youthful bloom, and replenish the natural oils of youth'.

Lucinda had already played her part by collating the findings of the three field research agencies they had used on this occasion, and there were moments when she felt anxiety in case she hadn't intrepreted them correctly. Did women, en masse, really want a cream that was perfumed, but delicately so it wouldn't clash with their scent? Did they really want it to feel fluffy to the touch rather than silky . . . when *soie* was the French for silk?

Lucinda realised with a sinking feeling that if she'd analysed the findings and presented them incorrectly to the directors, thousands of beautifully packaged jars of Mousseline-de-Soie were going to stay on display in the various stores for a very long time.

On her desk she found a memo summoning her to an urgent meeting in the boardroom. It didn't look good.

Julian had lent the car to his parents so they could go and view houses in

Surrey, their county of choice, William having been born near Guildford in 1940.

The heatwave had broken with a vengeance, and it was a blustery day, grey and damp, with an almost constant drizzle of fine rain. 'So wetting,' Jane complained, clutching her umbrella. It was the heavy greyness that depressed her most of all. It hung over what was very pretty countryside like a pall of gloom, not letting even the smallest shaft of light filter through. After the brightness of the Dordogne, where the sun dazzled and the very air sparkled and smelled fragrant, the sullen sky of Surrey seemed to press down angrily on Jane's head, chilling her bones and numbing her toes and fingers, although it was July.

'Let's look at the house in Epsom first, as it's the nearest to London,' William suggested, as they joined the M25.

'Epsom . . .' Jane echoed despairingly. 'But that's surburbia. We want to be right in the country, surely. Or else in the centre of London. But not in between.'

William nodded. 'I agree, darling, but it sounds like a nice house, with quite a big garden, and it is within our price range, so we might as well look at it.' He was beginning to have the awful feeling that Jane was going to find fault with every house they looked at.

'Can I have a look at the estate agents' descriptions?' she asked.

'Help yourself. They're in my briefcase on the back seat.'

While William drove at a steady speed, Jane perused the list of properties they'd arranged to see.

They hadn't gone house-hunting for sixteen years, when they'd driven leisurely through the Dordogne, falling in love with every property they'd seen. But this was different. This reminded her of when they'd first been married, had very little money and wanted a house when they barely had enough money for a small flat. The descriptions dreamed up by estate agents hadn't changed in forty years either.

In need of modernisation could be translated as: this house is a total wreck and requires to be gutted before being rebuilt. *Recently refurbished* was a dangerous one, too; it could mean anything from a pub bar, complete with beer pumps and high stools erected in a corner of the dining room, to cladding added to the exterior walls. *Charming bijou property* definitely meant the rooms were so small you couldn't even swing a mouse, far less a cat. And *fine example of Victorian architecture* could easily turn out to be a large, ugly, ornate, ox-blood red brick edifice, with an oppressive atmosphere.

'There's certainly a wide range of choices here,' Jane said drily. 'But I hate the idea of what they call a kitchen/breakfast room. I really do want a proper dining room, William.'

'I like the sound of the house in Shere,' William remarked. 'It used to be an extremely pretty village. I used to stay there as a child, with friends of my parents.'

'I very much doubt if it's a pretty little village any more,' Jane replied.

'It's probably bang on the edge of some terrible housing estate, with giant supermarkets and car parks.'

She shuffled through the pages of descriptions, trying to find it. 'Ah, here we are. "A delightful well appointed period house originating from the eighteenth century." That sounds all right,' she continued hopefully. Then her eyes fell on the fatal bottom line. P.O.A.

'Oh, God, William. It says Price On Application. You know what *that* means. It's so expensive they daren't put the price, or nobody would even bother to go and see it.'

'I gather they're open to offers for a quick sale.'

The announcement was almost more devastating than the confirmation of a takeover bid. The heads of the various divisions sat looking at Marc Leblanc, UK Managing Director, with shocked expressions. Lucinda's first thought was, How could it have happened?

Xanthe, a giant American cosmetic company, famous for its Golden Blonde range of products, and their chief rival, had stolen the formula of Mousseline-de-Soie, in spite of the secrecy that had surrounded its production, and were about to launch it, worldwide, as 'Chiffony-de-Rose by Xanthe'.

Even the packaging was similar: a frosted glass jar with a silver screw top, in a pastel box tied with a silver ribbon. The only real differences between the two products were that the Chiffony-de-Rose cream was tinted pink, something Lucinda had reported was a popular choice amongst a certain age group of women, but the directors had decreed looked 'cheap' compared to white, and the colour of the boxing; D'Aussoire, after endless research into which colour would appeal the most, finally chose a cool, soothing shade of pale green, once again declaring pink would look 'tacky'.

But they had both gone with a silver ribbon, so if their rival products were, by any chance, displayed on the same beauty counter, they would look like alternative shades of the same product. However – most galling of all – it looked as if Chiffony-de-Rose was going to be in the stores several weeks ahead of Mousseline-de-Soie.

'This is going to cost us millions,' Marc Leblanc declared heavily, looking at them all accusingly. This was a calamity.

'Do we know who's responsible?' Lucinda asked. 'Has the leak come from here or Paris?'

'Here,' Marc replied immediately. 'That much we know. What we don't yet know is, have we been infiltrated by someone in the pay of Xanthe?'

There were uncomfortable stirrings around the boardroom table, and then everyone started talking at once.

'Who could have done such a thing?'

'What's going to happen now?'

'*Mon dieu*! This is a calamity!'

'We have a traitor in our midst!'

Lucinda leaned forward, wanting facts not supposition. 'Are we scrapping the launch of Mousseline-de-Soie?' It would be possible, she thought, to keep the formula, change the packaging and the name, and launch it as another product in a few months' time. It would be damage limitation even if it was not an ideal solution.

'We've invested too much to do that, and besides, we're beyond the point of no return,' Marc replied. 'Advertising space has been booked for the next six months in all the glossy magazines. And we've bought airtime for TV ads to go out twice nightly for the first month of the campaign.'

She knew that was true. They had to go ahead.

Alain was looking deeply troubled. 'It must be someone with a grudge.'

'Or someone who has been offered a lot of money by Xanthe,' Lucinda pointed out.

Marc put his head in his hands for a moment, and then looked up, his eyes blazing with anger. 'But it must have been someone who had access to every stage of production, from the first prototype of the cream to the finished article, and everything in between. I want each of you to question all the employees in your division. *C'est l'espionnage!*' he added dramatically. '*Mon dieu . . . c'est très sérieux!* We must catch whoever betrayed us, and they must be brought to justice.'

Lucinda knew, with a feeling of dread, exactly what would happen next. The whole atmosphere at D'Aussoire would alter the moment this news got out, not just in the boardroom, but in the offices, the restaurant, the lifts, corridors and washrooms. Suspicion, even amongst old colleagues, would be rife and would spread like an evil smell. The whole of D'Aussoire was going to be rocked by this act of betrayal, which was obviously an inside job because of the strict security that always surrounded a new product.

When the meeting came to an end, Lucinda took the lift down to the staff restaurant on the seventh floor. She needed coffee, hot and strong, and something to eat because she hadn't had time for breakfast that morning. Taking her coffee and a warm flaky croissant to an empty table by the window, she sat for several minutes deep in thought. The idea of questioning everyone in her division was a nightmare. Offence would be taken. People would be hurt that she could even imagine they were guilty.

Marc's last instructions for their investigation had been: 'Always surprise the enemy.'

It was quite likely, Lucinda reflected, that the enemy would surprise them by turning out to be one of their friends, a colleague they trusted and liked.

Lucinda noticed that Jane and William were very quiet that evening, when they came for dinner.

'How did it go today?' she asked. 'Find anywhere you liked?'

'Can we stay with you in your new house?' Jamie cut in, looking up from playing with his toy car. 'Will it have a pool and a playground too?'

Jane shook her head, and then looked across at William, waiting for him to speak.

'Which do you want first, my dear?' he asked Lucinda. 'The good news or the bad news?'

'Oh, God, what's happened?'

'What's the bad news?' Jamie asked. He'd stopped playing and was sitting quite still, looking at his grandfather anxiously.

'Jamie, stop interrupting,' Lucinda scolded irritably, exhausted after her terrible day at D'Aussoire. She glanced surreptitiously at her watch to see how soon she could send him and Daisy to bed. Dinner was still to be cooked, and Julian, who'd promised to help, wasn't yet back from an auction in Hemel Hempstead.

'It's all right,' William said mildly, smiling at Jamie. 'I'm afraid this is awfully boring stuff, old chap, but of course you can come and stay in our new house.'

Lucinda sat upright. 'You've found a house?'

'It's very charming,' Jane said loyally. 'It's on the outskirts of Shere, in Surrey, where William used to stay as a boy, and it's got five bedrooms, so you must all come and stay.'

'It's a lovely house,' William agreed. 'Built in the eighteenth century, of white stucco which makes it look light and bright, with lots of big windows and a very pretty garden, not big, but big enough. Easy to maintain, you know, which is important as dear old Jacques won't be coming with us.'

'Is that the bad news?' Daisy asked, her face comically doleful.

William and Jane looked at Lucinda for guidance. How much did you let little people of six and eight know?

'Probably,' Lucinda said cheerfully, getting to her feet. 'Come along, darlings. Bedtime. And as soon as Daddy gets back I'll send him up to read you a story.'

'Why can't you read to us?' Jamie asked, his voice edging towards a whine.

'I have to cook dinner for Granny and Grandpa,' she replied stoutly.

'We'll help . . . we'll help,' they chorused eagerly. 'I can make a salad,' Jamie added. 'Delia lets me.'

'And Delia lets me roll out pastry,' Daisy added proudly.

'I know. You're both very clever, but right now it's time for bed. Kiss Granny and Grandpa goodnight, and one day you can cook lunch for us all, how would that be?'

'Can I make a pie with pastry?' Daisy asked, dragging her doll along the floor after her.

'Any sort of pie you like, darling.'

'I'll make the biggest salad *ever*,' Jamie declared robustly. 'With lettuce and tomatoes and cucumber, and . . . and . . . what else goes into a salad, Mummy? Mummy? Do radishes go into a salad?'

'Sometimes I long for the day when they're older,' Lucinda admitted laughingly, when the children were upstairs, not asleep as yet, but at least in their beds. 'Then I think the time is going too quickly as it is, and I'm missing so much of their childhood, and I don't really want them to grow up at all.'

She had delayed starting dinner in order to open a bottle of wine, which they now sat drinking in the drawing room. Something told her it was going to be a stressful evening and she didn't have to wait long to hear what had happened.

'It's ICC,' William admitted. 'They've gone completely belly up, and the government are not going to bail them out, and there are no rescue packages on the horizon, so I'm afraid, financially, all we'll have is the money from the sale of the château.'

'Oh, I'm so sorry,' Lucinda sympathised, knowing what this meant to them. 'Is there no hope at all?'

He took a gulp of wine and shook his head, finding it difficult to speak at that moment.

'We heard when we returned from the country this afternoon,' Jane explained. 'We'd just made an offer for White Willows and it had been accepted. We had planned to delay exchanging contracts for as long as possible, as we've been doing with the château, but now we've *got* to go ahead, or we won't even be able to buy another house. My only worry now is that the American couple will back out; we've kept them waiting for quite a while.'

'That is a worry,' William agreed, blowing his nose, and gulping some more white wine. 'They could have found another place by now, so I'm going to phone our lawyer in France first thing tomorrow and tell him we're ready to exchange contracts. Then we'll fly home.' He glanced sadly at his wife. 'I'm afraid we're going to have to sell a lot of our furniture, darling. It simply won't fit into White Willows.'

'I'd already realised that,' Jane replied bravely. Maybe, she reflected, the Kernahans would like to buy some of the bigger pieces, like the antique dining table that seated eighteen, unless, of course, they thought it was too *old*.

When Julian got home at last, they were all in the kitchen, Jane sitting at the central table, drinking wine, William leaning against the dresser, whisky glass in hand, while Lucinda prepared hake, smothered with a sprinkling of parsley and chives and double cream, and cooked in a foil wrapping. With it she was doing mashed potatoes, French beans, and for pudding chilled mango with ice cream.

'Getting drunk again?' Julian grinned teasingly, as he put his head round the door.

Lucinda turned to kiss him, her lips brushing his mouth sweetly. 'Hi, Julian. We're all commiserating with each other. Help yourself to a drink.'

He glanced anxiously at his parents. 'What's up?'

Briefly, William told him what had happened.

178

'At least,' Jane said, when he'd finished, 'we shall get to see a great deal more of all of you.'

Julian bent down to kiss her on the cheek. 'I call that very good news,' he said gently.

'Can you lay the table, Julian? Oh! and I promised the children you'd read them a story when you got back.'

'No probs.' He noticed her wine glass by the cooker. 'So what's your news, Bun, that's making you take to the bottle like an alcoholic?'

'Don't even go there,' she said with a warning look. 'You don't want to know. Go and see the children, and when you come down again dinner will be ready.'

'Have you any idea who's responsible?' Julian asked, when they were in bed and Lucinda had filled him in on the D'Aussoire situation.

'It could be any one of five hundred people. The leak came from here not Paris, apparently, and I haven't the faintest idea who's behind it. Meanwhile I, and all the division leaders, are going to have to create huge bad feeling by nosing around, questioning the staff.'

'But you're still going to be bringing out Mousseline-de-Soie?'

'I gather we're going to rush it into the stores even sooner than planned. It's too late to bring the advertising forward, but the PR department have been in overdrive all afternoon, trying to get journalists to write about it as soon as possible. Thank God I'm in market research and not in any of the other divisions, where all hell has broken loose.' She plumped up her pillows so they fitted more comfortably into her neck. 'By the way, I'm going down to Bristol on Saturday to deliver the letters and bracelet to Fenella Harrison. I can't get any more time off, so I've got to make it at the weekend which is a damned nuisance, but I want to get it done. This business of Dad's Will is hanging over me like a great dark cloud.'

Julian snuggled closer, putting his arms round her while he tenderly kissed her neck just under her ear, which always drove her crazy.

'The sooner it's over the better,' he whispered, 'and let's hope you'll never have to work again after that.'

'Then I can stay at home and I'll lock you in the house so you can't go out either, and we can make love all day long,' she giggled wickedly.

'I can't wait,' he groaned, pulling her closer.

Lucinda thought she was dreaming for several seconds, as the layers of sleep were peeled away by the incessant ringing of the phone. Then she felt Julian stir in the bed beside her, awakening her fully.

'Who the fuck's ringing at this hour?' he grumbled incredulously, reaching for the phone.

Lucinda peered at the alarm clock on her side of the bed. It was four thirty in the morning. She flopped back onto the pillow, cursing. Then she heard Julian speaking to someone, his voice registering increasing alarm.

179

'Oh, my God! No! That's terrible. What a catastrophe. Jesus, I can hardly believe it!'

She sat upright. What had happened? Had Sarah had an accident? Had Anne tried to commit suicide?

'Oh, *Dad* . . .' Julian was saying. 'I'm so sorry . . .'

Then it must be Jane. 'What's happened?' Lucinda whispered, frightened now.

He cupped his hand over the receiver. 'It's Dad. The château has been gutted by fire.'

'*What?*' Stunned, she lay beside him, trying to take in what this meant. To say that her in-laws, and especially Jane, must be distraught was an understatement. Everything they owned in the world was in that château. A lifetime of mementos and records of Julian's grandparents and great-grandparents, as well as forty years of marriage between William and Jane. Lucinda recalled the albums of photographs of Julian at every stage of his life from birth to the family snapshots taken recently, with Jamie and Daisy in the new playground William had built them. Souvenirs of a life shared with love and laughter, reduced to ashes.

Lucinda realised tears were sliding down her cheeks. The château was gone and she wondered what on earth her in-laws were going to do now? William had only said that evening that a lot of the furniture would have to be sold . . . now there was probably no furniture to sell. And no château for the dreaded Kernahans to move into, either. It was a tragic end to an era that had been filled with the gracious lifestyle of a bygone age.

She heard Julian say goodbye to his father before adding: 'See you later.'

'What's happening?' she asked, raising herself onto her elbow.

He rubbed his face with his hands in a washing gesture before lying down again beside her. 'Dad just got a call from Jacques to tell him that fire broke out in the château a few hours ago, and there's practically nothing left standing except for the walls and the chimneybreasts. Mum and Dad are flying back tomorrow and I said I'd go with them. Oh, God, what a disaster. Dad was told the roof fell in, apparently, bringing down the staircase. Everything's gone, Bun. Everything.' His voice broke.

Lucinda put her arms round him and held him close. 'I'm so sorry, sweetheart. No one's hurt, though?'

He shook his head. 'Jacques noticed smoke coming from one of the upper windows, just as he was finishing his supper. He raised the alarm, but the château is so isloated, you know, that by the time the fire brigade arrived the fire had already taken hold. Poor old Jacques. Dad said he was practically hysterical when he rang them.'

'But how did it start? No one's staying in the place at the moment, are they?'

'No, no one. God, what are my parents going to do? They really have lost everything now.'

'But they're insured, aren't they?'

180

'That's true, but there are some things that can't be replaced by all the money in the world.'

They lay, side by side, in silent troubled contemplation. Julian had been nineteen and about to go to Newcastle University when his parents had moved from Hampshire to the Dordogne. From then on he'd spent most of his vacations at the château, revelling in the warmth of the sun, the comfortable beauty of the house, and the relaxed atmosphere which pervaded every room, like a fragrance.

When he got engaged to Lucinda, he took her there immediately, because he wanted her to know and love it as much as he did. His parents had tactfully flown to Paris for that first weekend, leaving them to enjoy it on their own.

Now they had both come to regard it as a second home, as had Jamie and Daisy. Holidays in the Dordogne were the highlight of their year.

This is more painful, Lucinda was reflecting silently as she held Julian's hand, than the château's being sold. She could hardly bear to think how Jane must be feeling at this moment.

'Delia, I have the most enormous favour to ask you,' Lucinda said the next morning. They were getting breakfast ready between them and the children were still upstairs.

'Right, ask away,' Delia replied calmly.

Lucinda lowered her voice. 'Julian has to fly to France today with his parents because their home has been gutted by fire, but I don't want the children to know yet, because they're only going to get upset.'

'Oh, Lord! What happened?'

'We don't know yet. I'm just going to tell them Daddy's going away on business for a few days, but the thing is,' Lucinda took a deep breath, bracing herself to ask the favour, 'I've got to go to Bristol for the day on Saturday, and I wondered if you could possibly switch your weekend off, to next weekend, so you could stay and look after the children? I know it's an imposition, but . . .'

Delia grinned. 'That's OK. Actually it would suit me better, because Chris is going to a football match and you know how much I love football,' she joked. 'Maybe Jamie and Daisy would like to go to the Little Angel Theatre in Islington.'

Lucinda smiled with relief. 'Delia, you're a saint. An absolute angel. They love puppet shows and I'll give you extra money so you can take them out to lunch, too.'

'Thanks.' Delia beamed. 'So what's in Bristol? D'Aussoire have a factory there, don't they?'

'Yup,' Lucinda replied non-committally. It was true; they had a packaging factory twenty miles away at Portishead. But that wasn't where she was going.

* * *

181

'Everything OK, Tom?' Susan asked gently. He'd been very quiet recently, and rather morose.

'I'm fine.' His expression was weary as he sat slumped in front of the TV in her tiny living room and it was obvious he didn't want to talk.

'You don't look fine.' She reached out to take his hand. 'What's on your mind? Something is, I can tell.'

'No, no really. I'm fine.'

Susan eyed him anxiously. Was it his father's memorial service that had upset him? She racked her brains, trying to remember when he'd reverted to being subdued and diffident, but she couldn't place the exact moment. He'd seemed to withdraw from her gradually in the past week or so, almost as if he were apologising for his existence, but why? What had he to apologise for? He was contributing generously to the housekeeping, he paid most of the bills, he'd bought toys for the boys; it wasn't as if she was keeping him, and yet he seemed filled with humility.

It made her feel uncomfortable and for the first time she no longer felt at ease with him.

'Can I get you anything?' she asked. 'A cup of tea? Coffee?'

Tom shook his head, and smiled wanly. 'No, thanks. I might go up to bed in a minute.'

Susan rose from her chair and went to kneel at his feet, her arms round his waist, her expression earnest as she looked up at him. 'Tom, I've known you long enough to know when something's wrong. If you're not worried about something, then you're ill. And if you're ill I'm going to take you to a doctor.'

His eyes widened in surprise. 'I'm not ill, Susan. There's nothing wrong with me.'

'Are you sure? You would tell me if there was, wouldn't you?'

He spoke stiffly. 'I'm perfectly all right.'

She got to her feet again and turned away from him to hide the hurt she felt. 'Then is there something wrong with me?'

'Of course not.'

She turned sharply to look into his eyes to see whether he was just being polite or not, but she couldn't tell. He had that bleak faraway look he'd had when she'd first seen him buying sad little portions for one in Waitrose; a veiled gaze that told her nothing. It was as if he'd distanced himself from her when only a short time ago they'd seemed so close.

'I'm going to have a bath,' she said shortly. Upstairs, she looked at her naked body in the bathroom mirror, and her depression increased. Tom might not be Tom Cruise, but he had a good physique when he didn't stoop, nice dark hair, clear olive skin and very kind grey eyes. He was also only thirty-seven and a young looking thirty-seven at that. She was forty-one and as she examined herself in the looking glass, every line of her body betrayed her age. Her breasts, once high, rounded and voluptuous, had dropped and sagged. Her once flat stomach was ridged with stretch marks. Her thighs had cellulite and her upper arms were flabby. She turned away from the mirror in disgust, hating her body, hating herself. How in God's name could she compete with the sort of woman Tom should have as a girlfriend? He must secretly long for the smooth firm flesh of a young woman in her middle twenties. A woman with no inconvenient past, no children, no baggage of any sort. Just her gorgeous self to offer him.

No wonder he was withdrawn and depressed, she thought wretchedly. He'd seen the sort of groomed and glamorous woman Harry had been able to attract. He only had to look at his sister to see a perfect example of brains, beauty and charm.

Beside them she lacked looks, education, culture and elegance. She was the daughter of a builder, an unmarried mother with a very ordinary job. How could she even begin to compete?

When he came to bed an hour later, she pretended to be asleep. She'd remembered how he'd grown quiet and estranged even before Miles's memorial service, so the problem must lie with her. And if that was the case, she was going to have to get him out of her life, for his own sake, because he was far too kind a man to do it of his own accord.

'I know you said I needn't but I wish I was going with you to Bristol,' Carina said regretfully, on the phone the next evening. 'But Alex insists we go to Scotland at the weekend, and with things being so tricky between us I don't want to give him an excuse to be with *her*.'

'You're sure he's having an affair?' Lucinda asked, and then wondered why she'd said that. Of course Alex was having an affair; he was that sort of man. She remembered how he'd kept looking at Paula that night.

'He's having an affair all right,' Carina replied bitterly. 'I just hope that if I sit tight it'll pass, and he'll get bored with her. A seventeen-year-old bimbo in his office! Christ, what a cliché! Why couldn't it have been someone interesting, if he had to have an affair in the first place? Like a movie star? Or a Member of Parliament? Why do men always have to have affairs with their secretaries, for God's sake?'

'It's the close proximity that does it,' Lucinda replied. 'Like women often have affairs with their driving instructors.'

'Do they?' Carina sounded interested. 'My driving instructor was an awful old goat. I'd have had to be beyond desperate to have slept with him.'

'There is a certain intimacy within the close confines of a car though, isn't there?'

'Maybe. Why, did you have a thing with your driving instructor?'

'Of course I didn't. I was married to Julian by the time I got round to learning to drive.' Lucinda laughed.

'So? Married women do have affairs as well as married men, you know.'

'Some married women perhaps, but I couldn't. I'd never be able to handle the deception. I can't even keep a tiny secret, like the cost of a pair of shoes, from Julian.' She giggled.

Carina's laugh was slightly brittle. 'You'd be hopeless if you had a lover, then,' she said lightly.

Later that evening, Julian rang.

'How are you? What's happening?' Lucinda asked anxiously. She'd been trying to get hold of him all day, but the phone at the château, not surprisingly, was unattainable and his mobile was switched off.

'Sorry, Bun,' he said apologetically. 'God knows how, but I lost my mobile at Heathrow. I'm ringing from the local *chambre d'hôte* where we're staying.'

'So . . . how bad is it?'

'The good news is that Jacques and his family and some of the locals managed to rescue most of the valuable stuff from the ground floor of the château before the fire took hold. When we arrived we found paintings, the silver, some of the antique furniture and Mum's Chippendale mirror on the lawn. Thank Christ it wasn't raining. We've managed to store it all in one of the barns for the time being while Mum and Dad decide what to do.'

'And the château itself . . .?'

'Gone. Gutted. Nothing but the walls are left standing. It's the most heartbreaking sight you've ever seen. When one remembers what it was like . . . the only consolation is that no one was hurt. Thank God Mum and Dad weren't here. The fire experts say they'd have died from smoke inhalation before anyone even knew the fire had started.'

'Oh, Julian.' Lucinda felt quite sick with horror. 'How did it start, anyway?'

'At the moment they believe it started in the linen cupboard on the top floor, but they're not sure how.'

'God, how awful. How's your mother taking it?'

Julian gave a little sigh. 'In a strange way she seems quite resigned. Especially as the best stuff was removed in time. She loved the place so much that I think she feels it is more fitting that it's been destroyed by fire, rather than have someone else live in it.'

'Really?' Her mother-in-law must have loved it a lot to be so dog-in-the-manger, Lucinda reflected with sudden understanding. 'How long are you going to be away?'

'A few more days. The insurance assessors are coming down from Paris tomorrow, and there's a lot to sort out. Dad's dead on his feet and they're both deeply shocked, so I have to stay and help.'

'Of course.' They talked for a few minutes longer and Julian gave her the phone number of the *chambre d'hôte*.

'Let me know how you get on with your trip to Bristol.'

'Don't worry, I will. Providing I survive Hitler's mother.'

'I hope you don't expect lunch,' were the words that greeted Lucinda when she arrived at Fenella Harrison's grey stone cottage.

Glad that she'd asked the taxi driver to wait and then take her back to the station . . . 'I'll make it worth your while,' she'd told him earnestly . . .

Lucinda was able to reply with dignity: 'I've already had something to eat on the train, thank you.'

'You'd better come in then, I suppose,' Fenella said ungraciously, her lumbering figure leading the way into a dingy front room. Lucinda had expected it to be exotic, hung with ethnic fabrics, burning candles, crystals on every surface and the smell of incense. She felt quite cheated to discover it was a very ordinary, unprepossessing living room, with cream walls and paintwork, a shabby beige sofa, two upright chairs and a small square table in the window. It had about as much character as a room in a motel, and seemed devoid of any personal touches.

'I've . . . I've brought your letters and the bracelet,' Lucinda began, wondering whether she was supposed to sit on the sagging sofa, or on one of the upright chairs.

'Well, it would have been a waste of your time and mine if you hadn't, wouldn't it?' Fenella countered drily. She was wearing the grey shawl she'd worn at the memorial service, and under it a vast dark blue caftan. Her feet, in sandals, were not at all clean, Lucinda noticed. Suddenly, she wished she'd read some of the letters before coming here today. Her reason for not doing so was because she'd become sickened by the sordidness of her father's life, and by the sexual sordidness she was beginning to realise was all around her. Harry had been screwing Paula for her money. Alex was screwing his secretary for lust. Who would be next to indulge their desires amongst the circle of people she knew? At moments she wondered if anyone ever stayed faithful to anyone else? Would it . . . *could* it even happen to her and Julian? Then she closed her mind quickly, not even wanting to think about it.

'Here they are,' she said, handing over the letters. Her only reason for wishing she had read some of them was to try to understand the nature of her father's relationship with this unlikely woman. Could it really have been love? The surprising thing was that, unlike Miranda Warwick's affair with Miles, which had taken place nearly forty years ago when she'd been young and quite pretty, the affair with Fenella had taken place only ten years ago, when she must already have been over fifty, and no contender for a Miss World competition. Of course, Miles would have been sixty-three, and no Romeo either.

Fenella was flicking through her letters with interest, stopping to read certain sections, grunting at others, chucking them down on the table when she'd finished. She looked up at Lucinda and stared at her with piercing eyes from under the frizz of her heavy grey hair.

'You've read them, of course?'

'No, I have not,' Lucinda replied spiritedly, glad now that she hadn't.

'I saved his sanity, you know,' she said in a matter-of-fact voice.

Lucinda looked at her enquiringly.

'With my healing powers, using rose quartz, which symbolises love, and a mixture of other crystals, I gave him back his virility.'

'I don't think I need—'

'You see, it is vital to tap into a divine source, be it Universal Love, God, Light, or Energy. Miles needed to find his spiritual truth. With crystal therapy I restored his balance, spiritual and mental as well as emotional and physical.' As she talked she was stroking the pale yellow crystal hanging on a chain round her neck that she'd worn at the memorial service.

Lucinda nodded because it seemed the polite thing to do.

Fenella continued, hardly pausing for breath: 'In Miles's case, when he came to see me here, I placed a red stone, sometimes a ruby, sometimes a garnet, between his legs, at the base chakra. That helped him greatly. It's so sad for a man when he becomes impotent. Sex had always meant so much to him.'

Lucinda dived hurriedly into her shoulder bag. 'I can't stay because I've got a taxi waiting, but here is the aquamarine bracelet.' She placed the long slim leather case, and the receipt, on the table between them and rose to leave.

Fenella glared at her. 'Sit down again. You need my help, too. Your meridians are fearfully blocked. Aren't you tired all the time? You need to be stimulated by having crystals placed on strategic points around your body. Yin meridians, which are feminine, flow upwards on a path from Earth to Heaven along which *chi* passes. With Miles, of course, I made him practise the masculine Yang principles, where the flow is downwards from Heaven to Earth.' She got slowly to her feet, ignoring the bracelet, although she scribbled a signature on the receipt 'Come with me.'

'I really have to go,' Lucinda insisted. 'The taxi . . .' She was feeling trapped in this grim little house, with an obsessive woman who wouldn't stop talking. But Fenella had gripped her elbow, and with great strength for an older woman was steering her through the doorway, across the hall and into the room opposite.

'I want you to see something,' she said commandingly.

Lucinda realised instantly that this was a very different room from the bland living room. The curtains were drawn and there was just one dim light in the corner. A high treatment bed stood in the middle of the floor, and arranged on shelves around the walls were hundreds of crystals. Some glittered, some were dull, and they featured every shade under the rainbow.

'How interesting,' Lucinda said politely, fearing now that Fenella would insist on 'treating' her.

'It's more than interesting,' Fenella snapped angrily. 'You seem to be working on entirely materialistic levels. Miles would have been very disappointed in you.'

'He was disappointed in all his children,' Lucinda retorted acidly.

'That's because none of you looked *beyond*. He told me all about you, you know, and Tom and Harry. You don't seem to understand how much there was to your father. He had a quicksilver brain. An acute intellect. But most of all he had an *open mind*. Something I can see you don't have. Let me tell you something, Lucinda. I met Miles at a lecture on the Holistic Approach to

Health, ten years ago. I was studying crystal therapy for healing at the time and Miles latched onto me, because he was fascinated by something new. We were lovers for several years and he became my inspiration, and I was an imspiration to him. We were two souls in search of the truth. I helped him become a man again, with these . . .' She threw her massive arms out wide, indicating the crystals, as they glittered and glowed in haphazard profusion.

'Miles will always be with me,' she continued. 'Even after I'm dead we will remain in the atmosphere, held together by the harmony we created with the crystals.'

Lucinda said nothing, thinking that, after all, this was a rather sad woman.

'None of you understood Miles,' Fenella said angrily. Then she turned and stomped out of the room and into the hall where she flung open the front door. 'Off you go then. Your taxi hasn't turned into a pumpkin.'

Lucinda started, staring at her. 'Why did you say that?'

'Say what?'

'Pumpkin. Why did you mention pumpkin?'

Fenella stepped out onto her front door step, and her mass of curling, frizzy grey hair rose and lifted in the breeze like a vast halo around her head.

'You have a lot of negativity and I really should insist on treating you, but you're obviously not receptive,' she said severely. 'Goodbye.' Then she turned and went back into her cottage, and slammed the front door behind her.

'And the old cow didn't even thank me for going all that way,' Lucinda said indignantly, when Carina phoned her from Scotland that evening to find out how she'd got on.

'What a bitch! Did she like the bracelet?'

'She didn't even look at it. My God, Dad was mixed up with some strange women, wasn't he? And they're all so different.'

'I suppose each of them appealed to a different facet of his personality,' Carina replied thoughtfully. 'And you say she treated him for impotence?'

'Yes. A bit odd for a serial seducer, don't you think? I honestly don't know whether to believe a word she says or not.'

'And all this happened ten years ago?'

'Ten or eleven years ago, yeah.' Lucinda spoke with weariness. On the scale of Need to Know, the private details of her father's sexual performance came bottom of her list. 'Anyway, thank God it's over and I never need to see her again. How's your weekend going?'

Carina's voice took on a hard edge. 'Alex and the others have been fishing all day. I didn't go because I woke up with a stinking headache.'

'Do you feel better now?'

'Yes. I've been lazing about being waited on hand and foot by our hostess's excellent butler, and now I'm about to have a shower and change for dinner. There are eighteen of us in this houseparty, so I don't have to talk to Alex which is a relief.'

'Oh, Carina, it sounds miserable.'

187

'Believe me, lots of wine softens the edges. I hope that if I hang in there he'll get bored with his little tart, because I don't really want a divorce. I wouldn't be nearly so well off, you see. My standard of living would go down.'

Lucinda felt shocked. She'd been accused of materialism by Fenella, but she was a non-starter compared to her friend.

'It would be very bad for the children, too, Carina,' she said pointedly.

'Better for the children than living in a bad atmosphere. However,' Carina continued brightly, 'I don't suppose it'll come to that. There are times when husbands have to stray and my remedy for that is to take myself shopping.'

When she'd finally hung up, Lucinda realised she'd seen an entirely different side to Carina. Money and what it could buy obviously meant a great deal more to her friend than it did to her. Unless she was putting on an act, she seemed more worried about the financial outcome of Alex's liaison than about the emotional.

The next morning, as it was Sunday, Lucinda slipped into her alter ego, dressing as she did at weekends in peasant blouses and ankle-length cotton skirts, flat shoes, and letting her hair flow loose, with tendrils falling around her un-made-up face. This was in such contrast to the power suits, high heels and immaculate make-up that were necessary for work that the first weekend Delia had been with them she'd hardly recognised her. Julian called it her 'hippy look', aware that she needed to feel she was a domesticated wife and mother at heart, even if she was forced to be the professional businesswoman during the week.

Even her manner became dreamy and vague as she drifted around the kitchen, scattering herbs into the various dishes she was cooking, listening to Mahler's symphonies on the CD player, and making endless attempts to cuddle Jamie and Daisy, who after a few moments' submission wriggled out of her arms and rushed back to playing.

It was pouring with rain, so she allowed them to break the usual rules of only eating in the kitchen or dining room by setting up a picnic, on a rug, in the middle of the drawing room, so they could watch cartoons.

After delighted screams of 'Cool' and 'Wicked' they'd just settled down to sausages on sticks, miniature pizzas and bacon-flavoured crisps when the front door bell rang.

'Blast!' she exclaimed, annoyed. 'Who on earth can that be?'

'Blast!' echoed Daisy, scrambling to her feet.

It was Harry, about the last person she wanted to see on the one day she could relax with the children.

'Hi, sis! Thought I'd drop in for a spot of Sunday lunch as I was in the neighbourhood.' He strode past her into the hall and sniffed the air hopefully. 'How's everyone?'

'Julian's in France with his parents because their house has been burnt to the ground, Delia is upstairs, the children and I are having a picnic, and there *is* no "Sunday lunch". What are you doing in the neighbourhood, anyway?

It's miles from your usual stamping ground.'

'My, we are being ratty,' he remarked, wandering into the drawing room. 'Hello, kids! I hope you're more pleased to see me than your mother.'

'Hello, Uncle Harry,' they chorused politely, ruining the effect by adding: 'There isn't any lunch for you. Mummy only made enough for us.'

Harry did his best to hide his crestfallen expression. 'Well then, a nice glass of Burgundy wouldn't go amiss,' he said brightly. 'And maybe a sandwich, Luce?' The little boy lost expression was nailed to his face as he gazed at his sister.

Lucinda gave an exasperated sigh. 'It's your own fault, Harry. If you'd said you were coming I'd have fixed something, but I'm exhausted after yesterday, and . . . erm . . .' Too late she remembered she mustn't mention her trip to Bristol in front of her brother.

But he hadn't missed her sudden hesitation and instinctively he knew she was hiding something. 'So what happened yesterday?' he asked casually.

'Mummy went to Bristol to see someone,' Jamie piped up. 'When Carina rang in the evening Mummy said the woman was an old cow.'

There were moments, Lucinda had to admit to herself, when she could happily have strangled her children.

Harry looked at her sharply. 'Who did you go to see in Bristol?'

Without looking at him Lucinda replied loftily, 'You know D' Aussoire have a packaging factory at Portishead? I just had to nip down on a bit of business.'

He frowned and looked doubtful. 'On a Saturday?'

'We have a problem as a result of industrial espionage,' she said quickly. 'I needed to sort something out.'

Harry was immediately distracted and fascinated, as she knew he would be, at the mention of any sort of scam. Briefly she told him what had happened. It would be public knowledge within days, anyway, so she didn't feel she was being disloyal to the company. Then she made him a ham and salad sandwich, fetched a bottle of wine from Julian's 'cellar', and returned to her position on the floor with the children.

After a while, Jamie and Daisy wanted to play upstairs and, with a sinking heart, Lucinda had to let them go. She'd begun to suspect why Harry had come to see her, and it wasn't long before she realised she was right.

Fourteen

'It's obvious,' Harry said smoothly, 'that Dad had a couple of mistresses, and that they have something to do with the papers he left you. Why have you never let me see them? That stuff about their being publishers' contracts or notes for his lectures is bollocks and you know it.'

'They're confidential,' Lucinda said stubbornly. 'If he'd wanted the world to know about them he'd have left them to you. As it is he left you fifty thousand pounds, so I don't know why you're complaining.'

Harry's eyes narrowed. 'It's *because* he left Tom and me fifty thou and he didn't leave you anything that I'm sure the papers are valuable, in lieu of leaving you actual money.'

'So what are you complaining about? Let's suppose they're worth fifty thousand. And you're already getting the same amount . . . what's your problem?'

'The secrecy surrounding them makes me feel they're probably worth a lot more than that.'

Lucinda gave a short laugh. 'The fact is, Harry, they're more likely to be worth a couple of thousand at the most.' And that's the truth of it, she thought. If I end up with a piece of jewellery that in fact may only be worth a thousand or two, which is more than likely, then Harry's quids in and I'm the loser.

'Shall we put it to the test?' Harry asked nastily.

She frowned. 'What are you talking about?'

'If you don't show me, or even tell me, what those papers are, I'm going to tell Mum about the two women who turned up at Dad's memorial service, women he'd obviously had an affair with judging by the panic on your face, and what they were shouting at each other. I bet those so called "papers" are something to do with them, aren't they?'

Lucinda's face was a sickly shade of pale. 'You wouldn't dare! You wouldn't hurt Mum like that, after all she's been through.'

'Not for a few thousand pounds right now, I wouldn't,' he retorted swiftly.

She felt enraged. 'Why should Julian and I work ourselves to death to make a living when you do fuck all, and then have the cheek to ask me for money.'

'I'm in debt.'

'So you're in debt! That's not my problem. If you got a proper job and didn't try to keep up with heiresses like Paula, you wouldn't be in debt.'

'Don't talk to me about that bitch. Thanks to her, I'm homeless, and having to live with Mum.'

'You haven't asked Mum for money, have you?' she asked, appalled.

'No, of course I haven't,' Harry retorted, looking away. 'But I'll tell her about those women unless you let me have some cash now.'

'That's blackmail.'

'Call it what you like.' He jumped to his feet and went over to the writing case. It was unlocked. And empty.

He rounded on her furiously, and she wished Julian was at home. 'I'm losing patience, Lou.'

'There's nothing to *tell*.'

'You're lying. I know you're lying. Why did you get Carina to take that hysterical Italian off your hands after the service? Why did you take that great gypsy woman into a side room at the reception? You're up to something, Lucinda. And unless you help me out now, I'll tell Mum that Dad had mistresses and that you know all about them. That they're friends of yours.'

'You wouldn't!' But the look in his eyes told her he would.

'Try me,' he challenged recklessly. 'The bank is about to foreclose on my overdraft, Visa and Amex are about to sue me, and I've already got out of Mum all her spare cash, until probate is granted. I'm up against the wall and I'm desperate.' Harry was sweating now and the air between them was crackling with animosity.

She stared at him coldly, saying nothing.

He rose, hands deep in his trouser pockets, and started pacing up and down the room.

'I've had my life screwed up from the beginning,' he said, almost as if he were speaking to himself. 'Dad was a monster, and Mum was, and still is, a doormat. Everyone in my life has let me down, and Paula has been the worst of them all.'

'What did you expect? Paula obviously realised you were only interested in her money,' Lucinda pointed out.

'There was no reason for her to steal my idea. When she knew how desperately I wanted to get my scheme off the ground, and it would have been a good investment for her, no kidding, what does she go and do?' he demanded, swinging round to face her aggressively.

'What does she do?'

'She pinches my idea in its entirety, changes the name and then sets up a company of her own with offices and everything. Now it's her company and I'm left out in the cold.' Harry's lower lip started to tremble and she was fleetingly reminded of Jamie; that was how he looked when someone had broken his favourite toy. But then she remembered that Harry wasn't a child of eight. He was thirty-four and prepared to blackmail her. Her heart hardened. This was no time for sentimentality. Harry was rotten, through and through, but their mother must be protected whatever it cost.

Reaching for her handbag, she pulled out her cheque book. 'I'm giving you a thousand pounds, Harry, of my own hard-earned money which you don't deserve, which I hate giving you and am doing so against my better judgement, but I don't want Mum to get hurt.' She scribbled rapidly with her ballpoint. Then she looked up at him as she handed him the cheque. 'You're scum, Harry. I'm ashamed to have a brother who could sink so low. Take this but don't you dare come back for more, and don't you dare say anything to Mum, *ever*. If you do I shall inform the police; blackmailing is a criminal offence, in case you didn't know.'

Then she got to her feet, feeling sick and tired. 'Now get out,' she said, pointing to the door.

As she'd expected, everyone at D'Aussoire was in a stressed state the next morning. The enormity of what had happened had sunk in over the weekend and now people were whispering in corners, eyeing each other suspiciously, and getting paranoid that they might be thought to be guilty.

Lucinda still hadn't come up with any ideas about the members of her own team, but she was 90 per cent certain none of them were involved. For one thing they were only responsible for collating the information collected by the field research agencies. Whoever had sold the formula of Mousseline-de-Soie to Xanthe would have had to have access to every aspect of the product, and that meant someone in a high position, most likely one of the directors. Who else, she reasoned, as she studied the details of the people in her division, would have known details of the formula, the design, the packaging, and the advertising campaign, in order to be able to sell the whole package to their rivals?

This was an inside job and she was sure Marc Leblanc was going to have to look amongst his co-directors to find the culprit. Nevertheless, the friendly atmosphere had changed. Distrust stalked the aisles between the desks. Everyone was sure someone else was watching them over their shoulder.

At lunchtime, Julian phoned from France.

'I'm not going to be able to leave here today, after all,' he told her regretfully. 'Something really awful's happened.'

'What is it?' Her first thought was that Jane, unable to bear the grief of losing the château, had . . . Oh, God! 'What's happened?'

'Dad has been arrested by the *gendarmerie*, and so has Jacques.'

'*What*! How could they be?' she asked stupidly.

He sounded distressed. 'The insurance company are saying the fire was started deliberately. They've accused Dad and Jacques of arson. They've found out Dad lost all his money in ICC and that's why he was selling the château, and they think he got Jacques to torch it for him, while he was away in London, providing himself with a perfect alibi.'

'Oh, my God! But your father can prove that's not true, can't he? That's a terrible accusation.'

'Until the authorities discover exactly how the fire started, there's no proof Jacques didn't do it at Dad's behest.'

'Oh, that poor old man. He must be so scared, and your poor dad, too. What an absolute nightmare. Surely no one will believe the place was destroyed on purpose?'

'The insurance company are only too happy to believe it if it saves them shelling out several hundred thousand pounds.'

Suddenly Lucinda was struck by another devastating thought. 'Then that means, apart from everything else, that if the insurance company won't pay up, your parents have no money at all. No assets, absolutely nothing. They're homeless.'

'Yup.'

'Then they'll have to come and live with us,' she said impulsively. 'Bring them back with you, Julian.'

'Our house is too small, Bun, but it's a sweet thought and I'll tell them. Meanwhile, I have to stay here to try to sort something out. We're still at the *chambre d'hôte* so I'll ring you tonight. Hopefully Dad and Jacques will have been released by then, unless of course they're charged. The trouble is I've no idea how French law works so I'm not sure what the procedure is.'

'Give them my best love and tell them how sorry I am. And come home soon, I miss you, terribly.'

'Miss you too, Bun. Give my love to Jamie and Daisy.'

'Was the playground burnt, too?' Daisy asked, clambering onto Lucinda's knee.

'No, darling, the playground's fine.'

'But it's no use without the house,' Jamie pointed out pragmatically. 'Where would we sleep?'

Daisy's eyes filled with tears. 'Then our bedrooms have burnt, too? Have all the toys been burnt?'

Jamie looked at her scathingly. 'Of course they have, silly. If the house has been burnt, so have all the toys.' Then he looked at his mother, his face suddenly pale. 'Has Grandpa's train set been burnt?'

Lucinda put her arm round him and pulled him close. The day that William had told Jamie he was allowed to play with the beautifully preserved train set he'd had as a boy was one of the happiest days in Jamie's life. He'd stayed by the miniature track, with its signals and little station, and three trains rattling round and round, all day, refusing to go to bed until he'd been promised he could play with it again the next day.

'I'm afraid it's almost certainly gone, sweetheart,' Lucinda told him sadly. 'Jacques and his family managed to save some things, but probably not the train set.'

'Why not?' Jamie exclaimed, bursting noisily into tears. 'I l-loved that train s-set,' he sobbed.

'Oh, my darling . . .' She gathered him up into her arms, and held him on the sofa beside her, while Daisy, still on her lap, decided to burst into tears too. Lucinda rocked them both, knowing that the loss of the toys they'd loved was as devastating to them as the loss of precious artefacts was to her in-laws.

Delia came bouncing in from the kitchen. 'Look what I've got!' she exclaimed, giving Lucinda the shadow of a wink. 'Ice cream with hot chocolate sauce. Your favourite. Now, maybe if you're very good, Mummy will let you eat it in here instead of the kitchen. What do you say, Mummy?'

Lucinda grinned at her. 'You're a star, Delia. And yes, they can both eat it in here, on one condition.'

Jamie and Daisy looked up at her, their tears magically drying up.

'What's that?' Jamie gulped, wiping his nose on the sleeve of his dressing gown.

'That I can have some, too. Can that be arranged, Delia?'

'Oh, I think we can let Mummy have some, don't you?' she agreed, smiling broadly as she hurried back to the kitchen.

Tom was painfully aware that Susan seemed aloof these days, almost as if she didn't want him around any more. It was as he feared and had dreaded since the day Jim had got into the house and beaten him up. Immediately afterwards, when she'd brought him back from the hospital, bruised and battered and badly shaken, it had seemed the most natural thing in the world for him to move in permanently. She'd insisted on looking after him, and in a rush of emotion, because he was desperate to protect her in case Jim came back, he'd gladly agreed. Within a week he'd moved out of his miserable flat, bringing his possessions with him. But then it began to dawn on him, with sickening clarity, that if Jim *did* come back, he'd be no more able to protect Susan than he'd been the first time. He'd been kidding himself into believing he was able to look after her if anything happened.

The fact was, he'd failed her over his handling of her ex-lover, making her realise she was stuck with a weakling who couldn't even stand up for himself.

In spite of his confident manner at his father's memorial service, when he didn't want to let his family down, all his former low self-esteem had risen to the surface again, like floating wreckage in a river, and from that moment on he saw himself through Susan's eyes, and hated what he saw. He was spineless, a failure, a wash-out, just as his father had said.

'You'll never amount to anything,' Miles had frequently told him, taunting him about his poor exam results, his lack of prowess on the playing fields, his inability even to hold an intellectual conversation.

And now Susan had realised this for herself and she was no doubt disappointed and disillusioned. He ought to leave her, of course, instead of being another millstone round her neck, but right now he didn't have the strength. So was he going to wait until she told him to go, he asked himself, as he sat at his dreary desk in his dreary office, knowing his father had been right all along. He didn't amount to anything and he never would and Susan deserved better. Much better. She was the most wonderful woman he'd ever met, but he must let her get on with her life, give her the opportunity to find a real man, who was strong and successful, who would look after her; the question was . . . when would he find the strength to leave?

* * *

With Julian away, Lucinda decided to set about trying to trace Renée Hartman. She also wanted to read 'Pumpkin's' letters. In the past couple of days she'd thought a lot about Miranda's comment about her taxi turning into a pumpkin, and she realised she'd over-reacted, that of course Miranda had been referring to the Cinderella story. But maybe, just maybe, 'Pumpkin's' letters would reveal some little detail like the name of a mutual friend, or a place where they'd met, or *something* that would be a clue as to who she was.

Once the children were in bed, and Delia had gone to the cinema with her boyfriend, Lucinda made herself some coffee and then settled down by the drawing-room phone. Renée's old address, 67, The Avenue, Wainsley, York, was printed at the top of her writing paper and below it, a phone number. The area code looked out of date, and as the letters were all written in 1973 it no doubt was. Without wasting time she rang 192, and a moment later was given the more recent area code for York: 01904.

With trembling hands she dialled the number, composing in her mind what she'd say when she got through. A man answered.

'I'd like to speak to Renée Hartman, please,' she said as confidently as she could.

'Who?'

'Renée Hartman?'

He sounded puzzled. 'There's no one here of that name.'

'Is that 67, The Avenue, Wainsley?'

'That's right.'

'Then I suppose . . . how long have you lived there?'

The man hummed and hawed for a few moments before finally saying, 'We moved here in 1973, but I've never heard of a Renée Hartman.'

'Then you couldn't have bought it from her,' Lucy said in disappointment.

'Let me see now, hang on a minute . . . Muriel?'

She could hear voices in the background engaged in a lively discussion, then the man said: 'Are you still there? My wife says we bought the house from a couple called Derwent.'

'I see. I'm sorry to be such a nuisance, but have you any idea where they moved to?' She was thinking that perhaps Renée's married name was Derwent and that she and her husband had sold 67, The Avenue.

He was off again. 'Muriel?' he bellowed once more. 'Do you remember where the Derwents moved to? No, no, it wasn't Colchester. But it was somewhere in the south.' There was more animated talking in the background.

'Sorry about that,' he said, coming back on the line, 'but we're not sure. My wife thinks they went to Colchester, but I think it was more like Kent.'

Thanking him again, she hung up. She'd realised there was no point in pursuing a Mrs Derwent, because even if Renée had married after her affair with Miles, why would she give her name at the memorial service as Hartman?

So now what? Apart from putting another advertisement in the newspapers and hoping her mother had never heard of Renée, what could she do? She didn't come under the category of a missing person so those outlets were useless, and as for looking her up in an electoral roll, which one? Where would she start?

Dispiritedly, she put Renée's letters to one side, and moments later found herself immersed in 'Pumpkin's' warm and loving prose.

Beloved one, I am missing you more than words can say, and longing for your return after your trip. To hold you in my arms again will be sheer heaven. How I wish we could spend just one night together, instead of the snatched secret rendezvous . . .

I'm desperate to see you, my dearest love, soul of my soul, heart of my heart. When we are apart I feel I'm only half a person, but oh God, you've no idea how much I love you and need you . . .

Lucinda put the letters down, too embarrassed to read on. Her father, for God's sake, was the recipient of this purple passion, and she wished she'd resisted her curiosity and left them in the sweater drawer. Or had he wanted her to read them? But what sort of a man did it make him if that were so? He could so easily have put each batch in a sealed envelope with the name on it, and she would have been none the wiser about the contents.

And then, with horrid clarity, she remembered her father chanting nastily to her when she'd been about four: 'Curiosity killed the cat!' because he'd found her eavesdropping on a conversation between Tom and Harry about her being too young to go to a pantomime with them.

So was this her punishment? Did he guess she'd be tempted to read letters that would sicken and embarrass her? Had he left them unsealed on purpose, to teach her a lesson?

Without actually reading any more, she skimmed the pages for a name or a place that would provide a clue, but there were none. The whole tenor of the letters was of passionate love with the accent on sex. Whoever 'Pumpkin' was, Lucinda reflected, she certainly had a high libido.

'I'm stuck,' Lucinda told Carina later that evening on the phone. 'I've got no idea how to trace Renée Hartman, or find out who the hell "Pumpkin" is.'

'So you don't think "Pumpkin" is Paula Maxwell?' Carina sounded disappointed.

'No, I'm sure she's not. That was just me clutching at straws. But how do I find this Renée woman?'

'All I can suggest is that you go to York, and try to trace her from there. She must have had friends in York who have kept in touch. She must have banked there. Used an estate agent? There must be people in the town who remember her.'

'Hang on a minute, Carina . . .' Something wasn't adding up but she couldn't put her finger on what it was. She reached for Renée's bundle of letters again. Unlike 'Pumpkin' she had dated them very precisely, and they'd all been written in 1973. And yet the man she'd spoken to on the phone had said he and his wife had moved into 67, The Avenue, in 1973. Lucinda did a quick calculation. So had Renée lived with the Derwents? And if so, who were they and where had they gone?

'What are you doing?' She heard Carina's voice in her ear.

'Sorry, honey. I'm going to trace the Derwents. They will lead me to Renée.'

'Are you going to share your reasons with me for doing this? Or is it a private matter?' Carina joked lightly.

Briefly, Lucinda explained. 'There's only one snag,' she added irritably.

'What's that?'

'How am I going to get the time off to make all these enquiries up in York? God, I feel like a prisoner at the moment. There's so much I want to do, and I can't get away from work to do it.'

There was a moment's silence. 'I could do the spade work for you. I'd quite like to have something to do; it would take my mind off Alex and his bloody love affair.'

'Oh, Carina! Here am I going on about these wretched women when you've got so much on your plate,' Lucinda said apologetically. 'Honestly, don't worry. I'll find the time—'

'I mean it, darling,' Carina cut in. 'Truly. Let me go up to York for a couple of days, so I can scout around and find out what I can.'

'Really? You wouldn't mind? God, I'd be so grateful.'

'No problems. God knows, with Tara and Charles away at camp, there's only Michael, so I'm not pushed for time.'

'Thanks, you're an angel.'

'Is that you, Lucinda?'

Anne had never really learned that Lucinda did not like having personal calls at the office unless it was an emergency. It set a bad example to the rest of the staff and was generally frowned upon by senior management.

'Hello, Mum,' she replied, her voice low, swivelling her chair round so the others wouldn't hear.

'What's Harry up to, dear? Have you any idea.?'

Fear squeezed Lucinda's heart. 'I've no idea, Mum. Why? What's he been doing?'

'He keeps asking me if I know what papers Daddy left you. I told him you'd said they were just old documents and contracts but he seems to think you're hiding something.'

Lucinda flushed with anger. 'That mischief-making little bugger!' she whispered furiously. 'He's so afraid I've been left more than he has, he'll say anything.'

'There's no need to swear, dear,' Anne told her reprovingly. 'I told Harry it was nothing to do with him, but he said you were acting suspiciously—'

'I was *what*? I'll kill him! He's just out to make trouble. Pay no attention,

Mum. And don't worry. I've got to go now, but shall I pop in and see you after work this evening?'

'I'm having dinner with Granny, actually.'

'Then I'll give her a ring and ask if I can drop in to see you both.'

'That would be nice. There's one other thing, dear. Harry is really trying to persuade me to sell this house as soon as probate has been granted. He says, through contacts of his, he can get a really good price, and if we cut out the agents I'll make more money.'

Were there no depths to which Harry would not sink, Lucinda thought. Aloud she said, 'Mum, only sell if you want to. You like the house and it's entirely up to you, but whatever you decide, don't let Harry sell it for you. It's essential you use proper estate agents, otherwise you have no comeback if anything goes wrong.'

'I suppose you're right, dear,' Anne agreed vaguely.

'Granny? It's me.'

'Lucinda darling! I haven't heard from you for ages. How are you?'

'I'm fine. I'm sorry I haven't been in touch but life has been more than chaotic. I'll tell you all about it when I see you. Listen, Mum says she's having dinner with you this evening; is it a dinner party or Mum on her own?'

'Oh, on her own, sweetheart. You know how she hates any sort of party.'

'That's what I thought. I wondered if I could drop in to see you both, but could I arrive first so we can talk?'

'A very good idea. She's coming at seven thirty.'

'Cool. Can I come at about six thirty? I've got so much to tell you.'

'That would be wonderful, darling. And you'll stay for supper, won't you? And have Julian join us, too?'

'Julian's still in France with his parents, so I'm on my own.'

'Then you'll stay?'

In the nicest possible way Lucinda realised it was like a royal command, rather than a mere invitation. 'Of course I'll stay,' she rejoined stoutly. 'I can't wait.'

As Lucinda swung her chair back so that she faced her desk, she was aware of Alain Loubet standing looking down at her.

'Lucinda,' he said in his broken English, 'you seem very busy? Are you helping us to find the person who sold out to Xanthe? Or are you conducting your own affairs in our time?' There was a steely glint in his eyes, magnified by his glasses, and she realised he wasn't joking.

'I'm sorry, Alain,' she said, blushing and deciding to make a clean breast of it. 'Since my father died there have been a lot of problems in the family. My mother phoned me, worried about something, but I'll make sure it doesn't happen again.'

'Please do, Lucinda. We are at D'Aussoire to work, and at the moment we have a very serious situation to address. We need everyone to give it their undivided attention.'

'Yes, of course.'

But Alain had marched off, his beady eyes taking in everything that was happening in the open plan office that filled the ninth floor. Everyone, she noticed, was being careful to look busy. All the directors, as well as Alain, were prowling around these days, snooping and spying. The atmosphere was getting more uncomfortable all the time.

'Darling, how lovely to see you,' Sarah said, welcoming her as always with a hug, a glass of champagne, and an invitation to sit in the most comfortable armchair. Her drawing room smelled of gardenias and there were scented candles in a glass dish filled with polished grey stones.

'Now tell me all the news,' she said, as soon as she'd settled herself on the sofa facing Lucinda. She looked much better than she'd done at the memorial service and this evening she was wearing a smoky blue dress with becoming ropes of pearls round her neck.

Keeping it as brief as she could because she wanted to tell Sarah everything before Anne arrived, Lucinda told her all that had happened, including her trip to Bristol, and Harry's blackmailing activities.

'That's why I phoned you, apart from promising to see Mum tonight if I could. What am I going to do with Harry? He's never sunk as low as this before.'

'The trouble is,' Sarah said wisely, 'he's had a taste of the high life with this woman, Paula, and now she's double-crossed him he's angry, resentful, in debt, and probably missing living like a millionaire as well.'

'That's his problem,' said Lucinda unsympathetically. 'I'll kill him if he tells Mum about Isabelle and Fenella. Little does he know about all the others,' she added, raising her eyes to heaven.

'You shouldn't have given him any money, darling. Blackmailers must never be pandered to. He'll try to get more and more out of you.'

'But what was I to do, Granny? Mum will be distraught if she knows Dad cheated on her for their entire married life.'

'Actually, it's quite a pity that Paula wasn't stupid enough to invest in his idea,' Sarah said, smiling at the thought. 'That would have kept him quiet and taught her a few things about con men.'

They heard the bell ring. Anne had arrived.

'Remember, Granny, if Mum wants to sell the house, tell her she must go to estate agents and not let Harry handle it,' Lucinda said urgently.

'Quite,' Sarah replied fervently.

Lucinda had always believed in telepathy, and was therefore not at all surprised to bump into Paula Maxwell in the street the next day.

'Hello, Lucinda, how nice to see you,' Paula greeted her. 'What are you doing in this area?'

They were standing on a corner of Oxford Circus and Lucinda was on her way to buy a range of cosmetics produced by Xanthe, to check that they hadn't filched any more of D'Aussoire's ideas.

'I'm shopping,' Lucinda said briefly, not wanting to talk to her.

'How is Harry?'

'I'm surprised you're interested,' Lucinda retorted loyally. Harry might be a scoundrel but he was her brother.

Paula's eyes softened and there was a hint of apology in her tone. 'Of course I'm interested,' she said. 'He took everything the wrong way. I've been trying to get hold of him but his mobile seems to be turned off all the time, and I believe your mother's number is ex-directory, isn't it? I don't even know where she lives.'

Lucinda looked at her coolly, saying nothing.

'So could you give him a message when you see him? Could you ask him to get in touch?'

'If I see him,' Lucinda said curtly. 'Now I have to dash.'

'Of course.' Paula smiled graciously. In her high fashion trouser suit, pale blue pashmina and suede boots she did look marvellous, Lucinda admitted grudgingly. But what was it Sarah always said? Fine feathers make fine birds. Put her in a High Street outfit and she'd look no better than anyone else.

As Lucinda sat in the taxi on the way back to the office, a collection of Xanthe products in a smart carrier bag beside her, she tried Harry's mobile, but it was still turned off. Then she tried Anne's number but there was no answer. Her mother was probably out shopping and it was anyone's guess where Harry was. Probably chatting up someone in a pub as he planned another scam.

On impulse, she decided to ring Tom. Maybe he could talk to Harry, knock some sense into his head, and make him see how cruel it was to cause trouble with Anne.

Garson & Co was a far more laid back business than D'Aussoire and no one minded if the employees had personal calls. They were even encouraged to have gossipy tea breaks, as the chairman had taken to heart a new survey which said people actually worked better and achieved more if they were allowed moments of relaxation during the day.

Lucinda was put though immediately. 'Hi, Tom, it's me.'

'Hello, Lucinda. How are you?'

She could tell immediately by his tone that he was depressed. 'I'm fine, but you don't sound great,' she said with sisterly candour.

'I'm fine,' he asserted, 'just a bit tired. We've got a lot on here.'

Lucinda knew he was lying but she didn't press the point. Tom had always been a very private person and he would tell her in his own time what was wrong.

'I was wondering if you'd seen Harry lately?' she asked.

201

'No. I haven't seen him since the memorial service, why?'

For a moment she had a wild desire to tell him everything; about the mistresses, the letters, the jewellery, even the three million pound reward if she played the 'game' right, and also how Harry had got wind of what was happening and was threatening to tell Anne. Then she realised it was unfair on Tom. Why should he be burdened with the knowledge of their father's libertine past? And the added burden of having to keep it a secret?

'He's upsetting Mum, that's why.' Then she realised she'd have to tell him something. 'There were a couple of women at the service, friends of Dad's, and Harry proceeded to put two and two together and realised they were old flames. He also thinks the papers Dad left me are valuable or something. Anyway, he threatened to tell Mum unless I gave him some money.'

'He did what?' Tom sounded stunned.

'Yes. He was out to make trouble so I gave him a thousand pounds to keep him quiet.'

There was a long silence before Tom answered, and she could almost hear the cogs of his brain whirring round as he took in the information. Then he spoke angrily. 'You didn't! Lucinda, you shouldn't have done that. You can't let him blackmail you. He'll only come back for more.'

'Tom, what was I to do? But you're right. He still went ahead and tried to get Mum to tell him what sort of papers Dad left and now she's wondering what's going on. I'm at my wits' end and I wondered if you could talk to him?'

'What good would that do?'

'Who else is there? Do you know he's even borrowed Mum's savings, all she's got until probate is granted, because he says he's in debt?'

Tom sighed deeply. 'What about that girlfriend of his? I thought she was keeping him?'

'That's all over.' She told him what had happened. 'As a matter of fact I bumped into her in the street this morning and she wants to get in touch with him again.'

'Then why doesn't she?' Tom sounded immensely weary.

'Tom, are you really all right? You sound ill.'

'I'm OK.'

'And Susan? Is she all right? I thought she was so nice. Once Julian gets back from France you must both come to dinner. I'd really like to get to know her.'

'Well . . . we'll see. I'd better go now, Lucinda.'

After they'd said goodbye, Lucinda spent the rest of the journey wondering what on earth was wrong with Tom. He'd always been morose but today he sounded as if life was no longer worth living. Alarm shot through her so that her heart seemed to twist painfully. Maybe there really was something wrong with him. She was glad now she hadn't unburdened herself. It was just that with Julian away she desperately missed having someone to talk to and confide in. She missed the evening chats over a glass of wine when the children had gone to bed, and she missed even more the solid warmth of him in the bed beside her.

This evening she would ring France to find out how things were going. Surely the fire inspectors must have traced the cause of the fire by now?

The people in Lucinda's division were agog with some gossip that had made its way down from the boardroom on the tenth floor.

'What now?' Lucinda asked, unpacking her Xanthe purchases, which she intended to pass on to D'Aussoire's laboratory to be analysed.

Peter Harris, her immediate boss, was full of it. 'They're almost certain they know who sold out to Xanthe. They think it's someone from head office.'

'In Paris?'

'No.' He shook his head. 'Someone who *was* at the Paris office but who's been transferred here,' he whispered, so no one else in the department could hear.

'Do they know who?'

'They're questioning suspects right now. Actually,' he leaned closer, 'they think more than one person was involved.'

Lucinda nodded in agreement. 'That's more than likely.'

'There are six in this division for a start.'

'Six what?' she asked, startled.

'Six people who have come over from Paris to join us here in the past two years.'

Lucinda stared round the room at her colleagues, all of whom she trusted implicitly. But Peter was right. Six of them had been seconded from headquarters in the past two years. Was it possible that a huge betrayal had been going on right under her nose, and she hadn't noticed it?

The house was very quiet when she got home a bit earlier than usual that evening. She found Delia in the kitchen, finishing off a load of ironing.

'Where are the children?' she asked, dumping the fruit she'd bought for supper on the table.

'Playing upstairs.' Delia smiled placidly. 'Ever so good they've been today.'

'I'll go up and see them. Give them a surprise.'

She crept up the stairs quietly, loving to listen to their conversation when they were on their own.

Daisy's voice rang out loud and clear, not from the children's bedroom as she'd expected but from her own.

'Would you like more than one, sir?'

Jamie's voice was low and gruff. 'I think my wife would like several.'

'And in which colours, sir?' squeaked Daisy.

Intrigued, Lucinda tiptoed across the landing and peeped through the gap in the door, which was slightly ajar.

Her dressing table had been cleared of all the knick-knacks she normally kept on it, and all her make-up was displayed as if it were a shop counter. Daisy, her lips and cheeks heavily rouged and her eyes surrounded by black eyeliner, was acting as the shop assistant, while Jamie was sporting a moustache and beard and heavy eyebrows painted on with Lucinda's best mascara.

'What on earth . . .?' she exclaimed when she saw them.

'Can I help you, madam?' Daisy piped up. 'We have some very nice perfume you might like.' She seized her mother's bottle of Joy, the most expensive scent in the world, which Lucinda kept for special occasions, and sprayed the surrounding air liberally with it.

'*Daisy!*' Horrified, Lucinda seized the bottle from her. 'Stop wasting it!'

'We're playing shops,' Jamie explained. 'We're part of D'Aussoire. I'm buying lipsticks for my wife.'

Lucinda looked down and saw all her lipsticks had been opened, and their colours smeared on the glass top of the dressing table.

'That's our colour chart,' Daisy said proudly. 'Like you have at the office.'

'Little devils, I didn't know whether to laugh or cry,' Lucinda told Delia later, when the children had finally been scolded, scrubbed, given supper and sent to bed.

Delia grinned ruefully. 'I'm ever so sorry. My fault, I'm afraid. I left them playing upstairs good as gold. Then I got so involved with the ironing I forgot the time. Did they do much damage?'

'I've cleaned up the mess but they've ruined most of my lipsticks, eyeliner pencils and mascara. I think thcy presume, as most people do, that D'Aussoire give me all the make-up I want but of course they don't. Apart from the odd sample I have to buy everything.'

'That's a shame.' Delia looked scandalised. 'I thought you got given anything you wanted, seeing as you work there.'

'No such luck. It's understandable, though. Six hundred people are employed in the London office alone, spread between the eight different companies, so just think what it would cost D'Aussoire if people in the other offices around the world were able to help themselves to what they wanted? You're talking in terms of six thousand people. It would cost the company millions of pounds.'

Delia's jaw dropped. 'It's big business, isn't it?'

'It's one of the biggest industries in the world. It runs into hundreds of billions of pounds and it's the most savagely cut-throat business on earth. It's even worse than the rag trade.'

At that moment the phone rang and it was Julian. Lucinda's face lit up at the sound of his voice.

'How are you, darling? Tell me what's happening?' she asked eagerly.

'We're still waiting to hear how the fire started. The forensic department or whatever they call them in this country have been and we're expecting their report within the next twenty-four hours. Meanwhile, all this hanging around is a bit of a nightmare.' He sounded harassed and tired.

'I bet it is,' Lucinda sympathised.

'Dad daren't go ahead with buying the house in Shere, either, in case they don't get any insurance money. They heard today that other people want to buy it, too, so that's added to the gloom of the situation.'

'Oh, my God.' She could just imagine them, cooped up in the *chambre d'hôte*, not knowing what was going to happen next.'What about the Americans who were going to buy the château?'

'They've flown back to Florida in high dudgeon, saying they'll sue for their deposit if they don't get it back within seven days.'

'Oh, Julian. What a ghastly time you're all having. I wish I could be with you, sweetheart. Are your parents all right?'

'As soon as it's been proved the château was not torched, Dad will still have to fight for every penny he can get from the insurance company. They really are not happy at the idea of paying up. Ma and Pa are going to stay on here, but I'll be home the day after tomorrow.'

'You will? Oh, fantastic!'

'Bun! You sound like a teenager,' Julian laughed indulgently.

'I *feel* like a teenager, just about to go on a date with my boyfriend. It'll be marvellous to have you home again. You've no idea how much I miss you.'

'I've missed you like hell, too, Bun. See you Friday evening. OK?'

'I can't wait.'

Fifteen

Lucinda sat at a corner table in Quintino's, a trendy little restaurant near D'Aussoire, waiting for Carina. The atmosphere was cosy, with rose-coloured table cloths, subdued lighting, and the bustling air of an expensive but successful place to eat, for rich and successful business people. For Lucinda it provided privacy, away from her colleagues.

She scanned the menu while she waited. 'Tiny Blinis with Dill Mousseline and Smoked Salmon topped with Beluga Caviar' caught her eye. Well, what the hell! She might be a millionairess this time next year! Champagne should be drunk with such a delectable dish, but she settled for Perrier, with ice and lemon. She had to keep a clear head because the finger of suspicion was becoming more focused at work. At any moment the person who had betrayed the company was likely to be accused outright. Although it wouldn't affect her, it was nevertheless a moment she was not looking forward to. God knows what it would reveal, but the notion that it might be someone she knew and trusted was a deeply unnerving and unpleasant thought.

At that moment she saw Carina, gliding between the tables as she came towards her, looking stunning in a caramel-coloured suit, with an emerald green silk scarf wound round her neck and a lot of gold jewellery. Her blonde hair fell from a centre parting in a casually fashionable way, and she was smiling broadly.

Greeting Lucinda with a kiss on both cheeks, Carina dropped into the chair opposite with a look of triumph.

'You'll never guess what I've got to tell you!'

Lucinda's heart leapt. 'I don't believe it . . . you've found Renée Hartman?' she gasped.

Carina laughed. 'Just call me Sherlock Holmes.'

'Tell me! Tell me! What happened in York?'

'I've traced the Derwents.'

'You've . . . And . . .?'

A handsome young waiter was hovering over them. 'Can I take your orders, Mesdames?' he asked them.

'I'll have whatever you're having,' Carina said easily.

'And wine?' Lucinda asked.

'You bet! Yes, wine, please.'

Orders taken, Lucinda leaned forward and spoke rapidly. 'Well? Do they know Renée Hartman?'

'You could say that.'

'What do you mean?'

'Renée Hartman is their daughter. Hartman is her married name but she was divorced years ago. I know she's living with her mother, who is positively ancient now, because I phoned the number I was given for the Derwents, pretending I was from British Telecom. I asked if Renée Hartman lived there and would she like a separate phone line?'

Lucinda's face was a study. 'And . . .?' she croaked, stunned.

'She told me herself, in a gin-soaked voice, what I could do with my offer!' Carina laughed. 'She sounds really rough and raunchy. What *was* Miles doing with her?'

Lucinda remembered reading Renée's letters. 'That would figure,' she remarked drily, suddenly feeling nauseated. She took a gulp of water. 'So . . . I suppose I've got to get in touch with her now,' she said, wishing it was the last thing in the world she was required to do.

'Isn't that the big idea, honey? That's four down and one to go. You're doing well.' From her cream Chanel handbag she withdrew a sheet of folded paper. On it was a printout of Renée's address and phone number.

'Thanks a million, Carina. I'm really grateful. I think you've done miracles tracing her so quickly. I'll . . .' she took a deep breath, 'I'll phone her this evening.'

Their blinis arrived and Lucinda glanced surreptitiously at her watch. She still had thirty-five minutes before she had to get back to the office.

Carina spoke. 'Which piece of jewellery are you going to give her?'

'I'm not sure.'

'You've got to keep the diamond brooch for yourself. You'd be mad to give it away.'

'That leaves the ring and the pearl necklace.'

'Why not give her the ring? You're not even sure if it's a sapphire or an amethyst, are you? I doubt if it's worth much.'

Lucinda nodded. 'It would be suitable for an older woman, too. The pearls are for someone younger, in their thirties or forties, perhaps. Let's hope "Pumpkin", if I ever do find her, is youngish and glamorous.'

'She might well be. After all, Isabelle is still quite a looker, isn't she? Have you heard from her again?'

Lucinda cast her eyes to heaven. 'Mercifully, no. Not that I've got anything against her, per se, but she's a bit much, isn't she? All that emotion is so exhausting.' She giggled. 'God, if she knew she was one of five I really think she'd kill, don't you?'

Carina nodded, laughing. 'Without a doubt.'

'You're looking very pukka today,' Lucinda observed. 'How are things?'

Her friend grinned. 'Alex has sacked that bitch of a secretary. He's back in the fold, for the time being anyway. He's taking me to Rome next weekend.'

'Oh, I'm so glad, honey,' Lucinda said delightedly. 'You must be awfully relieved and happy.'

'It's OK. Until the next time, that is.'

'What do you mean, the next time?'

'Get real, Lucinda,' Carina implored. 'This is the twenty-first century. If

Alex has strayed once, and this isn't the first time, he'll stray again. It's hell while it lasts but it does go with the territory when you're married to an attractive sexy man. Not all couples are like you and Julian, you know.'

'But *you* wouldn't . . . would you?'

She looked levelly at Lucinda. 'If I did, no one would know about it. Not even you, honey.'

On the way back to the office, Lucinda went over in her mind what she'd say when she phoned Renée Hartman. Not that this was the first time she'd had to go through such an ordeal, but each woman had been different, and from her raunchy letters Renée seemed the most different of all. She glanced at the address and phone number Carina had given her. Romford, in Essex. Less than two hours' drive away, which was a damn sight better than getting to Bristol, or York for that matter.

Not wanting to give up part of the weekend, when Julian would be back home and Delia was off duty, she decided that, if she couldn't get through by phone, she'd go one evening the following week, after work. If she left D'Aussoire by six o'clock she could be at Romford before eight, providing the traffic wasn't too bad. There was a certain urgency to get this visit over and done with, too. It was like a treasure hunt, except that it was she who was giving away the treasures, and the end was almost in sight. How she was going to find 'Pumpkin' she still had no idea. Maybe something would turn up.

From the office she rang her favourite florists, Town and County Flowers, and ordered a fantastic bouquet of lilies and roses to be sent to Carina, as a thank you for all her efforts. As she was finishing the call, she saw Alain entering the office from the lifts on the far side. She saw him prowling around, sharp-eyed and critical-looking. By the time he got to her, she was studying a report on the findings by a field research agency on hair care products.

'What percentage of women are using hair colourants in this country, for the current year?' he asked, without even saying hello.

Lucinda looked up at him and without missing a beat replied: 'Forty-five per cent, according to the research carried out, starting age approximately nineteen, but rising sharply with the over-forties. We have the biggest share of the market. I also have reports on the findings on the twelve hundred and sixteen different lines of shampoos, conditioners, styling mousse, gel and hair spray on the market worldwide, if you would like them?'

Her tone was almost challenging. There was something about Alain that annoyed her deeply.

'Bring them to the director's meeting tomorrow afternoon,' he said casually, as he moved on to continue his inspection of the office. As he moved from desk to desk his presence had the effect of a Mexican Wave, as a ripple of apprehension, followed by relief as he passed, spread among the employees.

* * *

209

There was a surprise for Lucinda when she got home. As she entered the hall she heard movements in the drawing room on the left, and then Julian appeared, standing in the open doorway grinning at her.

'*Julian*!' she gasped, throwing herself into his arms and pressing her cheek against his. 'I didn't expect you until tomorrow night.'

He kissed her warmly. 'There wasn't anything more I could do. Mum and Dad have settled into the *chambre d'hôte* for the time being, so I decided to come home.'

She kissed him back. 'Am I glad to see you. You've no idea how much I've missed you.'

His eyes were serious as he looked down into hers. 'I've missed you like hell, Bun. I couldn't wait to get back to you.' He pulled her closer, and, fastening his mouth over hers, cupped the back of her head with one hand.

'How do you breathe and do that too?' piped a little voice from the top of the stairs. 'I wanted to try it with Jamie but he wouldn't let me. He said he'd get all my germs.'

Crumpling with laughter, Julian and Lucinda drew apart and looked up to see Daisy, in her nightdress, watching them.

'It takes practice, but it doesn't work with a brother,' Julian replied gravely.

'What doesn't?' shouted Jamie. There was a thunderous rumble as he came scampering out of the bedroom. 'What doesn't work with a brother?'

Daisy spoke sadly. 'Kissing. Now I'm never going to know unless I get married.'

'Who'd marry *you*?' Jamie shouted, leap-frogging over her. Now that his father was home again he relished there being another male in an otherwise all-female household.

'Mummy, *someone* will marry me, won't they?' Big tears welled up in Daisy's eyes and her mouth drooped.

Lucinda hurried up the stairs and drew Daisy into her arms. 'Don't cry, sweetheart. Lots and lots of people will want to marry you when you're a big girl. There'll be a long queue at the front door, with lots of lovely boys ringing the front door bell, all desperate to marry you.'

Daisy giggled wetly.

'Oh, no!' Jamie remarked, pushing past them. 'Then she'll be a tart.'

Later, when they were on their own, Julian started telling Lucinda all that had been happening. How the beautiful château was a blackened empty shell, and the garden trampled to a pulp by firemen with their hoses and fire engines. How the pool was full of filthy water and floating debris. How Jacques and his family were traumatised, because not only had he been accused of torching the house on the instruction of his employer, but without Château St Laurent there was no employment for any of them in the future. Generations of his family had tended the gardens and olive groves of the estate. In just one terrible night they had lost their home, their jobs and their future.

'What about these charges of arson?' Lucinda asked anxiously.

'We still don't know how the fire started. They are bringing in more experts from Paris.'

'Have *you* any idea how it began?'

Julian shook his head. 'It looks like it actually started on the first floor and then spread upwards, bringing the roof down so that everything crashed to the ground floor. Apparently people could see a glow in the sky as far away as Toulouse.'

'Oh, darling . . .' She rested her head on his shoulder, and held one of his hands in both of hers. 'Your poor parents.'

'The house in Shere has definitely gone, too.'

She sat up to look directly into his face. 'We'll *have* to have them to live with us, then. Maybe we could get a bigger house, so they could have their own quarters.'

'D'you know how much a bigger house than this would cost? Unless we move to the suburbs or the country. Then you and I would have to commute to the centre of Town every day, and think what that would cost in fares,' he added worriedly.

Lucinda nodded. 'We'll have to think of something, though. You're their only child, and they've already had this dreadful blow of losing all their money with ICC. To be homeless as well would be too much, at their age.'

'You're right.'

'We could afford a bigger house if I inherit the money Dad's left . . . providing I get this damned jewellery business right.'

'Oh, Bun.' He kissed the top of her head. 'That will be *your* money.'

She turned to glare at him with mock anger. 'Since when have we ceased to be "us"? You know perfectly well we always share everything.'

Getting the engaged signal every time she tried Renée Hartman's number, it was lunchtime the next day before Lucinda was able to get through. For some reason she was dreading this forthcoming encounter more than any of the others. She'd been nervous when she'd had to meet Isabelle, uptight when going to see Miranda, apprehensive at the thought of a second meeting with the overbearing Fenella, but this time she felt real stomach-churning qualms. It was Renée's letters, of course, that were the root cause of her dismay. What sort of woman likened her lover's performance to that of a 'raging stallion, thrashing and bucking', no matter where they were?

And that is my father she's talking about, Lucinda reflected, shuddering.

An elderly-sounding woman, presumably Mrs Derwent, answered the phone.

'Can I speak to Renée Hartman, please?'

' 'Ang on a mo,' she replied gruffly. There was a clatter as she put the receiver down and then Lucinda could hear her shouting: 'Ree-nee. Yer wanted on the phone.'

It seemed a long time with much rustling in the background before Lucinda heard a woman's voice ask: 'Hello? Who is that?'

It was a slightly more educated accent than Mrs Derwent's, but the tone was raucous.

Lucinda braced herself. 'You don't know me, but my name's Lucinda Cotterell, and my father was Miles Scott-Forbes.'

'Shit! Well I never!'

For the fourth time in the past three months. Lucinda went into the spiel about the letters and the jewellery. 'I wonder if we could meet so that I could pass them on to you?' she concluded.

Renée suddenly seemed awe-struck. 'I can't believe it. After all these years. Fancy your pa keeping my letters! And leaving me jewellery! I thought he'd have forgotten about me twenty years ago.' Then she gave a roar of crude laughter. 'My, we had a high old time, your pa and me!'

This was met by a moment's silence from Lucinda. For some reason, she found Renée's voice vaguely familiar, and this unnerved her.

'Can you come up to Town to meet me?' she asked. 'I'm working, you see, so it's difficult . . .'

'All righty! What do you suggest?' Renée asked brightly.

Lucinda's mind raced. Lunch would be a nightmare. Tea was out of the question because of work. Drinks . . .?

'How about we meet for a drink? There's a nice little pub called the Rat and Falcon in the King's Road, Chelsea. By World's End. How about next Tuesday evening, at six thirty?'

'Okey-dokey! How am I going to know you? I might pick up the wrong person by mistake.' She laughed suggestively. 'My luck might even change!'

Dear God, Lucinda thought wearily. Aloud she said briskly: 'I'll be carrying a black briefcase, and I'm tall with long dark hair pinned back.'

'Okey-dokey,' Renee repeated with touching amazement. 'Talk about a voice from the sodding past! I can't believe Miles remembered me.'

'Yes. Well, he did,' Lucinda remarked awkwardly. 'I'll see you next Tuesday, six thirty.' After she'd hung up, she hoped she'd sounded sympathetic and understanding.

Susan had cooked Tom's favourite supper – a steak and kidney pie with a gorgeously spongy suet crust and lots of thick dark gravy, which she was going to serve with potatoes, Brussels sprouts and baby carrots. She'd also made meringues stuffed with whipped cream to follow. But her face was set in sad lines as she laid the little table in the kitchen, and then opened the bottle of red wine so it could 'breathe'. Something Tom had explained was necessary with red wine for it to be drunk at its best.

Tonight was almost certainly something of a farewell last supper, because she was going to tell him, when the boys had gone to bed, that he didn't have to stay if he didn't want to. She still had her job. They had managed financially before she'd met him, and she'd manage again. Most importantly, she was determined not to plead, cry or appear sorry for herself.

There'd be plenty of time for that after he'd gone. Meanwhile, didn't she have Dick and Steve to keep her company? It wasn't as if she was going to be alone. At six thirty Susan went upstairs to change into her favourite blue dress, because she always felt confident when she wore it. She also knew Tom liked her in it, and if this gave her a tiny sneaking ray of hope that it would make him say he wanted to stay, well . . . who could blame her?

Tom, punctual to the moment, drew up outside the house at six forty-five. Watching him from their bedroom window, she saw how he stooped, looking tired and dejected, as he came up the front steps with a heavy tread. Susan's heart gave a painful throb. He hated living with her here, in this poky little council house. He found her dull, plain, uneducated. He was bored.

Susan hurried down the narrow stairs, a bright smile pinned to her face, a laughing lilt in her voice.

'Hello! How was your day?' She kissed him lightly on his grey cheek, before bustling ahead of him into the kitchen. Tom followed slowly.

'Fine.' He sniffed the air. 'Something smells good.'

'I hope so.'

'Have I time for a bath before dinner?' They always ate early because of Dick and Steve, and she was sure his family never 'dined', as his grandmother would have called it, until much later.

'Of course you have. Why not take a glass of wine with you up to the bathroom? Help you to relax.'

Tom looked at the neatly laid table and the opened bottle of Beaujolais. 'I think I'll wait. Thanks anyway.' Then he glanced at her. 'You're very kind and thoughtful, you know.'

Susan looked back at him but his eyes were veiled and she couldn't tell what he was thinking. 'Nonsense!' she said, more briskly than she'd intended because for a second she'd felt tears prick the corners of her eyes.

Smelling the fragrance of steak and kidney pudding, Steve and Dick came lumbering down the stairs exclaiming they were starving and when could they have their dinner?

'Oh, Mum!' they wailed, when Susan told them they must wait for Tom. 'What can we eat, then?'

'Have you finished your homework?'

There were grunts which she wasn't sure meant yes or no, but tonight was not the night to exert discipline. She needed all her strength to talk to Tom later.

'You can have an apple if you're hungry,' she told them instead. 'Dinner will be in about twenty minutes.'

When Tom reappeared, looking pink and refreshed, she could tell he was making an effort to be cheerful. He poured their wine, chatted to the boys about their day and asked if they wanted to go to Richmond Park at the weekend. He also offered to do the big Saturday shop for Susan, so she could sleep in late.

'You don't have to, Tom,' she said gently.

He gave her a strange look. 'Well, if you'd rather I didn't . . .'

It was a rather silent supper, and Susan found she could hardly eat anything, so sick with nerves did she feel at the thought of what she must say when they were alone.

Anne felt so uneasy and worried, alone in the big house, that she couldn't settle to anything. Instead of cooking the sausages she'd bought for her supper she made herself a cup of Bovril. There was nothing on television she wanted to watch, and she was unable to concentrate on the biography of Beethoven which she'd got from the library. Anxiety encompassed her like a web, tugging at every nerve ending, holding her in its grip. Instead, she found herself wandering from empty room to empty room wondering what to do.

What was it the estate agent had said to her, when he'd phoned at lunchtime? What had he meant when he'd said he'd been told she wished to sell her house immediately, as quickly as possible, and would she like him to value it for her tomorrow morning?

'Are you from the tax office?' she remembered asking stupidly. 'Someone has already been round to value the house for probate.'

No, he assured her cheerily. He'd got nothing to do with the tax office. In fact he only had good news for her. He had a client who was keen to purchase her house, but of course he had to go round it first, to see what was what, because he wanted to get the best price for her.

'But I don't want to sell it,' Anne had bleated repeatedly, but the estate agent had brushed her protests aside as if he were deaf.

'Tomorrow morning convenient, then? At ten o'clock?'

Then he'd hung up before she'd been able to say no. This was obviously Harry's doing, but where *was* Harry? He'd told her a week ago that he was off to stay with his old school friend, Bill Hamilton. But he failed to say where Bill lived. And she couldn't get through to him on his mobile because an electronic voice told her each time she tried that the number was unavailable. Did that mean, Anne wondered, that he hadn't paid his phone bill?

She reached for the phone several times, between sips of Bovril, wanting to ask Lucinda for her advice but then hesitating, because she didn't want to bother her. Lucinda had enough on her plate. Then she thought of ringing her own mother, but Sarah was giving a dinner party tonight.

That left Tom. Good old Tom might be able to tell her what to do. Anne dialled his number and Susan answered.

'I'll get him for you,' Susan said hurriedly, as if she didn't want to speak to Anne herself.

'Hello, Mum. How are you?'

'Oh, Tom!' Babbling nervously, she told him what had happened. 'This man is coming tomorrow morning and I don't know what to do.'

'Did you get his name and number?'

214

Anne hesitated. 'He did say which firm he was from, when he first rang, but I wasn't paying any attention. Harry is behind this, I'm sure, but he's away somewhere.'

Tom sighed. 'Typical. Listen, Mum, I'll be with you by half past nine so that I can head this chap off. I'll also ring Bernard Clarke to see if he knows when probate's likely to be agreed. Then it's up to you and no one else whether you want to sell the house or not. Don't let Harry try to make up your mind for you.'

'But what do you think I should do, Tom?' She sounded quite lost.

'That really is up to you, Mum. If you feel happy and secure there, then you should stay. On the other hand look how happy Gran is, in her flat. You should discuss it with Lucinda. She's very good at that sort of thing.'

'She's always so busy I don't like to bother her.'

'None of us are too busy for you, Mum.'

'Dear Tom,' she said fondly. 'Can you really be here in the morning to help me with this man?'

'Definitely. And when you see Harry tell him I want to talk to him.'

When they'd said goodbye, Tom went back to the kitchen. Susan was doing the washing-up and Dick and Steve were somewhere upstairs. He looked brighter and Susan glanced questioningly at him.

'Is your mother all right?'

Tom nodded. 'I'm going over there in the morning to help her get rid of a pushy estate agent who's urging her to sell her house. Harry is behind this really, so I've got to go and help her out.'

His tone, she noticed, was more confident than it had been for some time.

'She must be so grateful, Tom.'

'Well, at least I can be of some use to her, even if not to anyone else.'

She looked up sharply. 'What's that supposed to mean?'

He looked at her sadly. 'I'm not much use to you, am I? No wonder you secretly despise me for being so hopeless. God, I couldn't even stand up to Jim! I should have knocked the living daylights out of him for threatening you – and what happened? I ended up draped along the skirting board.'

Susan stared at him as if she couldn't believe her ears.

'*Tom*! Is *that* what's been the matter with you? You thought you were letting me down?' she added incredulously.

'Well, I did, didn't I? I was no match for him.' He shuffled his feet and gazed down at the floor. 'I've never really been a match for anyone, and I think I'm being unfair to you by hanging around. You deserve much better, Susan.'

There was a moment's stillness in the cosy kitchen as Susan stood with her hands resting on the edge of the sink. Then she spun round, her eyes over-bright, her voice wobbling.

'Tom, never let me hear you speak like that again. You are the most marvellous man I've ever met or am ever likely to meet. I love you to bits and if you walk out on me because you've got this crazy idea you're inadequate, I'll never forgive you. D'you hear me?' She was crying openly now. 'I thought the problem was *me*. I'm not young any more, and I was never beautiful. I'm not as well educated as you, and I've got a load of baggage from my past. But I love you and I never want you to go . . .'

Tom had his arms round her, rocking her gently from side to side as if she were a distressed child. 'It's all right,' he kept whispering. 'I won't leave you. I never wanted to leave you.'

They stayed like that for several minutes, shaken by the emotional crisis that had come and miraculously gone. Their hearts still pounded painfully in the aftermath of receding fear. The relief that everything was all right between them hadn't yet registered.

Later, as they lay in bed, Susan noticed her blue dress lying in a crumpled heap on the floor. She smiled to herself. It really was her lucky blue dress.

'I've just been talking to your brother,' Bernard told Lucinda the next morning, when she phoned him at home to arrange a time to come and collect the ring.

'What's he up to?' she asked cryptically.

'It was Tom I was talking to, not Harry.'

'Oh!' Her manner changed.

'In a way it's to do with Harry, though. You don't by any chance know where he is, do you?'

'I haven't the foggiest, Bernard. Why, what's happened?'

Bernard outlined Anne's fears and Harry's involvement. 'Oh, for God's sake!' she exploded. 'What's the matter with him? Why can't he leave Mum and her affairs alone?'

'I'm afraid we both know the answer to that,' Bernard replied drily. 'I think when Harry recieves his inheritance he'll be a lot happier.'

'Want to bet? Anyway, I'll be with you on Tuesday morning.'

'I'll look forward to it. You're doing extremely well, Lucinda, if I may say so. You only have one more person to trace.'

'I have a feeling I'm going to get stuck, trying to find "Pumpkin". I haven't a thing to go on, you know.'

'I wish you luck, anyway,' Bernard replied warmly.

Sir Humphrey Hodson arrived at Claridges in good time to meet Paula for lunch. While he waited in the foyer, standing near the mantelpiece with its real glowing coal fire, warming his hands, he nodded to several friends, who were on their way in to the dining room.

Sir Humphrey lunched in this grandest of old-fashioned hotels in the heart of Mayfair several times a week. He was always given the same table and welcomed with deference by the waiters, who looked as if they had stepped out of a scene in the thirties. Most of the ladies who lunched wore hats, just as they'd done in the old days, and Sir Humphrey loved the traditions associated with a place which was still a favourite with the crowned heads of

Europe, who never stayed anywhere else when they visited London. Even the British Royal Family were known to let their hair down at big private parties in the ballroom.

Paula arrived almost immediately, and her father smiled with pleasure to see her in an exquisite ruby red suit, with black accessories and a becoming turban-shaped black hat, which set off her ruby and diamond earrings.

'My darling . . .' he greeted her, kissing her on both cheeks. 'You're looking very well. Would you like a glass of champagne before we go in to lunch?'

'How wicked but how wonderful!' she laughed. Sir Humphrey loved to see her laugh. She reminded him of her mother, to whom he'd been utterly devoted until her death from cancer when Paula was still a child.

'How is everything, Daddy?' she asked as they sat on a sofa in a corner of the reception area, while a string quartet at one end of the room played excerpts from *My Fair Lady*.

Her father nodded, pleased. 'I've had a bit of good news, actually, but it's confidential so you mustn't breathe a word to anyone until it's officially announced next week.'

'All right,' she promised. 'What is it?'

'I didn't want to worry you, darling, but I invested quite heavily in a company called ICC. It got into big trouble a couple of months ago and I thought I'd lost the lot, but they've just been taken over by Hailybury, Gross and Powling, in a bid to make the company solvent again. HG&P have enormous assets, mostly in property, so they're going to be able to absorb ICC's losses without much problem. I don't think my shares are going to yield much profit for a while, but on the other hand I won't have lost anything, either.'

'Daddy, that's wonderful. I'm so glad.'

'And how's your new company going, darling?'

'Very well. Better than I could have hoped seeing we're only just up and running. People really are interested in tracing their family trees.' She smiled happily. 'We're going to make a profit in the first year at this rate.'

He raised his glass to her. 'Congratulations, my darling! You've been a very clever girl.'

Paula raised her finely arched eyebrows. 'Not really. It was Harry's idea. I just put it into operation.'

'Well, I think you've done brilliantly. You've kept the stock and chucked out the old bones. Now that's what I call clever. Serve that little bounder right.' Sir Humphrey sniffed. 'He may have had a good idea in the first place but he hadn't a clue how to get it up and running and he never would have had. Little men like him always end up with nothing and it's their own damned fault.'

'That's very harsh, Daddy.'

'Not at all. Thank God you got rid of him.'

'He left. I didn't ask him to go.' For some reason, Paula found she was always made to feel as if she were still a teenager when she talked to her father. The fact that she was a forty-four-year-old widow never seemed to cross his mind.

'Whatever.' Sir Humphrey spoke dismissively. 'He's gone and that's the main thing, and I'm jolly proud of you, my darling. Now let's go and have something to eat, shall we? I quite fancy some foie gras, and then perhaps grouse. What do you say?'

Nothing much had changed since she'd been a schoolgirl, she reflected with amusement, as she followed him into the high-ceilinged, ornate restaurant, yet at the same time it was enormously reassuring and made her feel comfortingly looked after. Lunch at Claridges had always been a highlight of the school holidays, alongside a shopping trip to Harrods to buy new clothes, a box at Covent Garden for the ballet, a picnic at Glyndebourne to see the latest productions, and tickets for the Centre Court at Wimbledon.

By the time she was fourteen Paula realised she had largely taken her late mother's place in her father's life. At sixteen she was acting as his hostess when he entertained. At twenty she was sophisticated and cultured beyond her years. It gave her an edge over her contemporaries, as did the large trust fund her father had set up for her. By the time she was twenty-one she had become isolated from her own age group and veered towards friendships with older people. She'd become attracted to older men, such as Neil, her late husband. He looked after her. He was already successful and worldly like her father. He'd made her feel safe and cherished, and when he died she felt like a lost child.

But that was four years ago and now she was done with older men. She craved firm flesh, a flat stomach, the clean jawline and the virility of a young man. And she desperately desired the smell of danger.

Paula sat quite still while her father ordered for both of them, without asking her what she wanted. This was a habit of his which had always irritated her. He even decided which wine they'd have, knowing she preferred white, but choosing red because he liked it better. But she said nothing, and smiled agreeably as she smoothed the white damask napkin on her lap, while glancing around at the other tables. Ex-King Constantine of Greece was seated discreetly in one corner, with a group of friends, and by one of the large windows Lady Thatcher was engrossed in conversation with two current politicians.

From the beginning Paula had decided she wanted this lunch with her father to be peaceful and convivial, because what she was about to do was going to enrage him so utterly, it was likely to estrange them for a very long time. In fact, she was prepared for the fact that he might never forgive her.

Sixteen

The Rat and Falcon was still fairly empty when Lucinda arrived. She glanced round to see if a single woman in her fifties was sitting alone as if waiting for someone but the bar was mostly filled with young men and women drinking Sea-Breeze and planning how they were going to spend the evening. To her surprise she didn't envy them their freedom and lack of responsibility. Twelve years ago she'd been like that, meeting friends every evening, spending her salary on pretty clothes, intent only on having a good time. And then Julian had happened and her life was changed for ever. Would she like to go back to being a single girl? Able to do what she liked? With no one but herself to please?

Lucinda smiled to herself as she ordered a gin and tonic. Her answer was simple. She wouldn't want to turn the clock back in a million years. The idea of life without Julian, Jamie and Daisy was unthinkable, even if she did have to work a twelve-hour day to hold the whole thing together. In fact, she felt quite maternal as she watched the giggling girls up at the bar in their casual clothes, and the young men trying to impress them. None of them had her security, and the warm comforting knowledge that she'd already got everything she wanted, and she felt quite sorry for them.

Settling herself at a small round table on the far side of the room, from where she could watch the entrance, she decided to make this meeting short and sweet. She'd buy Renée a drink, hand over the letters and the ring, say she had to get home to her children and then bid her goodbye. She was adamant about one thing. She did not wish to hear a single word from Renée about her father's sexual prowess.

An older man, followed by a couple, entered the bar, and a minute later two young women in their early twenties came swinging in and were greeted with a chorus of *Hi*s and *Hello*s by the young group who had set up their own enclave at one end of the bar. Orders were given. Ice being shovelled into glasses rattled noisily. The air hummed with the *phfizz* of bottles being opened and the *glug-glug* of drinks being poured. There was the constant *dring* of the cash till, and the crackle of bags of crisps being taken out of cardboard boxes.

It was hot, and the blue haze of cigarette smoke hovered like an evil-smelling miasma just above Lucinda's head. Beginning to sweat, Lucinda slipped off her jacket and wondered why on earth she'd chosen to meet Renée here, except that it was neutral territory, near home, and at the time had seemed like a suitable place to meet one's father's mistress.

There was a movement in the doorway. Lucinda looked up and, in a heart-stopping moment, recognised Renée Hartman instantly.

She was the tall, bone-thin woman with the red hair Lucinda had seen talking to Fenella Harrison after the memorial service. Renée had been in severe black then, but tonight she wore a dark red velvet and lace cocktail dress, a relic from the fifties, Lucinda imagined, and over it a long velvet coat trimmed with worn and moth-eaten mink.

'You must be Miles's daughter,' she declared in a husky voice as she lowered her angular frame into the opposite chair.

Lucinda tried not to stare, managed to smile, then asked Renée what she'd like to drink.

'Rum and Coke,' she replied without hesitation, taking a pack of Silk Cut out of her fake black leather handbag. Her heavily made-up face, painted with scarlet lips, crimson rouge, green glittery eyeshadow and kohl-edged eyes reminded Lucinda of an elderly clown trying very bravely to give one last performance.

'There we are,' Lucinda said gently, when she'd bought the drink and placed it on the table.

'Thanks.' Renée started coughing, and reached for the drink. Her arms were like white broom handles, her neck a series of stringy cords. She drank deeply, then drew on her cigarette again.

'I have your letters,' Lucinda continued brightly, almost as if she was talking to a child. She placed them on the table. 'And this is the piece of jewellery my father left,' she added carefully.

Renée opened the small square leather case, had another fit of coughing and dropped a trail of ash across the box, half obliterating the ring. She blew on it and then took the ring out of the case. The dark purple-blue stone and surrounding diamonds, set in silver, did not look very impressive in the dusky yellow light of the pub. For some reason, Lucinda found herself feeling embarrassed. It didn't look like much of a legacy.

'I can't believe he left me this,' Renée said, and great tears plopped onto the velvet front of her dress. 'It was so long ago. I'd never forgotten him, but I didn't think he'd remember me.'

'Well, he certainly did,' Lucinda said kindly, not knowing what else to say.

Then Renée picked up the letters and held them as if warming both her hands. 'He never wrote to me, you know. And I wasn't supposed to write to him. In the end he got himself a PO Box number, so I could.' She shook her head, a tangled riot of dyed red hair. The gravel in her throat rattled, and she coughed again. 'He was a wicked, wicked man, an absolute womaniser, and I always knew I wasn't the only one, but Christ, was he amazing.'

Lucinda shifted uncomfortably and took a gulp of her gin and tonic, but before she could divert the conversation Renée was saying: 'I don't know how your mother put up with it, I really don't, and that makes me feel guilty, you know? I saw her in the distance at his memorial service, and I could see she wasn't enough for him, but then what woman would have been? Maybe I and all the others did her a favour? At least he never left her, did he? She never had to face that humiliation, as I did, when my husband walked out on me.' She leaned towards Lucinda, her eyes pools of tragic pain in her painted face.

'I was a singer, you know. In nightclubs. Doing really well at one point. London was swinging then, as they say, and . . . oh, God! we all had such a wonderful time. My husband was Billy Hartman, the trombonist. He was in a band. I was . . . quite good-looking in those days.' Renée's face crumpled momentarily, and she groped in her handbag again, producing a dog-eared and cracked photograph. 'That was me, when I was singing at the Blue Angel.'

Lucinda found herself staring at a picture of a shapely, stunningly beautiful young woman in the likeness of Rita Hayworth. It was hard to reconcile that exquisite creature with the caricature figure sitting opposite her now.

'You *must* have had a wonderful time,' Lucinda agreed.

'Oh, I did! You young ones don't know what a good time is, in spite of your drink and drugs and discotheques,' she declared, cheering up. The ring was on the fourth finger of her left hand now, where it slipped round loosely. 'What a pretty ring. It'll go really well with some earrings I got in Woolworth's years and years ago.'

'I *think* those stones are the real thing,' Lucinda suggested carefully.

Renée looked scandalised. 'Oh, I'm sure they are. Miles would never have bought anything tacky or cheap. Is it a sapphire, d'you think?'

'I don't know much about jewellery, but I think so. If not it's an amethyst.' She hadn't the heart to say, as she'd planned, that she had to rush off. Renée Hartman had obviously taken great care with her appearance for this meeting, so Lucinda offered her another drink.

'Don't mind if I do,' Renée replied, brightening even more.

Lucinda didn't get home until nearly nine thirty, to find Julian waiting anxiously for her.

'That was the saddest evening I think I've ever spent,' she told him. 'Renée is looking after her elderly mother, they're on social security and housing benefits and all that, and she looks ill herself. Smokes like a chimney and has a terrible cough. But it wasn't just that . . . she's living in the past, hanging on to the glory days when she was a nightclub singer and her life was glamorous.' Lucinda shook her head. 'She really admired Dad, although she admitted he was a terrible womaniser. What surprised me was that she didn't talk in a vulgar and crude way, as her letters had suggested she might. She even sounded fairly ghastly on the phone, but tonight she was quite subdued and not really outspoken at all. Maybe she felt ill. She certainly looked it.'

'Nevertheless she doesn't sound like any of the other women Miles knew,' Julian observed. 'What with Fenella and her crystals, Isabelle the rich socialite, Miranda the blue-stocking and now Renée, the ex-showgirl, your pa certainly liked variety, didn't he?'

'Didn't he just.'

'I bet this Renée Hartman has that ring valued and then flogs it for whatever she can get.'

'You're probably right,' Lucinda agreed thoughtfully.

'By the way, Ian and Rachel phoned when you were out. They've asked us all to stay for the weekend after next. I said you'd phone her.'

Lucinda's face lit up. She hadn't seen Ian and Rachel since the nightmare dinner party when Carina had tried to goad Paula into admitting she was 'Pumpkin'.

'That'll be fun! We always have a good time when we stay with them. Remember the barbecue last summer? And that Easter weekend when Rachel organised a treasure hunt in the grounds for all the children?'

Julian grinned. 'I remember Jamie finding over twenty of those tiny chocolate eggs, and being frightfully sick everywhere, after he'd scoffed the lot.'

Lucinda buried her face in her hands at the memory. 'Talk about embarrassment! Especially as Toby and Archie always behave so well, too.'

The Comptons' boys, Toby and Archie, were the same ages as Jamie and Daisy, and they were always clean and tidy, very polite and definitely prissy. They'd been brought up to share their toys with other children in a playroom which was three times the size of Lucinda's drawing room, and at moments Lucinda wished her own children were as well behaved, especially in front of other people. On the other hand, Toby and Archie were a bit like robots, and Julian once joked that they were so repressed they were bound to end up as serial rapists or murderers.

'Come in time for dinner on Friday night,' Rachel told Lucinda when she phoned her a few minutes later. 'We've got several people for supper and on the Saturday we're giving a party for Ian's birthday. I'm doing a buffet lunch for about thirty people and in the evening I thought I'd do a formal dinner.'

'My God, Rachel, how do you do it?' Just thinking about all that cooking and preparation made Lucinda want to lie down on the floor and expire with exhaustion. Suppers . . . lunches . . . dinners . . . and no doubt a few people popping in for drinks at some point . . . it was really quite annoying. But Rachel always made it look so easy, so effortless. Like her children, everything was perfect. The house. The garden. The food. The flowers. Even the two little miniature dachshunds had never been known to pee on the carpet or do worse in the middle of the lawn.

'I do have a marvellous nanny,' Rachel assured her, laughingly. 'And two wonderful women from the village who clean and iron and all that. Anyway, you know I love cooking more than anything. It's my hobby. And I don't have a demanding full-time job like you, either,' she added generously.

Mollified, Lucinda laughed too. 'Rachel, even if I was at home all day I don't think I'd ever be able to entertain the way you do. I find the whole business of cooking really stressful.'

'It's just practice, Lucinda. Anyway, I'm thrilled you can manage the eighteenth. You'll know lots of people at the lunch on the Saturday so it should be fun. I'd hoped Carina and Alex would be able to make it but they've apparently got to be in Brussels. Something to do with Alex's business.'

'Oh, what a pity.'

'I know, isn't it maddening? Carina's always such an asset at a party. You'll both have to come another weekend, maybe in the autumn.'

As they got ready for bed, Julian, stretching his arms above his head, remarked: 'A luxurious weekend in the country is just what you need, Bun.'

She smiled at him from the depths of snowy pillows and duvet. 'Won't it be heaven? I'm going to fast for the previous week so I can do justice to Rachel's cooking, although I could do with a month's holiday.' She frowned, touching her face with her fingertips. 'Do you think I'm getting bags under my eyes?'

'Those are laughter lines,' he retorted, coming to stand by the side of the bed. He bent forward, looking closely at her. 'I've got frown lines *and* bags under mine, so think yourself lucky.'

She reached up, winding her arms round his neck and looking into his eyes. 'Perhaps we should both have plastic surgery if I get all Dad's money?' she asked with mock seriousness.

'And end up looking like Frankenstein and his wife? As Daisy would say, "I think not."'

'There's a call for you, monsieur,' the proprietor of the *chambre d'hôte* called out urgently, as William and Jane returned from their morning walk. They glanced at each other apprehensively. What new nightmare could this be? William's face turned white and Jane wondered how much more she could bear.

'I'll take it,' William said grimly, striding towards the old-fashioned telephone booth at the far end of the reception area.

Jane hovered uncertainly, watching his receding figure, her heart plummeting with dread. Supposing they really believed William had authorised the burning of the château? Supposing it couldn't be proved he hadn't? Weakly, she sank onto a chair to wait for him. The minutes ticked by, and she could see through the glass panel of the booth that William was still deep in conversation. He was nodding from time to time. Eventually, after what seemed like hours, she saw him hang up.

She tried to rise from her seat to go to him, to be supportive and sympathetic, but her legs seemed paralysed with fear. Coming towards her, she saw William's face was still pale. He looked profoundly shaken.

'What is it?' she asked tremulously.

He sank onto the chair beside her, shaking his head. 'I can hardly believe it,' he murmured.

'Believe what?'

William turned to look at her, his eyes glazed and expressionless with shock. 'ICC has been taken over by a property company called Hailybury,

Gross and Powling. It means we haven't lost everything after all.'

Jane's hand flew to her mouth as a dry sob broke in her throat. 'Oh, William . . .!'

'I can't believe it,' he repeated, dazed. 'After all that worry, the nightmare of thinking we'd lost all our money . . . well, we *had* lost it all, but this is the rescue bid I've been praying for.'

'So we can buy a house, now, can't we?'

He reached for her hand. 'Yes, darling, but one thing at a time. I'm still under suspicion for torching the château. There's a lot to be sorted out before we can make any plans.'

Excitement was beginning to ripple through Jane, in little surges and eddies like an incoming tide. Thank you, God, she kept thinking. Thank you. Thank you. Aloud she exclaimed: 'Darling, do phone Julian.'

'Yes, I will.' William glanced at his watch, confused. This unexpected reversal of fortune had disorientated him so that he couldn't think straight, had no idea what time it was, far less which day. The strain of the past few weeks had been so terrible that now it was almost over he felt quite ill from sheer reaction. 'I'll do it now,' he said with an effort. 'What's his number?'

Jane rattled it off by heart and looked at him anxiously. His face was very grey and she wondered if she should call the local doctor. A shock was a shock, whether it was something nice or not, and William was no longer a young man.

'Where's Geneviève?' Lucinda asked at lunchtime. She hadn't seen her all morning, and she was waiting for her to collate the demographics for the effect of a new line in sun block creams on pale skin through to ebony.

'She hasn't called in sick,' Magali remarked. 'Oops! Here comes Alain. He's going to want to know where she is, too.'

Alain strode from the glass lifts that rose and fell with sinister silence from the ground floor to the eleventh, and started looking around agitatedly.

'Where is Geneviève?' he shouted, looking suspiciously at Quennel, Solita and Lucinda, as if they might be hiding her under their desks. His eyes swept the rest of the room angrily.

'Where is she?' he shouted sharply.

There was a sudden terrible tension in the air. Something had happened and they all guessed Geneviève was at the heart of it. The vast area fell silent. Even the usually busy phones ceased to ring. There was no *tap-tapping* on keyboards, no rustling of papers. Everyone sat motionless, as if they'd forgotten how to breathe.

Alain stomped up and down the aisles between the rows of desks, getting increasingly fraught. 'When did you last see her?' he demanded of anyone who might answer him. 'Did she say anything?' He turned on Lucinda. 'Have you questioned her? Kept her under surveillance? I told you to watch everyone in this division! If she has slipped away . . .!'

Lucinda faced him boldly. 'Geneviève is above suspicion,' she told him coldly. 'I know her well and we've worked together for nearly three years.'

'No one is above suspicion where financial gain is concerned,' he stormed. 'Have you any idea how much Xanthe will have paid their informant for all the information? Have you any idea how much it cost *us* to get Mousseline-de-Soie ready to be launched? As head of this department you must be aware we spend six million pounds a year on field research *alone*?'

'Spread over many products, not just the Mousseline,' Lucinda interjected spiritedly. 'I'm perfectly aware that launching a brand new line can cost millions, but that is beside the point. Geneviève would never do such a thing. She's absolutely loyal to the company, apart from which she's not senior enough to have gathered sufficient information to be of any use to Xanthe.'

'I want to know where she is,' Alain insisted, ignoring Lucinda's remarks. 'As soon as she gets in, send her up to my office immediately.'

There was a note on the hall table addressed to 'Mummy'. Amused, Lucinda opened it, recognising Daisy's writing, in multi-coloured capital letters.

DEAR MUMMY, DADDY FONED TO SAY GRANDPA'S GOT HIS MUNY BACK! OH, MY WIRD!! WAT EXCITMINT! GONE TO DANCING. LOVE DAISY.

She was tapping in his mobile number when he arrived home, a few minutes later. One look at his face and she knew Daisy's note was true.

'I phoned you at the office but you'd already left,' he explained, kissing her briefly. 'And what's the point of having a mobile if you have it turned off, Bun?'

'Sorry,' she said apologetically. 'Have the insurance agreed to pay up, then?'

'Better than that.' He told her about the ICC takeover. 'It's the most marvellous thing, Bun, because it's restored Dad's self-confidence.'

'So he'll get the investment back?'

'Yup! And if Dad's got any sense they'll sell their shares in ICC immediately and put the bloody money in the bank.'

'So they'll be able to buy a house after all. God, what a relief.'

Like a homing pigeon she headed automatically for the kitchen, dumping her handbag on the table, and putting on the kettle.

'Have they discovered what started the fire?'

'Not so far.' He watched her get two mugs down from the dresser, and milk from the fridge. 'Bun, wouldn't you prefer a glass of wine? Do you really want a cup of tea? It's nearly dinner time.'

She looked vaguely surprised. 'I suppose it is. I've lost all track of time. It's been such a hellish day and I've no idea what we're going to eat. How about scrambled eggs on toast? Or pasta? I've got a jar of sauce somewhere in the cupboard.'

Julian caught her hand and spoke gently. 'Calm down, Bun. You're running on empty you're so exhausted. I'll open a bottle, and when we've had a drink I'll take you to dinner at that new Italian restaurant round the corner.'

'But the children . . .?'

'Delia's taken them to friends, hasn't she? They'll already have had something to eat and be ready for bed when they get back.' He glanced smilingly at Daisy's note, which Lucinda had put on the door of the fridge. 'Love the spelling.'

'I think we should frame it,' she laughed.

Seventeen

'There's nothing to worry about, Mum,' Tom told Anne. 'The estate agent won't be bothering you any more, and I've spoken to Bernard. He's arranging for you to have some money, to keep you going until probate's granted. I think it's a personal loan, because Dad's money can't be released yet, but he wouldn't want you to know that.'

'Oh, my dear, thank you. How kind of him. Thank you so much for speaking to him for me.'

'You've nothing to thank me for. I can't get hold of Harry, though. I think his mobile must have been cut off. I suppose you haven't heard from him?'

Anne couldn't hide the relief in her voice. 'Not a word. I've no idea where he is.'

'Good. And whatever happens, Mum, don't lend him a penny. You know what he's like.'

Although she remained loyally silent, Anne knew only too well what Harry was like. Hadn't she loaned him three thousand pounds, which she'd saved over the years for an emergency? She was too proud to let even her family know how stupid she'd been and how, as a result, she'd been forced to live on bread and tea for the past few weeks.

Aloud she told Tom: 'Don't worry, my dear. He'll be getting the fifty thousand pounds Daddy left him, so he'll soon be all right for money anyway. You'll be getting yours, too, won't you?'

'That's right.' Tom was planning to take Susan and the boys on holiday but they didn't know it yet. It was to be a surprise. With his self-confidence still fragile, and his sense of self-worth almost non-existent, his desire to prove himself worthy of Susan still dominated his conscious thought. He must do something special which would prove to her how much he loved her, and a good holiday was the best thing he could think of.

The fact that none of them had heard from Harry worried him not at all. Harry had always been able to look after himself, thinking up some new scam, getting involved with a bunch of con-artists, or worming his way into the life of someone rich and influential. If there was a tragedy in all this, Tom reflected, it was that no matter what, Harry always managed to blow it.

Anne blinked back the tears, but this was different. She wasn't crying for the loss of Miles, but because she was so touched by what the letters said about *her*.

She'd finally plucked up the courage to read all the letters of condolence she'd received when Miles had died, only to read lines like: *Without you Miles would have been lost*, and *We've always admired your loyalty; how lucky he was to be married to you.* Another wrote, *You were his strength and the one person he depended on,* and later, *Your love and devotion is an example to us all.*

All the letters were in the same vein, and Anne began to feel overwhelmed by the affection and friendship being directed at her. She could hardly believe it. Here she was being lauded as a heroine, and all the time she'd thought of herself as a devoted slave, unworthy of Miles's love. It put a whole new light, a fresh perspective, on their marriage. Perhaps she *had* been worthy of him, in a wife-like way if not as an intellectual equal. Perhaps she *had* deserved his love and loyalty? Would someone write: *Dear Anne, What a shining example you are of selfless love, and how long we have admired your caring attitude to Miles* if she hadn't been a good wife?

Once she'd read the letters, all of them, hundreds of them, it was nearly five o'clock in the morning. Anne didn't feel tired, though; she felt invigorated. It was as if she'd been given an award . . . something like a Lifetime's Service Medal for being married to Miles. That people should think so highly of her made her feel re-born.

Checking the stock of rich blue headed writing paper which Miles had always had printed by Smythsons, remembering he always ordered a thousand sheets at a time with envelopes to match, and finding there was enough for her requirements, Anne made herself a fresh pot of tea, settled herself at Miles's desk in his study, and started to reply to the letters. It might take her weeks but it was the least she could do when people had been so generous in their praise of her.

Lucinda's scream at the breakfast table a few days later made the children jump, startled Delia and caused Julian, who was never at his best in the morning, to demand crossly: 'For heaven's sake, what on earth's the matter?'

She was holding the *Telegraph* open at the Court Circular page and staring at it as if hypnotised.

'What is it, Mummy?' Jamie asked.

'Perhaps someone's died, like Grandpa,' Daisy assured him confidently.

'Listen to this,' Lucinda said in a stunned voice. She began to read aloud. ' "The engagement has been announced between Paula Maxwell, née Hodson, daughter of Sir Humphrey Hodson and the late Lady Hodson . . ." ' she paused, gulped, took a deep breath and continued: ' ". . . and Harry Scott-Forbes, second son of the late Professor Miles Scott-Forbes and Mrs Scott-Forbes." '

There was a moment's stunned silence, broken by Julian, who, forgetting the children were there, exclaimed, 'How the fuck did he pull that one off?'

Lucinda gave him a warning look.

'Pull what off?' said Jamie.

'What's fuck?' Daisy asked curiously.

Deeply shocked, Delia jumped to her feet. 'Daddy means how much *luck* Uncle Harry has had, finding a lovely bride like Mrs Maxwell.' She looked sternly at her employer before turning back to the children again. 'Come and brush your teeth, Jamie, Daisy.' Then she hustled them out of the kitchen, her back rigid with disapproval.

'Whoops!' Julian grinned sheepishly.

But Lucinda wasn't listening. She was reading and re-reading the announcement, her eyes staring unbelievingly at the newsprint. 'How *did* he pull it off? Is she mad?'

'What are you going to do, Bun?'

She glanced up. 'How do you mean?'

'Are you going to ring and congratulate them?'

'I'm not even talking to Harry at the moment after the way he's behaved. I wonder if anyone else in the family knew about this?'

Sarah, partaking of breakfast in bed, as she always did, turned to the Court Circular page of the *Telegraph* first, to see if anyone in her circle had died in the past twenty-four hours. The average age of the deceased could affect her emotions for several hours, too. Some days the majority of people listed were in their seventies, which made her feel she was outstaying her welcome and about to become a burden to her family. On other days the greater number seemed to be in their nineties and some even a hundred, and this made her feel very perky, so much so that she would contemplate going out to buy some new shoes, or even a dress.

Today was such a day. Ninety-two . . . ninety-seven . . . ninety-nine . . . she still had plenty of time ahead. Then she looked at what the Royal Family were up to, saw the Queen was working as hard as ever and even Prince Philip, nearing eighty, was keeping busy, and this inspired her, too. If *they* could still lead an active life, so could she.

Finally she turned to the Forthcoming Marriages column. Blinking, she thought for a terrible moment that either her eyes were playing tricks, or she was suffering from the first signs of dementia. But then she read the announcement again. So it was true. Harry had got himself hitched to the woman who had stolen his idea and was marketing it as her own.

Sarah had seen a lot of strange things in her life, but this struck her as bizarre. Why on earth should a beautiful rich widow in her forties, who had the world at her feet, want to marry a penniless thirty-four-year-old waster? Pushing her breakfast tray to one side, she reached for her phone on the bedside table.

Did Anne know what her son was about to do?

'I see your brother's got himself engaged, Tom,' one of his office colleagues remarked during the morning.

Tom frowned, looking blank. 'Engaged in what?' he asked stupidly.

'Engaged to be married, of course.' He flipped the newspaper onto Tom's desk. Tom read the announcement twice. Harry married. A stab of envy shot through him, not because he knew Paula Maxwell was rich and beautiful and lived in a marvellous duplex, not even because he was jealous of Harry, but because it must be so wonderful to get engaged in the first place. How fantastic to have your whole future happiness assured. To be accepted by the woman you love. To know you were going to spend the rest of your life with her . . . Tom sighed, knowing it was no use daydreaming. Susan wasn't the marrying kind, he feared. She'd reared Dick and Steve all by herself, with no need of a man to support them. She was strong and independent. Loving, yes. Warm, oh, yes. Passionate, caring and a born home-maker, definitely. But she didn't actually *need* anyone. If he was to drop dead tomorrow, she'd still keep going, bringing up her boys, earning her own living, and keeping those metaphorical home fires burning.

He glanced at the announcement once more, knowing that whilst he'd be euphoric at a time like this, Harry was probably revelling in the fact he'd never have to work again.

It was the hundred red roses that had done it, of course, hideously clichéd though the gesture had been. That, and the fact she was missing Harry in her bed so badly she couldn't sleep. Never in her whole life had Paula been as aroused by anyone as she was by him. Just to look at him turned her on. She'd become as sexually addicted as a drug addict is to heroin, and if he didn't actually feel the same way, and she had a feeling he didn't, at least he was able to perform to order.

When he'd stormed out of her apartment after she'd told him she'd adopted his idea, she'd presumed that when he'd cooled down and got over his anger he'd come back. But he hadn't.

Paula had really believed he'd eventually understand that what she'd done to him was exactly what he himself had set out to do to her. Couldn't he see they were two of a kind? And that this made them soulmates? Perfectly suited? Wasn't he aware that what she'd done was very wrong, but the sort of thing sharp businessmen did every day? It was the cut and thrust of commerce, and happened in the City all the time, with secret takeover bids, and a bit of share-pushing here and there. So why was Harry letting it affect their wonderful personal life? For once, she thought, he's not using his head. I could still give him the lifestyle he wants, without his ever having to work for it. Except in bed.

For three weeks she agonised, wondering where he was, wondering what he was doing, and wondering how she could get hold of him. Then she'd bumped into Lucinda in the street, and she'd had no contact with Harry either and Paula started to worry. Suppose he'd gone abroad and she never saw him again? Panic and regret began to consume her. She needed Harry as she'd never needed anyone before.

Then the roses had arrived one morning, with a note saying, *Can we talk? Love, Harry*. A frisson of sexual desire shot through her as soon as she realised they were from him. Memories of their adventurous lovemaking made her feel weak. It was going to cost her a lot of money, but so what?

Men bought women, in one way or another, all the time; what was wrong with a bit of role reversal?

She tapped in his mobile number and suddenly he was answering the phone, and at the sound of his voice she lost it completely.

An hour later he was round at her flat, in her bed, and there he remained for several days, while Paula, telling her maid he was ill with flu and mustn't be disturbed, waited on him hand and foot, a slave to lust if ever there was one.

She only left his side once, to have lunch with her father. She knew what the future held, if Harry didn't.

A week later, realising he had it made, Harry accepted Paula's proposal of marriage; how could he refuse? She even displayed a solitaire diamond 'engagement' ring, telling everyone Harry had given it to her. And as a sop to his injured feelings about Family Lines she appointed him chairman of the company, on a good salary plus 10 per cent of the profits.

He wasn't so stupid as not to realise it was a sinecure, but it would look good on the headed paper.

Sir Humphrey Hodson was incandescent when he opened the *Telegraph* that morning. Was this the work of that little shit Harry Scott-Forbes? Had he inserted this announcement in order to publicly embarrass Paula? Sir Humphrey seized the phone and was angrier than ever when he found the number engaged. Paula's mobile gave the busy signal, too. Goddammit! What was going on? If Paula thought she was going to marry that good-for-nothing gold digger . . . Then he paused, remembering she was forty-four, and not a malleable young girl any more. Her money was her own. She could do as she liked. And she *had* been sad and lonely since she'd been widowed.

But Harry Scott-Forbes . . .! For God's sake, surely she could have done better than that? Surely she could have found someone with at least *two* brain cells?

At the third attempt Paula answered her phone and he thought she sounded guarded.

'Are you going to tell me what's going on?' he asked abruptly.

'Harry and I are getting married, Daddy.'

'I gathered that, but in God's name, why? He's a waster, Paula. He'll bleed you dry. I don't want to hurt your feelings, but why do you think he's marrying you?'

'We need each other,' she said quietly. 'It's as simple as that.'

'It's obvious to a blind man why he needs you . . . but why the hell do you need him? You could have anyone you wanted! This is serious, Paula. I'm deeply worried about you.'

She spoke gently now, as if trying to make a child understand. 'I know what I'm doing, Dad. I've tied up all my finances so that no one else can get to them. Family Lines is mine and the company will be paying Harry a salary in accordance with his position.'

'You're *buying* him,' her father said, stunned. 'Paula, how can you . . .?'

'Dad, rich men buy women all the time, so why shouldn't I do the same? I love Harry. I want him in my life. I need him desperately, and I wish I'd handled adopting his idea in a more diplomatic way. I hurt him dreadfully over that, and I nearly lost him because of it. But he missed me enough to want to see me again and now we've made a deal and we're both happy. We both get what we want.'

There was silence on the line while Sir Humphrey tried to gather his thoughts. Then he spoke. 'But do you really think it will last, darling? People like us don't go in for these sorts of Hollywood arrangements.'

He detected a smile in her voice. 'Dad, I'm not a nineteen-year-old heiress. I really do know what I'm doing. That's why we put the announcement in the papers today. We wanted to present our relationship as a fait accompli in order to avoid discussions and arguments. I expect Harry's family will get a shock, too.'

The thought: she can always get a divorce if the worst comes to the worst, flashed philosophically through her father's mind.

'Then if you're really happy, my darling, I'm happy for you,' he heard himself say to his own surprise.

'Thank you, Daddy.' She was laughing merrily now and he knew he'd said the right thing if he wanted to keep her close. 'We're going to have a very quiet wedding and then a big party for everyone in the spring and I hope you'll come to both.'

'Try keeping me away,' he said with forced jauntiness.

The report was in French, but over the years William and Jane had become fluent in the language, so that posed no problem. Nevertheless, the words danced dizzily before their eyes, and it was several minutes before they dared come to a conclusion about the contents.

'Is that right?' Jane kept saying. 'It was the heater in the airing cupboard that started the fire?'

William nodded, frowning. 'Yes. Yes, that must be what they mean by *C'était un thermostat défectueux du chauffage électrique dans la commode qui était à l'origine du feu.* It looks as if the thermostat in the heated rail failed to work, and that some of the linen had got pushed against it. It would have scorched the fabric, it says here, until it got so hot it ignited.'

'Oh, my God.' Jane covered her face with her hands. 'I always hated that heater. Do you remember the time I burnt my arm when I was reaching for some pillowcases?'

'It was very effective, though. Everything was always beautifully dry and aired.'

'But that means you're off the hook, doesn't it? The insurance people may think it's negligence on our part because we didn't know the thermostat was broken, but they can't think it's arson now, can they?'

'I wouldn't think so.' He read the report again, terrified he'd misunderstood

232

it, but no, the fire had definitely started by accident. He hardly dared think about the future because he didn't want to raise Jane's hopes, but if the insurance company paid up, coupled with his restored investment in ICC, then . . . but no, he mustn't even think about that, far less daydream. They'd endured such a punishing time, they were too fragile to bear further disappointments.

'I don't think I'm ever going to find "Pumpkin",' Lucinda told Carina despairingly. The previous week she'd daringly placed another advertisement in the personal column of *The Times* and the *Telegraph*, on the same lines as the one she'd used to trace Miranda Warwick, but this time there'd been no response.

'Perhaps you should put in another appeal,' Carina suggested. She'd invited Lucinda and Julian to supper . . . 'just us, darling, so it's informal' . . . and while the men were deep in discussion about the government, they were catching up on the gossip.

'I suppose I could but I have a gut feeling it wouldn't help,' Lucinda replied, sipping her ice cold champagne. 'Maybe she's married and doesn't want to come forward. Maybe she's abroad, dead, or just doesn't read the newspapers. There's nothing more I can do. Her letters give no clue as to place or even time of her affair with Dad.'

Carina gazed down thoughtfully into her glass. Then she brightened. 'I tell you what you could do,' she said.

'What?'

'Why not *pretend* to the lawyer you've found her?'

Lucinda looked shocked. 'Oh, I couldn't do that.'

'Why not?' Carina spoke matter-of-factly. 'Why not?' she repeated. 'How can he be sure you've actually made contact with Isabelle, Fenella, Renée and what was the other one called?'

'Miranda.'

'Right. For all he knows you've burned all their letters and pocketed the jewellery for yourself. Why don't you tell him that by a stroke of luck you've discovered who "Pumpkin" is, and then you can wrap up the whole thing? Keep the diamond brooch for yourself, which I'm sure is the most valuable piece, and then collect the lolly? He's not going to question you, is he?'

Lucinda shook her head. 'I could never do that to Bernard, apart from which it wouldn't work. Each time I've collected a piece of jewellery he's given me a legal document, stating I'm giving such-and-such a piece to whoever, and they have to sign it, saying they've received it. Then I have to send it back to him. He trusts me, Carina. I wouldn't break that trust if I could.'

There was a long pause while Carina looked down into her glass, examining the bubbles whizzing up to the surface of her drink. 'You could forge the signature, couldn't you? Give "Pumpkin" some name or other . . . say Penny Wright or Pamela Jones, and then sign it yourself, disguising your handwriting?'

Lucinda's jaw dropped. 'Carina! How can you suggest such a thing?' she said, deeply shocked.

'Because I want you to inherit that fortune, and who would know? And who would you be hurting?' Carina argued. 'You've given this woman the opportunity to come forward, and so far she hasn't. Don't tell me you're going to throw in the sponge and let some bloody animal sanctuary benefit from Miles's secret fortune, because you've suddenly come over all moral?'

Lucinda flushed. 'But don't you see, I'd feel bad if I cheated? I'd always know I'd only won this bizarre game Dad set up because I hadn't played by the rules.'

Carina stared at her, her blue eyes suddenly hard. 'You're off the wall!' she said flatly. 'You've played along with his crazy scheme so far and now you just have to tell a lie . . . just *one* lie, in order to fulfil all your wildest dreams! How can you possibly say that's cheating?'

'But it *is*,' Lucinda retorted miserably. 'At the end of the day I've got to live with myself, and I'll never feel comfortable again if I can only get the money by forging a fake signature and lying to Bernard.'

'I'll tell you one thing,' Carina pointed out, 'if you *don't* lie about finding her you *will* be cheating . . . you'll be cheating yourself out of three million pounds and a valuable piece of jewellery.'

Lucinda looked at her in stony silence. 'I can't do it, Carina. If I lose, I lose. But there's no way I can lie to Bernard.'

The room was silent. Julian and Alex had stopped their conversation at the sound of the women's raised voices.

'I would just point out one thing,' Julian said mildly, catching Lucinda's eye. 'Miles was such a devious old fellow . . . what proof have we got that "Pumpkin" ever actually existed? Maybe she's a figment of his imagination, planted by him just to see if Lucinda would fall into the trap of pretending she'd found her? And if that was the case, Miles could have left another codicil declaring the whole "game" null and void because you hadn't played by his rules.'

'But she must exist. I have her letters,' Lucinda protested, alarmed. 'You don't mean . . .?'

'Miles could have disguised his handwriting and written them himself,' Alex remarked, joining in the conversation. 'Or he could have dictated them to someone.'

'Have you actually got proof he had three million pounds in the first place?' Carina asked suddenly.

'Christ! Could the whole thing be a prank?' Alex asked.

'Don't! Don't!' Lucinda wailed, burying her face in her hands. 'I thought I just had to trace this one last mistress, but now you're all suggesting . . . No!' she added suddenly, sitting upright. 'If Dad was a lunatic, Bernard Clarke isn't. He's on the level and I'd swear on my life about that. I'm sure "Pumpkin" exists. Anyway, Bernard explained how Dad managed to make so much money over the years, so let's not get carried away.'

'Then let's hope you find her,' Carina said peaceably.

'And let's hope he hasn't laid any traps for you to fall into,' Alex added warningly.

Lucinda couldn't get to sleep that night. She kept turning restlessly, her mind buzzing with thoughts of this damned woman who signed herself 'Pumpkin'. Who could she be? Anyone, came the answer. Where could she be found? Anywhere, whispered the night.

Beside her, Julian slumbered soundlessly, his ability to switch off as soon as his head hit the pillow filling her with envy. Eventually, frustrated by lying there doing nothing, she slipped out of bed and, in the darkness, quietly opened the drawer where 'Pumpkin's' letters lay. Then she crept down to the drawing room and, settling herself by a reading lamp, started to examine them once more, searching for any clue that might give away the identity of the writer.

I dreamed of you last night, saw your face, heard your voice . . . did you know that when you reach orgasm your dark eyes turn to black? Jet black. As unfathomable as a deep pool. What are you thinking, my love, at the moment when you pour yourself into me? Oh, how I want you with me now, how I long to feel your touch . . .

Lucinda picked up another letter, *Beloved one*, it began, *nothing will ever be the same again now that I know how much we love each other and how bonded we are . . .*

Glancing through the rest of the letters, and there were over twenty in all, Lucinda realised they were in much the same vein. There was really nothing to be learned from them. The affair had, as she'd realised before, been particularly passionate. Even more so than Miles's affair with the fiery Isabelle. This struck Lucinda as interesting because 'Pumpkin' was so obviously English she would have expected her letters to be more reserved. But maybe that was to adhere to the clichéd belief that all English people were undemonstrative.

But what really marked them as different from all the other love letters was the very distinctive handwriting, with its long loopy regular curves, making it resemble a stylised Byzantine design rather than ordinary handwriting. Who the hell wrote like that?

The night had grown chilly and Lucinda felt suddenly sickened by the unwanted knowledge she'd gained since her father's death. Why couldn't he have let the past die with him? And why, in God's name, had he chosen her to resurrect it?

Steve and Dick were so excited they didn't know what to do with themselves. They'd never had a proper holiday before and they were up at six o'clock in the morning, racing around the little house, making sure their bathing things were packed, the fishing rods Tom had bought them were in the boot of his car, and their beach towels were in their cases. No matter how often Susan reassured them, they were still hyper at the prospect of going away.

Tom was taking them all to Bude, in Cornwall, for two weeks. He'd booked two double rooms at the Burn View Hotel, a few minutes' walk from the vast sandy beach, and he'd promised them trips to Hartland Point to see the lighthouse, as well as Padstow, Clovelly and Tintagel. The last particularly excited the boys because they'd been learning at school all about the legend of King Arthur and the castle he'd built for Guinevere and the Knights of the Round Table, and how Merlin the Magician was said to have lived in a cave under the castle.

'Will we see the Round Table?' Dick asked eagerly.

'Sorry, lads, but most of the castle has been washed away by the sea, hundreds of years ago. It's just a ruin now, but a very exciting one with a marvellous view of the Atlantic,' Tom replied.

'You obviously know that part of the world?' Susan asked, as they set off after breakfast on Saturday morning.

Tom nodded. 'I did have a couple of very happy holidays there with a friend from school and his family. I haven't been back since I was twelve, but I remember it being a great place. Steve and Dick can go rock climbing, or fishing on the canal. I used to catch dogfish in the rocky pools on the beach, and tiny crabs, too. Then we'll get surfboards so we can all go surfing. That's brilliant fun.' He sounded so young and enthusiastic that Susan turned smilingly to look at him.

'It's going to be the most marvellous holiday we've ever had,' she murmured. 'A real family holiday,' she added wistfully. It wasn't really, of course. It would be if Tom even hinted at marriage, but he seemed to be ignoring its very existence, and she wasn't sure why. They'd never been closer or more loving. He was devoted to Steve and Dick and he couldn't do enough for her, but marriage . . .? It was as if it hadn't even crossed his mind. This made her worried, and saddened her, too. She thought they'd arrived at an understanding, neither of them feeling inadequate or undeserving of the other, and she'd rejoiced in their new rapprochement, thinking it was the beginning of a secure relationship. But nothing more had actually happened. Tom seemed happy with the way things were and she feared that he simply didn't want to commit to marriage.

'We'll have a marvellous time,' Tom was telling the boys. 'The surfing at Summerleaze Beach is the best on the west coast. You get Atlantic rollers coming in, right up the beach, and it's terrific.'

'Do you have to stand on the surfboards?' Steve asked doubtfully.

Tom shook his head. 'The boards we'll get are like thin planks of wood with a curved lip at the front. You just lie on your stomach and come in on a wave.'

'Cool!'

'Wicked! I thought we'd have to stand, like that advert on the telly. Wheeeeee!' The boys swayed from side to side on the back seat of the car, waving their arms, and pretending they were zig-zagging on incoming rollers.

236

Susan was laughing, excited herself. 'We'll never keep them out of the water, you know that, don't you?' she asked Tom.

'Just as well I bought us all wet suits then, isn't it?'

'Oh, Tom!'

'Wicked!' yelled the boys, swaying and bouncing harder than ever. 'Bags I first in the sea.'

Both Jamie and Daisy had sore throats and high temperatures.

'You must stay in bed today,' Lucinda told them, looking worriedly at their flushed cheeks. Their breathing was slightly rasping too, and they seemed happy to loll lethargically in bed, instead of romping noisily all over the house.

Delia had awoken Lucinda at seven o'clock that morning, to report the children weren't well.

'I think we should ask the doctor to drop in and see them,' Lucinda said anxiously.

Delia nodded. 'Can't be too careful. Lot of meningitis about.'

Lucinda felt like killing her for voicing her own fears. 'Lots of flu, too,' she retorted briskly. 'I'll ring Dr Haswell now. Will you be all right on your own today?' she continued, cold with guilt and misery. Shouldn't a mother stay with her children when they were ill? You can be home in half an hour if need be, said a voice in her head. 'Ring me if there's any change,' she told Delia. I shouldn't be giving her this responsibility. I should be here, with Jamie and Daisy.

'Don't worry, we'll be fine, Lucinda,' Delia was saying sturdily. 'I'll keep them warm, give them lots of drinks, and we'll see what Dr Haswell has to say.'

'Yes. Right. Thank you.' She hurried back to her bedroom, feeling distraught. Supposing they were sickening for a serious illness?

Julian was still in the shower. 'Everything OK?' he shouted above the gentle roar of the water.

'I'm phoning Dr Haswell.'

As she finished speaking to their kindly family doctor, Julian appeared at her side, his body steaming, a towel slung round his hips. 'What's wrong with them?' She could tell by his voice he was anxious too.

'Temperature. Sore throats.'

'They're probably coming down with a cold,' he said, relieved. 'You know how easily children run a temperature.' He towelled his hair vigorously. 'You're in a state because you've got to leave them and go to work, aren't you?'

'Aren't you?' she snapped.

'I wish we could both stay, though I don't think it's necessary. Delia's very competent, and in an emergency she can get hold of us immediately.'

Lucinda said nothing, but her mouth was tight as she stepped into the bath and her eyes had the blank look of deep anxiety, like an animal in pain.

237

When she'd dressed she hurried back to the children's room, but Jamie and Daisy were asleep again, their flushed little faces half hidden by their duvets, their hair sticking clammily to their temples.

Delia hovered in the doorway. 'They've had a drink but I thought it best to let them sleep,' she whispered. 'My ma always says sleep is the best medicine.'

Lucinda nodded. 'The doctor will be here during the morning. He didn't think it was anything serious, but he's going to have a look at them, anyway. You'll ring me if . . .'

' 'Course I will, Lucinda. They'll be as right as rain. You get off to work, and don't worry. I'll ring you when the doctor's been.'

'Thanks, Delia.' Lucinda looked at her babies again, finding it the hardest thing in the world to leave them when they were like this but knowing that she had to, especially at the moment, when things were so edgy at the office.

Julian came tiptoeing into the room. He peered at the children one by one, careful not to disturb them.

'They'll be fine,' he whispered. 'I'll keep my mobile on all day, Delia, if you need me.'

'So will I,' Lucinda said hollowly. She glanced at her watch. She was going to be late. 'I'll get back as early as I can,' she promised.

'Try not to worry, Bun,' Julian murmured as they hurried down the stairs together.

'I can't go on like this,' she told him. 'It's not fair on the children and it's not fair on us, either.' She was near to tears.

'Maybe I can get a better paid job, then you can give up work altogether.'

'Don't even go there,' she whispered, turning to kiss him fleetingly on the lips. 'You love your job. The sensible thing would be for me to leave D'Aussoire, and do something less demanding. With more flexible hours. Must fly now, see you tonight.'

'Have you heard . . .?' D'Aussoire was in crisis. There seemed to be a buzz of urgent activity on all eleven floors, as rumours and counter rumours flew around like angry wasps, no one knowing quite what to believe.

'What's going on?' Lucinda glanced around enquiringly as she hurried to her desk. People were huddled in groups, whispering nervously, looking shocked.

A silence as sudden as a radio being switched off fell over the vast office space. Colleagues looked embarrassed, feet shuffled, no one looked directly at Lucinda. Then she noticed Geneviève was missing.

'I don't believe it,' she said slowly.

'She wasn't alone,' Peter croaked, looking dazed.

Lucinda swung round to look at him. 'What do you mean, she wasn't alone?'

'Alain's gone too.'

'*Alain*?' she repeated incredulously.

The others nodded. Then they all started talking at once, pouring out the information in fragments, like bits of a puzzle, jumbled up.

'They were having an affair . . .'

'. . . they were in collusion.'

'Between them they were able to gather . . .'

'. . . information from both sides of the Channel.'

'Alain was in a state the other day because he thought she'd gone without him . . .'

'. . . to live in Mexico.'

'He's left his wife for Geneviève . . .'

'. . . Xanthe paid them twelve million for all the info.'

Lucinda stood still, as the words whirled around her like a spinning-wheel of chatter. She sat, trying to take in the enormity of what had happened. It didn't seem possible. Alain, yes. She'd never liked him, never trusted him, and it came as no surprise to realise that he had massively cheated the company of which he'd been a director for eleven years, but Geneviève . . .!

Lucinda shook her head, wondering how she could have been so wrong about the young woman she had so utterly trusted. Or had Geneviève been under Alain's spell? Madly in love with him, perhaps? But most of all she felt betrayed. These people had been her work colleagues; Alain had nagged her to try to find the culprit, Geneviève had pretended to be her friend.

Peter came over. Placing his hands on Lucinda's desk, he leaned forward and spoke to her in a low voice.

'It's not your responsibility,' he said, guessing what Lucinda was thinking. 'You were very good to Geneviève, turning a blind eye when she pleaded illness; backing her when she came in for criticism. You were always loyal.'

'I liked her,' Lucinda pointed out wonderingly. 'How could I have been so wrong? Now I feel dreadful. I should have known what was going on. Or at least suspected something.'

'I don't think anyone had any idea what she was up to,' Peter retorted stoutly. 'You couldn't possibly have known. I think Alain was always snooping around just to put us off the scent, don't you? Probably making sure Geneviève wasn't giving anything away, too.'

'Dear God,' Lucinda groaned, leaning back in her chair. 'This is a lousy business, isn't it? It's so corrupt. I have to go and buy cosmetics manfactured by other companies, pretending I'm an ordinary housewife, and then they get sent off to the laboratory to see if we can pinch any of their ideas, and other companies do the same to us. I hate it all, you know. The competitiveness. The rivalry. The way we all spy on each other. It's pretty disgusting, isn't it?'

'Don't let it get you down, Lucinda. People like you are needed in this industry.'

Lucinda spoke bluntly. 'Frankly, Peter, I don't think I can take much more of it. This business with Geneviève is the last straw. I befriended her when she arrived from Paris. Made sure she was all right, and had a place to stay.

And then she goes and does this and I never even noticed.'

Because I have other things on my mind right now, she reflected. Jamie and Daisy are ill and I should be at home with them. Julian deserves more of my time, too. And so does Mum. And Granny. Then there's the business of Dad's damned Will . . . And now this debacle at D'Aussoire . . . She could feel the beginnings of a tension headache starting and she wished she had the time to take up yoga or something.

Later that day, having been told by the doctor that he thought the children were sickening for chickenpox, and that they were to stay in bed, she phoned Julian.

'There is a lot of chickenpox going round, apparently,' she told him, 'so he's probably right.'

Julian was philosophical. 'Better they get these childhood diseases over as soon as possible. I had chickenpox when I was twenty-one and it was hell.'

Then she told him about Geneviève, whom he'd met a couple of times when he'd picked Lucinda up from work.

'I'm sickened by the whole thing,' she told him. 'It amounts to negligence on my part that I was completely unaware that one of the girls in my department was hand-in-glove with one of the directors, and that between them they were selling the details of a product to a major rival and I missed it because I thought Geneviève was a friend. I always thought Alain was a bastard, but at least I believed he was on the level. I'm absolutely gutted. And completely disillusioned. I'm going to resign, Julian. This is a corrupt business and I don't want to have anything more to do with it.'

'Poor Bun. Let's talk about it tonight, shall we? I think I can get away early, so I'll be home by half past four. That'll give Delia a bit of a break.'

'Great. I'll get back as soon as I can, too,' she told him. 'I've thought of something else, Julian. We may have to cancel our weekend with Rachel and Ian if Jamie and Daisy have chickenpox.'

He groaned. 'You're right. Let's see how they are tomorrow.'

Anne only stopped answering the letters in order to have a bath and something to eat, before returning to Miles's desk to renew her task. Only, strangely, it wasn't a chore. It wasn't a tedious duty that good manners dictated she do. It was highly pleasurable putting pen to paper, forming the words, shaping the phrases, lengthening a paragraph or choosing another adjective . . . it reminded her of something she'd enjoyed doing a long time ago. Something that formed an escape route from reality, that let her imagination take flight, that gave her a curious physical delight and a feeling of freedom such as she hadn't felt since she'd been in her teens.

For a moment she felt a pang of regret that because of Miles's caustic remarks she'd given up writing children's stories. Maybe she should get them out again and have a look at them? Maybe with a little jigging they wouldn't be the rubbish Miles had suggested they were?

Anne's blood flowed a little faster in her veins, as she finished yet another letter. Hadn't her mother said that older women sometimes started a new career, just when they thought their lives were over? Supposing . . .? She pulled herself together with an excited little tug of emotion. She mustn't get carried away. She must finish answering all these letters, first.

'Wicked! Look at those waves!' Steve stood on the narrow promenade, in front of the row of beach huts, and pointed to the grey-green sea as it stormed up the beach on an incoming tide.

'Cool,' Dick agreed, trying to keep the excitement out of his voice.

Susan hooked her hand into the curve of Tom's arm. 'It looks quite rough,' she observed, watching the threshing waves pounding on the sand before surging forward in a thundering frothy mass.

Tom nodded. 'It is a bit rough today. That's why the flags are crossed on that stand in the middle of the beach. There's a strong westerly wind coming in from the Atlantic, too.'

Steve looked impressed. 'Is it dangerous?'

'It can be,' Tom admitted. 'That's why they use the flags to warn people not to swim. There are always lifeguards on duty, of course, just in case someone gets into trouble.'

The boys surveyed the beach in silent awe. To their left, the causeway, built over a hundred years ago from large flat stones, looked like a submarine in distress as the waves hit it and silvery spumes of spray caused it to momentarily disappear, only to re-emerge again out of the heavy dragging pull of the water.

'It'll be fine tomorrow,' Tom observed knowledgeably. 'In the meanwhile, how about some fishing on the canal?'

'Can't we climb over there?' Dick asked, pointing to the right-hand side of the beach, where the rocks rose in jagged grandeur, their surface embellished with thick scratchy crustaceans.

'Not on an incoming tide,' Tom warned. 'It's easy to get cut off from the beach and stranded and then you're really in trouble. We'll explore them tomorrow at low tide, and do some dog fishing. There are some beautiful pools over there.'

Susan looked up at Tom with affection. 'You seem to remember it all,' she said. 'How long is it since you've been here?'

He did some quick calculations. 'About twenty-five years, I suppose, but it's the sort of place where nothing changes, thank God. Driving to the hotel just now, I recognised most of the shops; where we bought fishing line, and a beach ball and shrimping nets . . . and the corner shop that sold hot dogs and ice cream . . .' His voice faded away and he was smiling at the memory of the only happy holiday he'd ever had.

Susan hugged him to her side. 'We'll make this another happy holiday,' she murmured, reading his thoughts. 'It'll certainly be the best holiday the boys and I have ever had and that's for sure.'

241

Tom gave her a grateful look. 'It will be for me, too.'

They awoke the next morning to clear blue skies, a calm sea and a stretch of sandy beach that made Dick and Steve run to the water's edge, shrieking with delight, wanting to do everything at once; swim, surf, rock climb, fish, walk along the towpath on the downs overlooking the Atlantic, take a canoe up the canal to where Tom told them they would see what he'd used to call the Gingerbread House, have an ice cream, play ball, sunbathe, have a picnic . . .

'Can we, Mum? Can we, Tom?' they kept begging.

Tom laughed. 'We'll do it *all*, but one thing at a time,' he told them. 'Remember, we are here for two weeks. There's plenty of time. And we can come back next year, too, if you want.'

The boys looked deeply impressed at this last remark. So did Susan.

'Aren't children extraordinary?' Lucinda exclaimed in disbelief. Jamie and Daisy had completely recovered after two days in bed. Their temperatures had been normal for twenty-four hours, their snuffles had vanished, and Dr Haswell had pronounced them absolutely fit that morning.

It was as Julian had said; children can run high temperatures and have a slight infection one minute, and be perfectly all right the next.

'I'm glad we didn't cancel going to stay with Rachel and Ian this weekend,' Lucinda continued.

The Comptons had turned hospitality into an art form and when they drove up to the entrance of Stapely Manor on the Friday evening it was as if they were being enveloped in a cocoon of luxury. There was something sublimely reassuring and soothing about staying in a beautiful house, where everything was organised to perfection and a nanny whisked Jamie and Daisy off to play with Toby and Archie in a nursery that resembled Hamley's toy shop. It was as if they were children themselves again, stripped of responsibility or the need to make any decisions. Lucinda in particular found it a curiously free and light-hearted feeling.

'Come and have a drink in the garden, while Nanny gives the children supper?' Rachel suggested, after she and Ian had greeted them effusively. She led the way through an exquisite all white drawing room, onto a shady terrace which overlooked three acres of manicured lawns and flower beds. In the soft evening sunlight the shadows were long, the breeze was gentle, and the air was filled with the scent of nicotiana, jasmine and roses.

Lucinda looked around appreciatively, marvelling at the orderliness and perfection of everything, while Julian lowered himself onto a cushioned garden chair with a sigh of pure pleasure. Within moments a jug of chilled Pimms, brimming with fruit and sprigs of borage, had been placed on a low table by Ian, and they knew a weekend of unadulterated sybaritism had begun.

'This is the life,' Julian said, stretching his legs with a sheepish grin.

'Heaven to be here,' Lucinda agreed, feeling relaxed for the first time in weeks and suddenly glad she'd decided to pack her prettiest clothes, knowing she wouldn't be allowed to go even near the kitchen.

More guests arrived for the weekend. Hazel and Melvyn Anstruther, a newly married couple who giggled a lot and held hands self-consciously; Jemima and Edward Parsons, with their six-year-old daughter, Calista, who was wafted off to the nursery to join the other children as soon as she set foot in the drive. Finally Karen and Owen Randall arrived. They were jolly and boisterous, and burst in on the proceedings armed with tennis rackets and golf clubs, declaring noisily: 'We're *mad* about sport and we remembered you had a tennis court and were near a golf course.'

Rachel soon had everything under control, though, including her guests. Drinks over, they were tactfully dispatched to their various rooms, all of which had bathrooms en suite, it being made plain they should gather in the drawing room for drinks 'at eight o'clock, for dinner at eight thirty'.

Soaking in a tub of hot water perfumed with Jo Malone tuberose bath oil, Lucinda closed her eyes in a state of perfect contentment. Jamie and Daisy were now watching a video in the nursery with the other children, having been given a delicious supper, while next door Julian lay spread-eagled on the four-poster bed, drowsily flipping through a new edition of *Country Life*. She was determined to forget her worries this weekend. It was going to be a couple of days of self-indulgence. To hell with D'Aussoire; the sooner she left the better. And fuck her father's sick idea of turning her inheritance into a grown-up game of Treasure Hunt. It was over anyway. She'd never trace 'Pumpkin' now. But the diamond brooch was hers and so was the pearl necklace. At least she presumed they were, unless there was some diabolical little codicil Bernard hadn't mentioned, which stated she got absolutely nothing unless she got everything right.

If what Carina thought was true, the brooch was worth thousands of pounds, and the pearls were bound to be worth something. She would sell them, and that would give her financial breathing space while she looked for another, less demanding job. It was disappointing, but then she'd never really believed in the three million pound jackpot anyway. Fortunes like that didn't fall into the lap of someone like her.

'OK, Bun?' Julian asked, strolling into the warm scented bathroom.

She rose from the water and wrapped a fluffy white towel around her slim body. Her eyes were bright and clear and she looked as if she'd just shed a heavy burden.

'I'm absolutely fine,' she replied, smiling. And she was. The relief at having decided to leave D'Aussoire, and end her pursuit of 'Pumpkin' and settle for a more realistic future, made her feel terrific. Light. Free. Positive. And they were on the eve of a really enjoyable weekend.

'What's the time?' she asked.

Julian, undressing slowly, glanced at his watch. 'Half past seven. Plenty of time before we have to be downstairs again.'

'That's just what I thought,' she grinned mischievously, dropping her towel to the floor. She grabbed his hand. 'Come on. That four-poster bed wasn't only meant for sleeping in, you know.'

Tiffy and Ollie, the miniature dachshunds, lay on the hearth rug, their brown coats gleaming, their paws twitching from time to time as they dozed fitfully through the after-dinner chatter. Everyone had congregated in the drawing room, made merry by a carefully chosen selection from Ian's wine cellar.

'That was a fantastic dinner, Rachel,' Lucinda remarked, sipping her coffee. They'd started with *crème cendennaise*, a chicory, potato and leek velouté with croutons, followed by *délice de flétan aida*, which was a small fillet of halibut garnished with asparagus tips in a white wine sauce. For the main course Rachel had chosen roasted quail with butternut risotto, with white truffle oil, served with *pommes nouvelles* and *endives meunière*. Finally, there was ice-cream soufflé flavoured with Cointreau. Everything had been so exquisitely cooked, though, and the portions were so small and dainty, that no one felt uncomfortably full.

'It was super,' the jolly Randall couple declared loudly.

'Absolutely wonderful,' stated Edward Parsons, while Jemima patted her stomach and giggled that she wouldn't be able to eat for another week.

The others all agreed, enthusiastically. Rachel was a renowned cook amongst her friends, and in spite of producing four courses for ten people she still looked cool and immaculate, her pale blue dress not even creased. She laughed gaily, offering around a dish of home-made truffles. 'It's easy peasy,' she said lightly. 'I'm not even very original, I'm afraid. I take down recipes from everyone and everywhere. Messing around in the kitchen is my hobby.'

There were groans from the other women. 'Hobby? You actually *like* it?' 'I *hate* cooking.' 'It's so *boring*!' 'Thank God for Marks and Spencer.'

Then, from the newly wed Hazel: 'I don't much like cooking, but I love to make Melvyn's favourite dishes,' she gushed sweetly.

'You'll get over that soon enough,' Karen Randall told her briskly. 'I point Owen in the direction of the microwave, and then it's up to him.'

'I must say,' Lucinda said thoughtfully, 'I'd love to have a bit more time to spend cooking. I adored that halibut dish, Rachel. Is it very difficult?'

Rachel sparkled knowingly. 'With the white wine sauce and asparagus? Did you like it? Funnily enough, I got that recipe from Carina.'

'Carina?' Julian queried jokingly. 'Since when did she graduate as a Cordon Bleu cook?'

'I think she said she got it from her mother. Anyway, she gave it to me,' Rachel confided, as if she were giving away a state secret. She jumped energetically to her feet. 'I'll get it for you, Lucinda.'

'Oh, there's no hurry,' Lucinda said, but Rachel was gone, trotting off to the kitchen, her pale blue high-heeled sandals clicking across the parquet floor. A minute later she reappeared, the recipe carefully preserved in a transparent plastic sleeve.

'There you go.' She handed it gaily to Lucinda. 'You can copy it out and let me have it back tomorrow.'

Lucinda looked at the recipe, and the world seemed to drop off its axis and go spinning away in free fall. Shock tremors reverberated through her as if she'd touched a live wire. Realisation hit her in mounting waves of horrified awareness. She felt cold and sick and for a moment she thought she was going to faint.

'What's up, Bun?' she heard Julian say in a low voice. Her face had become a transparent white, and her hands trembled as she continued to stare disbelievingly at the recipe.

'The writing,' she whispered. 'But it can't be . . .!'

'What?'

Lucinda looked at Rachel as she skimmed past, still offering her home-made truffles, seeing her as if for the first time. Yet she had to believe the evidence of her eyes. The recipe was written in an extraordinary hand, large and regular with loopy lines and curves like a Byzantine pattern.

Julian was watching her with concern, unaware she'd reached the end of her treasure trail only to find herself sickened by what she'd found.

'Are you all right?' he whispered.

She hardly recognised her own voice, it was so croaky.

'It's "Pumpkin's" handwriting!'

It was very late now, and all the other guests had retired to their rooms, sated with food and drink. Rachel kept looking at Lucinda quizzically, too polite to suggest it was time to go up to bed but obviously vexed that they were lingering.

'Can you settle the dogs for the night, Ian?' she asked her husband pointedly, as she hovered by the drawing-room door.

Julian rose, glancing knowingly at Lucinda as he did so. 'Ian, I'll give you a hand,' he said, following his host into the hall.

'I really think we should . . .?' fluttered Rachel, looking at Lucinda expectantly, her hand on the light switch.

Lucinda held out the recipe, still in its plastic sleeve. 'So you're "Pumpkin",' she said slowly.

'Excuse me?' Rachel looked at her blankly.

'I recognise your handwriting, Rachel, so there's no use denying it. I've been trying to trace you for months. I'd given up, in fact, and then when you handed me this tonight . . . I presume Ian has no idea? Did you have the affair before you met him? There's no date on your letters.'

To her surprise, Rachel frowned, and then flew to her side, pulling her gently down onto the sofa, before sitting down beside her and taking her hand.

'I *thought* you looked unwell a little while ago. Is there anything I can get you?' she asked anxiously.

Lucinda stared at her, stunned. 'Why are you denying it?' she whispered.

'I know you had an affair with my father. I have all your letters to him, Rachel. I recognised your handwriting the moment I saw it. We've always talked on the phone, I suppose, so I've never actually seen your writing before, but for God's sake . . . it's so distinctive! It couldn't be anyone else's writing but yours.'

Rachel looked panic-stricken. 'Lucinda, you've made a terrible mistake,' she gasped. 'I never even knew your father. He was an old man, wasn't he? How could you think . . .?'

'But this is your handwriting, isn't it?' Lucinda asked accusingly.

'No!' Rachel's hands clutched spasmodically at the pearls around her neck as if they were choking her. She'd turned pale, and to Lucinda she looked profoundly guilty.

'Don't worry, Rachel. I'm not angry. In fact I'm relieved and thankful to have discovered who "Pumpkin" is at last,' Lucinda reassured her. 'It was just such a shock.'

'Lucinda, will you listen to me? I didn't write out that recipe.'

There was a moment's silence as the two women looked at each other.

'Then who the hell did?' Lucinda demanded suspiciously.

Rachel bit her lip and looked acutely embarrassed. 'I feel I should stay out of this,' she said nervously. 'I don't know what it's about, but I can only assure you I never even met your father.'

Ian and Julian came back into the room at that moment.

'What's going on?' Ian asked, looking at the two women.

Lucinda looked up at him. 'I just want to know whose handwriting this is.'

Ian shrugged. 'Can't help you there, I'm afraid. Does it matter?'

'Yes.'

'So whose handwriting is it, darling?' Ian turned to his wife.

'This puts me in a terrible position. I don't think I *can*,' Rachel bleated frantically, reminding Lucinda of a moth beating its wings against a window in order to escape.

Ian frowned. 'Why the hell not? I don't get it.'

Julian stepped forward. 'It's a very long story, and eventually Lucinda may be able to tell you all about it, but in the meantime it is vital for her to know whose handwriting this is. Her future could depend on it.'

Rachel looked at him quite crossly. 'But Carina is a good friend of mine, too. I owe her my loyalty as well as—'

Too late she realised what she'd said.

When they got back to London on Sunday evening, Lucinda realised she didn't remember much about their weekend with Rachel and Ian. She had a vague recollection of apologising profusely to Rachel, and of telling her the whole story, but after that it was as if she had dozed fitfully through a long film, only catching snatches of scenes where people gathered together to talk and laugh and eat and drink, while all the time the knowledge she had gained grew and grew like a mushroom in her head: Carina . . . her best friend; Carina . . . her father's mistress; Carina, the consummate liar; Carina . . . *who had promised to help her find Miles's five mistresses and had finally told her to pretend she'd found 'Pumpkin' so she could claim her inheritance.* And all along . . . the deceit hurt badly. Lucinda turned to Julian, who was equally shocked, and sought consolation.

'I can hardly believe it,' she kept saying, but Rachel had asssured her she'd watched as Carina had carefully copied out the recipe, even making a joke about her enormous and strange handwriting: 'It's too silly,' she'd laughed, 'if I write a thank you letter it takes up four pages. That's why I live on the phone, but so does everyone else these days.'

But she'd written to Miles, Lucinda reflected. Pages and pages describing her passionate feelings, as if her very soul had been forced to pour out the scorching depths of her emotions, as if only the written words, hot and impulsive, could do justice to her great love for him.

'But when . . . *when* did the affair take place?' Lucinda had asked Rachel, but Rachel couldn't answer because she'd never realised Carina had had a lover in the first place.

Back in London, Lucinda kept thinking about this.

'I've known her for twelve or thirteen years,' she told Julian. 'Did she already know Dad? Or did she meet him through me? Now I realise why she was so upset at his memorial service. That was the only time I've ever seen her cry.'

'So you think the affair took place before she got married?'

'I would have thought so, though she must have been very young. Perhaps it was just before he met Isabelle . . .!' She gave a sharp intake of breath. 'Oh, my God, and I asked her to look after Isabelle when we came out of the church! Do you think they guessed that . . .? Compared notes . . .?'

Julian looked at her quizzically. 'I think you'd have heard from Isabelle if that had been the case.'

'You're right. Phew! If Isabelle had realised Carina, Fenella *and* Renée had all had affairs with Dad, and that they were all at the service . . .!'

'Don't even think about it. When will you tell her?'

The last bit of the puzzle was about to be clicked into place. The final betrayal – a double betrayal now, Miles cheating on Anne, Carina lying to Lucinda – was about to be revealed, and Lucinda would soon be in a position to tell Bernard that she had completed her father's bizarre challenge.

Lucinda's mouth tightened. 'She's had her fun with me,' she said softly, 'now it's my turn.'

Susan lay stretched on the beach towel, realising she'd never been as happy in her life as she was now. The roar of the incoming waves and then the hiss as they were sucked back down the sand and shingle beach became a soothing rhythmic background to the happy shrieks of children playing ball games and building sandcastles and the occasional melancholy cry of a seagull.

Above, a cloudless blue sky hung like a canopy, dizzying in its pure, clear, unmarred depths as she gazed up at it and reflected on how much she loved Tom.

He lay on his stomach beside her, reading a book. Anyone glancing in their direction would think they were a staid married couple with a couple of sons, enjoying their annual holiday by the sea. Susan rolled over onto her front, too, stretching her bare legs behind her.

'Shall I rub some sun block onto your back?' Tom offered, placing his book face down. 'This is the most dangerous place for sunbathing in the world, you know,' he continued. 'One doesn't notice one's getting burned because the sea breeze is so cooling, but I remember my friend's mother got dreadfully burned when we were here. She had to go to the doctor and he said she could have achieved the same results by chucking a bucket of scalding water all over herself. She was really quite ill.'

'I'm being very careful,' Susan assured him, 'and I've made sure the boys have got a strong sun block on, too.'

Tom lay with his cheeks resting on his forearms, which were frosted with golden sand. Susan watched him for a moment longer before closing her eyes and saying to herself: just another five minutes relaxing then I'll unpack the picnic tea; jam sandwiches, shortbread biscuits, a Thermos of tea and some tins of Coca-Cola. What a wonderful holiday the boys are having. They aren't even missing the TV.

At first she thought the raised voices coming from the water's edge was a rowdy game of football being played by a large noisy family down from the Midlands who had been hogging the centre of the beach for days. But then she noticed an edge of urgency in their yells, and what sounded like a wail of panic. She glanced questioningly at Tom but he was peacefully absorbed in his book. It couldn't be anything much, then. She closed her eyes again.

Footsteps thudding thickly on the wet sand came nearer. Really, those parents should have more control of their children, she thought irritably. She raised her head to look round. But it wasn't one of the noisy family tearing up the beach, arms and legs working frantically, eyes wide with panic, mouth open in a struggle to breathe and yell at the same time. It was Dick.

'Mum! Mum!' he screamed, showering them with sand as he skidded to a stop. 'Steve can't get out of the water! He keeps being swept back into the waves!'

Even as he spoke Tom was on his feet, bolting down the beach with long desperate strides, shouting: 'Lifeguard! *Lifeguard*!' before he flung himself into the turbulent water where the undertow was so fierce and the currents were so strong that dozens of swimmers had perished over the years.

'Oh, God, please no . . .' Dry sobs were wrenched from Susan's lungs as she staggered to the water's edge, on legs that threatened to give way beneath her. 'Please God,' she muttered with a feeling of desperation that was too deep for tears, too deep for reason, a mindless blind panic that edged on insanity. 'Please God . . . *please* . . .'

Out at sea, the distance widening every second, Steve's head bobbed like a cork being tossed towards the rocks with their deadly jagged points. A crowd was gathering, huddling together, mothers grabbing their children and holding them close. Susan could see Tom's head too, battling against the current, in danger of being swept away as well although he was a strong swimmer.

Dick, watching fearfully, started to walk into the water again, was knee high to the almost spent waves, but with a feral scream of fear Susan grabbed him back, sinking to her knees, shaking all over, holding on to him tightly, sobbing: 'No, no.'

She was aware of frantic activity all around her, of a thick rope being unwound from a wheel high up the beach, of a terrible silence as the crowds watched, mesmerised by the sight of Steve's little head, popping up further and further out to sea. And of another head, and strong arms and shoulders . . . but would the swimmer reach the child in time?

'Didn't they see the flags were crossed in warning?' said a man to his wife, who was holding her children by their hands. 'Everyone knows it's dangerous to swim when the flags are crossed.'

Minutes before, the beach had been a glorious playground; now it was a doomed and savage place, cold, windswept, a setting for violent death. Kites and bats and balls lay abandoned. Holidaymakers strained to see what was happening, thanking God it wasn't their child in the water. They held their breath, willing the swimmer to reach out and grab the little boy before it was too late, knowing they were watching an impending tragedy, remembering this was real life, and not a film on the telly. Then a lifeguard came thundering past, tanned and muscular, the rope attached to the harness he wore.

For a moment there was a ripple of murmurs. Help was on its way. But in the distance a thin white arm appeared for a moment as if to wave goodbye before disappearing. Then there was no sign of the little bobbing head at all.

Groans rose and swelled and then the beach fell silent again. Several women broke down and started weeping, but Susan, still on her knees and clutching Dick, kept her eyes on the spot where Steve had vanished, willing him to survive, willing Tom to reach him in time, promising God anything he wanted if only he'd save her child. Everything was a blur to her tear-filled eyes now; both heads had vanished and the sea was an ugly deathtrap, swallowing up two of the people she loved most. Taking away from her the rest of her life.

Then she heard Dick speak hoarsely as he tried to wriggle out of her arms and she felt as if the world was dissolving, and she was dissolving with it.

'Tom's got him! Tom's got him!' he was yelling.

The ripple of murmurs had turned into a roar. People clapped and cheered. Tom was the hero of the hour. He was swimming with his back to the shore now, bringing Steve with him, the lifeguard hovering as if to assist, but this was Tom's moment. As he neared the shallows he stood up, lifting Steve in his arms, and the little boy, grinning wanly, clung round his neck as if he never wanted to let him go.

'I have my father to thank for that,' Tom mused wonderingly, when the boys were safely tucked up in bed that night. 'If he hadn't thrown me into that bloody loch when I was three, I'd never have learned to be such a strong swimmer.'

Susan looked at him, her eyes filled with tenderness and admiration. 'It was your own determination,' she told him, taking his hand. Then she took a deep breath. 'You're a wonderful man, Tom, and you've proved it, and I love you very much and if you don't marry me now I'll never speak to you again.'

Eighteen

Bernard Clarke's expression was inscrutable. 'So you're giving the rope of pearls to the last mistress on the list and keeping the diamond spray brooch for yourself?'

Lucinda nodded. 'I reckon it's the most valuable piece of jewellery, though it's not exactly my style. But that's what Dad wanted me to do, isn't it? Keep the most valuable piece for myself.'

'He did indeed, and I must congratulate you on tracing all the ladies in question. He set you an extremely tough assignment, as I pointed out to him at the time, but he said he was sure you'd do it.' He folded his hands and regarded her gravely. 'It can't have been the most pleasant of experiences.'

'It was . . . a learning curve as they say in America,' she remarked, raising her eyebrows. 'But I still have to assimilate the whole picture, try to fathom exactly what it was all about, and *why* Dad wanted me to go through this nightmarish rigmarole. So far the whole thing seems quite pointless, a complicated procedure that has taken me round the block a couple of times for no apparent reason. By the way, now that I'm giving the pearls away, are you confirming I'm eligible to inherit the money? That I have kept the most valuable piece of jewellery?'

'Not exactly.'

Lucinda sat upright. 'What do you mean, not exactly?'

Bernard looked at her sadly. 'I don't know the value of any of the jewellery. In the letter of instruction Miles left me, he said you were to take the piece of your choice to a jeweller, any jeweller, to be valued. Then you would know.'

She looked puzzled. 'But how will I know if we haven't had all the other pieces valued?'

'Miles said one piece was worth over thirty thousand pounds and that was the best piece. He knew the rest was all worth much less, so he saw no point it getting it all valued.'

'So if I've left myself with the wrong piece . . . I'll never know who I've given the right piece to?' she asked, appalled.

Bernard's smile was crusty. 'Isn't it better that way?'

She leaned back in the chair, nonplussed. 'I suppose so,' she said reluctantly, 'but it's pretty maddening, isn't it? Out of pure curiosity I'd like to know what everything was worth.'

'That's typical of Miles though, isn't it? Leaving you with a conundrum to the last?'

* * *

251

Lucinda laid the table with care, as if for a celebration. She put some pale pink roses in a small bowl in the middle, and pink candles in the glass candlesticks, although she knew it wasn't correct to have candles at lunch. Her grandmother would have been proud of her, though, for using the white lawn tablecloth and matching napkins, and she'd also got out her best dinner service and cut crystal glasses. She'd have preferred to have made it dinner instead of lunch but that would have been too complicated. Carina would have wondered, for a start, why she hadn't invited Alex, too. And why there was no one else there but the two of them.

A few minutes after one o'clock, Lucinda heard a taxi draw up at the house, and then the click of Carina's high heels on the front step, and finally the *ping* of the bell. She took a deep breath and went to answer the door.

'Darling! Lovely to see you! What a treat! Have you got the day off?' Carina came shimmering into the narrow hall in a white suit, all smiles, and groomed to perfection.

'You could say that.' Lucinda smiled, leading the way into the drawing room, which she'd tidied that morning. The children's toys had been put away, the magazines were in two neat stacks on the coffee table, and the cushions had been freshly plumped up.

'A drink? Champagne?' she asked casually.

'Lu-*cin*-da! Oh, my God, it's not your birthday, is it?' Carina looked aghast.

'No, why should it be my birthday?'

Carina's eyes narrowed. 'What is it, then? You've had promotion? Is that it? Or have D'Aussoire given you a pay rise?'

Lucinda laughed as she handed Carina her drink. 'You make me sound like a secretary in a typing pool. I do occasionally take a day's leave, you know, in order to become one of the Ladies who Lunch.'

'Good for you!' Carina raised her glass and Lucinda inwardly winced at the patronising tone. Had Carina always been like this? Or had she never noticed before? She wandered over to the fireplace now and was peering at the three or four invitation cards propped up behind the china ornaments. 'I see you're not going to the Kincardys' dance,' she observed. 'Pity, we could have gone together. Given you a lift.'

'We don't move in those exalted circles,' Lucinda said with gentle amusement.

Carina's flushed, embarrassed. 'The Kincardys are not *that* grand, darling. Anyway, how's everything going? I haven't seen you since your weekend with Rachel and Ian. Was it heaven? I wished we could have gone. So boring of Alex insisting we go to some bloody conference in Brussels. Did you have the most marvellous time?'

Lucinda replied with emphasis. 'Absolutely amazing. In fact, I've never had a weekend like it.'

'Oh! Who was there, then?' Carina looked quite put out at having obviously missed something.

Lucinda shrugged. 'Oh, I don't know,' she said ingenuously. 'The Anstruthers, and the Parsons, who have a sweet little girl, and the Randalls.'

'Un-huh?'

'That was it really. Rachel had surpassed herself, of course, with her cooking. It was all absolutely delicious.'

Carina nodded brightly, already bored. 'Yes. She cooks very well.'

'Actually, she gave us one of your recipes for dinner on Friday night.'

'*My* recipe? Darling, I don't do cooking.'

'I know you never cook, Carina, but you'd passed on to her one of your mother's recipes for halibut with asparagus tips; it was really delicious.'

Carina shook her head, her expression blank. 'I don't remember. It must have been ages ago, because Mummy died last year and she hadn't entertained for a while. Anyway, you had a good time?'

'The best. I've got a little something for you, actually, as a result of that weekend.' As she spoke, she rose and went over to the bookshelves on the right of the fireplace. She came back with a flat dark leather case which she handed to Carina. 'This is for you,' she said softly.

'For me, darling?' Then Carina frowned and looked suspicious. 'What's this?' She took it gingerly, as if it might explode in her hands.

'Open it and see.'

Carina's eyes darkened and she shot Lucinda a look of alarm. 'What is it?'

Lucinda's smile was lazy, amused. 'I think you already know what it is.'

Carina opened the box. The pearl necklace lay, pale and glowing, on a bed of cream velvet. The diamond clasp winked in the sunlight as it streamed through the drawing-room window.

'But why are you giving me this . . .?' she gasped, her frown deepening.

'These go with them,' Lucinda continued, handing her the bundle of love letters. The handwriting was visible, large and loopy and very, very distinctive.

'I . . . I . . .' But Carina couldn't go on. Her face was suffused with blood now, a deep embarrassed scarlet that spread down her neck in ugly blotches. Then she shrugged her shoulders defiantly. 'What can I say?'

'Try . . . I'm sorry I didn't tell you before; try . . . I'm sorry I lied; try . . . explaining why you offered to help me contact the other women? And why, when I finally couldn't trace "Pumpkin", you suggested I tell Bernard I *had* found her? And why, Carina, why you pretended to be my best friend, when all the time you were keeping this vital piece of information from me?'

Carina's eyes were cold and brazen. 'Actually, it was none of your damned business. My private life is my private life and I don't want Alex to know. If I'd told you, you'd have told Julian, and before you know it half London would have known.'

'For a start Julian does not gossip,' Lucinda retorted. 'Anyway, your affair appears to have taken place before you married Alex, so what's the big deal?'

'What makes you think it took place before I got married?'

253

Lucinda blinked, taken aback. 'Didn't it?'

Carina's voice was harsh. 'Who do you think Tara's father is, then?'

After Carina had stormed out, refusing lunch, but nevertheless taking the pearls with her, Lucinda sat alone, sipping wine, and feeling this was one shock too many.

She did some quick calculations. Tara was eleven. Carina and Miles must have started their affair at least twelve years ago. And Carina had been her friend for thirteen years, so whilst pretending to be faithful to Alex, and to have a steady and loving marriage, she was actually pregnant with Miles's child. A little girl, who for some unknown reason Lucinda had never taken to. Even when she'd been small there was something about her, a slyness, an arrogance, that made her so different to Charles and Michael.

Where and when her father had met Carina now seemed of little importance, though Lucinda remembered introducing her to Miles and Anne at someone's wedding. Not long after, Carina had given birth to Charles, and she'd had a milky glow about her, eyes shining, skin fresh, body voluptuous. All the men who'd met her at that time had been enraptured by this vision of a Dior-dressed Madonna. And so, apparently, had Miles.

But what was eminently more intriguing was the fact that when he'd finished with Carina he'd gone on to have an affair with Fenella Harrison. Talk of extremes, Lucinda reflected. From a glossy socialite who had London society at her feet to a grumpy aggressive old woman who looked like a gypsy and tied crystals to his groin.

Lucinda frowned, remembering his affair with Fenella had started ten years ago. So what had caused this change of direction? What had made him switch from Carina, and her bewitching glamour, to Fenella, and her healing powers?

'There are too many loose ends,' Lucinda groaned in frustration.

'The fact that Tara is your half-sister and you never knew is the most shocking revelation of all,' Julian remarked, as they lay in bed talking that night. 'At least none of the others produced children.'

'Her birth must have been a shock to Dad, too, because it looks as if he dumped Carina immediately.'

'It would be a shock to most married men to have their mistress produce a baby. Your father would have been sixty-two at the time, too.'

'How *could* she!' Lucinda burst out angrily. 'He was old enough to be her father, *and* she was married to Alex.'

'Do you think he knows?'

'Apparently not. That's why she didn't admit to me that she was "Pumpkin". And there she was encouraging me to believe that Paula was "Pumpkin". D'you remember that ridiculous dinner party we gave? With Rachel and Ian, too? God, if I'd known then what I know now.'

Julian drew his brows together in concentration. 'Do you think Tara resembles your father?'

Lucinda nodded. 'Poor child, I think she does, certainly her colouring is the same. Luckily for Carina, Alex is quite dark, otherwise there would have been problems when she was born.'

'It probably won't arise, because maybe you and Carina won't go on being friends now, but we'd better be careful Jamie doesn't get to like Tara too much, when they're older.'

Lucinda's eyes widened as she turned to look at him. 'Tara is his half-aunt, isn't she? My God, I never thought of that.'

'Will Carina tell her, do you think?'

'Not a chance, and perhaps that's for the best. She'd be devastated if she knew Alex wasn't her real father.'

'What a nightmare,' Julian groaned, putting his hands behind his head. 'Sex messes up more people's lives than anything else under the sun, doesn't it?'

Lucinda thought about this for a moment. 'But it's also the most wonderful thing under the sun,' she replied softly, reaching for him.

Sarah, in whom, as usual, Lucinda had confided, agreed that it would be cruel if Carina were ever to let Tara know the truth.

'I don't think there's any danger that Carina will,' Lucinda assured her.

'Quite. What good would it do?' Sarah said. 'It would just cause a lot of unhappiness and serve no purpose. I don't suppose you want to go on being friends with Carina, anyway,' she added.

'I don't think I can. It's spoilt everything.' Lucinda spoke sadly, almost with regret. In one week she'd known two types of betrayal. Geneviève was bad enough but this was a different matter. She'd looked upon Carina as an older sister. She thought they'd always been utterly honest with each other. And now this.

'She's behaved appallingly badly,' Sarah said, breaking into her thoughts. 'Having an affair when you're married with someone who is also married is bad enough, but having a baby as well is just sheer carelessness, especially nowadays, with all the types of birth control that were not available to my generation.'

Lucinda smiled at her grandmother. Sometimes Sarah could be amazingly up to date, and talk about pop stars who'd made it to the top ten, or the vagaries of some model's love life, but then she'd suddenly revert to the stiff, highly moral code of behaviour she'd known as a child and come out with gloriously Victorian remarks.

'I feel hurt that she couldn't trust me,' Lucinda explained. 'I've always told her everything, even confided in her about work, so surely she could have told me she was "Pumpkin"? I'd never have revealed it was her to anyone, if only for Tara and Alex's sake.'

'She was obviously very afraid it would get out,' Sarah observed.

'Then why did she take such an interest in the whole business of Dad's Will? Offer to help me find the various women, and all that?'

Sarah thought about this for a moment before answering. 'If you have toothache, you know how you can't resist probing the painful area with your tongue? I think she couldn't resist finding out about his other mistresses . . . maybe she had originally thought she was the only one, like Isabelle. To offer to help you find them was pure masochism, of course. Prodding the pain to see if it still hurt, whilst knowing it still did.' She gave a quick sigh. 'People bring such pain on themselves, as if in a strange way it was a source of comfort.'

Lucinda shook her head. 'I simply can't see why she was attracted to Dad, though. He wasn't sexy, like Alex, or amusing, or rich and sociable.'

'But he had the one thing that appeals to women, in the long run, more than anything else.'

'You mean brains?'

'Yes, darling. The greatest aphrodisiac of all, because these are the men who have power. And the thing that flatters women most of all is to be attractive to a man with brains and power. It makes them feel they must be very special, which of course most of the time they're not.'

Lucinda nodded in understanding. No woman wants to be linked to a stupid man.

'Now, what are you going to do next, darling?' her grandmother asked.

'Take the last piece of jewellery to be valued. Then I'll know whether I've hit the jackpot or not.' She took a deep breath, as if bracing herself to plunge into icy water.

'And the remaining piece is . . .?'

'A rather ostentatious diamond brooch, with really big stones.'

'And why did you decide that was the most valuable?'

'When I described them all to Carina, she said the brooch definitely sounded like the most valuable—' Something in Sarah's eyes made Lucinda break off. She looked at her grandmother anxiously. 'What is it?'

Sarah's brow furrowed worriedly. 'Carina hasn't, as it turns out, proved to be your most honest adviser.'

'I know, but . . .' Lucinda looked at her wretchedly. 'She wouldn't advise me to keep a worthless piece, surely? Would she? What would be the point? This was long before I knew she'd had an affair with Dad.'

'I'm sure it'll be fine, darling,' Sarah said soothingly. 'We mustn't give a dog a bad name. You'll let me know, won't you?'

'Of course I will, and we'll celebrate, Granny. Just you, Julian and me. Because we're the only people in the family, thank God, who know about it.'

'Thank God, indeed,' Sarah retorted, casting her eyes to heaven.

Anne took the yellowing handwritten pages out of the plastic carrier bag where they'd rested for the past thirty years and started reading the stories she'd written for Tom and Harry when they were small. With growing astonishment, and disbelief that she'd written them herself, she realised they were both amusing and clever. She'd written a series about five cats who lived on a farm. Their characters were all different, from the eldest, who was called Rowley, the wise leader of the pack who thought up daredevil adventures, to the flighty Babykins, who was always tripping over bowls of milk and getting into scrapes.

For the first time in years, Anne found herself laughing out loud. She had to admit they were amazingly good stories, which even adults would find entertaining as they read them to their children. So why had Miles damned them as rubbish? Of course they weren't great works on higher mathematics such as he had written, but nevertheless . . . Anne sat at his desk, thinking deeply, and thinking for herself for the first time in many years. There weren't enough stories about the cats to make a book, but supposing she were to continue the series . . . then have them all professionally typed . . .? Even, perhaps, find a clever artist to do the illustrations?

It was as if a beam of sunlight had burst through the thick dark clouds that had smothered her internal landscape for longer than she cared to remember. Her mother had been right. People *could* start over, even in their sixties, and even if the stories never got published it wouldn't matter. Writing would give her an outlet, an interest, and an absorbing way of filling her days.

Anne reached for one of the neatly sharpened pencils in the box Miles had kept on his desk, and, taking some plain white paper from one of the drawers, set to work.

'Do you want me to come with you, Bun?' Julian asked that evening. She'd arranged to collect the diamond brooch from Bernard at lunchtime the next day and then take it to Asprey's in Bond Street to be valued.

Her face lit up. 'Would you really? I'm going to be so nervous I'll probably leave it in a taxi or drop it down a drain or something. Oh God, it's scary. By this time tomorrow I may have inherited three million pounds, and be able to stay at home . . .'

'. . . and perhaps have another baby?'

'Julian!' She turned to stare at him, her eyes shining, her face flushed with excitement. 'Do you mean it? Another baby? Really?' she exclaimed disbelievingly.

'We could afford it, if that's what you'd like, and you could stay at home to your heart's content,' he assured her, kissing the tip of her nose.

She grasped his hand in both of hers. 'Oh, Julian, I love you so much. We're going to be so happy. Imagine, another baby! Wouldn't Jamie and Daisy be excited? They've always wanted us to have another baby. Perhaps we could get a puppy, too? They'd love that. And if I'm at home all day, it will be no problem looking after it.'

'Steady on, sweetheart. Let's not get carried away,' he laughed. 'Let's wait and see what happens tomorrow.'

'I shan't sleep a wink tonight. We must be the luckiest couple in the world, Julian.'

*   *   *

257

Harry adjusted his gold Cartier watch, settled into the driving seat of his brand new one-hundred-and-seventy-thousand-pound V12 Vanquish Aston Martin, unbuttoned the jacket of his handmade cashmere suit from Savile Row, and headed out of London. As far as he was concerned, this was as good as it got, and a damned side better than he'd ever hoped for.

While Paula was planning their wedding reception in two months' time with the banqueting manager of Claridges, Smythsons were printing the invitations, Town and County were designing the floral arrangements and Catherine Walker was making the wedding dress. She'd suggested that Harry go and find them a lovely house in the country where they could spend their weekends.

'Within two hours' drive of London, darling,' she'd instructed him, 'and with a swimming pool, tennis courts, several acres of mature garden, at least seven bedrooms with bathrooms en suite, and of course staff quarters. I leave it to you, Harry, you've got such good taste, but my budget is four million. Is that OK, darling?'

It was fucking OK as far as Harry was concerned. This was the life. He now had every fucking thing he'd ever wanted. A duplex in Eaton Place, a soon to be realised country mansion, the car of his dreams, handmade clothes, shoes from Lobb, monogrammed handmade shirts from Turnbull & Asser, Italian silk ties, at one hundred and fifty pounds each, from Versace, and a token job to make his whole lifestyle appear convincing to the outside world. The perfect job. He'd had the original idea so the glory was his, without having to do a day's work for the rest of his life. All he had to do was keep Paula happy, which wasn't difficult. Her list of priorities were good sex, constant praise about her appearance, regular red roses to assure her she was loved, a decent-looking man on her arm whenever she went anywhere, and a devoted slave who appreciated his lucky break.

Harry appreciated his lucky break, all right. As far as he was concerned, he'd never had it so good and the livin' was fucking easy.

Across town, Tom was in the process of buying Susan an engagement ring. Since the near tragic incident at Bude, he'd grown in stature and confidence in a way that had amazed even him. He actually felt, for the first time in his life, that he'd earned people's respect, and although he'd been embarrassed when the Cornish newspapers had blazoned his rescue of Steve on their front pages, with such dramatic headlines as HERO SAVES GIRLFRIEND'S SON, it did go a long way to assuaging the years of humiliation heaped on him by his father.

Susan's proposal had taken him aback, of course, coming as it did in a flurry of emotion within a few hours of Steve's rescue, but he'd accepted it, with a mixture of shock and delight. It was what he'd really wanted all along, but he'd feared rejection, and anyway he'd never really thought he was good enough for her. Not as a husband. Not as a stepfather for Steve and Dick.

But Susan had changed all that in one impulsive moment which had left them both stunned, gazing at each other breathlessly, until he'd said, almost crossly: 'Don't be silly, of course I'll marry you.'

Now, as he gazed in the window of the antique jewellers, his eyes alighted on a very pretty half-hoop ring of rubies and diamonds. The stones were quite small, of course; he couldn't afford anything lavish because he wanted to put the money his father had left him towards buying a bigger house for them, but he liked the setting, and it would go well with a gold wedding ring.

When he got home that evening, Susan was sweeping the paved garden, for the first of the autumn leaves were beginning to fall, and her tubs of flowers had the blowsy look of a beautiful woman whose bloom was fading.

'I thought we'd eat out here. It's so close, isn't it?' she remarked, looking up at the cloudy sky that seemed to be pressing the humidity down on their heads, so that she felt hot and sticky. Some time ago Tom had bought a garden table and four chairs at Homebase, to save dragging the kitchen table out every time it was warm enough to eat, and he'd also bought some cushions, and even a sunshade on a stand for when it was really hot.

'We could have a glass of wine out here before dinner, couldn't we?' Tom suggested, unwrapping the bottle of Chablis, already chilled, that he'd bought.

Susan grinned, delighted. 'I'll get the glasses.'

'Don't worry, I'll get them. You sit and relax.' He went off with the bottle to the kitchen. When he returned, he'd already poured out two glasses. Settling the tray on the table, he handed one of them to Susan.

'Thanks, Tom. Here's to us!' She raised her glass to him.

'Here's to us,' he echoed softly.

'When are we going to . . . Oh!' She started, frowning and gazing into the depths of her glass. 'What the . . .? Oh, my God. Oh, my God, Tom!' She lifted out the ring with dripping fingers, and the skin around her eyes suddenly turned pink. 'Oh, *Tom*,' she said brokenly.

'Is it all right? Does it fit?' he asked anxiously.

'If I have to break my finger, I'll make sure it fits,' she retorted spiritedly. It fitted. It slipped on her finger as smoothly as if it had been made for her.

'I can hardly believe it,' she kept saying, holding out her left hand so she could catch the light in the rubies and diamonds from different angles. 'It's beautiful, Tom. Thank you. Thank you. Thank you.' She leaned forward and kissed him generously on the mouth. 'You're the most fantastic man I've ever met, even if I was the one who had to do the proposing, and I love you to bits,' she told him, grinning.

Steve and Dick already knew they were planning to marry, but they hadn't told anyone else yet.

'When can we tell your family, Tom?' she asked.

'How about tomorrow?'

Julian went with her to Bernard's office. Now that the moment had come to collect the diamond brooch, on which her whole future hung, Lucinda felt sick with nerves. Her stomach was looping the loop, her heart was hammering in her ribcage, and her hands were shaking.

'Where are you going to have it valued?' Bernard asked conversationally, as he placed the leather jewel case on the desk.

'Asprey's,' Lucinda croaked, then cleared her throat, and repeated, 'Asprey's, in Bond Street. Do you think I should get a second opinion from another jeweller, too?'

Bernard considered this for a moment. 'I don't think that's necessary. You couldn't be going to a more reputable firm, but remember, you want a straight valuation of this brooch, but you also want, for your own personal use, a valuation for insurance purposes. If this brooch were to be stolen, it would cost a great deal more than its actual worth to replace, because of purchase tax.'

'Yes, I see.' She felt a tremor of excitement. The way he spoke it was as if he already knew the diamond spray was the most valuable piece in the collection.

'Is that it, then?' Julian asked. 'No more nasty little shocks Miles has left behind?'

For a moment Bernard seemed to hesitate, as if he was about to say something but wondered whether he should.

'What is it?' Lucinda asked warily.

'It's truly nothing to worry about,' Bernard said swiftly. 'He's left you a sealed letter, to be given to you one month from now, by which time . . . well,' he shrugged, 'the die will have been cast one way or another.'

'The die is going to be cast within the next two hours,' Lucinda pointed out. 'What horrid little message has he got for me in four weeks' time?'

'He did say,' Bernard continued hesitatingly, 'that it would take a month for the dust to settle, one way or another. And by that time you will be receptive to . . . what shall I say? . . . erm . . . you will be reconciled to the situation, whatever it is, and therefore better able to understand what your father has to say in his letter.'

'Patronising bastard,' Julian exploded heatedly. 'Hasn't he put Lucinda through enough? She's had to contact all his ex-girlfriends, and a weird lot most of them were, too, and she's suffered the agony of having to gamble in a ridiculous game of his invention for any inheritance at all, although her brothers were left fifty thousand each, and now she *still* has to wait a month to receive some final epistle from a man who was evil, manipulative, and enjoyed playing games with other people's lives.'

Bernard's smile was wintry. 'There's no need to blame the messenger, Julian, although I absolutely agree with what you say.'

'I'm sorry, Bernard, I didn't mean to have a go at you, but honestly! The man was a monster. He ignored Lucinda most of his life and now he's made her life hell ever since he died.'

'Maybe his letter will explain why,' Lucinda pointed out drily, 'although of course it could set me off on another wild goose chase. It's rather like a treasure hunt I took part in when I was in my teens. My friends and I were racing all over London, looking for further clues, and just when we thought we'd reached the end, there was another clue that sent us off again.'

'I believe the end really is in sight this time, Lucinda,' Bernard assured her.

'Well, here we go,' she said, rising and picking up the jewel box. 'I'll phone you later on today when I've got the valuation.'

'Yes, do. And the best of luck, my dear.'

'Thank you.' With the brooch in her possession, she felt her confidence returning. Everything was going to be all right. She felt sure of it now. As long as the brooch was valued at around thirty thousand pounds she'd be home and dry. That was the figure her father had said was required. Looking at the glittering diamonds, some big, some small, and all exquisitely set in what Carina had told her must be platinum, she was certain she'd got it right. All along, it had been the biggest, most impressive piece out of the six items he'd left. The pendant of peridots set in gold, the aquamarine and diamond bracelet, the finely woven gold earrings, the ring with the blue stone surrounded with diamonds; she was certain none of them were really valuable. The pearls she'd given Carina, of course, would have been extremely valuable if they'd been real pearls and not cultured, but was that likely? Wouldn't real matching pearls of that size have cost a king's ransom?

Lucinda and Julian were shown into a plush office on the ground floor of Asprey's and after a couple of moments a distinguished-looking, beautifully dressed middle-aged man joined them.

'Good afternoon,' he said, shaking hands. 'How may I help you?'

'My father has left me a piece of jewellery, and I'd like you to value it for me,' Lucinda explained, deciding an expurgated version of her father's Will was all that was necessary. She handed him the opened case, rather proudly now, and the diamonds looked dazzling under the overhead lights.

He took it and looked at it for several minutes, while Lucinda and Julian watched him expectantly. Then he lifted it out of its case, turned it over to examine the back, turned it again to look more closely at the diamonds, and then spoke.

'This, I gather,' he said, his brow furrowed anxiously, 'is a copy of the piece your father has left you?'

'A copy?' She looked surprised, but a cold hand closed around her heart. 'No, it's the actual brooch.'

'Do you know how he came by it?'

Lucinda shook her head. 'He left a lot of jewellery. That was one of the pieces. The best one, I think.'

The man's eyebrows shot into the air and he looked at her as if she were slightly deranged. 'But this is a piece of costume jewellery. A very good piece, probably by Christian Dior, but it would retail at about only fifteen hundred pounds, I'd say. And of course the second-hand value would only be thirty or forty pounds,' he added, as if to console her.

'But I don't understand . . .' Lucinda's hopes, her dreams, her aspirations

261

and the last lingering vestiges of respect she had for her father came crashing down around her, and she felt she was being buried under an intolerable sense of injustice. Julian reached out and took her hand. The charming man from Asprey's stood there, with the brooch in his hand, looking extremely embarrassed and sympathetic.

'I'm so sorry,' he said as if it was his fault, 'but anyone can make that sort of mistake. The costume jewellery today is really absolutely marvellous. It fools . . . I mean, it takes in so many people, because it can look like the real thing.'

'I don't know anything about jewellery, you see,' Lucinda explained in a flat voice. 'He didn't promise me it was genuine. I just thought it was.'

'Oh, Bun,' Julian whispered sympathetically. 'You weren't to know.'

As they left Asprey's, the fake brooch in Julian's pocket by now, Lucinda glanced at the glass showcases, containing millions of pounds' worth of diamonds, sapphires, rubies and emeralds. What a fool she'd been. Why hadn't she come here before, instead of just looking at books? Now, seeing a superb diamond necklace and matching bracelet, she could *see* the difference between the real thing and her piece of costume jewellery. The genuine diamonds had a depth of fiery brilliance that no fake diamond could ever achieve. The settings were finer, more delicate, too. Carina had been right about looking at the settings when advising Lucinda on how to make her selection, but she hadn't been right about the diamonds, had she?

They drove home in silence. Lucinda was too depressed to speak, and everything Julian thought of saying sounded clichéd and banal under the circumstances so he didn't say anything either.

She'd taken the afternoon off, thinking she'd be too excited to return to work, but now their little house was a haven, where she could nurse her blighted hopes. She was also angry with herself for getting it so wrong. *So* wrong. She hadn't even chosen a minor piece of real jewellery, like the peridot pendant, or the aquamarine and diamond bracelet. She'd picked a fake, a sham, an imitation bit of glitter that was worth nothing, and for no reason at all she suddenly remembered a scene in her childhood, when she'd been five or six. They'd all been having tea round the dining-room table, because Miles refused to eat in the kitchen, and she'd reached for the largest slice of a chocolate cake.

'You're greedy, Lucinda,' he'd bellowed furiously. 'You always go for the biggest of everything.' Then he'd seized the plate and taken it away from her. 'To teach you a lesson, you can watch me eat it, instead.' Which he'd proceeded to do, slowly and with sensuous enjoyment, licking his lips and finally scooping up the last of the thick dark icing with a teaspoon.

'Perhaps that will teach you not to be so greedy,' he said triumphantly when he'd finished.

Why should she remember that now? Because the brooch had been the largest, most dazzling item in the collection, and Miles had guessed she'd pick it to keep for herself, thinking that would teach her a lesson about being greedy, once and for all?

The more she thought about it, the more convinced she became that that's what had happened. It would be just her father's style.

'Why did Dad hate me so?' she asked, bursting into tears. 'He knew what I'd do, and he must be turning in his grave with laughter now. I did just what he prophesied I'd do. God, I could kick myself.'

'Bun, darling, wasn't it Carina who persuaded you the diamond brooch was bound to be the most valuable?' Julian protested, putting his arm around her. 'Don't be so hard on yourself. It was a lucky dip, anyway. I bet you none of the pieces of jewellery was worth thirty thousand pounds.'

Lucinda was so astonished she stopped crying and turned to look at him. 'You mean . . . no matter which piece I'd kept for myself, it wouldn't have been worth much?'

'Exactly! I think you've been had, Bun. Why didn't he give Bernard a list of all the valuations? Even if it was in one of his famous sealed envelopes, only to be opened after the event? It's just like Miles to get everyone wound up, and especially you, so that the choice of jewellery became a competition, which you either won or lost . . . and having lost, because there was no way you could have won,' he added slowly and carefully, 'there would be no need for three million pounds to be produced, would there? Because that probably doesn't exist either.'

Lucinda curled up in a heap on the sofa, trying to make sense of what Julian had said. 'But that's totally, utterly crazy and absolutely pointless,' she said at last. 'What the hell's it all been for?'

Julian shrugged. 'If he were still alive I'd say . . . ask your father. But he probably couldn't tell you either, because he just got his kicks from screwing up other people's lives,' he added angrily.

At that moment, Jamie and Daisy arrived, having been out for the afternoon with Delia.

'We must pretend nothing's happened,' Julian said quickly.

'Nothing has,' Lucinda retorted with asperity, as she blew her nose.

They all had tea round the kitchen table, with peanut butter sandwiches made by Lucinda because they were the children's favourite, and toast with Marmite made by Delia. As if she sensed Lucinda was despondent about something, Delia kept up a flow of merry chatter, getting Jamie and Daisy to tell their parents what they'd been doing that day.

Lucinda tried desperately to hide her depression, listening to Julian as he promised the children he'd take them all to Thorpe Park at the weekend, but a voice in her head kept repeating: Fool! You had your chance and you've blown it. You've blown it because you were greedy. You went for the biggest and what you thought was the best. Just as your father knew you would. Fool. Fool!

Her thoughts were interrupted by the front door bell.

'I'll get it,' Julian said, rising from the table.

Lucinda recognised Tom's voice in the hall and her heart sank as she wondered what he wanted. Tom was usually in the depth of some depression about his sad life, although he'd seemed more cheerful the last time she'd seen him. But the last thing she needed right now was someone who was as down as her.

But it was a radiant, tanned and smiling Tom who sailed into the kitchen, followed by Susan, whose hand he was holding.

'Hello, Lucinda,' he greeted her, kissing her on both cheeks. 'Susan and I wanted you to be the first to hear our news,' he announced with boyish excitement.

She looked from one to the other, and wondered when she'd last seen two people who looked so happy.

'We're getting married,' Tom burst out, unable to contain himself any longer. He put his arm round Susan and pulled her to his side. 'We're going to have a quiet wedding in four weeks' time and I wondered,' he turned to Julian, 'if you would be my best man?'

Julian beamed. 'Of course I will, Tom, and many congratulations. This is terrific news.' It was touching to be asked to be best man, but he knew the truth was that there was no one else; Tom didn't have any friends really.

'*Tom!*' Lucinda flung herself at him, putting her arms round his neck, her depression temporarily forgotten in her happiness for him. Tom deserved a good wife. Tom needed and always had needed love, companionship, understanding and someone who really belonged to him. And Susan, she knew instinctively, was the perfect choice. She'd be motherly, too, and really look after him.

'This calls for champagne,' Julian declared, going to the fridge, where he always kept a bottle ready chilled for unexpected occasions.

Jamie and Daisy were prancing around the kitchen, and even Delia's face was glowing with delight.

Lucinda hugged Susan, too, with genuine warmth. 'It's really wonderful that you're going to be part of the family,' she said with sincerity. 'I know you're going to be fabulously happy. I can just feel it.'

Daisy tugged Tom's arm and looked up at him. 'When you get married can I be the bride?' she asked hopefully.

Tom looked perplexed for a moment, but Susan dropped to her haunches so her face was level with Daisy's. 'The bridesmaid,' she corrected gently. 'If your mummy agrees then of course you can.'

'It's only going to be a small wedding,' said Tom, looking momentarily panicked. 'We're not going to have—'

'I know we're not,' Susan said, smiling up at him, 'but Jamie and Daisy and Steve and Dick must all take part, don't you think? Nothing grand. Just a quiet little family ceremony,' she added reassuringly.

Tom relaxed, relieved. 'That would be perfect,' he agreed. Then he bent down to kiss Daisy on her smooth little cheek. 'We'd love you to be bridesmaid, and perhaps Jamie, Steve and Dick could be pages or something?'

'We'll think of something,' Susan replied cheerfully, catching Lucinda's eye and giggling happily.

Lucinda insisted they stay for dinner, her mood lightened by the sight of Tom's sheer happiness, just when he'd become resigned to being lonely for the rest of his life.

It made her own situation, made wretched only because she'd allowed Miles to manipulate her from the grave, seem so much better.

'I know it's clichéd,' she whispered to Julian as she took a ready prepared chicken dish out of the deep freeze for dinner, 'but when it comes to it, having someone to love is so much more important than money, isn't it?'

'Love *is* the most important thing, clichéd or not,' Julian whispered back, kissing her swiftly on the lips.

Nineteen

'Can we meet?' Carina asked diffidently. Her voice over the phone was small and sounded crushed.

'Is it important?' Lucinda asked. It was Saturday morning, and she was just about to set off to Waitrose to do the weekend's shopping while Julian took Jamie and Daisy swimming at the local baths. The thought of having to spend time with Carina, listening to her justifying what she'd done, was the last thing she needed.

Carina spoke falteringly, as if she realised Lucinda didn't want to have anything more to do with her. 'I'd . . . well, no it's not, I suppose . . . but I'd really like to talk to you, Lucinda. I'd hate us to part company in this way after all these years.'

Lucinda felt tempted to tell her she should have thought of that before she embarked on a string of deception, but instead, and because Carina sounded so down, she said reluctantly, 'All right, but I haven't got long.'

'Can you come here? Then we can be on our own.'

Lucinda got in the car and drove straight to the Holland Park house, where for the past thirteen years she'd been wined and dined by a woman she'd trusted utterly. When she got to the house it had a curiously deserted air, so that for a moment Lucinda wondered if anyone was in, but when she pressed the brass bell she heard footsteps and a moment later Carina opened the door herself. She was wearing jeans and a dark brown loosely fitting sweater and Lucinda hardly recognised her.

The usually coiffured hair with its gold highlights was greasy and dull, and there wasn't a particle of make-up on her face, which was thin and drawn-looking.

'Come in, Lucinda,' she said without any of her usual enthusiasm and brightness. 'Thank you for coming.'

In a silence as oppressive as a funeral parlour, she led the way across the marble-floored hall into the large and gracious drawing room.

'Would you like some coffee? Tea?' Carina asked listlessly.

Lucinda felt awkward. Was this a sackcloth and ashes performance? A repentant act so as to appear more sinned against than sinning? Was she going to say Miles had seduced her? Made her pregnant on purpose? That everything was his fault?

'I'm fine, thanks,' she replied coolly.

What happened next took her completely by surprise.

'I just wanted you to know,' Carina said, 'before it gets out, that Alex has left me. And he's taken Charles and Michael with him.'

Lucinda stared at her, bereft of words. 'Why?' was all she could think to ask, and then realised it was a stupid question.

Carina looked down at her hands, her face pinched, her mouth tight with pain.

'Like a *fool*, I left the letters to Miles in my handbag, with the pearls. I was so upset you'd realised "Pumpkin" was me, and I was so angry with myself for letting the cat out of the bag about Tara, that when I got back here . . . well . . . I just lost it completely. I had a couple of drinks, and then a couple more. I lost track of time and finally went to have a shower. Unfortunately Alex had mislaid his car keys and he was late for a meeting, so he opened my handbag to borrow mine . . . and found everything.'

'Oh, my God.'

'I know. I can't think why I was so stupid. I had intended to burn the letters and pretend the pearls were some I'd bought for myself but . . . the world started falling apart at that moment. I never knew he had such a terrible temper.'

'But—' Lucinda began in protest, but Carina looked up and nodded, knowing what she was going to say.

'I know. I know. Hypocritical, isn't it? Typical bloody man. It's all right for him to have affairs but the minute he knows I had one *twelve years ago* . . . all hell breaks loose.'

'And he left you?' Lucinda askd incredulously. 'Just like that? Perhaps he's gone off in a temper and when he cools down he'll realise he over-reacted.'

Carina didn't answer and Lucinda knew there was something else.

'He's sure to come back,' she said consolingly.

Carina started to weep, great silent tears rolling down her cheeks. 'I lost my temper. You know what my temper can be like . . . I did it with you. I made the terrible mistake of telling him that Tara was Miles's child.'

Lucinda could just imagine the debonair, rich and successful Alex Somerset flying into a rage at the thought of his wife being impregnated by another man. And a man old enough to be her father.

'So Tara's still with you, is she?'

'Yes, poor little thing. She wonders what she's done wrong. I keep telling her it's me Daddy's angry with, but she wonders why he didn't take her with Charles and Michael.'

Lucinda covered her face with her hands at the thought of the confusion and misery the little girl must be suffering.

'Where is she now?' she asked, suddenly dropping her voice.

'It's all right, she's spending the day with a school friend.' She dragged a tissue from the pocket of her jeans and dabbed at her eyes. 'It's all the most appalling mess, Lucinda. He wants me out of this house within two weeks. He says he'll give me enough money to get a small flat for Tara and me, but the whole thing is hellish. And the worst part,' she concluded, her voice catching, 'is that I brought the whole bloody thing on myself.'

'I'm really sorry,' Lucinda said with sincerity. Then she searched around in her mind, trying to find something comforting to say. 'Surely Alex will change his mind when he realises what it's doing to Tara? He's obviously deeply shocked but I'm sure when he thinks about it he'll realise you've behaved no worse than he has, and that you were just unlucky.'

'He wouldn't call getting pregnant unlucky,' Carina said bitterly. 'He'd say it was bloody careless. He actually asked me why the hell I didn't have a termination? He told me I could have passed off the abortion as a "woman's thing" and he'd have been none the wiser. I'm afraid he hates poor Tara, now, almost as much as he hates me.'

'That's bitterly unfair. My God, the trouble and heartbreak my father caused.'

'You're going to ask why I ever got involved with him in the first place, aren't you?' Carina said, picking another tissue out of the box and blowing her nose.

Lucinda shook her head. 'I wouldn't do that. You must have had your reasons.'

'He fascinated me,' Carina said slowly. 'There was something hypnotic about him. I was utterly bowled over. I was crazy about him. I couldn't bear it when I didn't see him. I loved him more than anything in the world at one point. I was in his power and he could make me do anything . . .' she paused, then continued in a low voice, 'even when I didn't want to.'

'Can I ask one thing?'

'Go for it. I've no more secrets now.'

'Did he end the affair or did you?' Lucinda asked curiously.

'He did. Not long after I told him I was pregnant, he said it was all over. That was it. I said I'd bring up the baby as Alex's, and no one would know, but he wouldn't listen.'

'So he walked out on you?'

'Yes.' Carina seemed to hesitate as if undecided whether to say any more or not.

'What is it?'

'I know you'll hate hearing this, but you already know so much about your father that maybe it won't make any difference.' She drew in her breath sharply and her face looked trembly and white. 'He told me he only married your mother because she got pregnant, and that it had ruined his life. My getting pregnant seemed to bring it all back to him and he couldn't bear it.'

'I already knew that's why he married Mum, and the baby died, too. But it was very unkind of him to ditch you and not be supportive. After all, you were not asking him to marry you.'

Carina rose from where she was sitting and started pacing up and down, her trainers padding silently on the thick carpet.

'I don't think it was that. I think he was horrified that it had happened at all. He suddenly became impotent. It was as if his body was refusing to function, because of what it had done.'

Something seemed to click in Lucinda's mind. The timing was right. He'd become impotent, had needed help, and that was when he'd got involved with Fenella Harrison and her crystals. Hadn't Fenella said: 'I saved his sanity, you know'? and then '. . . using rose quartz, which symbolises love . . . I gave him back his virility.' And then again Lucinda remembered, as clearly as if she'd been talking to Fenella the previous week: 'I placed a ruby between his legs . . . It's so sad for a man when he becomes impotent. Sex had always meant so much to him . . .'

It occurred to Lucinda, although it wouldn't be tactful to say so now, that Fenella must have worked wonders, because after his affair with her, or maybe even at the same time, Miles had gone on to have a passionate affair with Isabelle.

'What are you thinking about?' Carina asked.

'Just that my father was utterly rotten.'

'I was at his funeral, you know,' Carina said quietly.

'You mean his memorial service,' Lucinda said.

'No, I mean his funeral. None of you saw me, because I stayed outside the chapel, and hid when you were all leaving, but I couldn't *not* go. I was shattered by his death. I had to say a final goodbye. He was, after all, Tara's father.'

Tara's father. The words sank into Lucinda's brain and she knew that that was how she'd always think of Miles. Not *her* father, or even Tom's or Harry's, but Tara's father. The innocent little girl whose life, this very moment, was being shattered by the wicked vagaries of a man Lucinda was now deeply ashamed to call 'Dad'. Tara had lost her home, her brothers, and the man she believed was her father. The rest of them would always carry the scars he'd inflicted on them, including Anne though she'd never realise it, but what about little Tara?

'Are you going to tell Tara that Alex is not her father?' Lucinda asked anxiously.

'What else can I do?' Carina's eyes flickered and she shivered. 'It would be worse if she thought Alex had rejected her for no reason, but kept Charles and Michael, wouldn't it? She'd never get over that.'

Lucinda nodded slowly, in understanding. She couldn't break off her friendship with Carina now, because of Tara. The child would need to have a sense of belonging to some family, even if they were of an older generation.

Carina had gone over to her pretty little escritoire in the corner.

'You might like to see something, actually, though it'll be peanuts to you now,' she said, fetching a folded sheet of paper which she handed to Lucinda.

Opening it, Lucinda saw it was from a Hatton Garden jeweller. It was headed: VALUATION OF PEARL NECKLACE.

Single strand, cultured pearl necklace, 33 graduated pearls measuring from approx. 12.20 to 15.60mm. Joined to a pavé-set diamond and white gold clasp. 18" long. Valued at six thousand, five hundred pounds.

'Very interesting,' she said, handing it back to Carina. 'You were right, they were only cultured pearls.'

'So how much was the diamond brooch worth?' For the first time there was a note of the old eagerness in Carina's voice.

'You don't want to know.'

'Why not?'

Lucinda made a little grimace. 'OK. Do you want to hear the actual value?'

Carina frowned. 'Yes,' she said uncertainly.

'Around forty or fifty pounds, if anyone's interested in a second-hand piece of Christian Dior costume jewellery.'

'Oh, *no*!' Carina's face turned ashen, and she clapped her hands to her cheeks. 'Oh, my God, that's ghastly. And it was I who advised you to go for it. Oh, Jesus, I feel even worse now.'

'No, you needn't. In all fairness, you never saw the piece, Carina. If you had you wouldn't have suggested that was the bit I keep. It's my own fault for not going to lots of jewellers and examining the real stuff. I don't know how I was so stupid as to think I could judge what was what, from mere books.'

But Carina was shaking her head, and running her hands through her hair, as if this was the last straw. In a matter of days she'd changed from a confident beautiful woman, sure of herself and her charms, to a pale vulnerable creature, whose eyes kept brimming with tears and whose mouth trembled.

'What a mess I've made of everything,' she wept.

'If it hadn't been for Miles, we'd both be better off right now,' Lucinda declared pragmatically. 'Come on, Carina. We've got to think about Tara. We've got to get through this together.'

Carina raised her blotchy and swollen face. 'Friends again?' she asked tremulously.

'Friends again. Miles can't be allowed to ruin everything.' Lucinda said firmly.

The next morning Lucinda handed in her letter of resignation to D'Aussoire. It was a brave decision, but one she instinctively felt she must take, although she now knew there would be no inheritance from Miles to cushion the drop in income from a highly paid position in a multi-million pound organisation to a part-time job with flexible hours. She'd worked for D'Aussoire for eleven years but now she'd had enough. The hours were too long, the job was too pressured, and the responsibility too great, and the corruption had finally got to her.

When she'd started, as a mere assistant to a market researcher, it had been easy. For one thing she hadn't been married then, and she'd been on the fringe of things; she'd even thought it was quite exciting to go incognito to various stores to buy the products of other companies, so D'Aussoire could see what they were up against. But as she'd gradually been promoted until she was head of the market research department, with an annual budget of six million pounds to ensure every product was thoroughly tried and tested amongst the general public for a period of over twelve months before it went into production, her job had become more and more political, devious and cut-throat.

'My quality of life is being ruined and so are my personal feelings of integrity,' she explained to Peter Harris, when he tried to persuade her to change her mind, later that morning. 'I'm sorry, Peter, but this is something I've wanted to do for some time now. I desperately miss not seeing enough of my children and they're growing up so fast. And I no longer want to be part of a giant company, which is forever fighting for dominance in the world of cosmetics. Life's too short.'

'How about we offer you an increase of salary? Better pension opportunities? Maybe more flexible working hours, Lucinda?' Peter suggested, desperate to keep her on board. He wondered how on earth he was going to be able to replace someone as conscientious and experienced at the job.

Lucinda smiled ruefully. 'Money no longer comes into the equation. I've just blown the opportunity of inheriting three million pounds, and that's suddenly made the thought of money seem meaningless.' She shrugged. 'One minute I thought I was going to be seriously rich, and the next, pht!' She clicked her fingers. 'My hopes were shattered and now it no longer seems to matter. What I want most of all is to be happy and to be a good wife and mother. Maybe I will return to a career when Jamie and Daisy have grown up, who knows? In the meantime I just want to potter along and relax a bit.'

Peter realised she'd made up her mind and could not be persuaded. 'At least you'll let us give you a farewell party,' he said. 'After all, you've been with us a long time.'

It was the last thing she wanted, but Lucinda smiled and thanked him graciously. It was agreed she'd leave in one month's time.

'You did it then, Bun?' Julian asked her that night.

She nodded. 'You don't mind too much, do you? We're not going to have nearly so much money, but I'll try to save on things that won't really affect you and the children. For instance, I won't need to buy expensive suits and shoes, will I? Or take taxis to work if I'm running late? And I can do more home cooking, and that will be a saving.'

He could see she was on the brink of tears and he knew she was torturing herself with the fear that she was being selfish by no longer wanting a high-powered job, and that the family were going to suffer financially as a consequence.

'Come here, Bun.' He wrapped his arms around her and held her close, his cheek pressed to hers. 'Everything's going to be fine. Don't worry. We all want more of *you* around the place, not the bloody money. I'm earning enough to keep us afloat, anyway.' Then he pulled away from her and looked down into her face, smiling broadly. 'I nearly forgot to tell you! Future

272

family holidays are assured once again, too!'

'What do you mean?' She could see he was excited about something.

'Dad phoned me at lunchtime with some brilliant news. The insurance company are going to pay out now that all charges of arson have been dropped, and what with being able to retrieve all the money he invested in ICC they're going to rebuild the château to its former glory! Mum says it's going to be even better than it was before. They're both so ecstatic at the prospect that I could hardly get a sensible word out of either of them, but it's good, isn't it?'

Lucinda's face was filled with genuine delight. 'It's fantastic news! Oh, I'm so glad for them, Julian. They've suffered so much in the past few months and the shock of it all is so bad for elderly people.'

Julian threw back his head and laughed. 'Don't let them hear you call them elderly. Mum likes to think she can pass for fifty, and Dad not much more.'

Lucinda giggled. 'They don't look or act their ages, and that's what matters. And won't the children be thrilled going back there again?'

'Don't let's tell them what's happening, Bun. When the château is ready, which probably won't be until next summer, Mum and Dad want us all to go over to France, telling the children we'll be staying in a hotel. Then when we turn up and they find the house restored, they'll get a huge surprise.'

'What a lovely idea.' She snuggled into his arms again, marvelling at the nice things that were happening in the family. Tom and Susan getting engaged, William and Jane's home being restored, Harry getting hitched to his millionairess, and Anne, now contemplating getting a flat in the same block as Sarah.

But Julian had other thoughts on his mind. 'How about having a shower?' he asked, kissing her tenderly.

'But the children haven't gone to bed yet,' she protested, nevertheless kissing him back.

'Since when has that stopped us?' he whispered, his kisses more ardent.

'Don't you want any dinner?' she teased.

'Later,' he breathed into her mouth, his arms tightening around her, holding her close so she was moulded to his body.

Lucinda needed no persuasion, and she thanked God, as Julian led her up the stairs, that this was one thing they could do as often as they liked, without its costing a penny.

The postman rang the bell aggressively. He was an impatient man, and hated to be kept waiting if there was a parcel that was too big to be slipped through a letter box.

'Registered package,' he said abruptly when Julian opened the door.

'Thanks.' Julian signed for it and glanced down at the handwriting.

'It's for you,' he said, putting it in front of Lucinda, as she sat at the kitchen table, cutting up Daisy's egg and bacon.

273

'For me? I wonder who it's from?' She turned it over. The sender's name was scribbled in the same hand. *Renée Hartman*. Lucinda frowned, her heart, for some reason, thudding uncomfortably.

'Why are you getting a parcel?' Jamie asked. He had a milky rim along his upper lip.

'Is it a present?' Daisy asked eagerly. 'But it's not your birthday.'

'I don't know what it is,' Lucinda replied, ripping open the packaging. 'I can't imagine why . . .' She gasped as a familiar-looking little leather jewel box was exposed. She didn't need to open it to know it contained the ring she'd given Renée.

There was also a letter, written on cheap writing paper.

Dear Lucinda, she read. *I am sending the ring back to you because I've got cancer and not long to go. I couldn't keep it anyway, because I couldn't afford the insurance. I couldn't bear to sell it because it means a lot to me, so I want you to have it. All the best, Renée.*

Attached to the letter was another sheet of paper. It was a valuation from a jewellery shop in Romford and headed: VALUATION FOR PURPOSES OF INSURANCE. It was then the room started to spin and Lucinda found she had difficulty in breathing.

A fine Moghul Kashmiri sapphire, 5 carats, cushion-shaped and mounted in a ring within a cluster of pavé-set old cut diamonds and with a platinum shank. Valued at thirty-two thousand pounds.

'Oh . . . Oh!' She handed the valuation to Julian, the tears streaming down her cheeks. 'Oh, my God,' she wept. 'I don't believe it! Poor Renée, she's dying . . .' Reaching for a roll of kitchen paper, she dabbed her eyes, and tried to control her emotions. 'That poor woman . . . and she didn't want to sell it because . . . because . . .' then she paused, remembering the children were listening, 'and she'd no idea what it means to me.'

Julian was re-reading the letter and valuation for the second time. 'That's extraordinary,' he kept saying, stunned. 'Quite extraordinary, that of all the pieces you gave away, this one turns out to be the one that . . .?'

'I know. I know.' Lucinda felt completely wrecked. In what should have been the most amazing and thrilling moment of her life, she was weeping for a woman she'd only met twice and not even liked much then.

'You'd better ring Bernard,' Julian told her.

Jamie looked at them both and then turned to Daisy, an expression of exasperation on his face. 'I jolly well wouldn't cry if someone sent *me* a nice present. What's the matter with grown-ups?' Then he looked at Lucinda. 'All you have to do, Mummy, is send a nice thank you letter. There's no point in stressing all over the place.'

Twenty

A month had passed and a delighted Bernard had arranged for the three million pounds to be paid into Lucinda's bank account. All that was left was for him to carry out Miles's final request.

'Here is the sealed letter from your father which I told you about, Lucinda,' he told her when she visited him at his office to tie up all the loose ends. She took it from him and saw there was even a sealing wax stamp on the back.

Lucinda slipped it into her handbag with a sinking feeling. She'd open it in the privacy of her bedroom when she got home. It was certain to be upsetting. Everything to do with her father always was. The very mention of his name filled her with dread now.

'He'd be very proud of you,' Bernard was saying, smiling at her.

'I doubt it,' she replied drily. 'It was only the generosity and good will of Renée Hartman that finally enabled me to claim my inheritance. I think Dad would consider that as winning by default. I still expect to be punished for not getting it right in the first place.' She patted her handbag. 'No doubt I'll find out what the punishment is in his letter.'

'He *was* cruel. I don't question that for a moment, but I believe he was trying to be cruel to be kind, but somehow never managed to convey his real motives. I also think he already knew he was ill with a brain tumour, you know. I mentioned to you that he looked ill when he came to see me to arrange all this. His illness may well have affected his mind. Anyway, it's over, and the best of luck to you, my dear. I'm really glad it's worked out so well.'

'This is finally it, is it? No sting in the tail that you know of?'

He shook his head, looking as relieved as she felt. 'None.'

'Do you know where he got all the jewellery from? I can't imagine him going out and buying it . . . except for the fake brooch.'

'The older pieces belonged to his mother, with the exception of the locket. I'm not sure where that came from.'

'He bought it for Miranda Warwick forty years ago, but never gave it to her,' Lucinda told him.

'Right. He also bought the modern gold earrings; he said something about having bought them as a present, but then changing his mind about giving them,' Bernard continued. 'I presume he also bought the fake diamond brooch.'

'As a booby prize,' Lucinda concluded. 'That would be just like him.'

'Maybe he mentions their provenance in the letter.'

'Maybe.' Even now, after a month, it hadn't really sunk in that she'd played her father's game, and won. Nobody won as a rule where Miles was

275

concerned. It had to be something of a first, she thought. More difficult to get accustomed to was the realisation that she was now a rich woman. She kept forgetting, kept thinking I must cut back now I've left D'Aussoire, be less extravagant with food, clothes, dry cleaning . . . and then remembering with a jolt that she'd never have to cut back again. It seemed unreal and she knew it was going to take time to get used to this new affluence.

But there was one thing she intended to do and that was tell Tom in confidence all about it, and to give him a wedding present of some of the money. Harry had feathered his own nest and Anne had been left well provided for, but Tom had suffered the most at the hands of Miles, who had broken his spirit and demolished his self-confidence. Considering how rich Miles had turned out to be, Tom deserved more than the fifty thousand pounds he'd been left. Now, he'd be able to buy a house, get a new car, and put a bit aside for the future.

Julian had absolutely agreed that it was the right thing to do. 'It'll be great to see Tom set up for life, especially now he's getting married,' he said. 'Who knows, hopefully he'll have children of his own as well, one day.'

'We might find we're both adding to the increase in the population,' Lucinda remarked laughingly. They'd decided having a baby was back on the cards, and now that she'd given up work she could hardly wait to get pregnant again.

The house was empty when she got back. Feeling suddenly nervous she decided to go up to her room and read Miles's letter straight away. No point in waiting. Bernard had said there was nothing more to fear, but she couldn't be sure. With hands that shook, she shut her bedroom door, sat on the edge of the bed, and broke the scarlet seal of the envelope.

Dear Lucinda . . . no affection there. I address my bank manager like that, she thought. The letter had also been written on a computer; perhaps he'd dictated it to a secretary and hadn't actually written it himself?

You must be wondering why I set you such a task, and why I chose you and not Tom or Harry to carry out my wishes. In truth, you are more receptive and intelligent than they are, so for you it will have been more of a learning experience than it would have been for them. I doubt, in fact, if they'd have lasted the course. You were always the one with the most promise, the one who was the most capable. When you read this letter you will have done everything I asked, and you will have collected your inheritance. My congratulations. What you will be thinking of me as a person now is no concern of mine. I wanted to show you the different types of love there are, without seeking affection for myself. I also wanted you to learn about the different types of betrayal, of which you will have come across many examples, mine own being the greatest.

Lucinda paused, resting the letter on her lap for a few minutes while she digested the contents so far. Her father had never opened up to her like this, and now to hear what seemed to be partly a confession made her feel

276

uncomfortable. This was an intimacy they'd never shared in life. Why was he presuming to intrude on her space after thirty-three years?

Taking a deep breath she read on with reluctance.

I salute your mother for her loyalty and her blind faith in me. That is a very special kind of love which I never deserved, but that does not take away from her selfless devotion, which I admired for itself. Bernard Clarke is another person you will have got to know well by now; I always admired his ability for true friendship. He did not like what I was asking you to do or the methods I chose to make sure you deserved your large inheritance, but his good will towards me never flagged. If you are reading this letter now, you have Bernard to thank for it because it means he will have carried out my wishes to the letter.

As for Tom, I hope he learns to overcome his fears, and grow stronger. I always tried to teach him confidence, but he responded with nervousness and weakness, and being cruel to be kind has not so far produced a man who believes in himself. Maybe you can buck him up. For myself, I fear I failed.

Lucinda, curled up on the bed by now, read on with growing fascination. Miles certainly wasn't pulling his punches and although, at times, he sounded unkind, she could see from his point of view where he was coming from.

On the other hand, Harry . . . She knew he'd be getting to Harry sooner or later, and she wondered what he'd have to say about his younger son. *If I was thought to be cruel to Harry my reason was to try to teach him humility. He has always been too full of himself and although this hides his fear of failure, he must be taught that work is the most important thing in the world, and to dream indolently of pie in the sky is a sin.*

Lucinda smiled, hearing his voice in his words. She wondered what he'd have thought of Harry's recent short cut to riches. Harry would no doubt have argued that there are more ways of becoming rich and successful than having to work for it.

By now, you will have encountered five very different types of women with whom I have enjoyed liaisons. Each will have something to teach you, as they taught me, and you may have already gleaned their particular gifts, for which I will always be grateful. Miranda, Renée, Fenella, Isabelle and of course Carina have given me so much . . . Here, Lucinda stiffened, wondering if he was going to mention Tara, and suddenly feeling an unaccountable little stab of jealousy; suppose Tara turned out to be his favourite child? . . . *I hope you extended to them all the courtesy they deserve and I hope you learned something about love from each of them because up to now it seems to me you have put ambition first and love second.*

She sat bolt upright, stung by his words. Put ambition before love? What the hell was he talking about? How dare he write to her like this? She loved Julian and the children more than anything else in the world. For the past eleven years she'd only worked to earn money. Hadn't she undertaken Miles's beastly tasks in the hope of eventually being able to afford to give up work?

Hurt and angry, she threw the letter down. What enraged her most of all was his suggestion that she could learn about love from his motley collection of mistresses. Had he no sensitivity at all? Didn't he realise that the thought of each of them was a blow to her heart on behalf of her mother, whom he'd betrayed again and again?

If, for a moment, Lucinda had felt herself relenting towards him, detecting a chink of humanity in his letter, the impulse was now swept away in a torrent of fury. He was the monster she'd always thought him to be. Clambering off the bed, she went down to the kitchen to make herself some coffee, determined not to read on. In fact, she'd tear up the letter and destroy its evil message, which was the philosophy of a malevolent man.

At that moment the phone rang. To Lucinda's relief it was Sarah, coming from a world where real love and goodness predominated. It was like opening a window and letting the sunshine and fresh air filter into her house.

'How are you, Granny?' she asked affectionately.

'Very well, my darling. How are you enjoying being a lady of leisure?' Sarah joked. 'God knows why anyone ever thought housewives and mothers were ladies of leisure in the first place, but I wondered if you'd like to come to lunch next Wednesday?'

'I certainly can, and one of the best things about giving up work is that I can see a great deal more of you.'

'That's wonderful, darling,' Sarah replied. 'Come at noon, so we can chat before the others arrive. I've invited the most charming young woman called Silvia Argent who is a budding dress designer, my old friend Ernest Warner – you know he's now chairman of Wantage's – Peter Sinclair, who breeds champion German shepherd dogs . . .'

But Lucinda wasn't really listening. She was relishing the sound of Sarah's enthusiastic voice and thinking how inspirational she was with her friends and her beautiful home, and the way she entertained with such generosity, although she was now nearly eighty-three.

It made Miles's life seem more sordid than ever, and his letter of explanation even more worthless.

'. . . are you all right, darling?'

'Sorry, Granny,' Lucinda apologised. 'Yes, I'm fine, just disgruntled by a sealed letter Dad left me.' Briefly, she told Sarah about it. 'I feel quite soiled from just reading it,' she concluded. 'I'm going to destroy it.'

'Is it the bit about you learning something from all his mistresses that's getting to you?' Sarah asked astutely.

'Yes,' she admitted reluctantly.

'Because you feel it demeans you as a woman?'

'Exactly,' Lucinda replied. 'I'm happily married to Julian, I love him and I love Jamie and Daisy; what have I got to learn from a bunch of women who helped him commit adultery?' She sounded deeply offended even to her own ears.

'Maybe,' Sarah said slowly, 'you'll learn than you've got nothing to learn?

278

That you're the luckiest woman in the world, and that these other women, for one reason or another, are to be pitied. Their lives are maybe an example of how *not* to do it, and how sad were the consequences for them, do you think?' she added diplomatically.

Shocked, Lucinda thought about this for a moment. 'Do you think I'm being too judgemental, Granny?' she asked at last.

'Why not finish reading the letter, and then see for yourself?'

'I suppose I could.'

'You sound very bitter, my darling. That's not like you.'

'This letter has really rubbed me up the wrong way. I can hear Dad's lecturing, critical, patronising voice in every line he's written and it takes me back to my childhood.' She sighed gustily. 'Once learned, something cannot be unlearned, and I'm afraid my mind is going to be stuck with the hideous situations he's made me examine for the rest of my life.'

'You'll only be stuck with them if you want to be,' Sarah told her gently, 'but it's up to you, and I'm here if you want to discuss anything.'

'Thank you, Granny.'

She went upstairs again and picking up the discarded letter started to read it again.

You're probably furious with me by now and I expect you loathed the tasks I set you. But I wanted you to learn about human nature and I wanted you to learn about tolerance and understanding. Qualities I know I lacked, especially towards Tom and Harry. I hope all this has broadened your knowledge of human failure and frailties, too. By now, in your journey through my past, you will also have learned that I have a daughter by Carina. This was such a shock to me, being the last thing I'd intended, that I nearly had a breakdown. The lesson you will have learned from this, Lucinda, is that it is more important to have regard for the results of your actions than to let yourself be carried away by a moment of madness.

Then came a paragraph that was enormously interesting.

In keeping your grandmother's sapphire and diamond engagement ring for yourself, you chose the most valuable piece of jewellery which is what I hoped you'd do. As to the other pieces, I shall never know how you distributed them, but I hope your intuition led you to give them thus: the peridot pendant I bought for Miranda many years ago and I hope she has it now. The pearls I feel should go to Renée, for their luminous glow reflects her personality. I bought the rather vulgar diamond brooch at a London store, as I thought it would do well for Carina because her appearance is deceptive like the brooch. Brilliant on the surface but with no real depths. When you met Fenella you realised she had healing powers and so I hope you used your intelligence and gave her the aquamarine bracelet. The gold earrings I bought as a birthday present for Isabelle, but I never gave them to her as I feared her husband might grow suspicious.

So there you have it, Lucinda. The puzzle solved.

There is much to learn from my mistakes, Lucinda, and I hope you will find a lot to learn from the people who became a part of my life, especially your mother. Love is the greatest gift of all and I did not deserve her devotion because my emotions are deeply flawed, but I hope that all I have put you through in the past few months(?) will have shown you an easier path than the one I chose, and that you will have learned from my wrong doings. Dad.

'I wept when I'd finished the letter,' Lucinda confided to Sarah when she arrived early for lunch on the Wedneday.

'I can understand that, sweetheart,' Sarah replied. 'He seems to have been a very complex man.'

Lucinda nodded. 'I doubt if I'll ever really understand him, or be able to forgive him for the way he cheated on Mum, and bullied Tom and Harry. I think he carried this Tough Love philosophy to cruel extremes.'

'Any man who hovers on the borderline between genius and insanity is mentally unstable, darling. In time I'm sure you'll see a more rounded picture of your father and be able to understand if not forgive his shortcomings. In the meanwhile be thankful that not only has everyone in the family survived his vagaries, but you're all making a good life for yourselves, too,' Sarah added.

Tom read and re-read the item on page three of the *Evening Standard*. It accompanied a photograph of Susan's ex, Jim Turnbull.

'Have a look at this,' he remarked, handing the paper to her.

'Serve him right!' she exclaimed, when she'd read it. 'If I'd been the judge, I'd have given him more than seven years for assault and battery and robbing an old woman. The man's a drunken thug.'

'Better destroy the paper before the boys see it,' Tom advised. 'It's awful to hear bad things about one's father,' he added quietly. Because he could trust Susan, he'd repeated to her all that Lucinda had told him.

'You're right,' Susan agreed. 'Do you wish you'd never known?'

Tom shook his head. 'In my case it's different. Now I know I wasn't a complete failure. It was just that my father made me feel I was.'

'You're anything but a failure,' Susan assured him, smilingly, as she leaned over and kissed him.

Harry awoke feeling deeply disgruntled. He'd been married to Paula for only a few weeks; but already he was deeply regretting what he'd done. The feeling was almost like having a bad taste in his mouth, after a heavy night's drinking. There was no danger and excitement now, closeted in her luxurious duplex, smothered by sex, his every wish pandered to.

In truth, he felt both disgusted with himself and bored. He'd awarded himself a life sentence in exchange for wealth, and as a result he felt like a male prostitute. A kept man in every sense of the word. There wasn't a pair of socks or a handkerchief in his dressing room that Paula hadn't bought him, along with all his clothes, his car, his watch, his camera, and various other rich man's toys. And she'd ended up buying *him*, as well; body, heart and soul.

His sense of identity had been wiped out by Paula, so he wasn't even sure who he was any more, and his imagination had dried up like a dust bowl in the desert, deprived of rain.

And it was never going to rain again if he didn't find himself once more. He needed to be dependent on his wits, have his mind sharpened by an edge of danger, live on a wing and a prayer if he were to survive at all.

Three months had passed and Sarah decided to give a little pre-Christmas drinks party.

'Mostly family and a few neighbours,' she told Lucinda, 'to celebrate your mother's moving into the flat above me, and the fact she's found a publisher for her children's book.'

'Isn't it brilliant, Granny?' Lucinda enthused. 'This has opened up a whole new world for her, hasn't it? I've read her stories about the cats to Jamie and Daisy, and they adore them.'

'She's writing a sequel, too. Now she's started she can't stop,' Sarah laughed. 'It's just what she needs.'

Sarah had also invited Tom and Susan, who arrived early, looking slightly bashful and holding hands. Harry and Paula arrived soon after, and it was plain they weren't getting on. Harry looked sulky and she had a strained look around the eyes.

'How's it going?' Lucinda asked him brightly, as she circulated amongst the guests.

Paula answered for him. 'We're moving into our country house in the New Year,' she said in a cold brittle voice. 'You must come and stay.'

Lucinda smiled politely and then caught Harry's eye. Behind Paula's back he slid his hand across his throat in a cutting gesture, and then shrugged.

At that moment, Tom and Susan came up, grinning broadly.

'We've got something to tell you,' Tom said in a voice shaking with excitement. Lucinda, looking at him, marvelled at how he'd changed since he'd known Susan.

'We're going to have a baby.'

Lucinda flung her arms around them both. 'That's marvellous,' she exclaimed. 'Does Mum know? And Granny?'

'You're the first person we've told,' Susan admitted. 'Tom and I hope you'll be a godmother.'

'If Tom will do the honours for me,' Lucinda shot back, grinning.

They both looked questioningly at her.

'I'm having a baby, too,' Lucinda said, her face flushing with happiness. At her side Julian nodded. His expression was amused as he told them: 'Jamie accused us yesterday of having S.E.X. for the *third* time!'

More guests arrived. The champagne flowed. The chatter had increased in volume. This was going to be a good Christmas and everyone was in high spirits.

At that moment Anne came up to Lucinda and Julian, looking younger and better than she had in years, wearing a pretty dress and jacket in a crushed raspberry shade, with matching lipstick and a rope of pearls around her neck.

'It's so nice living in the same block as Granny,' she commented. 'It's much nearer the shops and' – here she lowered her voice confidentially – 'I can keep an eye on Granny, you know.'

But Sarah had heard her. She glided past Lucinda a few minutes later, champagne glass in hand. 'It's more a case of my keeping an eye on *her*,' she whispered spiritedly, indicating her daughter. 'With the sort of social life she leads it's up to me to see she doesn't die of *boredom*!'